C000204725

SHE'S 𝐌𝐢𝐧𝐞

Claire Simone Lewis studied philosophy,
French literature and international relations
at the universities of Oxford and Cambridge
before starting her career in aviation law
with a City law firm and later as an in-house
lawyer at Virgin Atlantic Airways. More
recently, she turned to writing psychological
suspense, taking courses at the Faber
Academy. She's Mine is her first novel. Born
in Paris, she's bilingual and lives in Surrey
with her family.

C.S. Lewis (Grinyer)
THE QUEEN'S COLLEGE,
PHILOSOPHY AND MODERN LANGUAGES
1983-87

SHE'S MINE

Claire S Lewis

First published in the United Kingdom in 2019 by Aria,
an imprint of Head of Zeus Ltd

Copyright © Claire S Lewis, 2019

The moral right of Claire S Lewis to be identified as the author of this
work has been asserted in accordance with the Copyright, Designs and
Patents Act of 1988.

A CIP catalogue record for this book is available from the British Library.

ISBN 9781789541939

Aria
an imprint of Head of Zeus
First Floor East
5–8 Hardwick Street
London EC1R 4RG

www.ariafiction.com
www.headofzeus.com

For Clara and Louisa

Those who are faithful know only the trivial side of
love: it is the faithless who know love's tragedies.
Oscar Wilde, The Picture of Dorian Gray

And the king said, Bring me a sword. And they brought
a sword before the king.
And the king said, Divide the living child in two, and
give half to the one, and half to the other. Then spake the
woman whose the living child <u>was</u> unto the king, for her
bowels yearned upon her son, and she said, O my lord,
give her the living child, and in no wise slay it. But the
other said, let it be neither mine nor thine, but divide it.
The Old Testament Bible, I Kings 3 verses 24 to 26

I

Scarlett

I kick off my sandals and step from the boardwalk onto the beach. The sand scorches the soles of my feet and my head throbs in the glare of the midday sun. It's the hotel's private beach: just a long strip of coarse sand, crowded with sunbeds, between two rocky spurs jutting out into the wide bay.

In the heat haze above the sand everything is a shimmering frieze of colour – parasols, towels, and sunburnt tourists. I forgot my shades in the room and feel a little dizzy in the dazzling brightness, and detached, a spectator, watching myself on a movie set.

I'm loaded with towels and beach bags stuffed with Katie's gear – picnic box, sunhat, lotions and goggles. I stride out, ignoring the shifting eyes of middle-aged men, and flick back my hair, flaming in the burning rays.

Katie trails after me, humming softly, swinging a red bucket and spade in one hand and dragging a yellow lilo along the sand in the other.

Smells of barbecued fish and sounds of calypso drift across from the beach club restaurant where my employer, Katie's mother Christina, is enjoying a leisurely lunch (washed down with red wine no doubt) with her gold-digging fuck-boy-lover Damien – the latest in her string of unsuitable younger men.

I smile briefly at the hotel beach boys who wave and call out to Katie as she meanders by. They're sheltering from the midday sun, languishing on hammocks strung between palm trees, splitting coconuts or playing dominoes in the shade. More fool us, risking sunstroke on the beach.

'Come here Katie, under the parasol. Let's put on your cream.' She grabs my arm. For a child so fragile and slim, she's surprisingly strong.

'Where's Mummy?' she cries, fixing me with pretty blue eyes. 'I want Mummy, where's Mummy?' Her anxious refrain begins to grate but I can't resist for long and scoop her in for a hug.

'Shush, honey, stop whining, she'll be here soon,' I say, loosening her grip.

Smoothing a thick layer of cream over the little girl's pale skin, I gaze out to sea, squinting through searing vertical sunlight. The sky's a hard, metallic blue over glinting water. Arrows of light shoot in all directions. I'm hot and sticky from the cream.

'Mad dogs and English men...' I mutter crossly as I wriggle out of my linen sundress and squat on the damp, glistening sand, watching Katie who darts in and out of the foamy ripples at the water's edge. Christina's so distracted that she hasn't noticed that her blonde-haired baby will get sunburnt out in the midday sun. She wants to keep us both out of the way so she can get her kicks with Damien.

Katie's absorbed in her own watery world, now down on her hands and knees, rocking gently and sifting through the sand, searching for seashells to add to the treasure trove of golden olives, pale blue periwinkles, banded tulips and rose petal tellins she's collecting in her bucket. It's her latest obsession. Yesterday, I took childish pleasure in teaching Katie to recite the names of the smooth, shiny gem-like shells as we rinsed the sand off them in the bucket. Today, I feel too drowsy and queasy to join in.

The heat's oppressive and overwhelming, pulsing down. My head reels. Maybe it's the lingering jet lag? Perhaps I've caught a bug? Or could it be that Caribbean rum cocktail Damien forced on me at the poolside bar this morning?

'You may be a working girl, but you deserve a bit of fun too!' He had winked rakishly, handing me the glass. He kept insisting that one drink wouldn't hurt. Now I'm beating myself up for giving into him and taking the cocktail. It's the first thing I learnt at college – never touch alcohol when in charge of a young child. But just one drink, surely, shouldn't have left me feeling such a wreck?

Damien Covera – handsome, sexy and doesn't he know it! An Anglo-Italian city boy with classic Mediterranean panache. Clever too. He works in 'Derivatives,' whatever that means. Seconded from London to an investment bank in New York a short time before I came over from

England to start working as Katie's nanny. Apparently, he met Christina at some glitzy investors' art event hosted by one of the Wall Street banks just after he came to Manhattan.

He thinks he's such a charmer, God's gift to women – he's way too flash for me!

Katie adores him, of course but I'm not so easily taken in. I never trusted him. Even before 'that' morning in Christina's bedroom. It may be something to do with the fact that his eyes are just a shade too close together – though that doesn't seem to stop people thinking he's drop dead gorgeous. Our first encounter took place when he sneaked in one morning in April, just after I'd got back from dropping Katie at her new kindergarten. I spun round from stacking the dishwasher to find him standing right behind me, his crotch inches from my butt. He was peeling an orange with the long blade of the bread knife, and fixing me with his steady green eyes.

'Sorry, didn't mean to make you jump' he said, though he didn't look sorry. 'Christina gave me the key. Scarlett, isn't it? The new nanny.' He waved the blade towards my auburn hair. '*Scarlett Reyes*. Nice. Like the setting sun. Suits you.' Not sure if he meant my name, or my hair. He sat down on a barstool. 'How are you settling into life in the 'Big Apple'? Just say the word if you'd like me to show you around. We Brits should stick together.'

He caught me off-guard that day, not least because that morning I'd 'borrowed' Christina's soft brown leather jacket to wear on the school run and for a brunch date later that morning.

'You'd better take good care of that jacket,' said Damien with a sardonic smile, when he saw it tossed on the sofa. 'Apparently her first love bought it for her in Venice!'

Then one sunny Saturday in June, when Christina was summoned to deal with some crisis at her Wall Street hedge fund, he insisted on giving us a ride to Central Park in his borrowed open-top Chevy Corvette, and treating us all to ice creams.

'Don't mention this to the boss,' he had said, with a conspiratorial grin. 'I told her I was playing golf all day. You know how jealous she can be. Our little secret!'

I had watched as he had wiped a smudge of chocolate ice cream off the end of Katie's nose with a tweak of his thumb, twirled her high above his head until she squealed with laughter, then leapt into the Chevy, and driven off with a casual wave.

I've noticed, of course, that Christina, otherwise so cool, professional and glamorous, is smitten with Damien's boyish charm and though only five years his senior, feels uncomfortable in the role of 'older woman.' And I take secret pleasure in seeing how paranoid and jealous she becomes whenever he pays any attention to me, barely out of my teens.

Now, I rummage in the picnic bag for the snack I smuggled out from the breakfast lounge, and smile to myself. He certainly knows how to rattle her cage!

I find I've lost my appetite. I toss the sweaty cheese sandwich aside, retreat to the shade of the parasol, and struggle to focus on Katie, luminous and gleaming in her candy floss pink stripy swimsuit, a glimmering silhouette against the opaque backdrop of the sea. I listen to the splash of waves, rising and falling on the beach, the gentle fizzing sound of foam running through sand.

My eyes are stinging from chlorine and sun cream. I can't fight the urge to rest and lie back on the beach towel. What's happening to me? Maybe I have sunstroke, I feel so weird.

Now Katie is playing in the shallows, jumping on and off the yellow lilo bouncing in the waves.

She's going in too far, says a voice in my head. I will myself to get up and call Katie out of the water but remain motionless and mute. My legs are leaden. I'm a molten lump in the heat, struck dumb, unable to move or utter a sound.

My eyelids narrow and Katie's figure blurs into a muddle of light and shade.

I'll just close my eyes for five minutes. I lie here soothed by the sweet smell of coconut oil and roasted almonds wafting over from the hotel beach club. The rough towel beneath my sandy shoulder blades is coarse and comforting. I hear the muffled rumble of a speedboat crossing the bay and a light aircraft purrs overhead.

Then nothing.

I wake as the crimson sun sinks into the clouds at the horizon, roused by a splash of spray from the rising tide. I come to my senses with a start. Oh God – I must have fallen asleep! How long has it been? My head is turned to one side and I open my eyes to see Katie's red bucket tipped over on the sand right next to me. Empty.

'Katie, it's time to go,' I say as I sit up and look around. The beach is almost deserted, just a man at the far end walking his dog and a sun-scorched family, squabbling as they pack up their belongings.

It takes a few seconds before the panic begins to set in.

Katie, where are you?

I stand up.

She must have wandered down the beach. She can't be far.

My throat is tight as I shield my eyes from the sun and scan the beach to right and left.

Where is she?

I start to walk, then jog to the far end of the beach calling out Katie's name. I scramble on to the rocks, and strain my eyes to see as far as I can along the shore.

'KATIE! KATIE…!'

I race to the other end of the beach, frantically shouting her name again and again, and calling out to the family and the man with the dog, 'Have you seen a little girl with blonde curly hair, four years old, pink swimsuit?'

You've lost her.

I steel myself.

Get a grip!

Maybe Christina came and took her to the hotel play area or back to the room for tea? I grab my phone from the beach bag and punch out Christina's number. My heart thumps and my temples pulse…

Slow down, breathe.

As the ring tone kicks in, I lift my head and scan the shadowy water. A patch of fluorescence is rising and falling in the inky swell on the far side of the craggy rocks, reflecting the light of the scarlet rays – the little yellow lilo swept out to sea!

Oh God... this is not happening. Answer, for God's sake!

Christina's phone rings and rings until it diverts to voicemail. The rough timber splinters my bare feet as I sprint up the boardwalk screaming for help.

She's gone!

2

Scarlett

It must be only minutes but feels like an eternity until the rescue operation gets underway. At last the lifeboat is launched, and powers across the bay towards the yellow lilo that's barely visible as dusk gathers. A helicopter circles overhead, and paramedics and coastguards stride to the water's edge, setting up their gear. Now there are flashing blue lights and sirens blaring from emergency vehicles parked on the access road to the beach. Alerted by the commotion, hotel guests and staff stream out to see what's happening. Some stand there gawping. Others want to join the hunt and swarm along the shore, clambering onto rocks and pointing out to sea.

Not daring to look away, I stand by the water, rigid with fear, trembling and hyperventilating, clenching my fists, while I pray into the wind, praying for a miracle, hoping against hope that the lifeguards will find Katie clinging to the lilo.

★

As darkness falls, we're still here on the wet sand keeping silent vigil over the black water. Someone's thrown a beach towel across my shoulders. Christina's face is ashen and drawn in the shadows. Her cheeks are streaked with mascara and her red lipstick is smudged below her mouth.

Like a fancy-dress vampire, I think fleetingly.

Her arms hang limply at her sides. In one hand, she holds a pair of immaculate gold stilettos, in the other, the red bucket. Our eyes meet. Her eyes are vacant and glazed.

She shudders and turns away from me.

The coastguards haul the boat onto the sand, their faces grim. Katie's not aboard…

Now the accusations start, pounding round and round in my head. I am ashamed of myself. It's shocking, a nanny falling asleep when in charge of a child.

It's your fault, you idiot. You fell asleep. You let her drown. Katie, I'm so, so sorry. This can't be real.

I see the lilo, hanging over the gunwale, punctured and torn, the tattered strips of shiny yellow plastic illuminated by the searchlights set up on the beach.

Where is she?

A police officer touches my arm and asks us to accompany him to the hotel. 'There are certain formalities,' he says sombrely. 'Come, please.'

He leads the way, angrily brushing off a reporter who approaches, thrusting a microphone in his face. 'Any news, officer? What happened to the child?'

A team from the island's local news network has already set up camp on the beach and is broadcasting live. I catch snatches of the report as we trudge by,

'... *four-year-old girl missing... lilo swept out to sea... feared drowned... inflatable recovered... no sign of the victim... no body has been found... shark attack not ruled out ...all avenues of enquiry remain open... will update as soon as we have news.*'

I can't connect the words with Katie, my sweet little girl and constant companion since I came to New York. The bizarre sensation of watching myself in a movie comes over me again. Any second now, someone will shout 'cut' and I'll click back to reality.

I run to catch up with the police officer while Christina hangs back, fixated by the broadcast. Those words, *all avenues of enquiry remain open*, have broken through the virtual screen in my head that separates me from reality.

'Officer, please, there's something I need to tell you. Wait, please wait.'

My voice is shrill. It doesn't belong to me.

He keeps walking.

'I passed out. I was drugged. You've got to believe me. Someone spiked my drink at the pool.'

He pushes away my arm.

'Please, young lady. There is a protocol for these matters. We'll take your statement at the appropriate time.'

Now I'm shouting at his back.

'You've got to believe me. It looks like foul play. It could be relevant to your search.'

He turns and grabs me roughly by the arm. His voice is hard.

'Control yourself – or I'll arrest you for impeding the rescue operation. A little girl is lost at sea. That's all I care about right now. Do something useful. Look after the mother.'

I reach the boardwalk and wait for Christina. She hands me the bucket and leans against my shoulder. Oh, my God! It's so incongruous the care she takes in brushing sand off her perfectly manicured feet before she tugs on the ridiculous stilettos.

Suddenly it occurs to me:

'Where's Damien?' I say. She shrugs. Her face is rigid as a mask.

'I haven't got a clue. He told me he was meeting you and Katie at the play area. He told me to meet him there too. He never showed up.'

She stumbles towards the hotel, while I peer down at the empty bucket and wonder idly, whatever happened to Katie's precious hoard of shells?

The chatter in the lobby dies when the police officer ushers us through the entrance to the hotel. The receptionists are huddled at one end of the check-in desk conversing anxiously and ignoring the line of new arrivals, most still ignorant of the tragedy unfolding on the beach. The guests wait impatiently, waving passports and fidgeting with their suitcases. All I can hear is Christina's stilettos clicking like ice picks on the white marble as we are escorted in a walk of shame across the lounge and up the nearest staircase to two adjoining vacant guestrooms. The first is for me. The door shuts and I am left on my own to wait.

Suspended in time, I sit on the edge of the bed, staring at the pattern on the carpet, unable to move, locked in misery and remorse. Eventually, the tears come. I collapse onto the mattress and bury my face in the pillow, pounding my fists against the headboard until my knuckles are raw. I can't forgive myself for being such a fool. What was I thinking? To take an alcoholic drink when in charge of a child – especially a child who was – is – so vulnerable and needy as Katie? She would still be here, if it wasn't for that drink. I'm so mad at myself, and even more mad at Damien, the self-entitled bully who won't take 'no' for an answer – the man who always has to take the part of the dominant male and the playboy at the party!

My thoughts are interrupted when a police officer enters the room. She introduces herself as the family liaison officer and asks if I need anything. Then she sits down and takes out a notepad. She says her role is to make sure we are all OK, and to provide us with any support we may need in the tragic circumstances. She says it's not an interview but an off-the-record informal chat and while I take sips of tea she opens with questions about my welfare. Am I overworked? Stressed? Is this why I fell asleep on the beach? Mortified, I explain again that I believe I was drugged. I was well-rested and had been enjoying the holiday looking after Katie, I say. She moves on to questions about my relationship with Christina and Damien. She wants to know how long I've been working for Christina? Do we get along? Have there been any issues or anything unusual in my employment relations? I assure her that I have a good working relationship with my employer based on mutual trust and respect.

'We bonded over Katie,' I say. 'Christina knows I love her little girl to bits and she has full confidence in me. I'm like a second mother to Katie.' Though my words ring hollow now, I know they were true until the moment Katie disappeared.

'What's more,' I say, 'although I've only been working for Christina for three months, we've become great friends.'

Casting my mind back to my life in New York, that now exists only in the past tense, I tell the officer about our Sunday afternoon outings. Christina would occasionally invite me to join her browsing the second-hand bookstores on the Upper East Side. She would spend hours poking around in search of first editions of children's classics and vintage paperbacks. She loved finding a bargain and I was happy to go along with her even though I didn't share her passion for rummaging through stacks of dusty old books.

'Damien, on the other hand, protested quite openly that these outings bored him rigid,' I say. 'So we'd leave him at the apartment babysitting Katie. This gave him the opportunity to spend the afternoon watching cartoons.'

What I don't share with the officer is an account of my wild night out with Christina at the Brooklyn Bowl just two weeks ago, as I fear this might create the wrong impression. That was the night we really bonded as girlfriends. Generally stressed, anxious and overworked, Christina really let her hair down that night. She had surprised me by agreeing to come along to the hottest hip-hop, indie-pop and rap festival in town which, by lucky coincidence, was taking place on my night off. Being some fifteen years my senior, Christina's taste in music was radically different to mine but she was up for it. The truth is, I think she was lonely. Outside work, she hasn't any real friends. But getting to know me gave her the opportunity to get out and have some fun. That night, I did her make-up and lent her my leather skirt and heeled boots. After the frenzy of music and dancing, high on vodka shots and pot, we giggled and flirted like teenagers with sleazy men in sweaty bars well into the early hours. Damien was waiting up, morose and bad-tempered when we staggered into the apartment. He had agreed to babysit surprisingly graciously when asked by Christina earlier in the week but when we got back much the worse for wear, I could tell from the scowl distorting his handsome dark features that he was mightily hacked off we'd had such a fabulous time without him. Later I was woken by his shouting coming from Christina's bedroom and the following day I noticed a bruise on Christina's cheekbone that she had tried unsuccessfully to conceal with her foundation.

The voice of the police officer drags me back to the present.

'So how well do you know Damien?' she says, responding to my earlier comment. Her ears have pricked up with my mention of him doing the babysitting. I tell her that I met Damien after starting work with Christina and that I understand he works in finance in downtown Manhattan but personally know him only as Christina's partner.

'We get along fine but I don't entirely trust him,' I say. 'There's something about him. I can't put my finger on it...'

That's the truth, but not the whole truth. What I don't reveal to her is an incident that took place in Christina's bedroom the week before we flew out to the British Leeward Isles. I don't disclose it because the incident doesn't put me in a good light either! On Tuesdays, Katie does a full day at kindergarten so I have a little time to myself. I've got into the habit of using Christina's en-suite, luxurious, walk-in power shower and expensive beauty products following the weekly hot yoga class that I go to after dropping off Katie. So last Tuesday, I had just finished my shower and wrapped myself in Christina's bathrobe when I heard her bedroom door opening and then the sound of her antique roll top desk being unlocked.

I thought she must have come back early from work for some reason. There was nothing else for it but to come clean (literally!) and apologise for taking the liberty of using her bathroom without asking first. So I took off her bathrobe, draped a towel around me and opened the door. But it wasn't Christina. It was Damien with his back to me, checking the contents of the desk. Caught in the act. Hearing the catch he started and turned in alarm. He reddened but quickly composed himself and went on the offensive.

'What a vision of beauty!' he sneered as I stood there, my wet hair dripping onto the carpet. 'I didn't realise you and Christina were so intimate.'

'And I didn't realise you made a habit of going through her private papers!' I snapped back. I know very well that the desk, an old family heirloom shipped over from the UK, is a strictly no-go area that she keeps locked at all times. He just laughed and then cool as a cucumber, he slipped some documents into a green cardboard file under his arm, locked the desk, pocketed the key and marched out of the room.

'Just mind your own business and keep out of our affairs. Or you'll be going the same way as the previous nanny,' was his parting shot.

I understood this was no idle threat. Christina's so possessive and distrustful that I knew if she got wind of this brush with Damien, she would imagine the worst and I'd be out of a job. So I said nothing to Christina in New York and I say nothing to the police officer now as she converses with me in the hotel bedroom.

I decide to keep my suspicions about Damien to myself – for now.

For something that was supposed to have been a 'friendly chat' the questioning is intense. After asking about my relations with Christina and Damien she embarks on a list of questions clearly aimed at working out a timeline for my movements this afternoon. What time did I arrive at the beach with Katie? Did I speak to anyone? Did anyone approach me or Katie? Did I notice anyone watching her? What time did I fall asleep? What time did I wake up? When did I become aware Katie was missing? What did I do next? Did I see anyone on the beach when I was looking for her? How long did I spend searching the beach before raising the alarm? What time did I tell Christina her little girl was missing?

My head is pounding and I feel like a criminal by the time the family liaison officer finally puts her notepad away.

'These questions are nothing to worry about,' she assures me. 'We just need to establish the timeline for the disappearance of the little girl.' She ends the conversation by encouraging me to contact her 'any time, any place' if I need support or if I 'remember' anything else that may be relevant to the investigation. I half expect her to clap me in handcuffs and announce that she's putting me under arrest, when at last she says that I'm at liberty to go.

In a waking nightmare, we struggle on through the grief-stricken hours of the day making calls, badgering the search team for any new scrap of information and giving interviews to reporters in the belief that getting Katie's story out there might somehow help in her rescue.

The worst moment comes just after midnight when the operation is called to a halt. I collapse onto a chair in a quivering heap. All the strength has gone from my legs. Christina appears distraught, begging members of the police and emergency services to go on searching.

'There's nothing more we can do tonight. We'll resume at dawn. You should get some sleep,' says the commander sternly. Holding our despair at bay and unable to contemplate the thought of sleep, we pace the beaches and the rocky headland for the next two hours, tripping over stones in the darkness, our steps lit only by the moon and stars in the cloudless black sky and the light from our mobile phones.

I am lightheaded with exhaustion by the time I accompany Christina to her room in the early hours of the morning. We sit out on the balcony mesmerised by the sound of waves rolling on to sand. We are too tired to speak. I make tea and give her three sleeping tablets from a packet I find in her wash bag. Once the tablets take effect, I steer her to bed, her expression vacant and confused, as she lets me pull the covers over her. It's not until I shut Christina's door and go down the corridor to the room I'm sharing with Katie that it strikes me again. Where the fuck *is* Damien? I haven't seen him all day, not since he handed me the cocktail at the pool.

When I open the door, there is Katie's blue bunny, propped up on her newly-made bed. The tears stream down my face. The bedtime story I was reading to her last night is still open at the page we got to when her eyes finally closed. It's a beautifully illustrated copy of *Peter Pan* that Christina discovered in a quaint little bookshop called the Book Cellar, one of her favourite haunts for second-hand books. I glance down at the page. 'The Mermaids' Lagoon' – Katie's favourite chapter. She loves the colour illustrations of the mermaids diving in the waves. The doors to the balcony are open. I shiver in the sea breeze and step out through billowing curtains.

I stand there for a few moments still clutching Katie's bucket.

Lost. Drowned.

As I look out over the ocean, a shadow on the curtain catches my attention and I experience a sudden irrational leap of hope.

'Katie?' I call out, turning round to look.

Has she miraculously returned?

The room is empty.

I open the door, and call down the corridor,

'Christina?'

The corridor is empty and behind me in the room, the only sound is the flapping of the curtain.

Don't be an idiot! You're imagining things.

Still, I force myself to go out and quietly let myself in to Christina's room, with the spare key that she gave me on arrival, to check that she's OK.

She looks fast asleep. Knocked out by the sleeping tablets.

Am I losing my mind? It must be the adrenaline overload making me hyper-vigilant, my mind playing tricks on me. There's nothing more I can do until morning. I need to get some rest – to lie down at least – even though sleep is unthinkable. On autopilot I return to my room, walk into the bathroom and reach for my toothbrush.

My hand stops in mid-air.

$$D--IE-$$

The smudgy letters and dashes slice through my reflection in the glass, scrawled in my brand-new lipstick, bought in Macy's the day before we came away. *DIE.* The word screams out at me. The message is rammed home by a lipstick stick-figure of a hangman drawn next to the letters. I glance in the mirror at the open doorway behind and spin round sharply. My nerves are on a knife-edge.

What the hell is going on? Did Christina do this? Was it her who came into my room? But no. That's impossible. She's out for the count. More likely, it was one of the maids or one of the other guests. Word has got out. I'm the one to blame. The feckless, irresponsible nanny who let a little girl drown. Asleep on the watch. A child killer. From now on I'm going to be the object of everyone's hate

I grab a towel and start to rub at the letters frantically. Then suddenly it occurs to me that this could be evidence of something even more sinister – something connected with the fact that my drink was spiked. I throw down the towel.

Stop it now – you're being paranoid. Calm down... breathe...

Someone is fucking with my head: first spiking my drink and then – I look up and hold my gaze in the mirror – *sending me a death threat.* I grip the edge of the cold china basin. My hands are shaking. *Someone is setting out to intimidate and incriminate me.*

A cold chill comes over me.

This isn't just a threat. I'm being framed.

My stomach churns. The sickness I've been battling all evening, overwhelms me. Overcome by a surge of nausea, I collapse, retching onto the tiled stone floor.

3

Scarlett

At last the black night ends and dawn breaks over the sea. Through three tortured hours of darkness, I've been curled up on the bed with Katie's blue bunny, cold and shivering. The soft toy is soaked with my tears. Every muscle in my body aches from the tension of the previous day. After tossing and turning, I must have eventually fallen into a fitful sleep. As I wake, I reach out automatically to feel for Katie's sleeping form and the empty expanse of cold sheet brings me to my senses with a jolt. I'm gripped again by anguish and fear. The pain is brutal. I'm exhausted both mentally and physically.

I get up stiffly and rummage in my suitcase for migraine tablets. I'm still wearing my crumpled sundress from yesterday. It's stiff from seawater and smells of vomit. What happened to me? A rod of pain runs from the top of my skull down into the socket of my left eye.

I walk into the bathroom to splash some water on my face. I didn't imagine the gashes of red on the glass and the broken lipstick lying open on the shelf. Someone came into my room last night and wrote me a death threat. But, why?

I strip off my soiled sundress. Scrubbing myself in the shower, I relive the horrible confrontation with Christina on the beach yesterday afternoon like a newsreel unfolding. I can't erase the images of her hurtling down the sand towards me yelping like an injured animal. I wash traces of blood off my arms and wrists, still covered in scratches and bruises where she had grabbed and squeezed me frantically, all the while screaming, 'Where is she? What have you done with her? I trusted you, you careless bitch. What happened? Where is she?'

I can't get the words out of my head.

I recall sinking to my knees in the sand and hiding my face in my hands. She had carried on slapping me round the head again and again shouting, 'You lazy fool, I trusted you, you failed me,' until a police officer had pulled her away and she collapsed sobbing into his arms.

Eventually, Christina had managed to get a grip on herself and later even apologised for having lost control.

'It was only a matter of time,' she had said enigmatically.

Revived by the shower, I gaze at my suntanned face in the mirror. I don't look like a feckless loser or a child killer. Despite the traumas of yesterday, on the outside I'm bright-eyed and bursting with vigour. But on the inside, I'm broken.

I drag a brush through my wet, tangled hair. I must pull myself together for Katie's sake. Although the death threat written in lipstick on my mirror freaks me out, perversely it gives me reason not to give in to despair. I'm hoping against hope that Katie is still alive. I'm hoping against hope that some depraved soul is playing a sick joke on me and that she will be found safe and well. Thank God the letters are still legible. The police will have to take me seriously now.

Back in my bedroom, I pick up the business card I left on the desk. *Detective Sergeant Paul Costa*. The family liaison officer gave it to me yesterday.

'Sergeant Costa will interview you personally tomorrow,' she had said. 'He's asked you to come back at noon.' She had spoken with deference, as if this big shot would be doing me a special favour. Before he decides to throw me in jail, I've got to do everything in my power to find out what's happened to Katie. Someone's out to get me: first spiking my drink then the writing on the mirror. Something very strange is going on.

I tug on a pair of denim shorts, a faded T-shirt and my trainers. If Sergeant Costa's tied up until noon, I can't sit here in my room doing nothing until then. It'll drive me mad. I woke up in the night with an absolute conviction that Katie is still alive. It was almost like a vision – a vivid image of Katie running along the coastal path towards the little cove where Christina and I took her the other day to hunt for shells. This morning I intend to retrace our footsteps from that day and spend the morning scouring every cove and inlet I can get to along the coastal path.

I refuse to believe that Katie is dead. I cannot. Otherwise I'll just keep walking into the sea until the waters close above my head. It's possible that the lilo beached up on the rocks long enough for her to clamber ashore. It's possible she wasn't on the lilo at all but wandered off along the shore in search of shells. It's possible that she's sheltering somewhere lost and scared. I can't sit here tearing out handfuls of hair. I'll find her, if it kills me.

A few minutes later, I knock on Christina's door. There's no answer so I let myself in. The room is in shadows, the curtains drawn. There's just enough light to make out Christina's bundled shape twisted up in the sheets. Despite the three sleeping tablets, she must have been tossing and turning all night. Her face is pressed into the pillows and her stunning blonde hair ('beach-blonde, not bleach-blonde like the other school mums' she had remarked proudly when I paid her a compliment yesterday morning) spills out in a wave over the white cotton sheets. But Damien's side of the bed is empty, the sheet untouched and smooth. I shake Christina's shoulder. Still under the influence of the sleeping tablets, she moans, curls over and buries her head further into the pillows.

A message from 'unknown caller' sent at 3.42 earlier this morning flashes on the screen of Christina's mobile on the bedside table. I tap in the security code, which I know to be Katie's date of birth:

Sorry ambushed at golf club by Seb and Georgio. Heavy night at the Coco Shack – crashing at Seb's. Hope you had fun at beach with girls. Can't wait to carry on where we left off xxx D. Lost my phone at the golf club so sending this from Seb's.

Who is this Seb, I wonder? I'm sure I've never heard Damien mention him before...

I scan through messages Christina sent yesterday afternoon and evening to Damien – the first at 5.50 p.m. before she discovered Katie had disappeared:

I've been waiting for you in the play area for the last half hour!! Where are you??

And later on a series of urgent, panic-stricken texts and voicemails – seventeen in all – as she tried to locate him.

'Selfish bastard,' I say under my breath. Then scrolling back further, I come across an earlier message from Damien sent from his own phone yesterday afternoon.

Meeting girls at play area at half five

I screw up my lip. *Bullshit*. He never arranged to meet us at the play area, that's a barefaced lie. The plan was to come and find us at the beach.

I don't trust that fuckhead...

I stare at the screen for a few seconds, frowning, then replace the phone and leave without rousing Christina. Better to let her rest a little longer. To wake her would be cruel.

Not daring to stop for a coffee, I stride through the breakfast room and onto the palm-fringed terrace facing the beach. A few hotel guests, the early risers, are already tucking into the lavish breakfast buffet. Jake, the American grad student I drank with at the bar on our first evening, is sitting on the terrace. He glances up from a plate piled high with mango and papaya as I walk by, and looks away quickly. *Screw you Jake!* So much for our evening of 'flanter'.

Yesterday, I was turning heads in admiration, today they're turning away in disgust. Overnight, I've become a social pariah, the careless, lazy nanny who fell asleep on the beach and let a little girl drown – or something worse! It's so unfair. I want to turn round and shout at all those smug people, sitting there, looking the other way and judging me, 'It's not my fault. I was drugged.'

But there's no point making a scene. Right now the only thing that matters is to do everything in my power to help Katie – even if only the tiniest glimmer of hope remains. I hold my chin up and slide down my sunglasses. Come what may, I intend to clear my name. It's only too obvious that the police think I'm the one to blame. Passing out isn't a crime. God knows what my crime is but they're going to pin it on me. Today I'm going to insist they give me a drug test and I'm going to make sure it goes down in my statement that I was targeted too – someone spiked my drink.

Brushing past the lush frangipani and bougainvillea bushes spreading beyond the terrace, I breathe in deeply, calmed by the sweet fragrance of the blooms. I walk through the hotel grounds unconsciously softening my gait to the lilting beat of steel drums being played in the shade under the palm trees across the scrubby lawn.

Further off, I hear the throbbing whine of the search helicopter hovering just offshore and the jolting rasp of an outboard motor being started up on the lifeboat. Thank God. They're still searching for Katie. They haven't given up hope of finding her alive.

A boat is anchored out in the bay beyond the rocks where the punctured lilo was recovered. I walk down to the water's edge and look out towards the reef. Now my heart sinks as I make out the silhouettes of police divers donning masks and strapping on oxygen tanks as they prepare to enter the water. It seems the search-and-rescue operation has now become a search-and-recovery operation to find Katie's body. But I'm not giving up.

I set off on the hiking trail that winds over the rocky headland towards the next bay and see a police officer hanging on to a tracker dog, straining on the leash and wagging its tail in excitement. The officer is combing the waterline, allowing the dog to tug him in zigzags as the pair advance from one rocky cove or stretch of sand to the next.

The stony trail is set back about fifty metres from the beach. I scan the ground methodically from side to side as I walk, looking for anything unusual or out of place. I notice the occasional cigarette butt or discarded ice-lolly stick tossed between rocks beside the trail but otherwise the flora seems undisturbed. I'm planning to hike to the marina about six miles away, and then backtrack to the hotel staying close to the waterline. The sun is still low in the sky and a light breeze is coming off the glassy-smooth sea. It's going to be another scorching day but for now it's pleasantly cool, and my mind is focused and sharp, like the bright images of the landscape outlined in the early morning light.

The rhythm of my footsteps concentrates my thoughts as I replay in my mind the events of the previous day. Now that my head is clear, I recall in photographic detail the morning that the four of us spent together at the pool before Katie disappeared.

Damien and Christina spent much of the time reclining on poolside sun loungers, listening to music through headphones, reading and sensuously rubbing sun cream into each other's backs. Christina didn't go near the water but I had to admit, she looked a million dollars in her Calvin Klein leopard-print bikini. Damien did a couple of lengths of the pool showing off his stylish front crawl and his Orlebar Brown Hawaiian print swim trunks that he wears a little too tight and which I know cost him just short of three hundred US dollars. He spent the rest of the morning lazing around and flirting with Christina. Meanwhile I was in the water, entertaining Katie, giving her rides round the pool on the lilo, watching her on the waterslide, and helping her interact with two little girls on vacation from Texas who wanted to make friends.

Just before lunch, Damien took it on himself to go over to the pool bar and fetch us all drinks – a strawberry soda for Katie, a tropical mango pale ale for himself, a Diet Coke for me, and for Christina, the local poison, a Painkiller cocktail, that potent mix of pineapple juice, orange juice, coconut cream, nutmeg and Caribbean rum which slips down easily and tastes so fresh and delicious.

While Damien went off to the bar, Christina and I looked through the Spa 'menu' as we were planning to go over there for manicures later in the day. On his return, Damien told us that the bartender had boasted he mixed the best Painkillers on the island. I refused when he handed me the cocktail – 'I asked for a Diet Coke,' I protested. But he kept on pushing it in my face. He made out I was a being a killjoy, boring and square. Then he had a go at me for wasting his money. Even Christina had joined in to humour him, goading me gently.

'Go on, live a little,' she had said.

As I hike out along the trail, I'm struck by the contrast between my current lucidity and the bizarre, overwhelming feelings of intoxication I experienced yesterday. Must have been that cocktail. But it seemed quite ordinary at the time, didn't taste particularly alcoholic, shouldn't have made me drunk. And yet it set my head reeling, made me feel absolutely wretched. I remember feeling dizzy, nauseous and wasted... stoned – there's no other word for it. I'm convinced something in the drink made me fall asleep on the beach and then left me with such a dreadful headache and sickness last night. It must have been tampered with. I'm sure of it.

Could one of the barmen have spiked my drink? Unlikely. Damien ordered and paid for the drinks at the pool bar. Damien carried them over and handed me the glass. Is this his idea of a joke? Some joke! I left my cocktail on the table while I went over to cajole Katie out of the kids' pool and get her ready for the beach. Could Christina have dropped something in when I left the table? The sedatives she's always taking herself, perhaps? We were both drinking Painkillers. She could conceivably have dropped her pills into one of the cocktails and mixed up the glasses by mistake – or on purpose. My bet is that it was Damien who spiked my drink to try and make me look stupid and irresponsible in front of Christina. I think he's been trying to get me sacked ever since I caught him going through her desk. Maybe he thought it would be funny to discredit me with Christina by getting me high when I was on duty with Katie, and it all went horribly, tragically wrong.

The trail loops around the rocky headland, at times bringing me perilously close to the edge of steep limestone cliffs plunging down to turquoise sea. I can't bear the thought of Katie, if by some miracle she is still alive, perhaps wandering around out here on her own, lonely and confused – just one slip away from certain death.

Although I'm preoccupied, the rugged beauty of the coastline is not lost on me as I focus my attention on the surroundings for any sign of Katie. I trudge on for three or four miles. Nothing unusual catches my eye. Weirdly the feeling of panic and helplessness calls up flashbacks from the time our dog ran off when I was a little girl. Every fifty or so metres I stop and look around calling out Katie's name again and again, and then straining my ears for any response. I must look like a mad woman but I'm past caring. And there's no one to see me here. The track is deserted.

Eventually the trail winds through an outcrop of boulders emerging onto an elevated expanse of grassland from where I can see the panorama of the bay and the marina in the far distance beyond the hills.

The sun is now climbing in the sky, the cicadas are screeching, and the heat is building steadily. I'm beginning to tire. I pause at a viewpoint over the wide sandy bay to take a long swig from my water bottle and pull up my T-shirt to wipe my damp brow. I look out over the vast curve of sea, sand and green islands, known as Sugar Bay. The stunning vista would have enthralled me at any other time. At intervals along the beach, I make out red flags fluttering in the breeze. They must have been set up overnight by the coastguards to indicate that swimming is prohibited for the day. I shudder.

'Katie… Katie!' My voice echoes mournfully round the bay.

Come on out, where are you hiding? Where are you?

I scan the water, then the beach for any sign of a child, any sign of a body, any sign at all.

The flags call to mind the news I caught on local TV early this morning when leaving the hotel. Investigators are still waiting for the verdict of marine experts on whether rips on the lilo were caused by a shark attack. The newsreel referred to a recent attack by a rogue Caribbean reef shark on a tourist participating in an eco-dive in shallow waters off the reef. Local dive companies were blamed for provoking aggressive behaviour in the sharks by attracting them with lumps of meat.

I keep walking.

Scenes from the movie *Jaws* crowd into my head, overlaid with my last image of Katie splashing about on the yellow lilo…

But I'm letting my imagination get carried away. After all, the beach was crowded. Surely someone would have seen the lilo drifting out to sea? Why didn't someone raise the alarm...? Now that I think about it calmly, I find it hard to believe that not one of those fat, rubbernecking tourists sitting on that beach would have noticed a little girl being swept out to sea on a bright yellow lilo. There's something that doesn't quite stack up.

Beyond the viewpoint, the hiking trail runs close to the rough tarmac road leading from the main road to the hotel. There's very little traffic today as local beaches are closed and day-trippers have diverted to the beaches in the north of the island. An occasional van servicing the hotel thunders past as I hike the trail towards the marina. A police patrol car glides by slowly, then a second police car, about ten minutes later. Part of the search operation, I guess. Otherwise the road is empty and uncannily quiet. The sound of my trainers scrunching on loose stones and dry grasses fills the air along with the incessant drilling of cicadas.

I carry on hiking for another forty minutes or so when my reverie is broken by a clatter in the distance, the rattle of wheels bumping over rutted tarmac. The engine noise gets steadily louder as a vehicle approaches along the winding road. The noise is unnerving, yet somehow familiar. It sounds like a Jeep. Could it be Damien driving back to the hotel at last? Does he know about Katie? What on earth am I going to say to him? I shrink at the thought of having to break the news. Saying the unbearable words 'Katie's lost, she disappeared on the beach, we think she drowned,' will make it all the more real, more hopeless.

I stop uncertainly in my tracks. My mind is groping at something, that disturbing feeling of waking from a half-forgotten dream and struggling to remember some dark and threatening scene. My sense of foreboding grows. And it's not the black dog of guilt (yes, for all my bravado, I can't help but blame myself) that's been howling at me since yesterday.

Like a hunted animal, I sense danger. I quicken my pace, break into a jog. Now I'm sprinting down the track. The gorse rips against my arms but there's nowhere to hide, nowhere to run to.

As it rounds the bend, I immediately recognise the brassy orange jeep Damien rented at the airport.

An idea takes shape, a sudden creeping fear.

Oh my God… it's him, of course… it's Damien.

He's taken Katie. It seems so obvious now. It all fits. The image of the stick-figure hangman drawn in red lipstick, flashes before my eyes – both a death threat and a clue. The red letters 'D' 'I' and 'E', separated by dashes: spaces for missing letters? Like the children's game? Fill in the blanks and you get 'Damien.'

I've been such an idiot!

I should have told the police about his obsessive interest in Katie, and the trips to the park, and the time I caught him going through Christina's private papers in her desk, and the killer cocktail, and his lie about meeting us in the play area, and his mysterious absence from the hotel since yesterday afternoon. And the yellow lilo… yellow, like in Jaws… his sick idea of a joke?

'Oh shit!' I say out loud, as he spins to a squealing halt alongside me on the road.

He leans out of the window, leering, his head cocked to one side.

'Scarlett! Fancy meeting you here!'

He's unshaven, with wild eyes, and I smell alcohol on his breath. His white shirt is creased and stained. He looks as if he has slept in his clothes. As he lunges out, I take a step back from the Jeep and look quickly up and down the empty trail.

I'm on my own.

'Hop in, gorgeous. I'll give you a ride.'

Now I am truly scared.

4

18 October 1997: Oriel College, Oxford

Forgive me, you're not in this photograph but it seems like a good place to start – the end of your first week as an undergraduate in Oxford. I'm sure you'd remember the occasion. I kept the invite. The Oriel College Boat Club Freshers'97 Welcome Bop. You missed a great party, a party with a difference.

This was taken just after we arrived. We're standing a little awkwardly in St Mary's Quad posing for a group photograph in front of a black-and-white timber-framed building called, fittingly enough, 'The Dolls' House.'

What a stunning collection of extremely pretty, female undergraduates (and me, the imposter, but just as beautiful as the rest), all dolled up to the nines, a hand-picked selection from the intake of female freshers, outnumbering the male undergraduates in the photograph by about three to one.

The male undergraduates are also pleasing on the eye (all bar one, their puny cox) – eight tall, strapping second-year undergraduates with arrogant eyes and confident smiles, all wearing matching ivory boating blazers with navy blue piping and cuff rings bearing the three-ostrich-feather emblem on the left breast of the Oriel College Men's First Eight.

Look, there's James, holding out a champagne glass to that curvaceous brunette in the emerald-green cocktail dress. And over here, in the right-hand corner, it's me in your daringly low-cut, scarlet silk evening gown, clinking glasses with the president of the Boat Club. Do you remember him? Hamish Clarke, James' best friend.

We're all looking so very charming, restrained and civilised here. But believe me, by the end of the evening it was carnage.

We were so free in those days – before the tyranny of the Internet and the endless scrutiny of social media. I don't want to boast, but let's just say, the Monica Lewinski treatment was all the rage at the time.

We were so enthusiastic and so eager to please.

We gave those eight, presumptuous young gods (and their diminutive cox), more than their fair share – beyond their wildest imaginings!

It was coming to the end of Freshers' Week and Lara was enjoying her freedom and beginning to feel less strange in her new college surroundings. She was more than a little put out by the sudden arrival of Gabrielle, who was training in London as a fashion photographer and had driven up unannounced to Oxford, to ambush her for the weekend.

'What are you doing here?' said Lara in dismay as she opened the door.

'Why should you have all the fun?' laughed Gabrielle as she kissed her on the cheek. 'I want you to introduce me to some good-looking guys – and they've got to be rich and eligible too.'

Just when I thought I had got away from her, thought Lara. *Here she comes again, barging her way into my life...*

When Lara had gone down for breakfast on the Friday morning of Freshers' Week, she had found an invitation sticking out of her pigeonhole.

The rowers of the Oriel College Men's First Eight cordially invite you to Champagne and Dancing at the Oriel College Freshers '97 Welcome Bop this Saturday 18 October from 8 'til early. Venue: MacGregor Room, Third Quad, Oriel College. Dress: Sexy but smart. No plus ones.

Gabrielle spotted the invitation on Lara's desk the minute she barged through the doorway just before dinner on the Friday evening.

'Wow! This looks just the thing,' she said.

Lara groaned.

'There's no way I'm going to that. No one else seems to have been invited from my college and I don't know anyone at Oriel.'

'Oh, don't be such a bore,' said Gabrielle. 'Live dangerously for once in your life!'

'Anyway, I'm partied out,' said Lara 'I've been out 'til the early hours every night this week. I'm shattered.'

Gabrielle took the invitation and put it in the back pocket of her jeans.

'Well, if you're not going, I will. It sounds intriguing. I'm going to enjoy myself. There are bound to be some fit and lusty hunks among the rowers.'

She put on Lara's new lipstick and tried out a few poses in the mirror above Lara's desk.

'And, if you don't know anyone there, then no-one's even going to notice if I turn up instead. I'll just introduce myself as you.'

Gabrielle went through Lara's clothes.

'You must have something I can wear? Surely you didn't just bring T-shirts and jeans.'

Lara watched her, seething silently.

'I've worn most of my dresses already this week. We've had so many freshers' events. They're in the wash.'

'How about this one?' said Gabrielle, pulling a hanger out of the wardrobe and ripping the plastic cover away from a red silk evening gown. This would do. I'm sure it would suit me. What do you think?'

Lara yanked the dress away from her.

'I've never even worn that yet,' she said. 'You know very well it was my going away present. I'm saving it for the college Christmas Ball.'

But Gabrielle wasn't even listening. She was pulling off her jeans.

'Zip me up, please,' she said looking at herself in the mirror. She seemed very pleased with what she saw. She turned and looked over her shoulder to admire the back view.

'Yes, this is perfect. Thank you so much, darling.' She clapped her hands. 'I'm so excited. I can't wait!'

'You missed an amazing party,' said Gabrielle as the girls sat down for brunch in Queen's Lane Coffee House on the Sunday morning. The champagne had flowed, the setting was magical and what the Oriel men lacked in conversational skills, they made up for in stamina. Lara winced as Gabrielle boasted loudly of her conquests. She had defied the odds, and by the end of the night, in her own words, 'I got off with the three most attractive guys in the Eight – the number three, the number seven and the stroke.'

'I know you're an incurable flirt and a sex maniac,' said Lara 'but did you have to do it in my name?'

Lara was hacked off. She'd woken that morning to find Gabrielle sprawled naked on her sofa. Her red silk dress was in a heap on the floor covered in grass stains and ripped at the back where Gabrielle had put a stiletto heel through the hem.

'Don't be such a prude,' said Gabrielle. 'I was just beating them at their own game.'

Gabrielle spread butter thickly on the toast and took a large bite.

'I found out the big mystery. The cox cracked after his fourth glass of champagne - he couldn't keep his mouth shut. Just listen to this, it's brilliant...'

And so Gabrielle recounted the explanation for the mysterious invitation that had appeared in Lara's pigeonhole. The cox had boasted that it was traditional for the rowers in the Men's First Eight at Oriel College (one of the last remaining all-male bastions in Oxford) to mark their rite of passage to the heady status of Second Years (after their triumphs in Eights' Week and the rigours of sexual abstinence in the long vac), by 'welcoming' the new intake of female freshers to the university. This year's heroic campaign had been devised by the current president of the Boat Club (whose rowing position was number three – the powerhouse in the boat) and 'the adorable Stroke', over eight pints and six games of darts in the Oriel beer cellar. Their plan required each of the rowers in the Men's First Eight (plus the cox), to divide up the thirty-eight or so Oxford colleges between themselves, cycle round to the Porters' Lodge of each, pick out the most attractive female fresher from the undergraduate headshots posted on its college noticeboard, and leave an invitation to their party in her pigeonhole.

'Inspired, isn't it?' concluded Gabrielle 'You should feel honoured. You've been marked out as the prettiest new girl in your college.'

'Sexist pigs!' said Lara, who couldn't help feeling a twinge of jealousy for having missed out on such a lavish event. 'I can't believe they could be so elitist.'

'Well, I had a fabulous time with them all,' said Gabrielle. 'But I must admit Stroke was something special.'

Gabrielle leant back in her chair languidly as she described in vivid detail her last conquest of the night, making love in the moonlight on the soft, wet grass of Third Quad, to the strains of Elton John drifting from an open window…

And it seems to me you lived your life
Like a candle in the wind…

'What's he called?' said Lara, cutting her reverie short.

'God, I forgot to ask his real name!'

Gabrielle took out a cigarette and leant over to the girl sitting at the next table for a light.

'I just called him *Stroke* all evening.' She laughed.

'Since when have you been a smoker?' said Lara.

Gabrielle shrugged.

'He left me the packet.' She breathed in deeply, a dreamy smile on her face. 'Takes me back.'

Later that day Gabrielle drove back to Chelsea.

'Thanks for a wonderful weekend, darling,' she said cheerfully. 'I'll come and see you soon.'

On Monday morning Lara checked her pigeonhole for post on the way to her nine o'clock lecture at the English faculty on '*Sexual Innuendo and the Early Twentieth Century Novel, with reference to the works of D.H.*

Lawrence'. A single red rose was sticking out wrapped in a sheet of lined paper ripped from a notepad. She unrolled the scribbled note.

Can't stop thinking about you. Meet me at seven o'clock tonight at the PPP. I'll be sitting in the back row. I'm taking you to the movies! James (Stroke) x

Lara smiled as she fingered the rose.

Why not? She wrecked my dress, she used me, she trashed my reputation, she stole my identity… If this guy's all she's cracked him up to be, I think I might just enjoy a night at the movies with James.

The film had already started when Lara sat down in the dark on the back row of the Penultimate Picture Palace. The cinema was generally packed with students at weekends but on this Monday evening it was almost empty. The place smelt of stale cigarettes and she gagged as her fingers brushed against dried-up chewing gum stuck in the dark red fabric of the armrest. She'd arrived ten minutes late for their date but still he wasn't there. She sat looking at the screen in silence for a few seconds. Regretting her boldness, she was too distracted to read the subtitles and could make no sense of the black-and-white sequences flashing up in front of her eyes. But just as she was about to get up and flee, she felt a hand on her shoulder.

'You told me you love French cinema.' He sat down beside her. Even in the shadows, when James smiled

44

she understood immediately why Gabrielle had been so smitten.

She looked down. He'd placed a white rose on her lap.

'I'm sorry I was such a brute the other night,' he whispered. 'My behaviour was unforgiveable. I was so completely out of it. But I promise I'll behave like a perfect gentleman if you give me another chance.'

Less than half an hour later they abandoned the film and retreated to the bar for a drink. She followed him to a corner table.

'You're even more beautiful than I remember,' whispered James as he handed her a gin and tonic.

'Did I really tell you I was passionate about French cinema?' said Lara, changing the subject. 'That's so pretentious. And it's such a lie. I must have been trying to impress you.'

He laughed. 'I don't think you'd want me to repeat all the other things you told me you were passionate about,' said James pointedly. 'Though to be honest, the whole night is a bit of a blur. I dread to think of some of the crazy things I must have said to you!' He looked genuinely embarrassed.

She ran her finger round the rim of the glass and then sipped her drink.

'Tell me about you,' she said, to fill the silence. 'What are you passionate about?'

'Well, apart from you, of course,' he said, looking straight at her, 'I enjoy lots of things –rowing, cricket, classic British cars. But there's only one thing I'm really passionate about – my studies.'

He lit a cigarette.

'I probably never got around to telling you, but I'm reading Medicine. Once I qualify, I want to go into medical research.'

His eyes were earnest and intense, pupils dilated. She couldn't tell if this was all part of his chat-up routine – but it was working.

'I know it's a cliché but I want to make a difference, to discover something new that will help us to live longer and better.'

He took a long draw on his cigarette and gazed up at the wisps of smoke.

'That's really cool,' said Lara. 'It must be great to be so certain, to have such a clear vocation.' She hated how cringey she sounded. 'I haven't got a clue what I'm going to do after I get my English degree.' She picked up the white rose and began absently to pull off the petals.

'My big brother died of a rare form of bone cancer just before his seventeenth birthday,' said James. 'I idolised him.'

His tone was matter of fact.

She put down the rose and touched his arm.

'It left me feeling so angry and helpless. I don't ever want to feel that way again…'

'I'm sorry,' said Lara. She could think of nothing else to say.

'No, no I'm sorry,' said James. 'Stupid of me to speak of it on our first real date. I didn't mean to put a downer on things and make you feel awkward.'

He exhaled slowly.

'But… how can you?' said Lara, screwing up her face as she leant away from the smoke.

'I know… it makes no sense.' James smiled. 'It's my only vice. I promise.'

He stubbed out the cigarette and leant over the table to kiss her.

'Now it's your turn. I want to know all about you…'

5

Scarlett

Damien drives fast, like a lunatic. He hurtles along the hairpin bends towards the marina, flooring the accelerator and pushing the chassis and suspension of the Jeep to its limits. I grip the handle to stop myself lurching from one side to the other. The music blares, turned up to full volume. Even in profile, the expression on his face looks slightly manic, and I wonder whether he could still be high on some illegal substance – probably the same thing he spiked my cocktail with yesterday! I'm sure he's no stranger to substance abuse. After all, he's a regular at clubs in New York where it's easy enough to get hold of recreational drugs such as ecstasy and cocaine. And I know he's something of a Jekyll and Hyde: absolutely charming when he wants to be but with a more sinister side to his character – egotistic and brutish – especially when he's been on a bender. But I've never seen him in such a state as this.

'Slow down. You're going to kill us both,' I shout. I haven't dared to confront him about Katie's disappearance yet. 'I need to talk to you.'

He puts his foot down harder on the accelerator.

'Hey. I said I'd meet Christina at twelve o'clock. I need to get back,' I shout.

I've got to have it out with him. But I'm scared. He might lash out at me if I tell him what has happened. If he's innocent, he'll blame me. And if he's guilty, God knows how he might react if I make my suspicions known.

'Cool it, Scarlett! Let's have some fun,' he yells back. 'It's not often we get any time to ourselves. Christina can wait. I'll take you for lunch at the Coco Shack down at the harbour. I left my phone there last night. I'm on my way to pick it up. They do a wicked jerk chicken.'

Before I can reply, he eases the accelerator a fraction, and keeping his right hand on the wheel, leans over and throws the other round my shoulders. Then he yanks me in close and kisses me clumsily. I taste blood as his teeth clash against my lower lip. The car swerves wildly across the road, bumping in and out of the shallow drainage ditches at each side.

'I've been wanting to do that for a while,' he says. 'Ever since I first saw you leaning over the dishwasher in Christina's kitchen, in fact.' He laughs when he sees the look of disgust on my face and tilts back his head. 'You really need to learn to let your hair down sometimes, you know, Scarlett. You're a good-looking girl. And you've tits to die for! But you're such a tight-ass!'

I'm outraged but I'm no fool. His mood is dangerous. This is not the time to fight back or to accuse him otherwise things will get out of control. I reckon I can outwit him but I'm going to have to play it smart and pretend I suspect him of nothing. First I need to make him stop before he crashes the Jeep and kills us both. As he accelerates, I shout again above the blast of reggae from the speakers.

'Damien, for God's sake, slow down, you're going to crash.' I try to hide the panic in my voice. I know that if I lose my head there's a risk I won't come out of this alive.

There are viewpoints all along the scenic coastal drive with space for two or three cars, picnic tables, tourist maps and spectacular views over the bay. Just after the Jeep screeches round the next bend, I spy a police car partially concealed behind some bushes, parked up facing the road. It must be one of the extra police patrols involved in the search for Katie. My spirits rise – surely Damien's reckless driving will attract their attention and they will give chase?

A little further along the road forks. One fork is a dead end leading down to the isolated sandy cove known for its beautiful shells and gently shelving crystal clear waters where Christina and I came with Katie earlier in the week while Damien went off 'to play golf,' or so he claimed. The other fork continues on around the coast. I recognise this stretch of road because Christina and I returned this way by taxi with Katie after our 'girls outing' collecting shells. I remember that there's a viewpoint overlooking the bay located a few metres along the fork to the dead end. The beginnings of a plan start to form in my head. If I can stall Damien, even just for a minute or two, this might be enough to allow the police to track us down.

As we approach the junction, I stick my arm out. 'Take the left fork. Pull in at the viewpoint.' I flash him a smile. 'I'll let you kiss me properly if you stop the car.' It's the best I can think of on the spur of the moment.

Damien yanks the wheel and turns in sharply, skidding on the loose gravel. I feel a sharp crack of pain as my forehead thumps against the steel windshield frame.

'An offer I can't refuse,' he says, with a sideways glance. 'My lucky day.' He cuts the engine and pockets the keys. He's grinning but his tone is menacing. He takes a small package out of the glove compartment. 'Don't move' he says, stumbling out of the Jeep.

I'm sufficiently streetwise to work out that he's trying to stave off a comedown by going off to take another line of cocaine. My fingers on the handle, I hesitate. If I try to make a run for it, he's sure to catch me. He's got the car keys and there's no place to hide. I know I can't outrun him but this is my only chance to get away. I fling open the door and sprint as fast as my legs will carry me up the dirt track leading from the viewpoint back to the tarmac road. Suddenly, I hear sirens. Thank God my plan has worked. The police must have seen the Jeep careering down the road. They're giving chase. I keep running towards the roadway screaming as loud as I can and waving my hands above my head. But the police car doesn't slow and, gasping for breath, I watch in despair as it accelerates away in a cloud of dust in the direction of the beach.

A second later Damien is at my side.

'What the hell are you playing at?' he says. 'Are you trying to get me arrested for drink driving? Can't you see I'm over the limit?'

'That's the least of your problems,' I say.

He takes my arm and drags me back to the Jeep. 'Come on Scarlett.' He opens the car door for me. 'No more tricks, hey?' He slams it shut, locks the car and walks away jangling the keys.

While he ambles off to relieve himself behind a boulder (or more likely, take a line and dispose of his stash), my mind goes into overdrive as I work out my next move. I wonder if my imagination is playing tricks on me? Could he really be responsible for Katie's disappearance or am I being paranoid?

I lean over and stare into the rear-view mirror. I can't think straight any more – he's totally obnoxious when he's in this state but is he really capable of something as appalling and perverted as abducting a child from a beach? Am I simply looking for someone else to blame apart from my own stupid, negligent self? Imagining the most unspeakable crimes simply to blot out the horrible reality that I'm the one responsible for Katie's death?

My green eyes glare back at me accusingly.

I twist the mirror down further. I've got to play him right. If I can distract him for long enough, the police should come back looking for us when they see the Jeep's not down at the beach. I try out a smile, a tilt of the head, a pout of the lips.

Katie would never have drowned if I'd been looking after her properly – if I hadn't been careless and irresponsible.

There, I've accepted it now. There's no running from the truth: Katie is dead and it's all my fault. But this isn't the time to be beating myself up.

He'll be back any minute.

I'm running out of time.

In a frenzy, I rip open the glove compartment. A few maps, a metal hip flask, more than half empty. I unscrew it and sniff – he's been drinking rum. I take a gulp for Dutch courage. Save that he's been drinking and driving as well as taking drugs, there's no incriminating evidence I can see in the car. What am I looking for? Bloodstained clothes? A murder weapon?

I run my hands along the mats under the seats. Under the passenger seat, nothing. On the driver's side, nothing. But wait. Something small and hard. I hold it up to the light: an earring. It looks like one of Christina's treasured jade earrings, given to her by Katie's father. But how did it get here? As far as I know, she hasn't been out in the Jeep. Whatever! Christina would be gutted to lose it. I slip it into the pocket of my shorts. She'll be delighted to have it back.

I clamber up onto the seats and lean over into the trunk compartment hoping to find Damien's golf clubs – after all he told Christina he'd gone off to play golf. I could defend myself with a golf club, I think optimistically. But they're not there. In fact there's nothing much in the trunk, save for a suit carrier containing a stained tuxedo and a small black rucksack.

I grab the rucksack and yank open the zip expecting to find it stuffed with Damien's gear. But, no – instead it's stuffed with yellow plastic bundled up and pushed in tight. The same bright yellow as Katie's lilo… He must have bought two of them.

But here comes Damien, zipping up his jeans and swinging his hips. From the way he sniffs and rubs the back of his hand on his nose I can guess he's just taken a line of cocaine before disposing of his stash. I twist round quickly and slide back into my seat. He looks every bit the unreconstructed, redneck hero of an old-fashioned cigarette ad. I've got nothing to defend myself with, short of battering him over the head with the hip flask! He's finally got me cornered. Looks like I'm going to have to resort to desperate measures to keep him occupied until the police come back and find us.

'Damien, have a swig of this' I say, holding out the flask as he slams the door. 'Caribbean rum.'

I smile, tilt my head and pout my lips.

He looks into my eyes, takes a long slug, down to the last drop, and tosses the empty flask into the back of the Jeep.

'Now that's more like it', he says, as he turns his body towards me, caresses the tops of my thighs with one hand and slides the other inside my T-shirt.

I screw up my eyes and press my nails into the palms of my hands.

6

Photograph Two

15 June 1999: Trinity College, Oxford

Here we are partying again. Our Survivors' Photo, taken by the Oriel cox on my camera at six o'clock in the morning as dawn broke on the debris of the Trinity College Grand Venetian Masked Ball 1999. The image is a little blurred but camera-shake can be excused, considering the vast amounts of alcohol we'd all consumed by the time the sun rose over the festive scene.

We went as a foursome: you and James, of course, as you'd been going out together for the whole of the first and second Years – all thanks to my unconventional match-making at the Oriel Boat Club Freshers' bash; and I went with Hamish (or 'Number Three,' as I preferred to call him) who, as president of the Oriel Boat Club (and a rowing Blue to boot) had managed to pull some strings with the chaps in the Trinity College Boat Club and get his hands on two pairs of tickets.

The tickets were like gold dust. Hamish told me it was the most lavish and extravagant of the May Balls in that last year of the dying millennium and I believed him as we gyrated under a thousand lights to the beat of Coldplay in the purple haze of the sumptuous marquee.

By the time this photo was taken we were pale, dishevelled, spent and content after the revels of the night.

The four of us are sitting on the steps of Garden Quad, drinking flat champagne and munching soggy croissants, arms entwined, huddled together for warmth in the grey, damp, misty chill of morning.

We swapped masks and dresses just after midnight – look closely, I'm wearing your blue satin ballgown and you're wearing my black silk. They fit us perfectly. It was my idea, if you remember, to play a trick on the boys, to add a little extra spice and excitement to the night – as if that were possible.

They were so out of it by then, I'm not sure they even noticed...

And, if so, they didn't seem to care.

Gabrielle was so excited. This was promising to be the high point of her summer, the high point of her year. She was on a temporary contract working in the photographic department of an online fashion retailer. Though the job sounded glamorous on paper and was the first step in her career as a photographer, it was in fact extremely dull, being warehouse-based and involving spending her days processing literally thousands of digital images of clothing.

Her ambition was to manage her own photographic and film studio. This job bored her rigid.

The girls spent the whole day preparing for the ball – getting their legs waxed, their hair curled, their nails manicured, their make-up perfectly applied. By six o'clock in the evening Gabrielle was raring to go and impatient for the boys to come and collect them from Lara's room in college. It was a beautiful warm summer's evening. It was going to be a magical night.

Those hours of preparation had paid off. She and Lara looked exquisite, or so James told them, as he stepped through the door.

'You'll be the belles of the ball,' he said. 'We're the luckiest men in the world.'

James and Hamish also looked fabulous in black-tie and brightly-coloured silk waistcoats, both impressively tanned and toned from many hours spent training on the river. Gabrielle couldn't wait!

'Let's get the party started,' said James. He held out a champagne bottle to Gabrielle and while she struggled with the cork, he folded Lara in his arms and waltzed her round the room.

'You are so beautiful, you make my head spin,' he said as they tumbled onto the sofa.

The May Ball absolutely lived up to Gabrielle's expectations – and her expectations were exceedingly high. A spectacular and intoxicating night of live bands, wild dancing, discos, fairground rides, bumper cars, a full-size pop-up casino, decadent marquees, fine dining and endlessly flowing alcohol – all in a dream-like setting of beautiful historic buildings and spires, green lawns and ancient woodland. The atmosphere was electric. The exotic masks added an extra layer of excitement and intrigue to the night.

Hamish was all over her. He was an amusing and attentive host, plying her with alcoholic toasts and treats, and they moved like greedy butterflies from one entertainment to another as he romanced her through the night. He was showing her a good time and she was making it worth his while.

But Gabrielle just couldn't take her eyes off Lara and James – it was torture, seeing them arm-in-arm, laughing, kissing, so comfortable in each other's company, so much *in luuurve*! It made her sick. By rights, James should be hers. It was so unfair. Lara had stolen him. Lara would never have even met James if it hadn't been for Gabrielle. She had found him first and she was determined to take him back.

For Lara too, this night was the highlight of her year – celebrating the end of Trinity term exams and the end of her second year at Oxford. She and James had been virtually inseparable since their first date at the Penultimate Picture Palace on the Cowley Road. Despite her stunning good looks, she had undoubtedly been surprisingly reserved and insecure when she arrived in Oxford as a fresher but had since (in no small part thanks to James) matured into a confident and vivacious young woman who enjoyed life to the full and wore her intellect lightly. From the moment he'd dropped down beside her in the shadows on the back row of the PPP and presented her with another rose, white this time, 'as a peace offering', he'd won her over with his kindness and charm, lighting up her life. He was her best friend as well as her lover. He was her rock, supporting her though countless essay crises and hangovers, making her laugh when she was down, and, when he was not stuck in the labs or poring over medical journals, constantly at her side making her feel special, intelligent, beautiful and adored.

But Gabrielle was not one to be upstaged.

As the clock tower chimed midnight and the moon hung low over the dazzling set, Gabrielle had a brainwave. The four of them were standing in line, swaying in unison to the sensual rhythms of a jazz quartet performing under the stars.

'Let's play a trick on the boys,' she whispered in Lara's ear. 'Let's swap our masks and dresses and see how long we can deceive them. I'll bet you ten pounds they won't notice!'

Lara had drunk five cocktails and the best part of a bottle of champagne and was in no fit state to resist, so the girls slipped off to change.

Gabrielle didn't waste any time dragging off her dress. Soon she was back to the boys and playfully leading James away for a game of croquet in the dark. He had drunk three bottles of champagne and was up for the challenge.

*

By the time the clock on the tower struck one, Gabrielle knew her bet was won. The croquet mallets were abandoned on the grass. James was shackled at the ankles and wrists by the metal hoops she had hammered in with her mallet. He was her captive, trapped in exquisite torment flat on his back, watching the clouds scudding overhead. Their passionate embrace was shielded only by the moonlight shadow of the bust of Cardinal Newman, whose stony figure looked on in solemn distaste all the while she rocked to-and-fro.

Now the clouds had passed over. Lara's mask was tossed aside. Gabrielle had released James from the hoops. They lay still on the freshly mown grass in the Back Lawns of Trinity, satisfied and exhausted, their bodies touching, their heads reeling, their eyes sparkling with the most dazzling firework display she had ever seen lighting up the indigo sky.

7

Scarlett

At last I hear the shriek of a police siren.

Thank God!

I open my eyes. The sky is bright blue overhead.

Shaken and bruised. Humiliated but alive!

I shove Damien off as a police car pulls up beside the Jeep, its blue lights flashing. Damien tugs at his jeans and straightens his shirt.

'I know you're hiding Katie,' I hiss at Damien. 'Now for God's sake tell the police what you've done with her.'

Twenty minutes later I'm riding in the back of a squad car. Looks like I might get the chance to give Sergeant Costa my statement after all. The gargoyle face of the officer sitting alongside me leaves me in no doubt that I'm going to have some explaining to do. We're riding in convoy. I can see the back of Damien's dark head in the car in front. They clapped a pair of handcuffs on him and bundled him in, no messing. He's being 'escorted' to the police station, arrested on charges of dangerous driving.

When we pull into the police station, Damien's already on his way. I see only a fleeting view of him disappearing into the building, flanked by police officers. My car door is opened by a female officer. As she walks me to the entrance of the police station shielding me from a couple of stray reporters, a woman comes out of a café on the other side of the road. I don't recognise her at first but it's Christina, wearing a new pair of aviator sunglasses, a wide-brimmed sunhat and a flowery nipped-waist and full-skirted sundress I've never seen the like of before. Anyone would think she was trying to disguise herself! She's seething. She falls in beside me and starts firing questions.

'Where the hell have you been?' She can barely contain her anger. 'We were supposed to be here first thing to see the Commissioner.' She pushes back her sunglasses and gives me a look of pure contempt. 'What on earth were you playing at giving me sleeping pills last night? I didn't wake until after eleven o'clock, wasted the whole morning. You should've woken me up instead of going off alone.' Her eyes are puffy and bloodshot. 'And where the hell is Damien? He didn't come back last night or this morning. I've still heard nothing from him. Have you seen him?'

'You just missed him,' I say.

My first impressions of the police station, as we are led through the shabby painted doors, are not good. Officially we're here for an update on the investigation. But I've a sinking feeling we're being called in for further questioning as unofficial suspects.

The waiting area is crowded, scruffy and chaotic. It's flooded with light from the afternoon sun streaming through the bank of sealed, dusty and grime-stained windows along one length of the room. The police officer asks us to wait and disappears through the crowd of bodies down a corridor. We stand just inside the waiting room uncertain which way to turn. In her retro get-up Christina looks like a 1950s movie star. She's still wearing her silly aviator sunglasses to hide her sore eyes, bloodshot from crying. I guess this gives her the illusion of concealing her identity.

There's not a police officer in sight in the waiting area and nowhere to sit. The few hard, plastic seats are all taken and all those without seats are camped out on the floor. Some have their eyes shut, leaning back against the walls, others are listening to music through headphones or talking in loud animated voices recounting the ins-and-outs of some dispute or violation which has brought them to the police station. It reminds me of crowded train stations on inter-railing holidays when I was a student.

'What a dump.' I say. Christina looks around nervously, conscious of a stir in the room, and a hundred eyes looking at us, then a sudden hush followed by whispering, and pointing, none too discreet, which leaves me in no doubt that we've become reality TV celebrities overnight. I have a blurred memory of us having been accosted yesterday evening by one of the local paparazzi for a statement. Christina was clearly caught off-guard and almost speechless. When she opened her mouth, the only words that came out were, 'She's gone. She's still missing. Please bring back my little girl. Please don't give up.' The hotel manager had swiftly called over a security guard to bundle the pushy journalist and her crew off the premises. But no doubt our images and Christina's faltering words were flashing up in the island's 'breaking news' broadcasts.

Sure enough, when I look over at the screen fixed to the wall of the waiting area, the news channel is replaying a continuous loop of film cuts from last night's search operation: Christina's clumsy, awkward statement, pictures of us both on the beach, panoramic views of the bay, shots of the lifeboat coming into shore, a close-up of the deflated yellow lilo being ceremoniously taken away for analysis – but no Katie.

I feel sick.

I turn my back to the screen but I can still make out the reporter's voiceover: '... *no sign or sightings of Katie... Katie lost at sea... Katie, still missing... Katie last seen on the beach playing with the yellow lilo...*'

The land and sea search is continuing and as soon as any further information is available they will update their viewers immediately.

'What about someone updating her mother?' says Christina in a bitter tone.

As I walk restlessly round the room looking for someone in uniform to tell us what to do, I catch sight of a freshly-printed poster, tacked up on the noticeboard, in amongst other faded notices and mugshots of persons wanted for drugs and armed robbery offences, along with miscellaneous police guidance notes on burglary prevention measures, safe motoring, and the like. I drag Christina over to see it. She gasps and turns pale. The poster is a close-up photograph of Katie wearing her stripy pink swimsuit. The poster caught my attention immediately because I was the one to take the photograph. I emailed the picture to the police station from my phone late yesterday evening. It shows Katie, looking straight at me, her blue eyes shining with pride, as she holds out a handful of shells she collected on the beach, cupped in her sandy little palm. The single word, MISSING, is stamped in large black capital letters at the top of the poster.

Christina can't resist the impulse to reach out and touch the sun-kissed cheeks of her beautiful daughter. Her hand moves up towards the picture then she lets it drop. She peers more closely at the photograph. In the corner you can just make out the date and time recorded on my phone.

15:35 16.06.15.

She was still alive then…

It's chilling to see Katie's innocent face pinned up next to that of a former convict wanted for armed robbery, painful to imagine her out there, with all those dangers, all alone.

Like acquaintances at an art exhibition, we stand together reading the short police report printed below the photograph with a growing sense of dislocation, unable to connect the dispassionate words to Katie.

Police are seeking the public's assistance in locating a four-year-old female, Catherine ('Katie') Jamie Kenedey, dual national, citizen of the United Kingdom and the United States. The child, who answers to the name of Katie, was reported missing by her nanny at about 5 p.m. on Tuesday 16 June 2015 when she went missing on the beach at the Palm Reef Beach Club on Grand Carmola island in the British Leeward Isles (BLI).

Following receipt of this information, a land-and-sea search was carried out by British Leeward Isles Search and Rescue, the British Leeward Isles Police Force and members of the local community for several hours into the night. The search of coastal waters and the shoreline in the bay area resumed from 6 a.m. on Wednesday 17 June.

Initial inquiries indicate that the child may have been swept out to sea on an inflatable air mattress. Police are appealing for witnesses. No body has been recovered. Investigations are ongoing.

The four-year-old child is described as slim, white, approximately 102 cm tall and weighing approximately 16.5 kg, with blue eyes and medium-length wavy blonde hair. At the time of her disappearance she was wearing a pink-and-white striped swimsuit.

Anyone who may have seen her or know of any information relating to her whereabouts is asked to call 999 or contact the Criminal Investigations Department via Police Access number 206.

Christina turns away. 'This can't be happening' she says. 'I must be going mad.'

I reach into the back pocket of my shorts for my phone and the tips of my fingers touch the earring. I hold out my hand to Christina.

'I found this on the floor of the Jeep. I think it's yours.'

Christina hesitates for a second or two before taking the earring from my fingers.

'Thank you,' she says coldly. She puts the earring in her purse. 'I've been looking for it everywhere. I'd have been gutted to lose it.'

An awkward pause as she registers the irony, then, 'What were you doing in Damien's car?' Christina gives me an icy look.

'Oh, he gave me a lift.' I say breezily. 'I went out on the trail again searching for Katie. I woke up this morning tortured with the thought that she might be wandering about out there lost and alone.' Christina's lips quiver as she struggles to hold back her tears. 'Damien drove past on his way back to the hotel and stopped to pick me up.'

Fortunately my explanations are cut short when a police officer blusters up to us. I recognise him from yesterday. Today he's in full regalia, all shining buttons and buckles, and bulging holster. He must be in his late twenties or early thirties, tall, well-built with strong features. His shirt is bright white against his tanned skin. His eyes are unusually blue. He nods at me briefly and addresses Christina.

'Detective Sergeant Costa.' He shakes her hand a little too firmly. 'I am the officer in charge of this operation.' He has a studied, self-conscious, self-important screen-shot-police-cop air about him – a caricature of the cops in the NYPD movies. I've come across his type before – vain and power-hungry.

'Mrs Kennedy, thank you for coming in to the station. Come this way please.'

'It's *Miss*,' she says, 'Miss Kenedey, spelt *K-E-N-E-D-E-Y*.'

He gestures to me. 'Please come.'

We follow him into a small, windowless side-room containing only a bare wooden table, three chairs and a large clock on the wall.

'Please have a seat,' says Costa, pointing to the chairs. 'Can I fetch you some water? I will let the Commissioner know you are here.' He leaves us on our own.

'There's no sense of urgency round here,' says Christina. I hear the despair in her voice. Her eyes are glued to the old-fashioned clock on the wall, relentlessly ticking away the precious seconds. 'We're losing valuable time.'

From her bereft, frozen expression, I can imagine something of how she must be feeling – betrayed, numb, helpless, at a complete loss about what to do next. I put my arm round her. None of the police officers seems to care very much about her plight, or to have a word to comfort her.

She turns away.

'Is there someone we should call?' I say. 'What about your family? Have you told your parents? You should call them. You need their support.'

She must feel so very isolated and lonely with only me here by her side. And just the sight of me must make her sick. I've become a monster.

'There's no one. Please take your hands off me.'

The stuffy interview room is separated from the control room by a dirty glass partition wall. Through the glass I can see desks and workstations equipped with primitive computers and phones. Stacks of papers and files accumulate on the floor and every work surface. Wastepaper bins overflow with cans and empty take-away boxes. A grey-haired officer munches a sandwich at his desk, taking occasional bites, as he answers the phone and scribbles notes onto a large pad of lined paper; a younger officer, who looks no more than a teenager, lies slumped in his chair with his feet up on the desk and his eyes closed. His desk is littered with empty plastic coffee cups. Just on the other side of the glass, a third officer, a woman in her mid-twenties sits at a screen, touch-typing with one hand, and balancing a cigarette in the other. I can't help admiring her flawlessly polished purple nails. But if this is the hub of the search-and-rescue operation, it doesn't inspire me with much confidence.

My eyes gravitate to the wall and we sit in silence both watching the second hand, then the minute hand, turning. Seven minutes to four. Five to four. Eight minutes past four. Have we been completely forgotten?

After what seems like an eternity, the door opens and Costa enters the room with the Commissioner. Christina leaps to her feet.

'Have you found her? Have you got any news?' she says breathlessly.

'Ah, Miss Kenedey' says the Commissioner, stressing the *Miss* (he's been well briefed by Costa). He gestures for her to sit down. 'Thank you for coming. I'd like to update you on what's been happening today and to go over your statement,' he says sternly. He turns to me. 'And Miss Reyes'.' He nods curtly.

He starts the interview by repeating what we've already gleaned from the news in the waiting room. He assures us the search continues at sea and along the coast. Police boats are patrolling the shore. Tracker dogs are scouring the beaches. Divers are searching the waters close to the reef where the lilo was found.

'Have you got the report about the lilo?' says Christina. Her voice is shaking.

'I'm expecting the marine forensic report back any minute,' says the Commissioner. 'It's just a precaution, to eliminate this line of enquiry. Shark attack is most unlikely but we have to follow certain protocols when we have a victim at sea.'

She winces at the word 'victim', causing the Commissioner to change his tone. He becomes fatherly, condescending, pats her arm.

'Listen, my dear, we're doing everything we can to find your daughter. We'll find her. We'll bring her back to you safe and well. You must be patient.' His voice is calm and soothing but he avoids eye contact making me doubt his sincerity. He's just trying to avoid a scene.

They haven't found a body, he tells Christina, and they haven't given up hope of finding Katie alive. There are many small inlets and coves still being searched. She might have jumped off and made it to shore before the lilo floated out to sea. She could perhaps be taking shelter in one of the caves hidden in the coastal rock formations. She could have wandered some distance.

Well I'm not taken in and Christina doesn't appear to take comfort from his words either. Now she's got her elbows on the table and her head in her hands. The Commissioner's words ring hollow. Katie is dead, drowned. Swallowed up by the sea. It's no use clinging on to false hopes. The police know it and we know it. I take a couple of sips of water and say nothing.

I recall a grim statistic that caught my attention on the TV news coverage in the police station waiting area earlier on. Unusually, the British Leeward Isles has one of the highest drowning mortality rates in the world with over 20 per cent of deaths per year being recorded as such, most of them tourists. Despite this, the islands' most popular beaches still don't have lifeguards.

Katie is dead, drowned. She's become one of those statistics.

'Now Miss Kenedey, shall we begin?' Christina looks up into the Commissioner's impassive grey eyes.

'Let's take up where we left off yesterday...'

He flips over a couple of pages of her statement until he gets to the part dealing with the hours before Katie was reported missing. Costa's beside him, ready to take notes. He runs his hand through his hair. I can feel his eyes boring into me.

'Can you remind us what time you last saw your daughter?'

'I think it was about noon,' says Christina.

The Commissioner looks down at his papers. 'But I see from the coast guard's report that your daughter was reported missing at 5.03 p.m.? So where were you between noon and 5.03?'

'The four of us left the pool bar around twelve o'clock.' She gestures towards me. 'Scarlett and Katie went down to the beach. I had lunch at the beach club with Damien.' She shifts awkwardly in her chair. 'We stayed there until about two o'clock and then went up to the hotel room for a siesta'. I see Costa raise an eyebrow as he writes down the word.

'What did Scarlett and Katie do for lunch?' I'm sitting right in front of him. But I might as well be invisible as far as the Commissioner's concerned.

'They ate at the beach. Scarlett took a picnic,' says Christina. I nod in agreement. *If you can call a cheese sandwich a picnic!*

'Ah, I see, so you had lunch with your boyfriend and then went upstairs with him to your room for an afternoon *siesta*?' There's a shade of sarcasm in his voice. Clearly he doesn't believe they went up to the hotel room to sleep. Surely, he doesn't expect her to provide all the graphic details? 'And when your little girl went missing? Where were you? You need to tell us everything you can recall.'

'I'm not sure. I don't know exactly when she disappeared. As I told you, I was in my room all afternoon.' Christina averts her eyes from the steely gaze of the Commissioner. 'It's all very hazy,' she says, covering her face with her hands. 'I slept until about four o'clock. When I woke the room was empty, with the curtains drawn. I called out to Damien but there was no reply. I thought he must have gone down to the beach. I remember falling back onto the pillows and lying there listening to the waves and watching the ceiling fan spinning overhead.' For an instant, her voice is dreamy. 'The strange thing was that although I had a searing headache, for those few brief moments I felt happier and more carefree than I had felt in years.' She hesitates and coughs to clear her throat. 'Then I took a long, cool shower, dried my hair and dressed for dinner before going down to meet Damien, Scarlett and Katie in the play area. Damien had sent me a text telling me to meet him there at five-thirty.'

There's something pre-prepared and rehearsed about her speech. She looks directly at the Commissioner. 'It's here on my phone.' She scrolls through her messages and shows him the screen.

Hello beautiful! Gone for a swim. Meeting the girls by the swings at half five. See you there darling xxx

She points vaguely in my direction. 'But they never turned up...'

'That was a lie,' I blurt out. 'Damien lied. He told me they'd come to meet us at the beach.'

The Commissioner silences me with a dismissive gesture but I see Costa writing something down.

'What time did Damien leave your hotel room?'

'I don't know, he left while I was sleeping. It must have been between half-past two and four o'clock.' She glances at her phone.

There's a pause, and all I can hear is Christina's shallow breathing and the scratching of Costa's pen on paper.

This is so cruel. The Commissioner's treating her more like a suspect than a witness. At the very least, his line of questioning is designed to set her up and shame her as an irresponsible, neglectful mother, who abandoned her child on the beach. Anything to distract from the incompetence of the local police! She's getting the same treatment as me! She looks wretched – more than that, she looks humiliated. It can't be easy going over the details of her tawdry affair.

'Weren't you concerned or angry with Damien when he didn't turn up at the play area with Katie?' asks the Commissioner.

'I was annoyed that he had stood me up but I wasn't concerned,' says Christina. 'Scarlett was supposed to be looking after Katie.' She nods in my direction.

Your only concern was to get to the bar for your first gin and tonic of the evening to kick off another night of romancing under the Caribbean stars! My thoughts feel uncharitable.

'I remember noticing that the play area was unusually quiet,' continues Christina, 'There was just one little boy on the monkey bars with his mother watching him – and then the peace was broken by the helicopter circling overhead. But it was only when I walked into the hotel lobby and saw the hotel manager deep in conversation with two police officers that I realised something was wrong. When he saw me his jaw dropped. I was heading for the bar. He almost knocked me flying when he grabbed hold of me. He told me they'd been looking for me everywhere... that something dreadful had happened...' She rubs the tops of her arms that still show the marks of bruising where his fingers had dug into her flesh. 'I can't see how any of this is relevant.' She puts her head in her hands again and sighs.

At that moment a movement in the control room attracts my attention through the glass. The police officer with the purple fingernails stands up and walks over to a printer. A few seconds later she pushes open the door and hands a sheet of paper to Costa who places it in front of the Commissioner. My pulse is racing. I can scarcely breathe. I look over at Christina. Suddenly alert, she's gripping the table. Her knuckles are white.

'Is it good news?' she bursts out, and lashes out with her arm as if to snatch the sheet from him. The expression on his face is determinedly bland as painfully slowly he puts on his reading glasses and peruses the document. At last he looks up.

'It is good news,' he says. I take a breath. He reads from the report. '*In conclusion, Marine Forensics advise that lacerations on the yellow inflatable are not consistent with a shark bite... Lacerations were caused by protrusions of coral and rock from the reef... Microscopic analysis reveals trace particles of coral and other marine micro-organisms where the tearing occurred. No human DNA has been detected.*'

My heart sinks. Katie has not been found. Not even a sighting. So Katie was not attacked by a shark, but most likely drowned at sea. What kind of good news is that?

Christina slumps back in the chair, defeated.

'You're wasting your time,' she says.

She slams her palms down on the table, sending her water glass crashing down to the floor.

'I'm sick of all this crap! Katie wasn't eaten by a shark and I don't believe she drowned. Can we stop this ridiculous circus and get on with the search?' she shouts. 'I know she's still alive and you need to get out there and start looking for her.'

Christina pushes back her chair and stands up. 'Please can I go now,' she says. 'I need some fresh air. The air is stifling in here. These walls are closing in on me.' She looks white and clammy, as if she's about to faint. 'I need to get down to the beach, to see with my own eyes what's happening down there, to be part of the search to find my daughter. Time is slipping away. Shouldn't you be down there too, directing the operation?'

'Miss Kenedey,' says the Commissioner coldly, 'please don't try to tell me how to do my job. We are pursuing several avenues of enquiry. My officers are fully in control.'

He closes Christina's incomplete statement and stands up. Looks like she's offended him.

'You are free to leave at any time. Thank you for your help with our enquiries. If you remember anything more, you know where to find us.'

'What about my statement?' I protest. 'I want to have it put on the record that I believe I was drugged.'

Costa shuffles through the papers and hands a single sheet over to the Commissioner. Reading upside down, I can see that it's a few notes from my conversation with the family liaison officer yesterday consisting only of my personal details and a brief summary of the timeline based on my answers to her questions. There's no record of what I told the police earlier in the day about having been drugged; no mention that I suspect that I am the victim of foul play.

The Commissioner ignores my protest.

'I'm very sorry Miss Reyes, but we have to stick to proven facts in the record of evidence.'

'Then give me a drug test,' I say. 'That will give you all the proof you need.'

'A drug test at this stage will serve no purpose,' says the Commissioner. He gives me a hard glare. 'Even if it comes back positive that doesn't prove that you had been drugged against your will at the time the little girl disappeared. You could have self-administered drugs last night or this morning.'

He gestures for me to remain seated while he holds open the door for Christina.

'I do, however, have some further questions for you in relation to the events of this morning,' he says disapprovingly, as he dismisses Christina with a nod.

I groan inwardly.

Here we go, now he's going to grill me about what happened in the Jeep.

Twenty minutes later I rejoin Christina and an officer leads us through a maze of corridors to the back of the building, where an emergency exit leads out onto a backstreet away from the main square.

'There's about twenty of them round the front,' she says, 'waiting to jump on you with cameras and mics.'

As we walk through the door, Christina turns to the officer.

'What have you done with Damien?'

'We've taken him to a holding cell,' says the woman. 'He's been remanded in custody overnight for his driving offences. The bail hearing will be tomorrow morning.'

I'm so happy. He had it coming.

Christina stands on the kerb, hailing a cab. She's desperate to get going. But it's market day. The road is gridlocked with pick-up trucks belonging to market traders now packing up their stalls and driving away from the main square close to the police station. Just as a taxi driver finally responds to Christina's dramatic hand signals and pulls across the road towards us, I hear her name being shouted loudly and the sound of pounding feet.

'Stop, Miss Kenedey. Wait please.'

It's Costa, shoving past the shoppers as he runs, muscles rippling under his white shirt, waving a piece of paper in the air.

'Miss Kenedey, we've just received an email from the police dog handling team.' He waves the computer print-out in her face.

At 2.21 p.m. today, Sergeant Kingsley Blake, search-and-rescue dog handler, reported 3 positive alerts by detective dog, PJ, on a child's pink swimsuit located in a rock cavern at Crooks' Bay.

8

3 June 2000: The Cherwell River, Oxford

Do you remember the day this photograph was taken? 3 June 2000 – the first summer of the brave new millennium. We look so young and so impossibly happy, captured together in the punt, you and me, and James wedged in between us, raising a glass of champagne in a toast, and his flinty blue eyes staring straight at the lens of my beloved Canon SLR propped up on the tripod.

The afternoon sun is behind us and we're haloed by incandescent light, an image of gilded youth, our mingled strands of golden hair glimmering in the rays. And in the foreground, look, you can see the slender branches of the weeping willow framing the shot, dipping low over the water, the narrow pale green leaves dappling light and shade across the forward-facing stern. The weeping willow, symbol of sorrow and grief, but also of wisdom and everlasting life – ironic, don't you think?

Like Shakespeare's doomed Ophelia in the painting by Millais, you're almost horizontal, 'mermaid-like' above the 'weeping brook', reaching for the dangling willow branch as the punt glides past. But you're carefree and laughing, oblivious to your fate. James' hand is resting softly on your bare sunburnt thigh. The dark, green, murky water swirls around the dragging metal pole clenched in my fist.

And we are profiled in the shot, a mirror image, identical yet opposite, our faces turned towards James, leaning in flirtatiously and seeking his attention with our bright rapacious eyes.

Caught in the click of the camera, the instant before he told me your 'good news.'

Gabrielle drove up to Oxford for the day to visit James and Lara. The girls were celebrating their twenty-first birthdays. She was looking forward to a weekend out of London, away from the traffic and the sweaty grime, a chance to breathe and see more than just the jagged rectangle of blue sky visible from her kitchen window. Most of all she was looking forward to seeing James again. She hadn't seen or spoken to him since April when he'd spent ten days of his Easter vacation lying low at her Chelsea flat, making use of her spare room. They'd kept it a secret from Lara who had gone home to Stratford-Upon-Avon to read and study for her Finals. It'd been a delicious conspiracy between the two of them – heady, passionate, and dream-like.

The instant Gabrielle finished shooting at the modelling agency in Covent Garden where she now worked as a fashion photographer, she would race for the tube, and hot-foot it back along the King's Road to the flat. James would be waiting for her, lounging on the sofa bed, pretending to read medical journals, smoking, and looking so young and beautiful. He was lithe and sinuous, lying there on her soft pillows, like an exotic cat, thought Gabrielle

'You should be a model,' Gabrielle had told him, observing him with a photographer's eye as she ran her forefinger slowly down his chiselled profile. 'You've got much better features than most of the guys I get to photograph.'

'Stop leading me astray,' he had replied. 'I'm destined to make ground-breaking medical discoveries, remember.' He had grabbed her wrist and pulled her towards him. 'Anyway, right now I'm having too much fun to go out and get a job.' He kissed her. 'Just give me sex and cigarettes and I'm happy malingering here with you.'

Now, today, it was such a glorious Oxford day, the first brilliant hot day of the summer. Gabrielle was looking forward to finding a pretext to ditch Lara later on and spend some time alone with James. They had some catching up to do. The three of them whiled away the afternoon punting on the Cherwell. James had brought along a bottle of champagne and they drank it in the punt, carelessly leaning back against the vinyl cushions and laughing and looking up at the picture-perfect blue sky. They were sharing the one glass that James kept refilling until the bubbles frothed over and spilt onto their gleaming legs. Gabrielle's gaze was drawn to the myriad sources of light, glancing off the ripples on the surface of the water, ricocheting off the glass held high in James' hand, and piercing through the dappled canopy of leaves. She felt bathed in light, and closed her eyes sensuously, to capture the moment.

'We've got something to celebrate – I mean, as well as your birthdays,' said James, touching Gabrielle's hand softly. 'Lara's pregnant. Did she tell you?' Gabrielle opened her eyes and now the light was blinding and hostile, bleaching out the colours. James had a huge grin on his face. His white teeth sparkled. The cat who got the cream. The laughter had gone from Lara's deep, luminous eyes and they seemed to cloud over as Gabrielle stared blankly into them. Lara turned away and looked down at her hand trailing in the water beside the punt. 'No, she didn't say,' said Gabrielle. 'Well, congratulations!' she added darkly, after a long pause.

And so, instead of spending a steamy evening alone with James, Gabrielle went back with Lara to her room in college, where they passed the evening talking and sipping tea. Gabrielle got to work on Lara.

'You're going to get rid of it, surely?' said Gabrielle. 'It's not fair on James. He's got three more years before he qualifies. You'll wreck his career if you have the baby. He can't support you and the baby on his medical grant. He'll never be happy if you make him give up his life ambition.'

Lara listened, not saying much. Gabrielle kept on and on at her.

'And you worked so hard to get into Oxford – bored us all stupid going on about it since you were thirteen years old. Dreaming spires, college balls, Pimm's parties, a glittering future in academia and all that jazz. You've lived the dream these past three years. You can't just throw it all away now – you can't go back to being a provincial nobody.

Now, Gabrielle pointed down angrily at her stomach. 'And you'd be the laughing stock of the village. Imagine the embarrassment? The vicar's daughter – an unwanted pregnancy, an illegitimate child. It's too humiliating.'

Gabrielle felt the evening stillness almost vibrating through the open window. She caught wafts of perfume from the purple blooms of ancient wisteria growing outside the casement window, carried on the gentle breeze. She watched Lara leaning back in the window seat, breathing deeply, her hand resting lazily across her stomach. Although still slim and angular, she already looked unmistakably pregnant, thought Gabrielle. She had that self-satisfied, bovine look about her.

The calm of dusk was magnified by the chime of bells from a tower in the back quad. It was such a tranquil setting yet Gabrielle could sense the pulse of anger and jealousy ringing in her ears, like the bells. She had a sudden impulse to strike Lara, to shove her out the window.

The bells reminded her of childhood quarrels. She was transported back in time to a birthday party at the vicarage in Stratford. She remembered how choked with envy she'd been when Lara had ripped the pink tissue paper from her birthday present, a golden-haired, blue-eyed china doll. For her own birthday present that year, Gabrielle, 'the tomboy of the two,' had asked for a skateboard. She thought dolls were for sissies. But when she set eyes on Lara's lovely china doll, she was possessed with jealousy and desperate to do a swap. Usually so pliable, Lara was implacable. She kept the doll.

But not for long... it wasn't long before her pretty face was shattered.

She's not keeping that baby, thought Gabrielle. *She's not having the baby and she's not having James. I'm not the kind of person to sit around waiting for the scraps.* Her throat was dry and her chest was taut. She felt an aching sickness in the pit of her stomach.

She was a little girl again. Telling tales to her mother at the injustice of it all.

'He was mine first. She stole him from me. It's so unfair.'

This time her mother was not there to adjudicate.

Just the sort of thing Lara would do to get her man, just typical – get herself pregnant, then play the damsel-in-distress. *Well, I want him back. And I'll get him back. I don't care if she hates me for it.*

She was already planning her revenge.

I'll make her have an abortion. I can fix it up at the Chelsea clinic. And I'll make him fall in love with me again. Whatever it takes. If the scheming bitch thinks she can trap him with a baby, she can think again.

9

Scarlett

The alarm goes off at half past six and I wake from a broken, fitful sleep. In a state of semi-consciousness, I recall lurid fragments from my dreams – I'm screaming at Damien as he leans over Katie; he's dragging off her swimsuit while she giggles and licks her ice cream; I'm hitting Damien over the head again and again with a hip flask; I'm lying face up on the yellow lilo looking at the sky; someone is making love to me, he has strong hands, a searching tongue; I'm ruffling his dark hair, overcome with feelings of tenderness; I'm calling out a name, begging him to stop but willing him to go on; wanting this man, but who is he? A face comes into view above my head. It's not Damien but Detective Sergeant Costa, and he's bearing down on me, pressing his strong hands around my neck as I struggle for breath; I'm gasping for air, a police car is coming, the sirens are wailing…

The alarm is bleeping on my phone and a boulder is pressing down on my chest.

*

I'm due back at the police station with Christina at 9 a.m. The Commissioner has asked Costa to question me separately from Christina to go over my explanation for being found 'joyriding' with Damien in the Jeep. He clearly wasn't convinced by my answers yesterday – I told him basically that I had no choice about accepting the lift from Damien as I couldn't get away from him. There was no place to run. And as for what happened in the Jeep, well, I was scared of Damien and, in that moment, it was the only way I could think of to get him off the road and stall him for long enough to give the police time to catch up and take him into custody.

'You could call it *preservation sex*, if you like,' I had said, only half-flippantly. The Commissioner didn't understand that, of course, being a man!

Anyway, Costa's tasked with taking a full statement from me this morning. On the plus side he should have the results back from the drug test. After Costa showed us the email about the discovery of Katie's swimsuit, I persuaded him that what I had told the police about my drink being spiked needed to be taken seriously. So Costa took me back to the police station to administer the drug test while Christina went on down to the beach.

I knock on Christina's door just before seven as we had planned to breakfast in her room together, to avoid backhanded whispers of hotel staff and guests. The sight of us engaging in any normal activity seems to provoke outrage. But it's not as if we can survive on thin air. Christina opens the door and goes back into the bathroom to finish putting on her make-up. She's wearing the silk gown that Damien had surprised her with for the vacation. I perch on the edge of the bed and see her reflected in the bathroom mirror, slicking red lipstick over perfectly formed lips.

How can she bother with make-up when Katie is missing?

I pick up the hotel phone to call for room service. The jade earring is lying on the bedside table next to Christina's brown moleskin Gucci purse.

She's going to lose it again, I think with annoyance.

She never looks after her things. She's so careless.

I tell the maid we'll have breakfast on the balcony and she sets out a tempting tray of steaming coffee, croissants, fresh fruit and yogurt. My stomach is in knots but I need to keep my strength up.

Sitting on the balcony, the air is crisp, there's sunshine on the water. It's going to be another beautiful day, the second morning without Katie.

I look up at the cloudless sky. The sun is still hanging there. The sea is still blue. The tourists are still heading for the beach. And Katie is still missing... This can't be real.

Still missing.

I must still be dreaming...

Christina is still locked in the bathroom, making herself beautiful so I tap on the door.

'Breakfast is here' I call out. 'Fresh coffee.' It's the little things that keep you going, I tell myself guiltily.

As the door opens, I note the effort Christina has made with her appearance this morning. Her striking blue eyes are rimmed with navy eyeliner and she's even gone to the trouble of applying concealer to disguise the dark circles beneath them.

Clearly, old habits die hard. Perhaps with all those television cameras around she wants to look her best. To be fair, it might be that it's not simply her incurable vanity but rather an attempt to keep control, to hold it all together.

She's done her hair differently, pulled back from her face and twisted into a shiny knot on the top of her head. She's wearing the jade earrings.

'You look nice' I say automatically. 'Those earrings go well with your eyes.' Christina smiles absently.

It's only as I utter the trite words, that a thought strikes me. How very strange? The jade earring I found under the seat in Damien's car is sitting next to Christina's purse on the bedside table. I can see it there right now, catching the light. So that makes three…

She catches me looking.

I decide to say nothing.

While we're breakfasting on the balcony – or rather, while *I'm* breakfasting, given that Christina pushes everything away except for a scalding cup of black coffee – the phone rings. A package has been left at reception for Damien. I offer to go down and collect it.

When I hand over the thick brown envelope to Christina, she rips it open unceremoniously. Damien's mobile falls out onto the table. She puts the mobile straight into her bag.

'The police will want to see this,' she says.

Clearly, she doesn't want me looking over her shoulder while she goes through his calls and texts.

There's also a handwritten note and a sheet of paper with a list of transactions that looks something like a bank statement. She opens them out on the table. The note is on the official letterhead of the office of Leonard de Cruz, manager of the Black Jack Casino at Limetree Bay.

The note is dated yesterday, Wednesday 17 June.

Hi Boss, Good to see you last night. You forgot your phone – the concierge passed it over this morning. I've enclosed your account. Dieter's agreed to extend your credit until Saturday latest. Best I could do.

The casino manager's clearly on friendly terms with Damien as he signs himself 'Lennie' and says he's looking forward to the game of golf planned for Friday.

'He told me he left his phone at the golf club,' says Christina.

'He told me he left his phone at the Coco Shack,' I say. 'He wanted to go back for it and take me there for lunch. He should get his story straight!'

She gives me an angry look and I decide I've said more than enough.

While Christina reads out the note, I run my eyes down the printout. On closer scrutiny, the account turns out to be a list of bets placed by Damien at the casino from 4.15 p.m. on the afternoon that Katie disappeared until 3.35 a.m. the next morning. The print-out shows seventeen bets placed in just over nine hours and the tally of wins and losses during that period amounts to a staggering 13,335 US dollars owed by Damien to the Black Jack Casino! As if that wasn't bad enough, there's a note at the bottom recording that Damien made a payment at 3.39 p.m. of five thousand dollars as part settlement in respect of deferred debts on his account, but that a further 5,737 dollars is still due, in respect of those deferred losses.

'He's been gambling again,' says Christina. 'I knew he was lying. He wasn't at the golf club at all. While we were searching for Katie, he spent the night placing bets at the casino. I had no idea he had it this bad. It's an addiction.'

I think it best not to tell her what I really think of the slippery bastard. But I do register one important fact – the document provides Damien with an alibi. If he really was at the Black Jack Casino between 3.39 p.m. in the afternoon of Tuesday 16 June and 3.35 a.m. the next morning, then he can't have taken Katie.

Casinos are prohibited in the British Leeward Isles. The Black Jack Casino is in the US Leeward Isles – more than half an hour's boat ride from where our hotel is situated on the island of Grand Carmola in the British Leeward Isles. If the gambling debts belong to Damien then he must have already embarked from the island of Grand Carmola by three o'clock in the afternoon.

Our eyes meet and I wonder if the same thoughts are going through Christina's head.

Damien can't be Katie's abductor.

At 3.35 p.m. on Tuesday 16 June, I took a photograph of Katie playing on the beach, filling the red bucket with shells.

When we enter the police station on the dot of 9 a.m. pushing past the straggle of reporters camped outside the door, the duty officer on the desk greets us like old friends and ushers us straight through to the Commissioner's private interview room. The room is less shabby than the room we were questioned in yesterday. It's freshly painted and there's a comfortable blue sofa and armchairs in the corner. We seem to have been upgraded to VIP witnesses (or is it VIP suspects?). A computer and printer are set up on a polished wooden desk in the middle of the room. There are three black-and-white prints with views of Oxford displayed on the walls. He's clearly an English expat. It's more like a study in a university library than a police interview room in a small town in the Caribbean. As we sink into the sofa, Christina points to one of the pictures, a framed print featuring a building with a domed facade, dated 1920 with the title *A View of The Queen's College, Oxford* and says casually, 'How bizarre! Feels like a colonial outpost in here.'

The windows overlook a small dusty courtyard shaded by lime trees. I open the window. Mundane everyday sounds filter into the room above the whir of the air conditioning – a car horn, a dog barking, the endless buzz of cicadas. Sun streams through the branches of an acacia tree growing in a corner of the courtyard. A cat is stretched out on the warm stone on top of one of the walls. It yawns and rolls over.

Costa breezes in a few minutes later and Christina immediately hands over the brown envelope.

'I think you'll find these papers interesting. They may be relevant to your enquiries,' she says.

What about Damien's mobile phone. Why isn't she handing that over?

Costa runs his eyes down the list of bets placed by Damien at the Black Jack casino, frowns and puts the sheet to one side. He sits up straight, self-important. He's preoccupied with his own reveal this morning, pleased to be the centre of attention, now that the Commissioner has placed him in command. He sets a large metal box that looks something like an old-fashioned tool kit in the middle of the table.

We sit down apprehensively as Costa unlocks the box and removes a large yellow padded envelope stamped *Exhibit* which he lays on the desk in front of us. I place my hand over Christina's and hold my breath as he slits open the envelope with a paper knife and carefully pulls out the plastic exhibit wallet contained within it. I feel her hand trembling beneath mine. A child's pink swimsuit, balled up and covered in sand is visible through the clear plastic.

Costa explains that the item of clothing was found and positively identified by a police tracker dog at Crooks' Bay yesterday afternoon. The area around the rock cavern where the clothing was found has been cordoned off and a police forensics team is preparing to carry out a detailed inspection of the site. The team has requested a visual inspection of the item by witnesses to confirm the dog's positive alerts.

He clears his throat. 'Miss Scarlett Georgia Reyes,' he says, writing my name at the top of the witness identification form. I watch the pen held in his firm grip, gliding smoothly over the paper. His handwriting is surprisingly neat, made up of beautifully formed copperplate letters.

'Please confirm your name and address.' He pushes the sheet over. 'Am I correct in thinking that it was you who helped the victim to change into her bathing clothes for the beach?' he says, officiously.

'Yes.'

Costa unzips the exhibit wallet, and using a pair of plastic tongs, lifts out the damp swimsuit. It hangs limply. The pink and white stripes are unmistakable. Christina lets out a low moan.

'It's Katie's,' I say.

'Can you be sure?'

'Look inside,' I tell him, choking back my tears. 'I always draw a smiley face, you know, in black marker pen inside the clothes she takes to kindergarten... she can't read her name tag.'

Costa lays the swimsuit down on the empty wallet and draws apart the straps with the tongs. Sure enough, there's a smiley face staring up at him in smudged ink. Costa has one eyebrow slightly raised, and looks so pleased with himself that, with my emotions on a knife edge, for one instant I have to bite my lip to stifle a laugh and the next, I'm sobbing into my cup of tea.

'You understand what this means, of course,' he says to Christina, ignoring my distress. 'Someone must have taken her.'

He pauses for effect.

'We're looking at abduction.'

Christina groans.

'That's what I've been telling you since yesterday,' she says, holding her head in her hands.

I struggle to compose myself, my eyes glued to his steady, suntanned fingers as he signs the identification form, *Detective Sergeant Paul Costa, Chief Criminal Investigating Officer,* then slides the form, together with the swimsuit back into the plastic wallet, zips it closed, and writes the words, *Exhibit One,* in black marker pen on the outside.

Christina walks over to the window and watches the cat, still stretched out on the warm stone in the sunshine. 'What now?'

'The investigation continues,' he says. 'We reassess and we keep searching. From now on, this is a criminal investigation and I am the chief criminal investigating officer on the case.' He sits back and thrusts out his chest. 'I'm in charge.'

Christina was not party to my grilling by the Commissioner yesterday but even so I can tell she senses a hardening in the police attitude towards us following the discovery of the swimsuit. In their eyes, this isn't simply a tragic incident any more. Costa's body language makes it plain. There's a certain detachment in his manner. We are all suspects now – and the crime is child abduction.

He tells us that Damien was held in custody overnight, charged with offences of dangerous driving. Costa doesn't hide the fact that he regards him as a key suspect in the abduction of Katie. The driving charges provide a useful pretext for keeping him in custody. The bail hearing will take place later in the morning.

He looks from one of us to the other. 'Do you know of anyone who could wish Katie any harm?' he asks. 'Do you know of anyone who would wish to do you any harm? It seems as if Damien has a solid alibi.' He taps the list of bets. 'Can either of you think of anyone else?'

We both shake our heads.

'What about the child's father?' says Costa. He turns to Christina. 'Are you still in contact with him?' I can see where he's going with that one. In fact, I'm surprised he didn't ask the question sooner.

Christina lowers her eyes. 'Katie's father died before she was born,' she says.

There's a long silence, then Costa says, 'Do you think money could be a motivation?' Although the Black Jack record of Damien's bets appears to constitute a solid alibi, I can tell Costa's still thinking about his gambling debts.

'I have a good salary,' says Christina 'but I don't earn a fortune.'

'How good is good?' says Costa.

'Around one hundred and twenty thousand US dollars a year,' says Christina. I call that a fortune and from the look in Costa's eyes so does he – but I suppose in the financial circles Christina moves in, that's standard, and would it really be enough to attract the attention of a potential child abductor?

'What about your mother?' I cut in. 'You told me once that she is embarrassingly rich. You said she inherited a trust fund. Damien must know that.' Christina gives me a filthy look, and then turns to Costa.

'It's true my mother is wealthy. She inherited a substantial sum from her grandfather who made his money trading commodities in London. But my mother lives in England. I live in New York. Damien has never met her and I've never spoken to him about her financial affairs. I've had nothing to do with her since before Katie was born. So please can we leave my mother out of this?' Costa says nothing but he scribbles something down in his notebook.

Once I've completed the formal identification of the swimsuit, Costa announces that he wants to speak to Christina alone so he asks me to 'take a break' and report back to the police station in two hours' time. I can't help feeling a bit hacked off that he's made me come over so early, only to send me out of the room twenty minutes later. But of course, now that Katie's disappearance is a suspected abduction, he wants to interview us all separately. That way he can play us off against each other. He holds open the door for me. His aftershave smells expensive and my flesh tingles as I brush against his starched cotton shirtsleeves.

'Before you send me away, you could at least tell me the results of the drug test,' I say.

'Oh, yes, forgive me, of course.' He gives me a condescending smile. 'Negative. The result was negative. We'll talk about it later.'

10

Scarlett

I'm so angry that my ears are ringing by the time I get to the waiting area.

There must be some mistake, or the drug test was carried out too late – more than twenty-four hours too late thanks to the Commissioner and his investigation team. Costa seems to think I should be pleased with the negative result. OK, so maybe they won't be able to charge me for drug offences but it's going to make it so much harder to restore my reputation and prove I wasn't to blame for Katie's disappearance. If the police aren't going to help me clear my name, I'm just going to have to do it myself – beat them at their own game.

I soon get bored of perching on a sticky plastic chair in the waiting area watching the clock so I decide to get a cab back to the hotel and get started with a spot of sleuthing of my own. The way things are going, I'm the one who'll end up being arrested for criminal negligence or some other trumped up charge unless I can find the evidence to prove that someone else is responsible for whatever has happened to Katie. Judging by the tough questioning the Commissioner put me through yesterday, everyone seems to be treating me as one of the prime suspects. The Commissioner's already told me that he's appointed a psychologist to put me through a lie-detector test later today. And he's asked me to take part in a re-enactment, on the beach, of Katie's disappearance tomorrow afternoon. Then to cap it all, he's arranged a news conference for tomorrow evening at which Christina will make a public appeal for Katie's safe return from which he's specifically excluded me.

In this hostile environment, I can't afford to lose any time. What's more, I can't help noticing that Christina's been acting weird. I know she's in shock and I don't want to judge her but somehow, she doesn't seem upset enough! God knows, I feel broken. In her place, I'd be in pieces. And one thing is really puzzling me. Why didn't she hand over Damien's phone? It's obvious that the phone is key to the police investigation. Why would she hold back such important evidence? It doesn't make sense unless she's trying to cover for him.

I slam the taxi door and head straight for Christina's room. I can't shake the suspicion that she and Damien are in on this together. She's hiding something. I want to find out why. The coast is clear when I tap quietly, so I let myself in with Christina's spare key and lock the door behind me. I'm surprised that the police haven't already taken steps to preserve and record any evidence that might be found here. I know that in a missing persons case they would normally do this within the first few hours. But I guess we were all fooled. All the early signs were that Katie had drowned. Still, they've known since yesterday when Katie's swimsuit was discovered that she may have been abducted. This delay looks like negligence or incompetence at the very least.

Feeling more like a thief than an amateur detective, I start to work my way swiftly and methodically through every drawer, cupboard, suitcase and bag in the room. First, the safe. It's tucked inside the wardrobe. The code has got to be Katie's date of birth – 140211. Christina uses that for everything. Sure enough, the safe door buzzes and swings open. Christina and Damien's passports are there. Not Katie's – but I have that in my safe. It occurs to me that the police have been remiss in not confiscating all our passports. This just confirms their incompetence. There are also a few twenty-dollar bills, house keys, six credit and store cards belonging to Christina, and a small leather jewellery roll containing a gold necklace, a couple of bracelets and the perplexing third jade earring that she must have moved from the bedside table into the safe.

I find nothing suspicious in the drawers – just a ridiculous quantity of clothes. My boss seems to have brought her entire wardrobe along with her. I count five pairs of shoes and seven cocktail dresses – designer brands. All those hours spent shopping on Fifth Avenue. Damien clearly also has a weakness for designer brands – his boxers, swimming trunks, and shorts are all Ralph Lauren, also three pairs of Levi's and a collection of flamboyant Versace shirts. Oh, and, not one but three tuxedos together with matching bowties! Why he would need to bring three dinner jackets to a Caribbean island is beyond me. He was obviously planning on taking Christina to some classy establishments or spending all his time at the casino.

Christina's left two books on her bedside table, *Brideshead Revisited* and *The Picture of Dorian Gray*. She has literary tastes in fiction. Both are well-worn with yellowing pages and broken spines. The novels must be old favourites. They're annotated in her handwriting with pencil under linings and scribbles in the margins. As I turn the pages, a photograph drops to the floor. At first glance, I think it's Damien. The man in the faded black-and-white portrait is very young but bears a striking resemblance to Damien – a softer, more romantic version – with the same engaging dark eyes, the same strong jaw line, and the same thick hair parted and swept to one side. Perhaps her first love? It's rather sweet that she keeps his photograph as her bookmark!

Seeing the likeness, I begin to understand why Christina fell for Damien even though they seem such an improbable match – he reminds her of a childhood sweetheart. All the more so, I guess, because he's a few years younger than her. While I feel nothing but disdain for Damien, I can't deny he has charisma. He's quick-witted and funny when he wants to be, and he knows how to turn on the charm. Let's face it, when I reflect on Christina's life in New York, what isolated, professional single mother in her mid-thirties wouldn't have her head turned by the attentions of a suave Wall Street boy who takes her to the theatre and the movies and wines her and dines her in all the best bars and restaurants? – especially when he takes an active interest in her child and looks like a male model to boot!

There's a stack of papers on the floor on Damien's side of the bed. I crouch down and rifle through them: boarding passes and other printed documents from the outward journey; a printout of the hotel reservation; car rental papers; a green cardboard file containing travel insurance documents and a document with the heading 'Moorings Lease'; a list of possible places to visit; maps, and some receipts for island excursions Damien booked on the day we arrived.

I recognise the green cardboard file from my encounter with Damien in Christina's bedroom in New York and wonder if some of these papers could be the documents I saw him taking from her desk that day?

I flip back to the insurance documents. It's Christina's annual travel policy, automatically renewed each year. An amendment adding Katie to the policy was made last month. I wonder if it was Damien who prompted Christina to include Katie when she hadn't got around to doing this in the past four years? Could Damien (with or without the connivance of Christina) have dreamt up the idea of faking a tragic accident to make it look like Katie was drowned at sea with the intention of making a false claim on Christina's travel insurance? Is this too far-fetched? I check the small print in the accompanying booklet.

Personal accident: If you are physically injured on a journey and the injury is caused by violent, visible,

external and accidental means only, we will pay you or
your legal representatives up to $25,000 if your injury
or accident leads to death or permanent disability.

I'm not sure that this would cover a drowning accident –
and twenty five thousand dollars would scarcely pay for
his gambling losses. And there are so many exclusions (that
I can't even understand) and legal hoops to get through.
Still, perhaps I'm not being completely ridiculous. He's
so up to his neck in gambling debts that he may have
resorted to desperate measures. I put the document to one
side. Costa needs to see it – just in case.

Then I look again at the moorings lease. The rental
period covers the whole month of June and the document
is signed 'P. D. Covera'. Damien doesn't own a yacht. I
didn't even know Damien could sail. He's never mentioned
it before. So why would he need to park a yacht in a
marina? I should show this to Costa too. I pull out the
document and place it on top of the travel policy.

Next, I slide my arm under the mattress and inside
the sheets and then go round the room on my hands and
knees looking under the furniture. From my position on
the floor, I notice something pushed under the bed in the
small gap between the bed base and the tiles. I slide in
my hand and pull out a dog-eared back copy of *Playboy*
magazine. I start turning the pages, partly out of curiosity.
The magazine falls open at the double-page spread,
Playmate of the Month, and I gasp in shock to see what
falls out: a black-and-white portrait photograph of Katie
as a toddler – disgusting man! – together with the original

of Katie's birth certificate. Now what legitimate reason could there possibly be for bringing the original of Katie's birth certificate on holiday? And why would it be hidden inside a six-month-old issue of *Playboy* magazine? This is the strongest evidence yet that Damien's involved. I bet he stole these from Christina's desk! I add the photograph of Katie and her birth certificate to the cache of papers that I'm gathering for Costa.

Suddenly, I hear the key turning in the door and scramble to my feet. Damn! *Must be housekeeping. Just my luck.*

I'm about to call out for the maids to come back later when the door opens and I catch a glimpse of blonde hair. Christina must have come back early from the police station. Still holding the copy of *Playboy* magazine, I dive into the bathroom and lean against the bathroom door, my heart thumping at the fear of being caught red-handed.

I hold my breath. I hear rustling on the other side.

'Scarlett, are you in there? What are you doing in my room?' Her voice is clipped and impatient.

'I picked up your key by mistake,' I call through the door. 'I'm feeling sick, I'm sorry. I had to rush in here to use your bathroom.'

I hear movement in the room, opening and shutting cupboards and drawers. 'I've come back for some documents,' she says. 'The police want them for the investigation.' While I wait for her to leave, I continue absently to turn the pages of *Playboy*, until right at the back of the magazine I come to a collage of shots that makes the blood rush to my cheeks. There's no mistaking it. It's me in the photographs, captured in a sequence of compromising positions in an outfit that leaves very little to the imagination. How did they get hold of my images? Is that why Damien kept the magazine, because I'm featured in it? Was he planning to discredit or blackmail me?

My thoughts are interrupted by the voice on the other side of the door. 'I'm going back to the police station now. I'll see you later.'

'Sure, see you later,' I say and make a big show of running the taps and flushing the toilet a couple of times. When I come out of the bathroom the room is empty and the documents I had placed on the bed are gone. She must have taken them with her.

II

Scarlett

I'm at the beach with Christina. We're not talking, just lying on sunbeds under a parasol, looking out to sea. Christina is sullen and irritable today. I can imagine only too well the malicious headlines if the paparazzi see us now – *heartless mother sunbathing while the search for missing daughter goes on* – but we have to be somewhere, we can't hide in our rooms all day, and this is as good a place to be as any.

Overhead the sky is blue but out to sea it's a menacing grey. There's going to be a storm. On the horizon there's a bank of bullet-grey clouds massing and moving in our direction. A dark sheet from the clouds to the sea marks the line of approaching rain. I reckon we've got about thirty minutes before we get soaked.

After the frantic efforts of the last few days, exhaustion has set in, numbing the intensity of my grief but making my mood as desolate as the leaden skies. If I were a cartoon character in a graphic magazine, I'd be drawn with a big black cloud right above my head.

We found a spot at the very far end of the beach hoping to be left in peace. Ever since Katie disappeared the local hacks have been prowling round the entrance to the hotel, and there's always a risk of coming face to face with them if they get the chance to dodge the security guards. They loiter in the grounds or stalk the beach in the hope of snapping a picture of us or scooping an interesting quote from one of the guests. I always thought I'd like to be famous. But this kind of celebrity is not for me. If you believe half of what's been said or written about me in the press and on social media, I'm negligent, lazy, drunken, promiscuous, disgusting, evil, perverted; I should crawl under a rock and die. As for Christina, it's even more vicious. She can't do anything right! I'm sick of their vitriol and lies. If I could get away with it, I would smash their cameras on the rocks.

Christina didn't say much about her interview with Costa this morning. She was tight-lipped and withdrawn when she came back from yet another trip to the police station. It's becoming part of the daily routine for each of us – a one-to-one session with Costa. I didn't dare ask her what Costa made of the documents she came back for yesterday because I didn't want her to know I'd been going through her private papers in her room (but in truth I can't actually be sure whether she gave him the papers or just took them away because she didn't want the police to find them). I've got my suspicions but I want to give her the benefit of the doubt.

Over coffee she opened up a little and told me that Costa's in the process of getting witness statements from all the staff and guests at the hotel. He's also about to launch a new poster campaign. He's still quite upbeat, hopeful that something positive will come of the enquiries: if Katie was abducted or wandered off at the beach while I was sleeping under the influence of drugs, someone must have seen something. They've had the dogs in action again too – scouring the beaches and coastal paths in a ten-mile radius from the hotel and from the site where Katie's swimsuit was found. But so far, nothing new… The trail goes cold at the cave.

We've been kicked out of our rooms this morning while they are being searched. The police are looking for evidence and recovering fingerprints. About time too! I suppose Costa finally realised a police search of both our hotel rooms was long overdue. Better late than never but if they wanted to 'secure the scene' they should have done it as soon as Katie went missing. So many people have been coming and going. Inevitably, it's going to look bad for me. They'll find my fingerprints everywhere in Christina's room. What hope of clearing my name!

Before I left my own hotel room this morning, a police officer asked me for the code to the safe. I've been using the same code as Christina – Katie's date of birth. The officer put on her white cotton gloves and emptied the contents out onto a dustsheet she'd placed on the bed.

'I'll check over the safe first then you can put your valuables back in before you leave the room,' she said.

She itemised everything – my passport, jewellery, wallet and keys and started to dust the passport and my wallet with a soft brush for fingerprints.

'Anything missing?'

'Yes, yes something's missing,' I said. 'Katie's passport is gone and a pink *Sleeping Beauty* purse that she insisted on putting in the safe.' Tears pricked my eyes as I recalled how pleased with herself Katie had been, feeling so grown up as she placed her purse in the safe along with my wallet. 'On the first day of the holiday, Damien gave her ten dollars to buy ice-creams. She was so excited.'

The police officer looked up. 'The child's passport is gone?' she said. She pulled out her pager to report this finding.

'I haven't touched the safe since the day we got here.' I felt my cheeks begin to burn. 'Christina must have taken it. Look in her safe.'

Naturally this incident has added to my unease, even though Costa insisted the search of our rooms was routine procedure, now that the investigation has changed from a search and rescue operation to a case of suspected abduction.

'Nothing to worry about' he said cheerfully but I knew he was being disingenuous. Our rooms are being treated as potential crime scenes now and the police are belatedly taking steps to preserve, record and recover evidence

'Let's go and get some lunch' I say to Christina, jumping up from the sunbed. 'You need to keep up your strength and we're going to get soaked if we stay here much longer. The strengthening wind, blowing through the branches of the coconut palms, creates the sound of pattering raindrops as if the downpour has already started. 'The restaurant should be quiet now,' I say. 'It's almost three o'clock.'

I lead the way as we amble over to the Reef Terrace where there's an empty table in the corner, sheltered by a fig tree. My favourite summer hit is playing on the beat box…

I wanna dance in the waves 'neath the Mexican sky
Are you with me? Are you with me?

The refrain takes on a new mournful and haunting quality in my head, strangely incongruous and ironic, yet reawakening memories of heady beach parties and night clubbing from a former life.

The metal chair scrapes as I pull it out and a lizard darts off into a chink between the stones.

One blink and he's gone.

'Let's start outside,' I say, 'and we can take cover when the rain comes.'

Christina says she doesn't care where she sits or what she eats, she's not hungry anyway, so I order the daily special for us both – grilled snapper and conch fritters.

'Sounds delicious' I say brightly.

The rain's coming down in sheets, we've retreated to an indoor table and my stomach's rumbling by the time the food arrives more than half an hour later. I bolt it down while Christina picks at her fish and scarcely touches the fritters. I detect a shadow of reproach as she eyes my empty plate.

'There's nothing wrong with your appetite,' she says reproachfully.

Despite the suntan, she looks exhausted, eyes circled with dark shadows, fragile and angular. She must have lost at least five kilos since the day Katie went missing.

'Did Costa take your fingerprints?' I ask her. 'He asked me to give my fingerprints "on a voluntary basis, to facilitate their enquiries". I mean God, I could hardly say no.'

Christina shrugs.

'I gave mine too. It will help them to distinguish between our fingerprints and any unexpected ones they find.'

I can't believe she's so cool about it. I'm indignant.

'He's treating us like criminals,' I say. 'Does he think that we've taken Katie, that we're hiding her somewhere?' The hypocrisy of what I'm saying (given my own doubts about Christina) only hits me when the words are out.

Christina looks at me blankly.

'He's just doing his job,' she says. 'Can you stop asking questions for one minute? Leave me in peace.'

But I can't let it go. As we drink our espressos, I probe Christina a little further to find out what Costa said to her. He's asked us both to keep our interviews with him private and not to discuss the investigation. But seriously, what does he expect? We're not going to sit here talking about the weather!

'Of course we're going to compare notes,' I say. 'And what we choose to talk about in private is really none of his business.'

'He's giving us the official line,' she says wearily. She pulls a face as she swallows two pills down with her coffee. 'It's the only way I can get through the day,' she says crossly, when she notices me looking disapprovingly at the packet of sedatives.

Her voice is tired and depressed.

'The harsh reality is that in his eyes all three of us, not only Damien, are now suspects – and each of us could be acting alone, or with an accomplice, or all three of us could be in it together.' Her voice rises as she says angrily. 'For all I know, you could have planned this with Damien. You could have hidden Katie away somewhere on the island hoping to collect a reward for her safe return before making a run for it.'

For the second time today, I feel my cheeks flush.

'Thanks…' I say bitterly. 'At least she'd be alive, if only that were true…'

Christina covers her face with her hands.

I bite my lip. That was cruel. I need to be more careful choosing my words.

On reflection, I have to accept the wisdom of Christina's words. I'm flip-flopping in what I believe myself. One minute I'm convinced it's Damien who has abducted Katie and that Christina is the innocent patsy, the next that she's a part of the plot, and the next that she's mentally unstable and has staged the whole abduction. I just keep getting this uncomfortable feeling she's hiding something from me. So here we are. We're both suspicious of Damien and we've both got our suspicions about each other – it's a triangle of distrust.

In truth, I don't know what to think any more, I don't even trust myself.

'Costa's poisoning your mind against me,' I say. 'He's trying to turn us all against each other. It's a deliberate strategy – *divide and rule.*'

I pour Christina some more coffee and she drinks it in silence.

'His attitude is making us paranoid.'

I give vent to my frustration.

'What makes Costa so sure that any one of us had a hand in it? Even Damien could be innocent. I know he's a jerk and his conduct has been appalling...' I hesitate but somehow I doubt she'll take offence any more to me referring to him in these terms. '... It's just possible he's telling the truth? Maybe he did go on a bender at the casino?'

I drop three sugar cubes into my coffee and stir briskly. This isn't the time to be worrying about my waistline.

'Surely the most likely scenario is that Katie was abducted by a stranger, perhaps someone already known to the police – some psycho who wandered up to her on the beach, maybe someone who's been watching her since we got here, waiting for his opportunity. When the sick bastard noticed I was asleep, he took her by the hand and walked off with her. It happens...'

Christina doesn't flinch, just sips her coffee and gazes out to sea. The sedatives must be numbing her pain and grief.

'Well, officially stranger abduction is still the police first line of enquiry, or so Costa claims,' she says, her voice clinical and detached. 'As I told you, they're now launching a proper appeal for witnesses, this time to Katie's abduction. In the next forty-eight hours they're going to try and speak to every member of staff and every guest now staying at the hotel, and they're also going to email everyone who was staying here when Katie disappeared who's now gone home. The hotel manager tried to veto it to avoid the bad publicity but Costa got his way.'

'Well, that's a start. But it's too little, too late,' I say. 'They should be going online, using the power of social media. Katie could be anywhere by now. Someone might be hiding her on the island. But she could just as well have been taken off the island. I know they've been monitoring the airport but they can't search every boat heading out to sea. They can't be watching every marina, every dock, every stretch of coastline.'

I tip the dregs of my coffee down the back of my throat, savouring the bittersweet taste.

'Our best chance of finding Katie is if someone recognises her and reports it to the police. We need to get her image out there so that everyone's on the lookout.'

'That's exactly what I said to Costa this morning,' says Christina impatiently. 'I'm all in favour of using mass publicity and social media when the time is right. He says he's fighting the powers-that-be on this one. The authorities don't want him doing anything that's going to sully the reputation of this place as an island paradise. They'll try to block anything that will damage their precious tourist industry. A mass online publicity campaign will be bad for business. That's the official line. It's as cynical as that.'

That stinks. But I know it's true. It will suit everyone here much better if the police can prove that Katie's abductor is someone close to her, a foreigner visiting the island, rather than an unidentified local who could strike again.

'Well, if he won't do it, I will,' I say. 'It'll be easy enough – I can get all my Instagram followers to help... I've got thousands, literally. We can make Katie's picture go viral. Just say the word and I'll do it.' I scroll through my phone. 5,759 followers, correction, that's just gone up to 5760... as we speak. It's a very good place to start.

'For God's sake, Scarlett, this is not all about you! If you start messing around with social media, it's going to disrupt the investigation. All sorts of fake leads will be flying round causing distractions and wasting police time.' Christina loses her temper and thumps her fists down on the table setting the crockery clattering on the metal top. Heads turn to check out the commotion but Christina's past caring. 'This is not the *Scarlett Reyes Reality Show!*' she yells. 'All you seem concerned about is salvaging your reputation, interfering in the investigation and putting yourself out there as some kind of Lara Croft character in an action-adventure movie. You're one of the main suspects, don't forget. Just let the police do their job.' She kicks back her chair and stands up, gesticulating wildly, as she prepares to walk off. 'This is not all about you!' she hisses at me. 'If it was up to me, you would have been arrested by now. To say you were criminally negligent is the most charitable interpretation of your behaviour.'

A waiter hurries over to ask if he can be of any assistance. His presence at her shoulder knocks the wind out of Christina's sails. She knows she's making an exhibition of herself. She sits down and says calmly, 'Anyway, how come you've got so many followers? You're a nanny, not a film star!'

I'd rather not go into details and I'm scared it'll set her off all over again if I do, so I keep my response brief. 'Oh, I've done some modelling and a few short films for YouTube channels when I was a student,' I say evasively. 'It's easy to pick up followers.'

When she hears this, Christina looks alarmed but doesn't explain why. She twists her hair nervously round her fingers. I note that she's had her nails manicured at the spa. Bright purple! The media will pounce on that if they see it – anyone would think she hadn't a care in the world!

'Let's wait. Give the police another day,' she says sternly. 'I'd like to wait and see if anything comes of this witness appeal they're working on right now. Costa seems to think he's got some important leads to follow up. He prefers the softly-softly approach,' she continues, 'to keep the investigation under the radar.' She must sense the fact I think she's being weak because she raises her voice once more. 'I couldn't give a damn what the authorities think but the key point is mass publicity could put Katie in more danger. We must tread carefully. A media circus could lead the abductor to panic, to harm Katie, to kill her and try to dispose of the body. It's really tough but I'm going to have to be patient.'

I look at Christina in astonishment – those sedatives really are numbing her brain. How can she bring herself, so coldly, to even contemplate the possibility of this horrific fate for Katie? In her place, I'd be screaming at the police to do anything and everything in their power to find my daughter, and to do it now.

Yet on reflection, maybe she's right. If Katie is in fact in the hands of a stranger, possibly a mentally deranged sexual predator, then mass publicity could drive him to the final horrific act. At the very least, it could drive him further underground.

'OK,' I say. 'Let's give Costa forty-eight hours. I'll get it all set up and if the police appeal comes to nothing, we can press the button on our own social media campaign.'

The waiter clears our plates and stands awkwardly by Christina's chair while she signs the bill to the room. I feel sorry for him. He's not sure how to treat us. The usual big smiles and friendly banter are naturally inappropriate, yet expressions of sympathy would be an intrusive and unwelcome familiarity. It's the same for all the staff, and the other guests too. We're spoiling their fun. Our presence at the hotel has just become an inconvenience and an embarrassment.

'Since we're banned from the rooms for the afternoon,' I say, 'let's walk to Crooks' Bay. The exercise will do us good and we can see what progress the police are making down there. We've got to do *something* and it'll be a chance to get away from the hotel and the tourists and the hacks.'

It's a two-hour stroll along the beaches to Crooks' Bay. We set off in an easterly direction along the coast – the opposite way from where I walked the other day. The storm has passed. The clouds have cleared and the sun is setting behind us sending shafts of golden light across the bay and lengthening our shadows into elongated monsters advancing on the sand. Ahead the coastline is formed of a succession of scenic ridges and peaks interspersed with white sand beaches and rocky shores, all bathed in the warm glow of late afternoon sunlight.

We talk a little as we walk along the seafront, leaving parallel sets of footprints in the sand. An uneasy truce is re-established between us. Further along the beach out of sight of the hotel, there are a few dilapidated beach huts nestling among the coconut palms. Here the beach is scruffy and unkempt, strewn with seaweed and dried coconut palm fronds, littered with plastic bottles and other debris washed up by the sea as well as rubbish dumped outside the huts. Leading down from the huts I notice two sets of footsteps – big footsteps and little footsteps. An adult and a child joining our direction of travel, and continuing along the beach but not in a straight line – weaving in and out of the water, diverting up the beach, converging, abruptly stopping and backtracking, ending with a patch of disturbed sand, a scuffle of hands and bottoms and feet at the water's edge. Beyond this point, there are no more little footsteps and only the big footsteps carry on along the beach. I crouch down to my knees.

In my new state of hyper-vigilance, my imagination goes into overdrive. Could these tracks in the sand mark repeated scuffles, attempts to run away, a final struggle? Abandoning Christina, I race along the beach, my heart thumping, following the single set of big footprints until I round the bend to the next cove. There not far ahead of me, I see him, a man carrying a child on his shoulders.

The child is hanging on to a small, bright green kite swaying in the sea breeze. The man bends down to let the little boy off his shoulders and he darts off along the beach laughing and swinging the kite.

I see her everywhere but she isn't here.

12

Scarlett

We have walked about a mile further along the coast when a text comes through on Christina's phone. It's Costa with an update on the outcome of Damien's bail hearing.

'Damien didn't get bail.' I can hear the relief in her voice. It seems at last the scales have fallen from her eyes. He's not the golden boy she once believed him to be. 'He's been remanded in custody for another twenty-four hours to give the police some more time to investigate the "reckless driving charges".' She indicates the quote marks with her fingers.

Thank God for that!

I am the main witness to those charges and Costa's using evidence he got from me during my interviews to substantiate them. Why he had to drag me into it, I don't know. I'm mortified at the prospect of having to testify in court – so far I've been circumspect – given the desperate measures I had to resort to in self-defence, my statement was selective, to say the least.

We both understand that the real reason Damien's still being detained is to give the police more time to investigate and gather evidence on the assumption that he played some part in the abduction of Katie. The driving charges are a convenient pretext for keeping the main suspect behind bars.

'If nothing else, they need some time to check out his gaming alibi,' says Christina. 'No doubt they're also hoping that the search of our rooms will throw up some leads. And they've impounded the Jeep. That's what the police are most interested in.'

I look up from the sand.

'A forensic team and sniffer dogs are all over it as we speak,' says Christina.

It didn't occur to me when they impounded the Jeep that it would be taken for forensic testing. But it's obvious, of course, that the Jeep is a potential crime scene and constitutes the most significant police exhibit.

'Costa's convinced that if Damien's implicated in this, he's got the best chance of finding evidence to prove it in the Jeep.' Christina sounds more positive and hopeful than she's ever been since Katie vanished.

I dread to think what the forensics team will make of it. My DNA must be all over the Jeep! It will convince Costa (if there's any doubt at all left in his mind) that I'm working as Damien's accomplice.

God knows what Christina will think! I've never really explained to her how I came to be there with Damien, or why I was escorted back in a police car with smudged lipstick and a torn T-shirt. No doubt, she and Costa have been debating the probabilities of Damien and I being partners-in-crime. The only reason she still tolerates me is because she needs me or because she's waiting for me to incriminate myself. She doesn't trust me any longer. She'll never speak to me again once the results of the forensic tests on the Jeep come in!

As for my own suspicions about Christina, I've decided not to say anything to Costa unless, and until, I get some solid proof. Costa doesn't fool me with the intimate, *I want to be your friend,* confidential chat. He's also waiting for me to make a false move. I don't trust him any more than I trust her.

Now the waves are lapping our ankles as we walk barefoot along the waterline. I'm looking down at the sand, shell-spotting by force of habit. Christina's bright purple toenails catch my eye. So, she had a pedicure too… that really is rather self-indulgent in the circumstances. There are scattered shells in among the seaweed and I bend down to pick up a few of them.

'Banded tulips,' I say, opening the palm of my hand to show Christina. 'These will be great for Katie's collection,' I blurt out. Then, 'I'm sorry, that was thoughtless,' as she gives me a killer look.

Between us, there's a Katie-shaped black hole echoing with her little girl's laughter and cries, and I feel like I'm falling into it. Katie's the one person I daren't allow myself really to think about. It's too painful and terrifying to imagine what might be happening to her and what will be going through her head. It's bad enough to know that she will be suffering emotional trauma – confused, frightened, distressed and lonely. That she may have been harmed, abused or even worse is literally too painful to contemplate.

So we continue to explore the twists and turns in the investigation and skirt around the black hole that is her absence.

I hold out my hand to Christina.

'Aren't they pretty?' I say. Then, 'There's something I've been meaning to ask you. Did you come into my room on the night that Katie went missing?'

She gives me a strange look.

'After you went to sleep. Sometime after midnight. I was out on the balcony. I thought I saw you leaving my room.'

'Listen to yourself! You're not making any sense,' says Christina. 'How could I have been in your room when I was asleep? The stress must be getting to you.'

I slip the shells into my pocket. 'I'm saving them for Katie,' I say defiantly.

The route takes us past Coral Point, a small fishing village with a busy working harbour.

'Perhaps this is where Damien was planning to bring me for lunch.' I bite my lip. Christina's giving me a dirty look.

Along the quayside, beyond the fishermen's boats with their twisted nets and ropes, there's a line of brightly painted blue-and-white motorised rowing boats tied up along the harbour wall. There's a sign by the boats with the words,

Available for hire – USD 20 per hour.

'Katie would love to go out in one of those,' I say.

This time, Christina's look is openly hostile as my hand flies up to my forehead to cover my eyes. We trudge on in silence.

Crooks' Bay is about two miles further on from Coral Point. As we approach, the path weaves through a labyrinth of boulders sticking up out of the sand close to the shore. The access to the beach is through a looming archway of rock, hewn away by the sea. As soon as we come through the arch, I see that a section of the sandy beach is cordoned off with red-and-white ticker tape. There's white plastic sheeting pulled across the entrance to a cavern, one of many formed (according to the guidebook I read on the plane) over the millennia by waves crashing into the gigantic boulders guarding the beach. There's a relentless slapping sound as the plastic flaps against the rock in the brisk sea breeze.

Christina claps her hands to her mouth and stumbles on a stone in the sand.

'Maybe this wasn't such a great idea,' I say.

Even her sedatives can't block the agony of seeing this.

A couple of men dressed head-to-toe in white plastic protective overalls are going about their business. The cavern and over half of the surrounding beach has been transformed into a crime scene. A mound of sand is partly blocking the entrance to the cave.

'That must be where the swimsuit was found,' I say. We stop in our tracks, staring like rubber-necking tourists, not knowing what to do next.

'What I don't understand is this.' I take my phone out of my pocket and snap a picture of the scene. 'Why did the abductor leave the swimsuit behind? It doesn't make sense, such a careless mistake. If you were trying to cover your tracks, you wouldn't forget to take away the incriminating evidence, would you?' I insist.

Christina turns away, and says softly,

'No... unless whoever took Katie didn't want to hide her tracks, unless she intended to leave a trail, unless she wants us to follow her, unless she is laying a trap for us.'

'You took the words right out of my mouth...' I say.

Lost in thought, I watch Christina's golden silhouette as she tramps off across the sand, backlit by the setting sun.

Her... She...

The words resonate in my head.

If she's not referring to herself, what makes Christina so sure Katie's abductor is a woman? I wonder.

Christina's head is bowed. It's the first time she's made any comment about the possible motives of an abductor. Could this be the moment to ask her about the third earring and the documents she took away from the bedroom when I was hiding in the bathroom? Can she shed any light on these mysteries? Is she on the point of making a confession? Is Damien blackmailing her? Are they in on this together?

... And why didn't she hand in Damien's mobile phone!?

'I've thought of another reason...' I say, running up behind her. '... Why the swimsuit was left behind, I mean. It could be a decoy. While the police are putting all their efforts into recovering evidence and excavating the cave, this gives time for the abductor to spirit Katie away. If the investigation team think she's buried here under the sand, they won't be searching for her anywhere else.'

I register Christina's look of horror at my thoughtless speculation, as she turns her back on me and makes her way over to a police Range Rover, parked up at the end of the dirt road running down the steep hill to the beach. The front door is open and an officer in shirtsleeves and shades leans back against the reclined seat, one leg hanging out of the vehicle, speaking into a walkie-talkie. Once again, I feel like I'm walking onto a movie set. He's straight up out of an American cop movie. I've never seen him before or I would certainly have remembered him. As Christina goes up to the car, I watch him come forward and take her in his arms. How very forward! She pulls away awkwardly. I notice him eyeing me up as I join them.

'Any news?' she says. She looks flustered.

'Nothing further as yet. We've got a few more hours' of digging before nightfall.'

Suddenly I'm struck by the tragedy of what's actually going on here.

As Christina turns abruptly away from the officer, she's looking even more tense and drawn than usual: her hands are shaking and her eyes are glazed.

Too much sun and she scarcely ate any lunch. It's all too much for her.

'He seemed a bit over-friendly,' I say. 'Have you met him before?' I take her arm and steer her over to the shade of a palm tree. 'Come over here, Christina. We need to get you out of the sun.'

'It's just a migraine,' says Christina, 'nothing important. I'll be OK.'

'That looks like a café, up there,' I say, pointing up the hill. They'll have cold drinks and ice if nothing else. 'Let's go and get you some iced water,' I say. 'It'll make you feel better. Then we can call for a taxi.'

It's a steep climb up the dusty dirt road that cuts into the side of the hill. In places, the rough surface is waterlogged and muddy where spring water trickles down over the vertical rocks, oozes across the road, and continues down towards the beach.

Picking my way across the waterlogged section, my eyes follow the parallel lines of tyre tracks running through the mud. Then something catches my attention. A set of deep S-shaped tracks marking the wild swerving line of a car skidding through the mud. Going too fast and out of control. Looks as if it almost went over the edge. I notice that the tyre tracks of the skid don't match.

Suddenly, I'm engaged.

Now that's a strange coincidence!

I take out my phone and take a couple of shots of the skid marks in the mud. Just in case...

Christina looks on, with a bemused expression on her face.

I'm hot and sweaty by the time we reach the café at the top of the hill, a simple affair, just a wooden shack, with a few tables and chairs whose dark green paint is faded and peeling. While we sip iced water, I steel myself to ask Christina about some of the things that have been nagging at me. But first I ask her.

'What did that officer say that upset you so much? You seemed so distraught after he gave you a hug.'

'He was acting and talking like he knew me but I've never met him before. I need some time to think. I don't want to talk about it.'

'Surely you can share it with me?' I say.

She turns away and we drink our glasses of iced water in silence.

'Let's call the taxi,' she says. 'I want to get back to the hotel.'

'I'm sorry I forgot to bring any money,' I say as we get up to leave the café. Christina rummages in her bag. She pulls something out. But it's not her moleskin *Gucci* purse. It's the small beaded purse with a picture of *Sleeping Beauty* printed on one side. Katie's purse. The last time I saw it was when Katie put it into the safe in my room.

'How did this get here?' She's looking scared. 'You didn't put this in my bag, did you, Scarlett?' she asks. Her voice is shrill.

'No, I promise you. Katie put her purse in my safe but I haven't opened it since the day we arrived. When the police went through the safe this morning the purse was gone. Katie's passport was gone too. I thought maybe you'd taken them and put them in your safe.'

Christina's hand is shaking. 'This is insane,' she says. 'I haven't touched Katie's passport and I know her purse wasn't in my bag this morning. The police officer carrying out the search of my room made me empty everything out on to the bed and she insisted on photographing the whole lot before she let me through the door.'

Christina won't look at me. There's something fake in her insistence. Is she lying to me? She would have had the opportunity yesterday morning (while I was faking sickness in her bathroom) to take things from my safe.

'It's confusing,' I say.

'It's a set up,' she says. 'Someone's trying to make me look guilty. The only time my bag's been out of my sight all day is when I left it in the changing room locker at the spa while I had my treatments.'

I don't want to intensify her panic but more importantly, where is Katie's passport? I think to myself.

She unzips the purse and tips the contents out onto the table. I count them out. Five little oval shells scatter over the formica top. Rose petal tellins – a delicate shade of pink. The ten-dollar note is gone. I wonder if these are some of the shells I found with Katie on the beach.

'Why five, I wonder?' I look at Christina. 'Any ideas?'

She touches each shell, one after the other, with the tip of her finger.

'Why five?' she echoes. A look of dismay spreads across her face. She covers the rose petal tellins with her hand.

I can't get another word out of her.

'Stop touching.' I say. The police might be able to get some fingerprints. It could be important evidence.'

I zip the shells back in the purse and wrap it carefully in a napkin.

'If we wanted proof that Katie's been abducted, not drowned or disappeared in some tragic accident, here it is. And whoever's got her wants us to know about it.'

I kick back my chair.

'Stay there, I'll be back.'

I sprint back down the dirt track as fast as I can go, losing my footing in the muddy section and sprawling on to the ground. When I reach the officer, I look down to see my legs and white shorts are splattered in mud. Not quite the image I'd like to present to him – cool, collected, seductive – as I run up to the Range Rover but that's too bad.

'Sir, I've got something for you.'

He looks up from his papers.

'Hi there, you're back. What happened to you?'

He smiles slowly, exposing a jaw full of perfect white teeth.

'Katie's purse containing some shells,' I say.

He lifts his shades and his eyes settle on my skimpy vest.

He takes his cap off the passenger seat and throws it in the back.

'Come and sit in the car. It's cooler inside.'

I hand over the purse folded up in the napkin.

'May be important for fingerprints.' I say

He shuffles through his papers and pulls out a blank form.

He leans across towards me until our shoulders and knees are touching.

'I just need to take a statement from you,' he says, 'to record the Exhibit.'

Before he can stop me, I swivel away from him and leap out of the car. I've no intention of getting trapped behind a steering wheel again!

'I'm sorry I need to get back to Christina, I'll get her to call DC Costa when we get back to the hotel.'

I start running back up the track as he jumps out of the car.

'Stop!' he shouts 'Can you give her a message?' He points up to where Christina is standing in the middle of the track waiting for me.

'Tell her I'm on night duty at the Shack again tonight. She'll know what I mean.' I turn to go and he shouts once more. 'Hey! Wait. If you've got anything more for me, it's DC Kramer, Matt Kramer. At your service.' He grins. 'Give me a call sometime.'

Not bloody likely!

What on earth is Christina playing at?

I give him a quick wave and keep running up the dirt road to join her.

When I catch up with Christina, I decide not to pass on the message to her. I'll tell Costa instead.

'What was all that about?' she says.

That's exactly what I was thinking.

'Oh nothing,' I say. 'Is the taxi on its way?'

We sit in silence on the taxi ride back to the hotel and I reach a decision. As soon as I get into my room, I'm going to make the final touches to my online appeal and press the button to activate. I won't say anything in advance to Christina or Costa. They'll find out soon enough once the social media campaign to find Katie has gone live.

13

Photograph Four

21 June 2000: University Schools, Oxford

*I took this photograph on the day you finished your
Finals – Midsummer's Eve. You're standing on the
pavement in front of the University Schools from where
you have just emerged, after a three-hour paper on the
'Aesthetics of Poetry in the Romantic Age.' That's how
invested I was in your studies and your future! You've
probably forgotten everything about that afternoon but
it is so real to me still that even after all these years, I can
remember the subject of your last exam and feel as if I
shared in the intensity and stress of writing those complex
and wordy essays.*

*I came up from London (leaving my studio early and
cancelling an important photoshoot), especially to bring
you chocolates and flowers to celebrate the end of your
gruelling week of Finals. James came to meet you too,*

of course (still carefree and oblivious to his offspring's fate – our guilty secret). For him, it was a short, fast cycle ride from his accommodation on the Cowley Road. And there he is on the right of the shot, his arm held high in a triumphant salute, clutching an empty bottle of champagne that he's just shaken and uncorked all over your head, his battered bicycle slung carelessly against a peeling black painted lamppost.

You're bedraggled and tired but lovely as ever. There are dark circles under your eyes and your mascara has streaked in the drops of champagne. The regulation black 'sub fusc' gown worn for your exams gives you a solemn and funereal air.

You should be so happy. You survived! But you look so drawn, and so sad, and so bitter! You're not even pretending. You're looking past me, over my shoulder as I take the shot, and you can't even be bothered to make the effort to twist your face into a smile.

Gabrielle had found the number for the 'family planning' clinic in her *Yellow Pages* telephone directory while Lara was staying at her Chelsea flat revising for university Finals. It was a private clinic, with the advantage of being only a twenty-five-minute ride in a black cab from Gabrielle's flat and advertising a 'quick, efficient, convenient and confidential service.' The very next day she left work early and took a detour to drop in and pick up the clinic's sales literature. Their advertising pitch set out the advantages of *'choosing to pay for private care in our clinic which is licensed and approved for the carrying out of privately funded abortions.'*

'This is just what we're looking for,' said Gabrielle by way of greeting, as she poured herself a glass of wine. 'Sounds just the job.' She handed the sales brochure to Lara who was sitting on Gabrielle's sofa trying to concentrate on *Wuthering Heights*, one of the set texts for her Gothic literature examination in two weeks' time.

'Read this,' she said. Lara scanned down the page.

> You may wish to pay for your abortion care as it will be quicker to get an appointment and you may feel more comfortable contacting our clinic directly rather than having to make an appointment with your GP and waiting for an NHS referral.

> At your initial consultation you will be offered counselling. You will also take a pregnancy test and have an ultrasound scan which will indicate how many weeks pregnant you are and what procedures are available to you.

'Did you see this?' said Gabrielle, pointing at the page. 'You can get it done same day. You can even arrange to get it done at the weekend. That way, you won't have to miss any tutorials.'

'It's very expensive,' said Lara. 'I can't afford it.' She put down her book reluctantly and glanced at the brochure while Gabrielle peered over her shoulder.

Our prices range from £250–1150. The earlier
you are in your pregnancy the less expensive the
abortion will be. You will be charged a small fee
of around £60–£80 for the initial consultation.
If you decide to proceed with treatment after the
consultation, you will be required to pay this in full
prior to treatment being started. If you opt for the
weekend service, you will be expected to pay an
additional small fee of around £50 on top of the
standard abortion costs.

'Well, it's just lucky I came up to Oxford to get you
yesterday,' said Gabrielle. 'We need to get on with it as
soon as possible. You got yourself into this mess. Now we
need to deal with it. The sooner we get it over and done
with, the less expensive it will be.'

'*We?*' said Lara. 'What do you mean, *"we"*? This is
my baby and I'm going to decide what to do about it.
I've had enough of you pushing me around and trying
to manipulate me. Anyway, I've already told you, I can't
afford an abortion.'

'And I've already told you, I'll lend you the money and
organise it all for you, since you're so clueless.' She leaned
over Lara's shoulder. 'Look, it says they offer a payment
schedule so we can pay by instalments.'

She finished her wine and poured them both a gin and
tonic. 'I'll pay for it out of my savings and you'll just have
to pay me back after your Finals, once you get a job. I'm
even willing to push the boat out and sub you for the
weekend service.'

She handed Lara a glass and then walked over to the phone.

'We can keep it a secret. We don't need to tell a soul. It'll be our secret – just you and me.'

Lara read the last paragraph of the leaflet.

> All your records will remain confidential and no one will find out about you having a private abortion unless you tell them or agree to them being told. This includes your GP and your family.

She put the brochure to one side and went back to her book.

'What about James?' she said, without taking her eyes off the page. 'Surely I should discuss it with him.'

'Fuck James!' said Gabrielle. She picked up the phone. 'It's your body. You get to choose. I'll call them now before they close. We'll book it in for next weekend. That'll give you a full week to get over it before the start of your Finals.'

14

Scarlett

I wake in the early hours of the morning. Images of freshly painted blue-and-white rowing boats are drifting through my head as I open my eyes. It's pitch dark. I throw back the covers and leap out of bed.

I've got to speak to Costa.

Last night Christina told me Damien has another bail hearing at ten o'clock this morning. Unless the police have enough evidence to charge him in relation to the suspected abduction, they'll be forced to release him since the dangerous driving charges don't carry a custodial sentence.

Costa also told Christina last night that the police have checked out Damien's alibi. The gaming entries are genuine. The manager of the Black Jack Casino took them through the books and the casino's computerised records show that Damien placed the bets. If his alibi is rock solid, there'll be no grounds for keeping him in jail. He'll be released after the hearing.

But there may be a chink in his alibi. I've just woken up with a blue-and-white painted brainwave bobbing in my head, and it won't wait until morning.

He said we could contact him any time, day or night.

I send a text to Costa, and five minutes later, grab my mobile again and punch out his number.

'Can't it wait 'til the morning?' he says.

I tell him I can prove Damien's alibi is shaky. I plead with him, crying into the phone. I know that if he thinks my state of extreme agitation is because I'm about to confess or lead him to a dead body, he'll have to agree to my plan.

He hesitates.

'Give me an hour,' he says. 'I'll collect you at the hotel.' I gush out my thanks. 'You'd better make it worth my while,' he says.

I'm sound asleep again when my phone rings at exactly 4.30 a.m.

'Detective Sergeant Costa is waiting for you in the lobby,' says the receptionist.

'Tell him I'll be down in two minutes,' I say.

I splash some water on my face, drag on my leggings and pull a sports hoodie over my camisole, slip into flip-flops, and make my way to the lift. I almost walk past Costa who's sitting at the table calmly drinking a cappuccino and checking out his reflection in the glass. He's kitted out in pressed blue Levis and a spotless white cotton shirt. I've never seen him in civvies before. A leather jacket is draped across the chair next to him. He raises an eyebrow.

'Nice to see you've dressed to impress,' he says sardonically, taking in my tangled auburn hair and flip-flops.

'I was expecting to see you in uniform.'

'This is strictly off the record. Unofficial business. I didn't get a chance to square it with the chief. Didn't want to disturb his beauty sleep.' He fixes me sternly with his penetrating blue eyes. 'Best not to draw attention to ourselves, don't you think?'

It is still dark outside and the forecourt of the hotel is deserted save for the sleepy doorman and the security guard. Costa's silver sports car is parked in the drop off zone outside reception, gleaming under the security lights. The car's flashier than I would have expected for someone on a police officer's salary. Must be good kickbacks in a place like this, a tax haven with lots of dirty money swilling around.

So much for not drawing attention – he might as well have come with the sirens blazing!

He unlocks the car and swings open the door for me with a chivalrous flourish.

'This better be good, young lady.' His voice sounds hard, without a trace of irony. 'I've come from the warmth of the conjugal bed for this.'

We're the only car on the road as he drives smoothly and swiftly through the black night towards the harbour.

'What did your wife say?' I ask.

He turns briefly. His expression is inscrutable.

'She's used to me being out all hours,' he says. 'Comes with the job.'

He hands me his mobile. The screensaver photo is of an attractive woman in her mid-thirties with her arm round a pretty child with dark curls, brown eyes and a big smile.

'That's my little girl, Sofia, she's seven years old. Well, as you can imagine her mother is 100 per cent with me on this case.'

I'm touched. He can't completely hate me, if he's willing to share this. Or is it simply a tactic to get me off my guard – to put my trust in him, to coax a confession out of me?

He drives on for a mile or so in silence then as we turn off the coastal road towards the harbour, he thrusts his hand into the glove compartment and pulls out a copy of Damien's betting records.

'I printed it off,' he says. 'I spent two hours with Leonard last night. Every entry has been cross-checked and verified with the casino's cashiers and accounting department.'

He's going through the motions, I tell myself. But it's clear he thinks Damien's alibi is rock solid. The only reason he agreed to take me out at this ungodly hour is because he thinks I'm guilty and about to break. He thinks checking out Damien's alibi is just a pretext on my part and that my real agenda is to confess and alert the police to where Katie is hidden.

But he's wrong. I run my eyes down the list of bets I partly memorised the day before.

'Yes, here it is' I say, jabbing my finger at the entries about halfway down the page. 'This is what I was telling you about on the phone.' Most of the bets were placed at intervals of under half an hour. But at 4.35 p.m. on the afternoon Katie disappeared, there's a gap. Damien placed a bet at the Black Jack table, and then there's a gap of well over an hour until he placed his next bet at 5.49 p.m. I wave the paper under Costa's nose. 'This puts Damien back in the frame.'

'Doesn't prove a thing,' says Costa. 'Doesn't invalidate his alibi. Perhaps he went for a drink at the bar, perhaps he was hungry and went to eat at the café, perhaps he met a friend and stopped for a chat...

'Perhaps he did... and perhaps he didn't,' I say. 'Perhaps he went for a boat trip instead...' He gives me another sideways look.

As Costa swings the car into the road leading to Reef Point harbour, my eyes are drawn to a flashing purple neon sign:

Coco Shack Nightclub
Turn Left 50m.

'Now that sounds familiar,' I say, remembering the text from Damien I saw on Christina's phone the morning after Katie's disappearance... *Heavy night at the Coco Shack*. And that officer yesterday, he mentioned it too. 'Tell her I'm on duty at the Shack'.

'Popular night spot, is it?' I ask.

'Popular with the local crack cocaine dealers and drop outs,' says Costa. 'A real dive – we get called in there every other week to bust the place.' I make a mental note to tell

Costa about my weird encounter with Kramer yesterday at Crooks' Bay.

Costa parks behind the Coco Shack and we head down to the quayside where I walked with Christina yesterday. The blue-and-white painted wooden boats are shrouded in shadows and shimmer in the moonlight. Far off, the first glimmers of dawn are breaking through where the sky meets the sea, as the dense black cloud thins and lightens to a luminous grey.

'This one will do.' He leans over and fumbles with the rope tying one of the boats to the harbour wall.

'Shouldn't we ask someone first?' I say. 'Won't we get into trouble with…' I'm about to say 'the police' but my voice tails off lamely.

'You're already in trouble… and I am *the police*.' He scowls. 'I don't need to ask for anyone's permission round here, everyone knows me.' The boat lurches under his weight as he jumps in from the harbour wall and reaches out his hand.

'Get in. We're going for a ride.'

Losing patience with the wet fibrous knot that has been pulled tight by the tension of the boat, he gets a penknife from the inside pocket of his leather jacket, and slashes the rope.

I wouldn't want to mess with him!

There's an oar in the bottom of the boat. He grabs it and shoves hard against the slimy wall to push us away. Then he leans over the outboard motor and yanks the fraying starter cord until it splutters into life.

It is still dark. But a few fishermen are emptying out their lobster pots in the gloom and other shadowy figures are beginning to emerge onto the quayside, carrying crates, unrolling nets and preparing to board their boats. It's like a stage set coming to life at the opening of a play. As Costa sits down to steer, a man runs out of a nearby shed waving his arms and yelling.

I feel like a thief in the night as the boat chugs away in low gear from its moorings.

Costa turns round briefly and laughs.

'It's only Mitch. He owes me. I'll deal with him later.'

I'm fearful that he won't be able to navigate safely in the dark over hidden rocks and in between the looming hulks of sailing boats. But he takes command at once.

'I know these waters like the back of my hand,' he says. 'My father was a fisherman.'

'Was?' I say, softly.

'Yes, he was lost at sea in a storm when I was thirteen years old.'

'That's so sad,' I say.

Beyond the shelter of the harbour, there's a brisk sea breeze rippling the water. I shiver and curl up against the wind. Costa takes off his leather jacket and slings it over to me. The little boat bumps over the waves, jolting me up and down on the wooden bench where I'm sitting in the bow facing him.

'After my father died, I took up deep-sea diving. If I could find him again anywhere, it would be under the waves.'

'How romantic.' Then I bite my lip. What a stupid thing to say! He must think I'm such a shallow, immature girl.

His head is turned away from me. He's looking past me, at the water ahead, almost talking to himself. In the gloom, I can just make out his profile, and only just catch his words, carried on the wind. He glances towards me, but then shifts his gaze to the water beyond and concentrates on the steering. For an instant, I get the feeling he's trying to win my confidence, to establish some kind of intimacy between us, and it makes me feel uncomfortable, as if he's preparing the ground for my confession.

'Check the time' says Costa, changing the mood abruptly.

4.48 a.m. I wedge myself further into the bow as he steadily pushes the throttle up to maximum speed. He's in his element now.

'You seem to enjoy adventures, Miss Scarlett,' he shouts over the noise of the wind and the sea and the roaring engine. I throw back my head and laugh, breathing in a lungful of salty air. My skin's tingling with the splash of seawater as the boat canters along at its top speed. Though half-ashamed to be feeling this way given the tragic circumstances, I can't deny I'm having fun, excited by the turn of events, excited and exhilarated. There's an edge of fear too, of the vast expanse of sea and of being alone in this little boat with this man (who I can tell is a street fighter at heart despite his civilised veneer), that makes it all the more tantalising. Costa may think I'm a fraud or worse and I can't decide if I like him or despise him, but I sense a certain chemistry between us.

He steers the boat close to the coastline under the sheer cliffs where the Caribbean gulls swirl overhead then swings the rudder and heads in a straight line across the water to the cluster of bright lights on the looming landmass just visible on the other side. It's St James, one of the US Leeward Isles and he tells me that the lights we can see in the distance are the lights of the *Black Jack Casino, open twenty-four hours.*

'5.17 a.m.,' I call out. Costa ties the boat to a rusty iron mooring at the casino's private dock. 'Twenty-nine minutes exactly.'

'Let's go in,' he says. 'I'll introduce you to Leonard, he's the boss round here. They do a good breakfast. Then we can test your theory.'

'Hey, Lennie,' he calls, as we walk in. 'When do you sleep, man? Here's the girl I told you about. Scarlett Reyes. She claims to be a gambling virgin as well as an amateur sleuth!' His voice bristles with sarcasm. 'Can you show her the tables?'

I'm happy to be shown round the casino, instantly at home in the bling red velvet décor of the establishment. Even though it's dead at this hour, I love the luxurious decadence of the place and the thrill of the tables and games of chance. There's hardly anyone at the tables, just a couple of ashen-faced, die-hard punters who've made it through the night.

After I've chanced my luck at roulette a few times 'on the House,' Lennie leads me back to the breakfast room just as two plates loaded with sausages, eggs, bacon and tomatoes are carried in.

'You're back.' Costa's sitting down ready to tuck in to the feast.

'She's a quick learner for a girl...' Lennie touches Costa's arm. 'Great sleight of hand. Could be a pro.'

I give Lennie one of my best 'put down' looks.

'Ah! Those green eyes!' says Lennie. 'Gambler's eyes.' He's got no shame, leering into my face. 'And gambler's fingers, so slender. Never seen such beautiful hands before...' He winks at Costa as he takes my fingers in his plump, sweaty palm while I become aware of some unspoken communication between them. I wince as his warm, wet lips touch my cool skin but smile sweetly.

What a complete prick!

'I'll come back one day, when I'm properly dressed for it,' I say, pulling my hand away and plucking at my hoodie in a mock, self-deprecating way. I'm regretting not having taken the time to make myself look decent.

'What was that all about?' I ask once Lennie sidles off to deal with a drunken overnight guest causing a scene at the cashier's desk. I sense that Costa is using Damien's alibi check as an opportunity to check out his own theory that Damien and I are gambling partners as well as partners-in-crime.

'Don't worry about him. He's just trying it on.' Costa smothers a sausage in hot mustard and cuts it neatly into bite-size segments. 'Let's hear it then.'

'OK so this is my theory,' I say. 'Our journey this morning from Coral Point harbour to the Black Jack moorings took just under half an hour. We know that Damien made a payment at the cashier's desk at 3.39 p.m. which means he must have left the hotel by three o'clock latest even if we allow only ten minutes for the drive down to the harbour and less than half an hour for the boat trip. Well, we know that I was sitting with Katie watching her play until at least 3.35 p.m. That's when I used my phone to take the photograph of Katie collecting shells on the beach that's on all the police posters. So clearly Damien can't have taken Katie from the beach himself. If he is responsible for her abduction, he can't have been acting alone.'

'You didn't get me out of bed in the early hours of this morning just to tell me that Damien has an accomplice, did you now, young lady?' says Costa, lifting his eyebrows offensively.

'No, there's more, if you'll hear me out.'

I take a sip of scorching tea.

'Right, so let's assume Damien arrived at the Black Jack Casino some time before 3.30 p.m. intending to spend the night gambling. He's addicted to gambling. It's worse than being an alcoholic. I know Christina rumbled him just before we came away on holiday – there was a huge scene at her apartment when he came back from one of his poker nights downtown.'

Costa's now slicing his bacon with the precision of a pathologist carrying out a post-mortem.

'Damien's such a loser in all senses of the word. Christina told me she found out he'd run up massive gambling debts in New York, had even 'borrowed' her credit card to pay them off. Though I don't think he even thinks of it as stealing, and nor does she, as they're both so careless with money.'

'Cut the backstory,' quips Costa, tapping his fingers. 'She gave me this information yesterday.'

'OK, so, Damien arrives here at the Black Jack at around 3.30 p.m., pays off part of his debt to the casino and starts placing bets. As well as having a compulsion to keep gambling all night, Damien needs to set up an alibi, and as well as wanting to establish an alibi, he's also tasked with a mission. At 4.35 p.m. he places a bet at the Black Jack table. He plays a round then throws in his chips and leaves the table, walks straight down to the moorings where he's left the boat he hired at Coral Point, jumps into the boat and speeds off in the direction of the reef.'

Costa yawns.

'Now here's the clever bit – Damien didn't buy just one yellow lilo, he bought two.'

I look up triumphantly to let this vital piece of information sink in. 'There were two lilos – number one, the lilo Katie was playing with at the beach, and number two, the lilo that was salvaged from the reef.'

'I'm not an idiot,' Costa snaps. 'I can count…'

'The lilo Katie was playing with when she disappeared was a present from Damien. He gave it to her in the morning – the morning of the day she disappeared. Christina seemed mad at him. She had sent him off after breakfast to buy a bucket and spade for Katie to collect her shells and he came back with the lilo instead. She made out that they're dangerous for little kids, of course. But Katie's face lit up with delight when Damien took it out of the bag, and Christina said she hadn't the heart to stop him. Anyway,

Katie got to keep the lilo but I remember that Christina sent him back to the shop for a bucket and spade.'

I pause for a breath while Costa taps a cigarette impatiently on the table, his face impassive.

'Now, my theory is that Damien didn't buy the lilos at the local shop at all. For one thing, I know that it opens half an hour later than the time he got back to the pool. And for another thing, I know they don't sell yellow lilos because I checked it out yesterday. They only have two colours – pink and blue. I'm convinced he already had both the yellow lilos hidden in the Jeep.'

'This is getting dull,' says Costa. He lights the cigarette and blows the smoke into my face. 'You've spent too long with pre-schoolers.'

I decide to ignore his rudeness. 'So anyway, he gave one lilo to Katie that morning. She played with it at the pool and she played with it at the beach. I think that's the lilo I found stuffed in a rucksack in the trunk of the Jeep. But as I say, there was a second yellow lilo, identical to the first, and that's the one Damien took with him on the blue-and-white motorised rowing boat he hired at Coral Point.' Costa pours himself another cup of black coffee. He looks bored rigid but I guess it's all part of his interview technique. 'So Damien places his bet at 4.35 p.m., jumps in the boat and heads for the reef. When he gets alongside the reef, he drops anchor, blows up the second lilo and throws it overboard just where it will get caught up in the current and drift along the reef and past the rocks until it is in full view of the beach.' He lights the cigarette and blows smoke across the table. 'Damien then turns the boat and navigates across the water to Crooks' Bay. There he meets his accomplice, who in the meantime has abducted Katie from the beach and driven her down to Crooks' Bay along the coastal road in the Jeep.' I pick up my knife and fork.

At last Costa is beginning to look interested.

'What happens next in this grand theory of yours?' says Costa.

'Something happens which means the trail goes cold at Crooks' Bay,' I say. 'We know that from the tracker dogs.' Suddenly, I can't face the thought of breakfast and push away my plate. 'Perhaps Katie never left the beach... perhaps she's still there – that's why your people are now digging up the sand. Or perhaps she was taken aboard the boat and dumped out at sea. But I can't bear to think of these things. I refuse to believe that Katie is dead. I believe that she is alive and I'll carry on believing and searching until there is absolute proof to the contrary.'

I stand up and walk over to the window looking out at the spectacular sunrise, an impressionist palette of pinks, purples and grey over the sea, then turn to face Costa.

'So this is what I think happened: the accomplice takes Katie to the cave, where she changes her out of the swimsuit into her clothes. Then the accomplice hands Katie over to Damien who takes her away in the boat to some isolated spot along the coast or on another nearby island where she is to be hidden away until arrangements can be made for her to disappear for good.'

Costa stubs out his cigarette, wipes his lips with a serviette and comes over to where I'm standing. He puts his hands on my shoulders and looks into my eyes very intently.

'You seem to have thought this through very carefully,' he says. He makes a long pause. 'Is there anything more you need to tell me Scarlett?' I let his slur on my innocence pass and continue quickly.

'Having dropped off Katie at the pre-arranged location, he then full-throttles back to the casino where he bounds up the steps, slicks back his hair, adjusts his designer shades, casually orders a drink at the bar, and strolls back to the black jack table in time to place his next bet at 5.49 p.m. Mission accomplished and his alibi intact.'

I pause for breath. Costa leans back against the wall and crosses his arms.

'You've pitched it well, got every scene worked out in that pretty little head of yours, haven't you!' I can feel myself blushing with anger. 'You sound like a second-rate crime novel,' he says. His voice oozes contempt, even though he's smiling at me like a perfect gentleman. 'So what was the point of launching the lilo, in this set up of yours?'

'Well, the lilo was a decoy, of course. At first, the abductor wanted everyone to think that Katie had been drowned or even attacked by a shark. I mean, it's obvious isn't it? God, even the colour – a yellow lilo! You must've seen *Jaws* when you were a kid? The little boy splashing in the water, and then a few seconds later, he's gone, and all we can see is a patch of blood-stained water. It was a play on everyone's emotions and a play for time – maybe even having a sick joke at our expense? But if Katie really had drifted out on the lilo from the beach, surely someone would have seen it happening? Even though you don't have lifeguards in this God-forsaken place someone would have raised the alarm. There were enough people sitting on their butts gawping out to sea.'

'Yeah, well maybe they were more interested in checking out the hot young totty on the beach than checking on the little kids in the water...'

'Very funny.' I say.

'I've got another question for you,' he says. 'If you're right about this, what happened to the first lilo, the one Katie was playing with in the water before Sleeping Beauty crashed out on the sand?'

I don't rise to it.

'It was carried away from the beach. Katie's abductor took the lilo with her and stuffed it in a rucksack in the back of the Jeep.' He shoots me a quizzical look. 'As Damien intended,' I continue, 'lilo number two that he launched near the reef drifted into a position where it was visible from the beach and could cause a distraction. Later that afternoon, I came to my senses on the sand to find that Katie had vanished, spotted the lilo, and raised the alarm, thinking that she'd been caught in a rip tide and swept out to sea. While all eyes were on the search-and-rescue at the reef, Damien's accomplice gained a few hours to remove Katie and cover her tracks.'

I walk back to the table, take a gulp of tea and look across at Costa.

'Her?' he says, suddenly alert. His head's tilted to one side. 'That's the second time you've used the word, "her" to refer to Katie's abductor. A few minutes ago you used the word "she".' He's observing me cynically. 'I know you women are not to be trusted but what makes you so sure Damien's accomplice is a woman? Do you have someone particular in mind?'

I say nothing.

'Let's go then' he says, kicking back his chair and pushing away the plate. 'Perhaps I can make you talk later? The sooner we check out this story of yours, the sooner I can get back to bed.'

15

11 September 2000: Twin Towers, New York

I love this picture because James took it. We came over to spend a week with you in New York just before you started your semester at Columbia University taking a post-grad course in Twentieth-Century American Literature. I was doing a project shoot for an exhibition I was putting together in my studio in Chelsea, on the theme 'Together and Apart.' I'd chosen to represent the theme in the form of bridges, and to feature views of bridges spanning the East River.

And there were other reasons for coming too. We wanted to check up on you. Make sure you had got over the upset of the miscarriage and were enjoying your time in New York. And, most importantly, we wanted to tell you face to face. To tell you we were engaged – didn't seem fair to let you find out from one of our friends.

So, we broke the news, over brunch in a little café in Tribeca, and you admired my engagement ring, a platinum band with a 1.5-carat flawless solitaire bought at Tiffany's earlier that morning. (James almost died when the manageress whispered the price!) Afterwards we took a boat trip around Manhattan, heading south down the East River and then round to the Hudson on one of those tourist steamboats. And I took lots of photographs of bridges from many different angles. You and James leaned over the railings looking at the views, chatting of nothing in particular, or rather he talked, and you just nodded and looked across the water.

Then as we rounded the river in front of the Twin Towers, James grabbed the camera from my neck. 'Come and stand over here. This would make a great shot – the two most beautiful girls in the world in front of the Twin Towers.'

And here we stand, side-by-side – together and apart – in front of those iconic, tragic towers soaring above our 'spot-the-difference' pretty faces. At first glance there is no difference – no way of telling us apart, unless you look very closely at the photograph. For you were always good at dissembling. But look again, at our double image. Our lips are parted, smiling, yet your eyes are dull, and in contrast, my eyes are shining as brightly as the diamond that's glittering on the fourth finger of my left hand.

I have to admit; the composition is good. There's clarity and depth. And there's symmetry and symbolism. Not at all bad for an amateur – all things considered. And, who knows, maybe the image has some historic value today.

Heart-rending to think, that exactly one year later the Twin Towers collapsed and disintegrated into dust.

Revenge is sweet. You triumphed in a punt on the Cherwell. I trumped you in a steamboat on the Hudson. Our most vicious duels always seem to take place afloat, in boats! All at sea, on rivers, adrift in the current... like today, we're always messing about in boats, funny that. But today you're my captive.

Gabrielle didn't hang around. As soon as Lara's abortion had taken place, she embarked on her campaign to win back James, if only to get one over on Lara and restore the rightful balance of power.

Her first move was to flatter his ego. She spent hours in the photography suite at her studio, perfecting black-and-white prints of pictures she had taken of him during his stay with her in Chelsea. She revelled in the alchemy of the darkroom – there was something magical, almost supernatural, in the process – standing over trays of pungent chemicals alone in the red glowing darkness conjuring faces and captured moments on blank sheets of white paper. Of course, she had had to move with the times, and engaged more and more in digital photography for her commercial work, but when working for her own pleasure (as in this labour of love), she opted for the witchcraft of the darkroom every time. She was thrilled with the results. They were indeed fine portraits of James. He made a good model, with his regular features and dark eyes that were at once expressive and nonchalant.

She experimented with different finishes and effects and produced a portfolio album that was worthy of submission to modelling agencies. She sent it to him at his student lodgings in Cowley Road, carefully wrapped in purple tissue paper, with a note:

My gift – as promised. You've got what it takes – If you want to take it further, I'll be here for you.

Of course, James was flattered, and attracted by the lure of fame and success. Despite his high ideals of wanting to make the world a better place, he was also vain and ambitious – an impressionable and dangerous combination. Although the same age as Gabrielle, she had an air of sophistication and experience that he could not match, working in London, earning her own living, owning a flat, and with access to all the best modelling agencies in the world of high fashion. When Gabrielle telephoned him in Oxford to check that the package had arrived safely, he declined her offer to get him photographic work on the basis that he was going to be a doctor, not a male model. Besides, he told her proudly, he already had plans for the long vacation – with the encouragement of his tutor, he had successfully applied for a vacation studentship grant with the British Pharmacology Society and would be undertaking a six-week summer research project, working alongside researchers in a laboratory engaged in the testing of new experimental cancer drugs. But Gabrielle was not so easily deterred – without saying anything more about it, she sent out his images to her clients. Within a few days she was on the telephone to James again. She had shown his shots to an influential client who was keen and was willing to offer James a few days' work. It was a fabulous opportunity, she told him, once in lifetime, very well-paid. Three telephone calls later, he capitulated; what harm could it do? It shouldn't interfere too much with his research internship. And he needed the extra cash. He would just have to call in sick to the lab on a few days. They wouldn't be any the wiser.

The following week (and less than two weeks after Lara's abortion had taken place) Gabrielle drove up to Oxford to celebrate the last day of Lara's Finals. She wasted no time in pressing home her advantage with James. After the traditional post-last exam ambush on the street, the three of them spent the evening with other drunken undergrads, quaffing Pimms and beer, and taking shots of tequila. By the end of the evening Lara was completely wasted and James (though pretty much the worse for wear himself) started to get concerned. He grabbed the tequila shot she was holding up to her mouth and dragged her out of the circle of drinkers on the floor and up onto the sofa.

'You need to stop drinking. It's not good for you – or the baby...' he hissed in her ear.

Together, Gabrielle and James half carried Lara back to her college room and Gabrielle told James she would put her to bed. As soon as the door closed, Gabrielle sat Lara on the bed and gripped her hands.

Lara was swaying from side-to-side, with her eyes closed, giggling to herself. Gabrielle slapped her hard round the face.

'Look at me, Lara. Open your eyes. I need to speak to you. Does he know? Lara, Lara, shut up you idiot! You bailed, didn't you? You haven't told him.'

Gabrielle watched the marks of her fingers spreading across the side of Lara's face. Suddenly sober, Lara opened her eyes and looked straight at Gabrielle. Her eyes were indignant, brimming with pain and anger.

'I've got to tell him, but I'm scared,' said Lara. 'He's a Roman Catholic, for God's sake, even though a lapsed one. Once a Catholic, always a Catholic and I know he's against abortion, believes in the sanctity of life and all that... He's going to hate me for it. I should have talked to him first. It was his baby too.'

Gabrielle grabbed her hand. 'You did what you thought was right. You did what you thought was the best thing for you and what you thought was the best thing for him too. You were being unselfish. You were thinking of him as much as yourself.'

'That's such crap,' said Lara. 'You know it's not true. You made me do it. You bullied me into it. You didn't give me any time to think... I didn't think at all...' She covered her face with the pillow and Gabrielle leant forward to hear her muffled words. 'And now I'm going to regret it for the rest of my life. I have to tell him. And he's going to hate me. And I'm going to lose him. I've lost everything. I got rid of his baby. I should kill myself too.'

Gabrielle yanked away the pillow.

'Pull yourself together, you're being ridiculous, hysterical. You're not the first person ever to have an abortion. It's a routine procedure. You'll feel better in a few days. It's just your hormones making you feel this way.'

She sat down on the bed next to Lara and put her arm round her.

'I've got a plan. You really don't need to tell him you had an abortion. What's the point of making him mad? Just tell him you had a miscarriage. Tell him that's why you were in London with me. That you were feeling ill and exhausted so I came to fetch you so that you could have a quiet weekend at the flat, and on the Saturday night the miscarriage started and we took you into hospital and you were too upset to talk about it before your Finals and then you didn't want to upset him before his end of year exams, so you decided to keep it a secret from him until now.'

Lara's expression was horrified, hostile. 'You want me to lie to him about the most important thing that's ever happened between us. We've spoken of the future, of getting married once we've finished our studies, he wanted me to have this child. OK, so we're young and naïve but we thought we could make it work – and then you barged in and took control and destroyed any hope of happiness we might have had. You just can't bear to see me happy! If I can't be honest with him about this, my relationship with James is over. If we stayed together, I'd be living a lie for the rest of my life.'

'Trust me,' said Gabrielle, 'it's the only way. If you tell him you had an abortion, he'll never forgive you. If you want to keep him, you've got no choice. Tell him it was a miscarriage.'

Gabrielle walked over to the window. The clock in the tower was tolling midnight. The room reverberated with the chimes. She slammed down the window. The cracked, dusty frame shook. 'How do you ever sleep with those bloody bells!'

The next day, well-coached by Gabrielle, Lara cycled up the Cowley Road with a pounding head and a heavy heart to tell the tale to James, and Gabrielle drove back to Chelsea but not before leaving a note in James' pigeon hole inviting him to come to her studio in Convent Garden the following Tuesday for a photoshoot – 'You've got talent! I'll give you some tips that will come in useful.'

But Lara was right. The lie came between them, like a flash flood forcing them apart. When Lara told James about her 'miscarriage' he broke down in tears. She was taken aback by his reaction that she considered self-indulgent and weak despite her own horrible feelings of shame. He said the loss reawakened the grief of losing his brother as a child. Almost believing in her own deception, Lara felt she was the one who needed his support. She needed him to be strong to help her cope with the loss and the grief. She had to admit that he pulled himself together very soon and in the following days he was there by her side whenever she needed him, offering sympathy, cups of tea and a shoulder to cry on.

But as time passed she became aware of a change in his mood. He embarked on obsessive research about the causes of miscarriage and blamed her for the loss of his baby. He accused her of having been irresponsible for drinking to excess in early pregnancy and for not having looked after herself properly. She was irritated by this constant sniping and became more and more withdrawn from him. She hadn't the strength of character to struggle and fight against the torrent of sadness and guilt. The bad feeling between them erupted in a blazing row after supper one balmy summer's night in July at The Trout Inn on the banks of the Cherwell. The next day Lara announced her intention to contact Columbia University to ask if it would be possible to reinstate their offer, made to her some months previously, that she had turned down when she discovered she was pregnant. In the second week of July, her Masters placement to study American literature was confirmed and ten days after that she was at Heathrow boarding a Virgin Atlantic plane for JFK, while James was heaving his trunk from the platform at Oxford station onto the London train.

Gabrielle was there to meet him at Paddington station and take him home to her flat where he stayed for the rest of the summer vacation indulging in her exotic cuisine and insatiable appetite for sex. When not working in the lab for his internship at the London Institute of Oncological Research, he was out earning extra holiday cash freelancing as a male model for Gabrielle's network of fashion photographers. He had little time to think of

Lara or to dwell on the sadness of the miscarriage and the bitterness of their break up but deep down he missed her dreadfully. This late summer romance felt like a 'through the looking-glass' fantasy with Gabrielle, who was a sparkling reflection of Lara, and a delightful distraction from his real life. But before too long he intended to do everything in his power to get back together with Lara – his first and true love.

But Gabrielle had other plans. One evening in late August, as she sat curled in James' lap on the sofa in her flat, sipping a shared glass of dark red Châteauneuf-du-Pape, she decided that the time was right to twist the knife. She gently stroked his hair and decanted her poisoned tale of truth and lies.

'There's something I need to tell you,' she said. 'Lara didn't have a miscarriage. She had an abortion. Here in London. At the Chelsea clinic. I begged her to think again. I begged her to wait, to go back to Oxford, to talk to you. But she was so determined. She was desperate to get rid of that baby, said she couldn't face going through with it, that it would put an end to her studies, wreck her life. And she couldn't face telling you because she thought you would put pressure on her to keep the child. I'm so sorry. I tried so hard to make her change her mind. I know how much this must hurt. I thought it was only fair that you should know.'

By the end of the September, Gabrielle's deceit had worked its magic. James had overcome his initial black depression and recovered his usual cheerful disposition, transferring his affections lock, stock and barrel to her. His anger with Lara tipped the balance in favour of Gabrielle. He put aside any lingering thoughts of trying to get back together with his first love. Cementing his relationship with Gabrielle was the best way to punish Lara for having disposed of his baby. In his head, Gabrielle had become Lara's avatar.

For Gabrielle, victory was sweet. They were inseparable, madly in love, the hottest new couple in town. Some weeks later Gabrielle suggested a long weekend in New York (all expenses paid by her), the pretext to check up on Lara, the true motive to press home her advantage and to torture her rival with the spoils of her passion.

James was up for it. It would be nice to see Lara again. He was in the mood to be forgiving. He'd always wanted to visit New York.

And fortunately for James, he had saved up enough money from his photoshoot assignments to feel suitably relaxed and pumped with testosterone when Gabrielle suggested that they should 'drop by Tiffany's' before taking Lara out for brunch.

16

Scarlett

I click the stopwatch on my phone as Costa starts up the engine and we hurtle across the water towards the reef.

6.25 a.m.

The shadows of dawn have melted away. It's daybreak and sunshine is streaming into my eyes, bouncing off the surface, lighting up the spray. I'm alive and at one with the sea and the sun.

6.49 a.m.

Costa steers the boat alongside the reef, cuts the power and drops anchor.

I click the stopwatch.

'Twenty-four minutes.'

The boat bobs in the water. It's peaceful without the straining engine. The surge and suck of waves breaking on the reef and lapping against the wooden hull provide a soothing soundtrack. And now that we've stopped, the heat of the rising sun is building steadily. For the first time since Katie disappeared, I feel optimistic. Costa seems to think my account is credible. I think we're going to find her.

Costa stands in the prow with his back towards me and his head turned in profile. He takes off his leather jacket and undoes the top buttons of his shirt. He has the kind of body that looks constrained by city clothes. It occurs to me that on this boat I'm completely at his mercy, and I get the feeling that he knows it and it's going to his head. Now it's so quiet that I can hear his breathing. His eyes are fixed on the reef at the point where breaking waves funnel through a channel between two ridges of coral.

Suddenly the peace is broken by the garish ringtone on his mobile phone.

Could this be news of Katie?

I hold my breath. I watch him – the deepening frown as he takes the call and his curt response: 'Not now, I'm busy. Send through the report, I'll get back to you.'

My heart is thumping.

'Bad news?' He ignores me.

The gulls are swooping overhead. Save for them and two fishing boats far out to sea, we're alone. The boat's hidden from the shore by the topography of the coast and the overhang of the cliffs. Only someone walking along the coastal path on the cliff edge would be able to see us.

Costa seems lost in thought.

When he turns to face me, I sense a change in his mood and start to feel uneasy. His eyes are hostile, cold, shining with distaste. He crouches down next to where I'm sitting, uncomfortably close. The boat rocks under his weight.

'So what happens next?' he says quietly. 'Tell me more, Scarlett. You haven't told me everything that's going on in that pretty head of yours yet, have you? Who took her from the beach? If Damien couldn't have done it on his own then who is his accomplice?' He puts his fingers under my chin and tilts my face until I'm looking directly into his eyes.

So he thinks it's me.

I hold my breath. 'Her mother,' I say. 'Christina.' My words gush out. 'She took her from the beach and drove her down to Crooks' Bay in Damien's Jeep.'

For a second, I think he's about to strike me. His face is so close to mine that I can see beads of sweat glistening on his forehead and a muscle pulsing in his jaw. Then he turns away as if he can't bear the sight of me.

Slowly, realisation dawns on me. Now I get it. He thinks I'm lying, trying to frame the victim's mother to cover up my own guilt. That's why he agreed to this outlandish trip in the first place. He's been pretending to believe in me, and all the time he's just been giving me the opportunity to incriminate myself. He's a more wily detective than I gave him credit for. I've fallen into his trap. I've made myself his hostage – caught *between the devil and the deep blue sea* – and on this boat he can interrogate me to his heart's content, as tough as he pleases. Damien and I are his main suspects, and as the *chief criminal investigating officer* he will do anything to wring a confession out of me.

But there's no stopping me now. While Costa watches the waves breaking on the reef, I tell him why I'm suspicious of Christina. She's behaving in a strange and secretive way. She seemed distracted and distant from her daughter the first couple of days of the holiday. Then there was something over-the-top and fake about her grief when Katie disappeared. I can't put my finger on it but her grief doesn't ring true. She's hiding something.

'Damien's controlling her,' I say. 'She's besotted with him. As you've seen, he's a compulsive gambler with huge debts and expensive tastes – a morally bankrupt risk taker. My hunch is that Damien forced Christina to go along with his plan to stage the disappearance of Katie, to make it look like she'd died in a tragic drowning accident and to hide her away somewhere, before finding some way of either fraudulently claiming on her travel insurance or claiming a reward for information leading to her discovery. I guess he was desperate to get his hands on a lump sum to pay off his gambling debts and continue with his life of decadence in the sun. But his arrest screwed up the plan and now I think Christina's got cold feet and is desperate to find a way out…'

I'm sticky and breathless. The heat is building, the breeze has dropped and the endless listing of the anchored boat is making me feel seasick.

'I can't bear this any longer,' I say, tugging my hoodie from over my head and twisting my hair back into a ponytail. Again, I wish I'd taken the time to dress properly before leaving my room when I catch Costa eyeing the outline of my breasts through my camisole. He turns away quickly.

'I'm listening,' he says quietly. 'Carry on.'

Now I've got his attention.

'The beach was crowded when Katie disappeared,' I
say. 'If she had drifted out to sea on the lilo or been taken
by a stranger someone would have seen it. Surely one of
the scores of staff and guests you've been interviewing
would have noticed something. She's such a beautiful
child that she attracts attention. From the day we arrived,
we were there on the beach each day, all day long, back
and forth collecting shells. Everyone knew her. But no one
intervened, no one reported anything suspicious at the
time and no one's reported it since.'

He shrugs. 'It was a crowded beach, lots of people
coming and going. Anyone could have abducted her while
you were asleep.'

I shake my head. 'You don't know Katie. She's a
delightful, sweet little girl but if something upsets her,
everyone knows about it, believe me. She's a highly
sensitive child and she doesn't like strangers. She'd have
had to be dragged kicking and screaming off that beach if
someone she didn't know had tried to take her away.' He's
scrolling through a text as I talk, with a deepening scowl.
He taps out a response to the text then turns to me again,
stoney-faced.

'Do you think the child's still alive?'

'Yes…' I hesitate. 'Yes, I do believe that. I don't think
Christina would ever do anything to place Katie's life at
risk. I believe she's acting under Damien's orders and I
think he's doing it in order somehow to get money to pay
off his gambling debts and fund his drug addiction.'

'What makes you so sure Christina drove the car?' says
Costa.

'Because I found her earring under the driver's seat the morning after Katie disappeared. It must have dropped out while she was driving to Crooks' Bay.'

'It could have dropped out earlier in the week,' says Costa.

'Damien didn't hire the Jeep until the day before Katie disappeared.' I say. 'I remember it clearly because Christina picked a fight with him for missing supper that night. He said he'd been delayed by a puncture after collecting the Jeep. He'd called out a mechanic to change the wheel. What's more, I remember noticing that Christina was wearing her jade earrings at the pool on the morning of the day Katie was taken –She was wearing a bikini and kimono in matching blue – same colour as her earrings.'

He takes a long swig from a water bottle. I'm parched but he doesn't offer it to me.

'If Christina took the car, how did Damien get down to Coral Point?' he says.

'I've no idea. He's got plenty of friends here. Any one of his golfing or gambling buddies could have given him a lift. You should check with the cab companies too. Obviously, he wouldn't have wanted to park the Jeep down at the harbour as it would have given away his timings and movements.'

'Anything else?' says Costa.

'Look at this.' I hold out my phone and scroll to the pictures of the skid marks in the mud that I took yesterday when Christina and I walked up from Crooks' Bay. 'Look at the tyre tracks – an odd pair. The tracks caught my eye. I remember Damien complaining that the Jeep was driving badly because the replacement wheel wasn't compatible with the others. If the tracks match the treads on the tyres, there's your proof that it was driven down to Crooks' Bay.'

'But not who was driving it!' Costa mutters. 'Send me the pictures,' he says. 'I'll get my team to check out the tyres and talk to the mechanic who changed the wheel.'

He could be more gracious. It's a key piece of evidence. Once again, I get that sinking feeling I'm top of his list of suspects.

'I've got a question for you,' says Costa. 'The child's swimsuit was left behind in the cave. That seems very careless. Why would the abductor discard a key item of incriminating evidence?'

'Maybe she's distracted. She must have changed Katie into dry clothes in the cave. Perhaps she's under so much pressure from Damien that she's losing her head – she could have just forgotten it by mistake. Or maybe the swimsuit was a decoy – to make it look like murder. The abandoned swimsuit makes Katie's disappearance look like a case of a stranger abduction by a paedophile. So this draws the attention away from those closest to her. It changes the line of enquiry, confuses and stalls the police hunt, gives time for Katie to be taken away to another secret location while all the focus and effort of the police investigation is on the crime scene at Crooks' Bay.'

I'm feeling quite pleased with myself. I dip my hand in the water and lean over to peer down at the corals just below the surface.

'What's more, I'm convinced it was Christina who defaced my mirror with lipstick on the first night,' I say. 'I caught a glimpse of her sneaking out of my room. She's enjoying herself playing games with us – leaving death threats on the mirror, pretending Katie's purse was planted in her handbag – all to make it look like Katie's been targeted by a psychopath. She'll do anything to derail the investigation and deflect the suspicion from herself. She's not behaving logically.'

'And you're not thinking logically…' says Costa. He settles himself down beside me on the wooden bench, so close our thighs are touching. His bulk is enough to intimidate me and he knows it. But I'm determined to make him hear me out.

'Christina came on a few sailing holidays to the Caribbean with her family when she was a teenager. She must know someone here who could have been duped or bribed into hiding Katie away for a few days. It seems like a great plan. But it all falls apart when Damien goes on a bender at the casino and is arrested for reckless driving the next morning.'

'It's a great story,' he says, 'What does Christina do next, once she's installed Katie in her hiding place?'

I shift along the bench.

'She steals back to the hotel, changes into her evening gear, and makes her way down to the play area. Then she makes her grand entrance in the hotel lobby, and so the drama begins. You know the rest…'

I stop uncertainly.

'Well, you've certainly got a good imagination.' He grins at me.

His phone bleeps and he checks the message, his face inscrutable as he scans down the screen. He taps out another response then looks up.

He's not smiling any more. The boat rocks wildly as he stands up and leans over me, drags me up from the bench, grabs my wrists and pins them firmly behind my back.

'You've really got a nerve,' he says, 'trying to make a fool out of me.'

Then he pulls me forward, towering over me, crushing my frame against his chest. I can feel his heart thumping against my cheek.

'There's just one problem with your story. I don't believe it. It's second-rate fiction and first-rate fabrication,' he says in a low voice, bending his head down towards my ear. Suddenly, he loses patience. 'I haven't got time for this. Katie's life is at stake.'

With one hand he traps both my wrists in the small of my back and with the other he yanks my ponytail, pulling my head back until I'm looking up at the dazzling sky and my body is arched backwards, almost horizontal to the water.

'From everything you've just told me, *you* could be the accomplice!'

His eyes are locked on mine.

'Look at me,' he says in a dark tone. 'It's my turn to tell you a story.'

He cups the palm of one hand behind my head, like a ballet cavalier supporting his female partner. Though he's still bearing down on me at least this stops me toppling back into the water.

'There's another woman who could have walked off that beach with Katie without drawing any attention to herself... another woman that Katie would have followed without having a meltdown... another woman who'd been seen by everyone, coming and going with Katie down to the beach and round the hotel... and that woman is you. My hunch is that you stole her in plain daylight.'

'That's just ridiculous,' I say, with a strangled laugh.

'Not so ridiculous.' His lips are tight and for a moment I think he's going to spit in my face. But he releases his hand and shoves me upright, not a minute too soon. My head is spinning and I'm about to be sick. 'My turn now. In my version, you and Damien are deep in this together. Your claims about the spiked cocktail are a pack of lies. All the tests came back negative. Damien is your lover and partner-in-crime. You targeted Christina in New York because she's rich, and vulnerable, and alone. You saw she was lonely and fragile and preyed on her and her innocent child.'

There's no possible excuse for interrogating me in this way. The power has gone to his head.

'While Damien seduced her, you made yourself useful, even indispensable. Christina became more and more dependent on you to take care of Katie while she was working long hours in the office. Her short evenings and weekends were spent with Damien who bewitched her with romance and sex. In the meantime, Katie formed a strong attachment to you, and Christina was so grateful that she let you interfere more and more in her personal life, giving you unlimited and unsupervised access to her flat, her financial affairs and her online communications. Day-by-day, you found out everything about her and were in a position to monitor and control her every move.'

I hang my head as Costa berates me.

'So Christina believed you to be her faithful friend and employee and Katie's devoted and trustworthy carer. And she believed Damien was in love with her. But she was being deceived by both of you. While the money she was earning in Manhattan was being spent on Damien's gambling debts, he was also cheating on her by carrying on a wild, sex-crazed love affair with you.'

'No, no,' I cry. 'You've got it all wrong. I scarcely know him. Christina always made a point of keeping us apart.'

Costa laughs loudly as if I've just made the most hilarious joke.

'I've just been sent the results of the forensic tests on the Jeep, and the search of the hotel rooms. You saw me looking at the emails. Made for very interesting reading. The evidence confirms that you are indeed very well-acquainted with Damien, that you know each other intimately, in fact. Your DNA is all over the Jeep, mingled with Damien's. How do you explain that?' He makes an offensive gesture with his fingers.

'Not only that but Christina's room is riddled with your fingerprints – the drawers, the cupboard, the safe: all the evidence we need to show you've been acting in a highly suspicious manner, rifling through all her personal belongings.'

Abruptly, Costa flips me round so that I'm facing the ocean.

This time he crouches behind me, hooks one arm round my waist, and forces my neck forward until I'm looking down into the water.

He's enjoying this too much.

'Is she down there, Scarlett, is she down there in the ocean? What did that sad bastard do to her? What have you done with Katie? You can trust me, Scarlett.'

'If this is your interrogation technique, it's certainly not professional,' I say as I hang bent double over the water, entirely at his mercy. *Just because he knows he can get away with it! How dare he!*

Yet I can't deny that his methods are compelling. Perversely, there's something about knowing that I'm completely within the power of this trumped-up bully that gives an almost erotic edge to my fear. The urge to confess something, anything, if only to please him, is overpowering.

'You'd never get away with this in England,' I say, struggling to escape his hold. I've read enough trashy detective stories to know that exerting undue pressure on a witness renders the evidence inadmissible.

'I make the rules around here,' he says grimly. 'I've been doing some research of my own, Scarlett. I know you're not the person you claim to be. You lied to Christina. You don't have a childcare qualification. You dropped out of college after two years. Your certificates are all forgeries.' I squirm to get free but I'm held in a vice. 'And after dropping out of college, you worked as a waitress at the *High Kicks* pole dancing club in Soho…'

So that's why he thinks he can get away with treating me like this!

'… before moving to New York, where you spent six months training to be a croupier at the *Great Gatsby Casino* on Long Island – that's until you were sacked from your job for having an affair with one of the regular punters. Came to light when he started winning a bit too often! After a couple of months living off friends, you then signed up for a modelling agency with a sideline in soft porn and completed several assignments before taking up your position as a nanny working for Christina. It's not exactly an exemplary record for a "childcare professional".' He pauses for dramatic effect and to take a breath.

I have to admit it doesn't sound great. But he's twisted it all – made it sound so much worse than it really is.

He loosens his grip enough to allow me to stand up straight but he's still got my arms pinned behind my back.

'How did you dig up all this dirt on me? You're making me sound like a criminal?'

'It's called the Internet, darling. Carried out a few technical searches myself, last night – I'm not a complete caveman! And I have friends in London. I can call in a few favours when it comes to information sharing. Can you deny it? You're a fake and a fraud.' He leans in closer and whispers in my ear. 'Let's face it Scarlett, you've got history'

I know he's trying to force a confession out of me but this is going too far. 'For God's sake let me go.'

But he continues. 'And my guess is that the Great Gatsby Casino is where you hooked up with Damien who was there 24/7 indulging his gambling habit, and together the pair of you came up with the plan to swindle Christina by abducting her child.'

'Now I get it. So that's why you got Lennie to show me round,' I say. 'You asked him to check me out.'

Still standing behind me, he takes my hands in his and brings them up in front of my face.

'Lennie's got sharp eyes. He stalks the tables and watches the punters' hands with the eyes of a hawk. He's got a fixation with them – how a punter deals the cards, shuffles the pack, throws out his chips. He's looking out for cheats but it's helped me out a few times too.'

I wrench my hands out of his.

'You've got beautiful hands, Scarlett. You wouldn't hurt Katie with these beautiful hands now, would you?'

'I would never lay a finger on Katie,' I say. 'And I think you know that.'

Costa ignores my protest.

'Lennie never forgets a pair of hands and most of the island's scum passes through BJ's at some time or another. Now funny thing is, he could tell from the way you deal the cards that you're a pro.'

'You've got it all wrong. It's just absurd to think Damien and I could be partners-in-crime. I despise the guy. And whatever you think of me, and my lifestyle, I swear I never set eyes on Damien until I started working for Christina. The first time I met him was in her apartment in Manhattan. You would never dream of interrogating Christina in this disgustingly inappropriate way,' I shout.

'You know, Scarlett, in my book, there's a double-barrelled name for girls who dress and act like you. If you go around half naked, what do you expect?'

If he weren't a policeman, I would slap him.

'Sit down,' he says coldly, pointing to the bench 'I haven't finished yet. Calm down. So, this is my version. On that fateful day you take Katie to the beach. You play with her by the water for a while. Then you take her for a walk along the coast. You pass a few people as you stroll along the sand, smile and say hello. There's nothing to arouse any suspicion, a charming sight, an attractive young woman and a sweet little girl, walking hand-in-hand, collecting shells in a red bucket. You walk as far as Crooks' Bay. There you change Katie out of her swimsuit back into her clothes. You leave the swimsuit in the cave to make it look like she's been abducted and murdered. You meet up with Damien who takes Katie away in the boat and leaves her at the pre-arranged hiding place. You walk back to the beach and pretend to fall asleep on the sand. Sometime later the yellow lilo launched at the reef by Damien drifts into view. You raise the alarm and the rescue operation begins. The next morning you go out early and Damien picks you up along the coastal road. You're planning to go on together to the place Katie is hidden. God knows what you are intending to do with her. But your base instincts get the better of you both and you decide to stop en route. He fucks you in the Jeep and we arrest Damien for reckless driving. But we're no closer to finding Katie.'

At last he backs away and I slide off the bench and sit huddled in the bow of the rowing boat.

'Now what we really need to know, is what have you two perverts done with her, is she dead or alive, and where in God's name have you hidden her?'

'You're crazy,' I say, looking up. 'I'm doing everything I can to help in the search for Katie. As you know, I spent hours working to get that social media campaign up and running on top of volunteering for all the searches on the ground. I came out this morning because I had an idea which might help you to find Katie. I didn't expect you to attack and insult me and falsely accuse me. You won't bully me into a confession. I won't let you intimidate me with your distortions and lies.'

Costa's face is set, indifferent. 'None of that proves you are innocent. In fact, most of it is unwanted interference.'

'You're not going to get away with this' I say. 'I'm going to report you for assault.'

'All in a day's work,' he retorts. 'It's a different world out here.'

'Flunking my exams and dropping out of college doesn't make me a child abductor,' I say. 'And my jobs working as a waitress and trainee croupier and as a model for the photographic agency were all entirely legitimate gap year jobs. I took up anything I could get because I had to earn good money to clear my university loans, not because I'm some kind of depraved nymphomaniac. Once I'd cleared my debts, I went straight back to look for a job in childcare. That was what I really wanted to do.'

I warm to my theme, outraged and indignant.

'As for what happened in the Jeep. Shame on you, for being so insulting. I was in fear of my life. Letting Damien think he could seduce me was the only way I could get him to stop the car for long enough for the police cars to catch up with us. And it worked. Thanks to me, you've got him under lock and key.'

Costa looks a little sheepish at last, thank God, sitting at the other end of the boat, looking out to sea.

'You're as bad as him. Just because you're a police officer doesn't give you the right to abuse me in this way.'

He holds up his hands.

'And my fingerprints are all over Christina's room because I was searching for clues – something that your lot should have done days ago. I've already given you plenty of information to show that Christina is somehow mixed up in all of this but we need to work out how and why.'

All at once I'm exhausted. I curl up on the wooden planks, hold my head in my hands and sob loudly. All the pain and sadness of the last few days hits me.

I miss Katie.

After a minute or two, Costa comes over and pats me gently on the shoulder.

'Relax, Scarlett, relax. I'm sorry. I was too hard with you. Got carried away.' His tone is soothing. I'm not taken in – he's playing the two roles in this interrogation – both *bad cop and good cop.*

'Why won't you take me seriously?'

'I'm just doing my job. Come on, Scarlett. Cheer up. Crying doesn't suit you. Tell me where she is, Scarlett. It's not too late. I can get you out of this mess. I want to be your friend. You're an impressionable young thing.

Misguided. I know he made you do it. We can sort this
out. We can make it right.'

This time he lets me push him away.

'So you still don't believe me?' I say. 'Take me back to
the hotel.'

As the boat approaches the harbour, I turn to Costa.

'There's something else you need to know. I had my
doubts about Christina but deep down I really didn't
want to believe that she was involved in the abduction
of Katie – until yesterday. I know she loves her little
girl… and nothing I've said changes that. But what finally
convinced me to share my suspicions with you was what I
witnessed yesterday afternoon down at Crooks' Bay. That
cowboy overseeing the search down there, DC Kramer, I
think that was his name, well, she's had dealings with him
before. He seemed to know her pretty well.'

Costa cuts the engine.

'And as far as I could make out, he arranged to meet
her last night at the Coco Shack.'

He stands there, looking out over the harbour in silence
for a full two minutes then he turns.

'Well, Scarlett, that's the most interesting thing you've
said to me all day.'

Driving back to the hotel, Costa goes some way to
apologising.

'I'm sorry I was tough with you. Police tactics round here are rougher than where you come from. And there's no time to lose. I was trying to break you. I went too far.'

'Just because I'm a woman you think you can use the power of your position to humiliate me and try to force a confession out of me,' I say. 'You've made it pretty clear you think I'm guilty as sin.'

'Right now, it's my job not to trust anybody. Nobody's ruled in or out.'

We pull into the hotel and I can't get out of the car quick enough.

He lowers the window and leans over.

'If you're going to keep interfering with the investigation, Scarlett, then you might as well do something useful. Thanks to that social media campaign you pushed the button on yesterday, there are more than five hundred documents sitting on my desk containing possible witness sightings and photographs sent in by the public. We're completely overwhelmed. You can go through the files in case we missed anything important. I'll be expecting you in my office first thing tomorrow.'

This offer (or should I say order) takes me by surprise. Why would Costa give one of his prime suspects insider access to the investigation? I wonder if he's using this as an excuse to observe me more closely, in the hope I'll 'give myself away'?

'Is this another of your traps?' I say.

'Don't be such a cynic!' he says. 'As I've told you, we do things differently round here. I make my own rules. You provoked this deluge. Now you can help to process it.'

I want nothing more to do with him but I can't turn down this opportunity to get on the inside of the investigation.

'I'll do it,' I say. 'As long as you promise never to lay another finger on me.'

17

Scarlett

Costa drops me at a service entrance to the hotel and I go up the back stairs to my room. I crash out on the bed. I stir briefly before lunch when the maid knocks on the door, send her away with a muffled 'please come back later,' and then fall back onto the pillows. I wake just in time to catch the end of afternoon tea served on the verandah under the lime trees. As I'm loading up my plate with cupcakes and scones, I hear a familiar, sarcastic voice…

How could I forget that voice?

'Hey Scarlett, good to see you've still got a hearty appetite!'

It's Damien, propping up the bar and toasting me with a Mojito. I make no attempt to hide my shock and irritation. He's had a shower and a shave, and now looking as handsome and smug as ever, is quick to tell me that the bail hearing went 'swimmingly well' this morning. So all my efforts with Costa on the boat came to nothing.

He tells me that the judge 'was a pretty decent bloke, quite a good sense of humour actually, built up quite a rapport.' He's obviously been trying to charm his way out of trouble. The judge ruled that the charges for reckless driving did not warrant further detention and was more than happy simply to fine him five hundred dollars and release him from custody on bail while the police investigate further unspecified charges. It sounds like a brown-paper-envelope-under-the-table deal to me. I wouldn't put it past Damien. No wonder the judge was so cheerful!

Costa has betrayed me – didn't take any of my accusations about Damien seriously. Not surprising, I guess, given his own astounding comportment on the boat. They're two of a kind, predatory males, closing ranks. And despite my best endeavours trying to prove that the betting alibi doesn't hold water, Damien's release suggests that I failed. Costa's still obstinately clinging to his simplistic, unambitious opinion that there's insufficient evidence to bring charges against him for the abduction of Katie. I ask Damien if he's seen Christina and he tells me they had a late lunch together and she's now gone up to the room to rest. I am aghast. What is she playing at? So, all is forgiven it seems! In her position, I'd be tearing him to pieces.

As I work my way through the cupcakes, Damien leans back in his chair and takes it on himself to regale me with anecdotes about the dodgy characters he met in jail. He obviously felt quite at home. Not once does he mention Katie.

When I've licked the last crumb off my fingers and Damien has downed his Mojito, he grabs my arm.

'Let's get out of here, everyone's staring at us.'

'Get your hands off me,' I snap at him. I'm sick of being manhandled.

We wander out to the gardens.

'I want to apologise for my outrageous behaviour the other day,' he says. 'No hard feelings, I hope.'

He puts his arm round my shoulders. I shake him off and head in the direction of my room.

'Come on Scarlett, we need to talk. It's important – for Katie's sake.'

Reluctantly I follow him through the hotel gardens and along the beach, to get away from the flapping ears and prying eyes of the tourists.

I can barely talk, too angry to be scared of him. I'm fuming, appalled and astonished that he's been granted bail, and silently raging at Costa for not taking my allegations more seriously or warning me of his return. I remain convinced that he's the one behind Katie's disappearance. He seems so shockingly casual and unaffected. But when I challenge him, he goes off on the offensive himself, accusing me of looking for others to blame.

'Don't you dare try to guilt-trip me. If anyone's to blame, it's you. If you had been doing your job properly, Katie would still be here. What kind of nanny goes to sleep when the little girl she's supposed to be looking after is playing on a lilo in the sea?'

He rants on and on, says I'm incompetent and lazy and irresponsible. Well, I'm not taking that from him of all people. So pretty soon we've stopped in our tracks in the sand and we're both shouting, causing a scene. The red-faced sunbathers turn to stare disapprovingly. I scream accusations at him. I don't care who hears me. I don't care what they think of me. I accuse him of spiking my drink, of deliberately drugging me, of taking Katie away, of trying to make it look like she drowned, of framing me to make it look like I'm the one at fault.

'I've worked out your game,' I say. 'You think there's some money in this to pay off your gambling debts. You're desperate... you'll do anything.'

He just stands there, one hand on his hip, smirking. Suddenly, I can't hold back any longer. I snap. I lunge at him; the sand flies and I karate kick him between the legs with my bare foot. He crumples. For a moment he looks stunned. Then he straightens, clenches his fists, and I cover my face, thinking he's about to whack me. But seconds later he drops his hands and laughs, a loud, masculine, guffawing roar, as if I'm the funniest, most idiotic creature in the world.

'You've lost your mind,' he says. 'You're a fine one to dish the dirt. Flaunting your body at police officers like a cheap tart. Making false allegations about me. Tampering with the evidence. Strutting around as if you're in charge of the investigation. Who do you think you are – Pamela Andersen in Baywatch?'

He takes a packet of Lucky Strike out of his pocket and lights a cigarette.

'Didn't know you smoked,' I say.

'There are lots of things you don't know about me.' He takes a long drag and half closes his eyes, looking like he hasn't a care in the world.

'I've found out a few home truths about you too,' he says, slowly puffing a cloud of smoke into the sea breeze. 'I know you failed your childcare exams and were kicked out of university because of your conviction for possession of cocaine. And I know you were virtually unemployable after being sacked from the Great Gatsby Casino until you decided to have a go at modelling for a soft porn photographer.'

I barely flinch but he clocks it.

'Not many people would choose to employ a disgraced former trainee croupier with a cocaine habit as a nanny for their precious little darlings!'

He takes a couple more drags. Then he says, 'And I know you faked your security checks to hide your conviction for possession of cocaine when you applied through e-Face for the job with Christina. There's no way she'd have given you a job as Katie's nanny unless your references were squeaky clean.'

His words send a chill down my spine... like a bucket of icy water being tipped slowly over my head.

'I don't know what the fuck you're talking about,' I say, as I swivel in the sand and march back to my room.

Despite my show of bravado, I'm shaking as I walk away. My chequered employment history is not something I'm proud of. How the hell does Damien know about my conviction for possession of cocaine? Costa didn't seem to know about it this morning – or he would have added this offence to the litany of my sins in his character assassination of me on the boat. It's a spent conviction. I've gone out of my way to keep that episode of my crazy student days a secret. I've never told any of my family or friends and it never got out there on social media. Once again I get that sinking feeling.

I'm the one being who's being framed for Katie's abduction.

In reality, my 'crime' wasn't as bad as it sounds. I was the victim. I picked up a conviction for possession of cocaine in my second year at university thanks to a shitty, casual boyfriend who stuffed his stash into my bag when the police raided a wild student party we had gate crashed on a whim. I think the police had a pretty good idea that I'd been stitched up. My so-called boyfriend was the son of the local MP so they didn't ask too many questions. I was the 'fall guy'. Come to think of it – I begin to see a pattern.

And I never intended to get into modelling soft porn. I fell into it. It was just a way of paying off my university loans after I got kicked out from university and unfairly dismissed from my temporary job as a trainee croupier. I wanted a fresh start. I felt a real vocation to work with children. But let's face it, being a convicted drug offender isn't a great recommendation if you're looking for a job in childcare. So after about a hundred rejections, I decided to have a go at becoming a model. I got some photos taken and sent them off to all the agencies I could find online.

I was completely honest with them and declared the conviction on the application forms – thinking it wouldn't be such a big deal for a job in modelling. Most of them didn't bother to reply. I got a few automated responses. A couple got back to me saying they liked the photos but needed someone with experience. I had almost given up hope. Then on the very morning I was planning go and sign up at the welfare benefits office, an email pinged up on my laptop as I was eating breakfast.

We don't have any openings in London right now but we note from your resumé that you also have training in childcare. Our sister company which deals with overseas placements for nannies and home helps in the United States has a number of vacancies for positions working as a nanny for expatriate British families based in New York. If you are interested, we are happy to forward your resumé for consideration.

God what a fabulous opportunity! I'd always wanted to work in New York. I was jumping up and down. I read on:

If you are successful in obtaining a position in New York we are also happy to offer you up to five unpaid photoshoot assignments (reasonable expenses to be reimbursed) with our trainee Boudoir photographers in New York to enable you to establish your modelling portfolio.

I was so excited. This was a dream opening – a job in childcare and a chance to develop my career as a model, and the once-in-a-lifetime opportunity to work in one of the most exciting cities in the world. I had no idea what Boudoir photography consisted of. But I was keen to learn. As it happens, Boudoir was an understatement – a euphemism, to say the least. But I've never had too many scruples on the sexual front.

More importantly, there was the small problem of my drugs conviction. Had it been overlooked? I had noted it on the application form.

Later that day I received a phone call from the owner of e-Face agency. The woman seemed very professional. She assured me it shouldn't be a showstopper. She could smooth things along. She promised that confidentiality was assured. She would take care of my security clearance and then forward my resumé (which she would prepare on my behalf) to her sister company which had identified a family based in Manhattan that was interested in employing an English nanny. The very next morning she emailed me the completed, signed and certified child protection security clearance documents, along with a job offer – and before the end of the month, I was on my way to the Big Apple.

If anyone faked my security checks, it was her not me. It was the agency's doing.

When I reach my hotel room, the maids are in there cleaning, so I head back to the pool and find a free sun lounger in the shade of a coconut tree.

How on earth did Damien dig up all this dirt on me? I settle onto the lounger. I gaze absently at the coconuts hanging high above my head. I remember reading somewhere that more people are killed each year by falling coconuts than sharks. I look up anxiously. Knowing my luck, a coconut will fall on *my* head.

Damien's right. Christina surely didn't have an inkling of the drug conviction or she would never have offered me the job as Katie's nanny. So, the information must have come from Costa. He must have received a tip off from his police contacts in London and then grilled Damien about it during interviews. While Costa pretends to take me into his confidence, he's secretly gathering evidence against me, stabbing me in the back – and Damien will be more than happy to strike a second blow!

What's really baffling me is how Damien knows about e-Face and the faked checks. There's no reason why the British police would know anything about that. Is Damien an undercover agent leading a double life? Surely that's too far-fetched. As far as I can see, the only way Damien could know anything about these things is if he's connected with the modelling agency himself.

I shift my sunbed slightly so that I am not in the direct line of gravity. No point taking any chances with falling coconuts. And then I remember that trip to the park with Damien boasting about having worked as a male model and escort. Maybe he was on the books of e-Face too? That's the only possible explanation. To be fair I can't deny he has the body for it. He certainly looks good in those designer swimming trunks that he's always swaggering about in!

Just a quick swim in the pool and then I'll go and find him at the Reef Club. He's bound to be there – propping up the bar.

I dive into the cool water and swim the length of the pool underwater. As I surface, my head clears and with it comes a new certainty. He worked for e-Face. That's how he knows so much about the agency. He must have been in communication with the same woman at the agency who recruited me. So much for him working in finance in downtown Manhattan. I bet that was all made up. He's a complete fake – a fake and a con artist.

Later on in the evening, there's a soft knocking on my door. It's Christina. She's come by to let me know that she and Damien are driving out for dinner to Clamities, an upmarket seafood restaurant on the other side of the island that's fashionable with the floating-gin-palace set and well-heeled locals alike. It's one of her favourites, a beautiful location right on the waterfront in a secluded harbour, serving traditional gourmet dishes. She says she's desperate to get away from the paparazzi stalking her at the hotel. I try to dissuade Christina from driving out alone with Damien to such an isolated place. I've got a bad feeling.

'The clue's in the name,' I say. 'Clamities! Don't go with Damien. I don't trust that man.'

Anything could happen. But Christina closes me down.

'Damien's already made the reservation.' Her eyes could turn me to stone. 'Just keep out of it. I'm a grown woman. I can look after myself.'

*

I order room service and spend much of the evening on my laptop. Eventually I succeed in setting up the sporadic Wi-Fi connection and pull up my old email correspondence with e-Face. There it is, the agency's slogan 'e-Face for Unforgettable Faces' – ironically, I'd forgotten it!

I haven't had any communications with e-Face since taking up my position with Christina. I fire off an email complaining about the breach of confidentiality and request someone to contact me by return. I look up the website address and type it into my search bar. A message comes up. The website address no longer exists. A couple of minutes later there's a ping from my laptop. My email to e-Face has bounced back undelivered. Effaced, literally! Looks like they've gone bust – or perhaps been busted by the police?

Could there be some connection between the fake modelling agency and the disappearance of Katie? I call Costa. If I'm right and Damien worked for e-Face too, then this needs to be investigated further.

His phone goes to voicemail. I send him a text.

Call me. I've got a new lead for you.

Before shutting down the laptop, I decide to check out the location of Clamities. I find it straight away. According to TripAdvisor, it's the top-rated restaurant for 'Romantic Dining in Clearwater Bay'.

★

Needless to say, Costa doesn't call me back. Family commitments I suppose. Eight o'clock in the evening; he'll be busy at home with his wife and kid. It's lonely here with no one to talk to. Everyone's shunning me at the hotel. I'm desperate for a drink and I need a change of scene so I call down to reception. I can't stay here on my own.

Besides I want to check out the Coco Shack. It must be one of Damien's hangouts. The bar staff might have some useful intel. If I'm right that he hired a boat at Coral Point, he could have stopped off there after he returned it. Tonight, I can kill two birds with one stone. *What was it that cowboy Kramer asked me to tell Christina?*

I'm on night duty at the Coco Shack.

It'll be interesting to find out what Kramer's up to down there if he turns up expecting Christina for their shady rendezvous.

I dial o for reception.

'Hi, could you get me a cab please as soon as you can? I'm going to the Coco Shack... Yes, down at the harbour. That's for room 96, in the name of Scarlett Reyes.'

When I push open the saloon doors of the Coco Shack, a barrage of smoke and sweat and pounding rock and roll hits me. It's like a set from Thelma and Louise, a throwback to the early 1980s. The guys are rough-looking, dressed in faded blue jeans and leathers and stained sleeveless vests, their tattooed arms slicked with sweat. I feel as if I've strayed into a bar deep in Texas; there's nothing Caribbean about it at all and it's certainly not a classy nightclub – it's a dive.

A few guys are gathered round a pool table.

Native white trash.

One of them turns, grins and wolf-whistles as I walk in. He shares a joke with his mate, then picks up his beer bottle and strolls over towards me. From the way he moves, I can tell he's had a few. He's unshaven – but there's nothing designer about his stubble – and lean, and riddled with tattoos.

My taxi's already driven away and it's too late to back out the door, so I'm just going to have to tough it out.

'Hello stranger,' he says. I nod and sidestep round him to the bar. He plants himself next to me, resting his elbows on the greasy counter.

'Get a tequila for the lady,' he hollers at the barmaid, 'and another one for me.' His eyes stray to my cleavage as he strikes up a conversation. 'You look like a tequila-drinking kinda girl.' His breath smells of black rum and stale cigarettes.

'I'm looking for my friend,' I say. 'He was here a few days ago.' I pull out my phone and flick to a photograph I took of Damien and Katie by the *Alice in Wonderland* sculpture in Central Park, the week before we came here on holiday. It's the only photo I have of Damien. He's carrying Katie on his shoulders but I don't want to advertise my connection with her disappearance so I've cropped her out of the top of the shot. All you can see is her bare legs hanging down on either side of his neck and her cute little feet, in the pink jelly sandals she was so excited about wearing to the beach the other day. Damien's holding onto one of her ankles.

The man peers down over the screen and belches loudly.

'Never seen him before,' he says. 'Who's the little dame hanging round his neck?'

'Low life,' snarls the barmaid. 'Give it here'. She speaks in a low Southern drawl, must be an ex-pat from Georgia or Louisiana.

I snatch back my mobile and pass it to her.

She grabs a pair of horn-rimmed specs and squints at the photo on the screen.

'Don't recognise the dude,' she says, 'but I could swear I've seen the woman before.'

I hadn't noticed but it's Christina. There, in the background. Her features are out of focus. I zoom in on her face.

'Yup, that's the one. Stuck-up cow with an English accent. She was here the other night. Didn't stay for long. Just drank a beer and asked if she could buy a bottle of vodka and a packet of Lucky Strike, then walked out.'

She hands the mobile back to me. In the photograph, Christina is standing about ten paces behind Damien and looking away from the camera laughing. I remember now, she was watching a red squirrel that had stolen a boy's cookie.

'This is about the little girl, isn't it?' she says. 'The little girl, Katie, who's been on the news. Poor kid. Is that witch her mother?'

'Text me if you have any information,' I say, and scribble my number down on a beermat.

I can't wait to tell Costa that Christina's been seen hanging out at the Coco Shack.

18

20 May 2003: Stratford-Upon-Avon

Here's another happy memory of the three of us. I'm sure you'll remember this only too clearly, my wedding day. Here we are in the churchyard of the delightful Saxon parish church in the village of Ledstone, near Stratford. Remember? We were blessed with beautiful spring sunshine that day.

James is looking so handsome in his tux, smiling that irresistible, puppy-dog smile of his, facing our family and friends as we prepare to drive away, one hand holding mine and the other reaching to open the door of the bright red E-type Jag we hired for our honeymoon on the French Riviera. And I must admit that I do look something of a stunner in that fitted, off-the-shoulder, ivory lace wedding dress. We spent hours in a little boutique in Mayfair trying on dresses before finally settling on that one. Do you remember? Call me vain, but I have to say, it sets off my neck and shoulders beautifully.

The cobbled path leading from the church is strewn with confetti – white, pink and red petals. A few have come to rest on my bare shoulders and in my twisted braids. In the foreground a flurry of red petals catches the light, frozen in mid-air as the shutter closed.

My left hand is stretched out towards you and there's a blur of swirling colour, spiralling in an arc between us – my bouquet. Your hands are raised high above your head, which is thrown back as you look up towards the whirling flowers. You're clutching the air and there's a hollow below your ribcage rippling the smooth grey silk of your bridesmaid dress. You could be laughing. But I don't recall. Your face is hidden in the shade of the dark red blooms.

Tell me, Lara, did you screw him in the Bluebell Woods that day?

Gabrielle was desperate to get into the Jag and drive away, to leave them all behind, and to be on her own at last with James. To an outsider, it would have looked a picture-perfect day in almost all respects. But she had reached saturation point after spending less than twenty-four hours in her childhood home. Lara, in particular, had done everything she could to irritate her and blacken the mood with her gloom and sullen silences on the one hand, and her flirtatious treachery with James on the other. She couldn't wait to see them all receding to nothing in the rear-view mirror of the Jag.

The arrangements had mostly gone smoothly, marred only by a last minute hitch with the flowers. The florist who lived in an isolated hamlet about ten miles away was supposed to deliver the wedding party bouquets and buttonholes to the family home at ten in the morning. She had phoned at half past nine to say that her car had broken down and she was stranded.

James, with his usual punctuality, was ready hours early. He was always one for grand gestures, and, in keeping with tradition, was supposed to be keeping out of sight of the bride-to-be. He offered to save the day by driving over to fetch the wedding flowers. As he had never been to the place before and wasn't sure how to find it, Lara (whose hair and make-up had been done already) jumped up smartly and offered to keep him company and help him to navigate the country lanes.

'Great idea,' he said. 'We haven't had much time for a catch up and that way you'll get a spin in the Jag. It's such a gorgeous day. We can put the top down.'

So instead of staying dutifully with Gabrielle while the hairdresser and the make-up artist fussed over the final touches, Lara slipped out of the house with James. Gabrielle was seething when her mother told her where she had gone.

'What does she think she's playing at? She's my chief bridesmaid, for God's sake, supposed to be helping me, calming my nerves and keeping *me* company on the morning of my wedding. That's her job as my chief bridesmaid, isn't it? Any opportunity she can get to try and get her claws back into him. On this of all days... I don't believe it. Disloyal bitch. I wish she'd never been born.'

And she was furious with James. 'Just like him too,' she said bitterly to her mother. 'He can't bear to be on his own for five minutes. Always wants to have his cake and eat it. Can't resist putting out the charm and getting his ego massaged by having a pretty woman sitting beside him in the car. She's his ex and it's our wedding day. Doesn't even cross his mind that it's completely fucking inappropriate!'

Her mother just hushed and tutted.

'Come on Gabrielle. She doesn't mean any harm. They used to be close but that was a long time ago. She's had plenty of boyfriends since they broke up. They're just friends and he's almost family now.'

You just haven't got a clue, thought Gabrielle.

Then Gabrielle turned away and sat down in front of her mother's walnut dressing table. She opened a small velvet box and took out a pair of jade earrings.

'Those are so pretty,' said her mother. 'The colour is perfect with your eyes.'

Her anger ebbed away.

'He bought them for me in Venice' she said. 'A few weeks after he proposed to me in New York, we went away to Venice for the weekend, to have a proper break, just the two of us, without her. He gave them to me when we were floating in a gondola under the Bridge of Sighs. Have to admit it was a bit clichéd, but very romantic, more romantic than his proposal actually. I virtually had to drag him into Tiffany's to buy the ring.'

Her eyes were a little dreamy as she gazed at herself in the mirror.

Lara was alarmed. James was driving badly, tearing round blind corners on the country lanes, with no thought for oncoming traffic or cyclists or horse riders who might be just round the next bend.

He turned towards her and smiled the smile that had captivated her from the first. 'I'm so glad we got away. I wanted some time with you alone. How's life in New York? How are you? I mean, how are you really? Are you OK?' He put his hand on her knee.

'For God's sake, keep your hands on the wheel,' said Lara, 'I'm fine. Just fine. It's a bit late to ask now, anyway, isn't it? I'm making a new life for myself, away from Gabrielle, away from you, escaping the toxic triangle once and for all. I had to get away, to be alone, to be myself, to live my own life, to find my own identity at last. Not always defined as someone's best friend, someone's other half.'

The lane dipped into a valley and then rose on the other side passing through a shady tunnel of trees. It brought back memories.

'*The Bluebell Woods,*' she said. 'I haven't been here for years. We used to steal food from the church kitchen, play truant from school and cycle over here for a picnic at this time of year. Look, they're carpeted with bluebells.' She sighed. 'That's what Gabrielle wanted anyway, isn't it, what you both wanted – to get me cropped right out of the picture. You made your choice.'

Without warning, James swung the Jag off the country lane, up a farm track that led under the trees, cut the engine and got out of the car.

'Come with me. I've got something for you.' He opened the passenger door and pulled her by the hand.

They walked into the woods a little way, trampling the bluebells underfoot. James took something out of the pocket of his wedding suit then tossed it down over the wild flowers.

'Here, this is perfect. Use my jacket.'

She lay back on his jacket looking up at the criss-cross of branches and bright green leaves of early summer patterning the blue sky.

He held out a small velvet box.

'Don't tell me you're going to propose?' she said ironically.

'Don't mock me, Lara. I want to give you something. I believe it's traditional for the groom to buy presents for the bridesmaids but I don't want to give you some stupid trinket or box of chocolates chosen by the bride. Take it, please.'

She leant up on her elbows and opened the box.

'They're beautiful,' she said, touching the jade stones of the earrings, 'my favourite colour.'

'I chose them especially for you in Venice. I found them in a jewellery shop just behind the Piazza San Marco. I thought they'd be perfect for you. But don't show Gabrielle. You know how jealous she can be.'

He picked a fistful of bluebell stems and tucked them into her cleavage then kissed her playfully on the lips. For a moment she resisted, then she let herself fall back onto the carpet of wild flowers. 'I'm sorry. I'm so sorry the way things turned out,' said James.

They lay on their backs, his head pillowed on Lara's stomach, looking up at the sky through the green mosaic of leaves.

'You didn't give me a chance to try to make things right between us,' said Lara.

'I still can't forgive you for getting rid of my baby,' said James. 'Even after all these years, it hurts. How could you do it, without even telling me?' He turned his face into her soft, flat belly. 'I know I was a player back then. And you and I were so young and foolish. But you girls played me too, you know. I was your plaything, caught in the tug of war.' He rolled away from her and looked up at the sky. 'I was infatuated and obsessed with you both, tormented by your dual beauty. But it was only you I was in love with. I had made my choice. I was ready to give up everything for you. I was ready to be a father and your husband. But you were so determined to have an abortion and conceal it from me.'

'Is that what she told you?' Lara sat up rigid. 'She was the one who swore me to secrecy. And what she told you is a lie. She's twisted it all. I wanted to keep the baby. She forced me to have the abortion. And then after it was done, I wanted to tell you the truth. And she stopped me. It was all part of her evil plan to get her claws into you.'

She closed her eyes and lay back.

'Scheming bitch.'

★

'Where the hell have you been?' Gabrielle screamed as Lara burst into the bedroom. 'And what the hell happened to your hairdo? We've got to leave for the church in twenty minutes.'

'We took a wrong turn. Got lost in the lanes.'

Gabrielle took in Lara's glowing, dishevelled appearance, the windswept hair and smudged lipstick, the renewed spark in her eyes, and she knew.

'I hate you,' she said. 'I hate you. I wish you were dead, and I hate James. Where is he?'

'He dropped me at the house and he's gone straight to the church with the buttonholes for the men. Your bouquet is downstairs with the garlands for the bridesmaids. I've put them in vases of water to stay fresh. We didn't forget anything. It's all sorted. You can relax.'

Gabrielle watched her chief bridesmaid pull her cotton dress down over her shoulders and hips, and let it drop to the floor.

'I'll be ready in five minutes,' said Lara, as she slipped off her bra and tossed it on to the bed. 'I just need to rearrange my hair.'

Gabrielle bent down to pick up a wilted bluebell stem that had fallen at Lara's feet.

'I knew you would betray me, but did it have to be today?' she said, crushing it in her hands. 'I wish you were dead.'

Lara took the grey silk bridesmaid dress off its hanger, stepped into it and turned her back to Gabrielle.

'Could you zip me up please? Then I'm ready to go.'

At last they went out the front door into the rose garden of the vicarage, where the photographer was waiting.

'Where's my bouquet?' said Gabrielle crossly. 'You're hopeless!'

Lara ran back to collect the flowers from the hallway. As Lara handed over the bouquet, Gabrielle looked up at her perfect, inscrutable profile and felt sick.

They crossed the lawn to where the photographer stood adjusting his lens.

'Nice earrings, by the way,' said Lara quietly, as together, they turned to compose identical smiles for the camera. 'Did you get them in Venice, by any chance?'

Gabrielle closed her eyes and flung the flowers as hard as she could towards the smiling huddle of family and friends gathered along the path and the lawns leading from the church. When she opened them, she was looking straight at Lara, of course, and the flowers were winging their way towards her.

She's always there. Why does she always have to be there, like a shadow, right on my heels, always there to fight over the spoils?

Her smile froze as she watched Lara scrabble for the catch and fumble it. In an instant, James had let go of her hand and he raced over to where the scarlet bouquet had fallen on the path at Lara's feet.

Gabrielle watched him playing to the crowd. With a flourish of dramatic chivalry, he dropped to his knees, scooped up the flowers and handed them to Lara, who seemed almost to swoon with delight. All went quiet for just one beat. Gabrielle's nails cut in to her palms as her fists tightened. Then someone clapped, and everyone exhaled and joined in the clapping and cheering, all except for Gabrielle, as James strolled back to her side.

19

I'm drying my hair when the barmaid from the Coco Shack calls me on my mobile. I wasn't expecting to hear from her so soon. It's not even 7 a.m. I recognise her Deep South accent immediately but she's so agitated she can barely get the words out.

'I was taking the garbage out first thing this morning and I found her shoes – those little pink sandals, all covered in mud, stuffed in our trash cans. Same ones she was wearing in your photograph.'

The hairdryer drops to the floor.

'Don't touch them,' I say. 'You'd better call the police right now. Ask to speak to Costa, Detective Sergeant Costa, he's in charge of the investigation.'

'The police were down here last night,' she says. 'They must know something.' Her voice is breathy and raw. 'I saw a police officer talking to the girl's mother in the parking lot – they were standing by the bin store when I went out to get more beers, just after you left. You only missed her by about five minutes.'

Damn! I was right – Christina's up to her neck in this.

'I'm shit-scared,' she whimpers. 'The police must think something happened here. That lowlife who was talking to you at the bar last night and his gang of scum-fucks – any one of them could have done it.'

I'm scared too.

'Did you get the tip-off about the shoes?' I say, the instant I walk into Costa's office. He's told me not to interfere in the investigation without his permission – he wants to keep me under his control. But that's tough. 'Are your people searching the premises?'

'I've sent a car down,' says Costa. 'It's probably a red herring. My guess is it's another plant to keep us away from the girl's real hiding place. We know it's a diversionary tactic but we have to get forensics to investigate the site anyway. It's a waste of valuable time and resources. Slows things down.'

'Christina's been seen hanging out at the Coco Shack,' I say pointedly. 'The barmaid recognised a photo of her on my phone.'

'Ah! Were you down at the Coco Shack yourself last night?'

Oh God, so now he thinks I planted the sandals!

'I was going to ask you the same question,' I say. 'The barmaid told me the police went down there last night too. At first, she thought it was another police raid but they didn't arrest anyone. And then she saw an officer talking to Christina in the parking lot.'

He looks uncomfortable.

'Was it you… or Kramer?'

He shuts the door and pulls out a chair for me at his desk.

I stay standing. 'The barmaid saw a police officer handing over a package to Christina,' I say. 'My guess is one of your men is using his uniform as a cover for dealing drugs and has been supplying them to Christina – either for Damien's personal use or for resale to raise money to clear his debts. Could this somehow be linked to Katie's disappearance?'

'Best you don't go snooping around at the Shack,' says Costa, closing me down. 'It's got a bad reputation, drinking den of the local dealers. It's not safe for a young woman like you.'

Well, that's a bit rich after the way he harassed me yesterday!

'Well, you should get down there,' I say. 'Surely it's a crime scene now.'

'Just keep out of it.' His voice is hard. 'You seem to forget that I'm the one in charge round here.' He orders me to sit. Then he opens the blind on the panel screening his office from the control room. 'OK, let's get down to business. If you really want to help, I've got a job for you.' He opens a thick file crammed full of papers that's lying on the desk. 'Go through this lot and highlight anything you think deserves a second look.'

He leans over my shoulder, uncomfortably close. The smell of his musky aftershave is all too familiar.

'You're probably in a better position to spot a likeness than any of my officers in there.' Through the glass, I see his team lazily setting up for the day with cups of coffee and muffins. 'If you can't stop meddling at least you can do something useful.' He sweeps the clutter to one side. 'You can work here. I'll be out all morning. Then you can debrief me over lunch.'

He flips through the file like a deck of cards. 'There was a time not so long ago, when we were limited to door-to-door enquiries and face-to-face interviews.' He's sounding almost paternal now. 'But in this new age of the Internet and social media, the whole world wants to help. It doesn't make the job any easier.'

He touches my shoulder and I stiffen.

'I blame you for this,' he says sternly. 'You provoked this deluge with that damned Instagram campaign! Now you can deal with it. We've got 518 reported witness sightings... Five hundred and eighteen people who claim to have seen Katie or her abductor. That's just what came in 'til midnight yesterday. Email messages, tweets, photographs...'

He nods towards the control room.

'Your appeal has gone viral. It just keeps on coming. We've never seen anything like it. They're putting more files together in there now.'

He straps his pistol into the holster on his hip and swaggers to the door. I stifle a giggle. I can't take him seriously after our close encounters on the boat – a would-be big shot and bully who thrives on having his ego massaged. But I need to keep in with him if I want to stay on the inside of the investigation, so I smile sweetly.

'Sure, I'm happy to help.'

'I'm off to the Shack to check up on the forensics team and make some enquiries. For a start, I want to interview that barmaid.' He slams the door, then five seconds later he sticks his head round it again. 'By the way, you were right about the lilos. They weren't bought on the island. We checked the brand – manufactured and sold in the UK.'

I can't help feeling proud of myself as I skim through the file, scanning scores of photographs and messages sent in to the police in response to the police appeals and my own social media campaign. For the most part the images are of blonde-haired girls, about the same age as Katie – on the beach, in the queue at the airport, lined up to board a ferry, walking in the street, playing with other children, paddling in a pool – sent in by well-meaning members of the public.

The images vary in quality. Some are high definition close-ups, others grainy images taken at long range, some blurred, some cropped, some showing facial features, others shot in profile, some taken from an angle or from the rear.

Many of the images bear a passing resemblance to Katie, a collection of pale-skinned little girls, light hair, blue eyes, pretty smiles. One or two show a striking resemblance – I have to stare at these long and hard to be certain it's not her. Others are so way off the mark that I wonder if they've been sent in as a prank – pictures of dark-haired and dark-skinned little Caribbean girls, pictures of swarthy teenagers, pictures of boys. One joker has even sent in a picture of a dog.

They've all been carefully documented, indexed and filed by one of the officers on the team. But no attempt has been made to log the evidential importance of each item. It's all just been filed in order of receipt. Now I understand why the police operation lacks direction and focus. They're not short of leads, but the problem is they're swamped – literally hundreds of possible sightings and potentially interesting lines of enquiry have landed up on Costa's desk. The challenge now is to evaluate the credibility of each fragment of evidence, eliminating unnecessary diversions and pursuing those leads that warrant further investigation. That's where I come in!

The positive is that the thickness of the file proves that the locals and tourists are really getting behind the campaign to find Katie. There are scores of witness statements given by islanders and tourists setting out detailed accounts of suspected sightings or encounters with Katie and her abductor. Being something of a cynic, I can't help thinking that the huge response may have something to do with the fifty-thousand-dollar reward up for grabs for any information leading to her discovery. Costa cautioned against it warning that such a substantial amount would be too tempting and could result in false information being sent in. However, Christina put her foot down and insisted on advertising the reward. The money has been pledged by an anonymous donor from the BLI billionaire banking community who approached the police when my social media campaign was launched.

And, yes, I'm proud of that! God knows, if there's a chance the reward might 'soften someone's heart' then why not? What harm can it do?

I'm on my third espresso and three quarters of the way through the file by the time Costa blusters in carrying two iced beers and a takeaway pizza.

'Thought you might be getting hungry. We can share.'

He rips off a slice and hands it to me. Not exactly what I had in mind when he spoke of lunch!

'I don't drink beer,' I say.

He shrugs. 'Too bad. How are you getting on?'

I show him a few grainy shots of girls about the same height and colouring as Katie taken at various locations around the island.

'I can't give you a positive ID but these are the ones I can't rule out 100 per cent.'

He takes them through to the control room.

'I'll get Brenda to follow up. She can make enlargements and send someone out to interview witnesses.' She's the one with the immaculate purple nails.

'Oh, and there's something else I've got to show you,' I say, as he sits down beside me. 'I've saved the best 'til last.' I flip to where I've propped the file open with my sunglasses. It's the mugshot of the dog.

He can't resist a wisecrack.

'Have you gone barking mad?' He squeezes my knee.

'Not the dog, you idiot!' I say, swinging my leg away. The shaggy, brown mutt featured in the foreground is standing guard with its hackles raised, gaping wild-eyed, open-mouthed at the camera. 'In the background, down here right in the corner.' I point. 'Look. What can you see?' A little out of focus, the background consists of a line of over-sized, floating gin-palaces, moored along the quayside. It looks like an exclusive port or marina. 'There, in the right-hand corner of the photograph. Can you make out the name?'

Costa snaps it with his phone. The name of the boat is painted in black italic letters on the side of the keel. The letters are fuzzy and indistinct but as he enlarges the image on his screen they become legible.

'P – H – A – N – T – A,' he spells out. 'The rest of the name is cut off.'

'That's what I thought,' I say. 'Just wanted to be sure.'

'What are you driving at?' says Costa.

'The name of the yacht…'

'Phantom… Phantastic… Phantasm…' Costa throws out a few possible endings. 'Phantasy…'

'That's it…' I shout. 'But with a pun on the word 'sea' at the end.' I thump the palm of his hand in a triumphant high five. *The Phantasea*. Yep – that's the name on the rental mooring agreement.'

I don't know what you're talking about,' says Costa.

'I thought Christina showed it to you the other day,' I say. 'An agreement for the rental of a mooring space for a yacht in a marina. She came back for some documents while I was in her bathroom. She said she was taking them in to the police station to show you.'

'The Phantasea,' he says softly. 'No, I've never seen the name before. I would have remembered. Christina never showed me those documents.'

If he's telling the truth then Christina is behaving very suspiciously. It looks as if she's got something to hide. If she was innocent then surely she would have disclosed the documents. They could be important to the investigation.

He's beginning to take me seriously now.

'So you think this photograph could be a tip off?' he says, nudging the photo with his pen. 'You think Katie may be on the yacht?'

'It's worth checking out at least,' I say. It's certainly consistent with my theory. The Black Jack betting record shows that Damien would have had sufficient time to pick up Katie from Crooks' Bay and ferry her in the motorboat to a yacht waiting out at sea. His movements would have passed unnoticed in these island waters where the leisure yachts of the mega rich are everywhere.

'It would explain why the trail goes cold at Crooks' Bay,' I say. 'The tracker dogs have nothing further to follow. Once Katie was on the yacht she could have been taken anywhere or she could still be hidden onboard.'

Though he doesn't admit it, I can tell from the look on Costa's face that he thinks we might be on to something. He enters the control room and goes over to Brenda. Through the glass I see her pull a face as he puts the photograph on her desk and his arm round her shoulder. But a few minutes later, she comes in looking pleased with herself in a nonchalant kind of way.

'I checked with the Marine Registry. There is a yacht called The Phantasea on the register. The boat is privately-owned. Registered owner is recorded as J. Hamilton.

That's all they have on the register.' I watch as she taps her long nails restlessly on the desk.

So now we know the boat exists, we need to find out where it was moored. Costa turns to me.

'Did you notice the name of the marina on that moorings rental document?' he says. 'If not, we should be able to identify the marina from the photograph.'

I close my eyes and try to visualise the sheet of paper which I had found in the stack of papers piled next to Damien's bed. As I concentrate, an image of Playboy magazine, now stuffed in my bag, comes into my head. 'That reminds me, I found this under Damien's bed,' I say. I've been putting off handing it over to Costa because I didn't want him to see the compromising photo-sequence of me at the back of the magazine. His eyes light up. I drop it on the table face down. By chance my eyes fall on the postage label printed on the back. The magazine is addressed to P. D. Varcoe at an address in Notting Hill.

Suddenly, I get a lightbulb moment. 'Hand me a pencil,' I say. 'Covera – don't you get it?' It's almost too easy – like one of those intelligence tests I used to do in school. I scribble out the letters in a circle on the page, then draw lines between them, to rearrange the order, and cross them out one-by-one as I spell the name,

Varcoe.

'Got it! Q.E.D. It's Damien. I'll bet you a hundred dollars our friend Damien Covera is operating under a false name. His real name is 'Varcoe'.'

Costa swings into action. He radios the police coastal patrol and orders the launch of patrol boats to search for the vessel. He calls in an assistant to bag up the copy of *Playboy* for fingerprinting and DNA analysis. Then he orders his team to contact their counterparts in London to do further identity and security checks this time in the name of P. D. Varcoe. 'The slippery bastard must be using a false ID.' He straps his pistol onto his hip. 'Given the time difference, we won't get the results back from London for at least twenty-four hours,' says Costa. 'But in the meantime we can search for the vessel.'

He flashes me a smile. 'Hey, Scarlett, at last we're getting somewhere. You did good! Now let's have another look at that mutt.'

He examines the photograph more closely.

'Where was it taken? You must recognise the marina,' I say.

'That damn dog's butt is right in the way,' says Costa 'Could be one of the ports in the US Leeward Isles.' He presses the button on his pager. 'I'll call in Jack, he deals with the smugglers, knows all the ports this side of the Caribbean. He'll know.'

About half an hour later a burly man in torn denims and a dirty grey T-shirt bursts through the door. 'Hey man! Thanks for coming over,' says Costa. 'Meet the Jackal, meanest drugs buster in town' he says to me, clapping the man on the shoulder.

As I look him over uncertainly, he says.

'I try to blend in with the scum.'

'Talking of scum,' says Costa, 'Were you down at the Shack last night?'

The Jackal picks up the photo in his oil-stained hand. 'Nope, any reason?'

Costa goes over to the coffee machine. 'Strong, black, two sugars?'

He nods in my direction. 'Barmaid told my witness she saw a police officer talking to the kid's mother at the Shack last night – handed over a package.' I glow inwardly at my promotion from 'suspect' to 'witness'.

The Jackal raises his eyebrows and mouths the word 'Kramer.' They exchange a knowing look.

Jack slurps his coffee as he peers at the photo. 'Yup. I got it,' he says. 'Clearwater Marina, up in the north of the island.' So it is one of the ports on Grand Carmola. 'Look, there's the harbour wall.' The Jackal thrusts the photocopy towards Costa. 'And the orange buoy over there—' he points an oily index finger '—that's the warning marker for submerged rocks – site of the 1895 Smugglers' Shipwreck. It's an unusual angle. The shot was taken from the west quay, by the dive school, looking out to sea.'

Clearwater Marina – that figures. 'Can I see it again,' I say, holding out my hand. In the top corner of the picture is a dark-green awning above a restaurant and I can just read the name of the establishment which must be emblazoned in large white lettering across the fabric.

'Clamities,' I say. 'That's where Damien and Christina went for dinner last night.'

At that moment, Brenda bursts in with a message.

'I got through to the harbour master at Clearwater Marina. The Phantasea left her moorings yesterday with clearance for US waters in the St Croix cruising area.'

'How quickly can you scramble your crew?' asks Costa.

'We'll be on the water within the hour.' The Jackal makes to leave.

I leap up. 'I'm coming,' I say. 'Take me to St Croix. If there's any chance that Katie's onboard, I've got to be there.'

'Covert operations, no place for a lady,' says the Jackal. He slams the door as he strides out.

20

Scarlett

Costa turns to me. 'Jack's the best man to track The Phantasea. He commands all our covert operations. The US cops know him. We do some joint operations with US sea patrols busting the cartels so they won't ask any questions. They don't need to know the true nature of this operation. Not yet. I don't want them butting in. There's more chance of getting Katie back unharmed if we get our men on board first. Our US buddies can be trigger happy.'

He walks over to the window. It's a beautiful, still afternoon.

He turns to face me. 'You're having dinner with me tonight at Clamities'.

'Isn't your wife expecting you home?' I ask.

'Movie night with her girlfriends.' As I start to protest, he picks up his keys. 'Strictly business,' he says. 'We might pick up some useful intelligence from the harbour master and the restaurant staff.'

While the prospect of another boat trip with Costa makes me anxious, it seems that I've been promoted in his estimation from a suspect who must be broken to a trusted confidante. Though this intimate camaraderie is equally unprofessional and inappropriate in the circumstances, I'm happy to go along with it if it means I can be at the heart of the search for Katie. Also, I have to admit to a certain curiosity about seeing where Damien took Christina for dinner last night.

This time, Costa drives me in his official car, blue lights flashing, showing off his driving skills, dodging through the heavy afternoon traffic at speed.

At the harbour we transfer to an unmarked police boat, a sleek, navy blue motor launch, manned by a couple of cheerful young officers from the BLI marine patrol unit dressed in civvies. Looks like they're giving us a ride round the headland to Clamities.

As we approach Clearwater Marina, Costa gets on the radio to log our arrival with police headquarters. He announces the official version of our mission (enquiries at the marina's administrative office and at Clamities restaurant), and I hear Brenda's rich laughter coming over the radio waves.

'Sure boss, enjoy your dinner.' The radio crackles in the brisk sea breeze and cuts out. A few minutes later Costa's radio bleeps once more. Above the hiss, I hear Brenda's voice again. 'The Jackal just checked in,' she says. 'He's been granted permission to enter US waters off St Croix for an offshore drugs patrol.' Costa hands me a bottle of iced beer.

'I told you, I don't drink beer,' I say.

'This isn't that warm, dreary swill you drink back home. It's liquid sunshine,' says Costa. 'Try it: *Island Hoppin' IPA*, local brewery – you'll love it.'

He opens one for himself and sits down beside me.

'Aren't you supposed to be on duty?' I say.

Costa leans back to let the sun fall on his face. 'Jack's got everything under control.' he says. 'If he finds The Phantasea he can do the board and search. I've been doing eighteen-hour days. Reckon I'm owed an evening off.'

The view from the deck is achingly beautiful with the flaming crescent of sea backed by rippling sandstone cliffs and the sun dipping behind purple hills. Three beers later, I'm filled with a warm glow – a renewed surge of optimism convinces me Katie will be found on board The Phantasea, safe and well. Having eaten only a few mouthfuls of pizza all day, the beer has gone straight to my head. I stand at the rail, light headed and ready to forgive all wrongs.

'There's something I've been wanting to ask you.' I look into Costa's eyes. 'Your eyes, they're so blue. It's unusual for round here.'

'Well, my mother was from Tennessee and my father from Puerto Rico. Going back further, one of my great-grandfathers was Scottish. Don't laugh at me, it's true, he was a fisherman and a redhead like you, emigrated here from Skye. That explains the blue eyes. So, on the forms, I tick the box Mixed-Heritage Hispanic – covers a multitude of sins.'

'That's weird. My great-grandmother came from the west coast of Scotland,' I say.

Six degrees of separation and all that.

'So you see, we've got something in common,' he says.

My thoughts turn to Christina. I haven't heard from her all day. I was so preoccupied going through the files that I didn't have the headspace to concern myself with her unusual radio silence. She's usually bugging me every five minutes with texts. But she hasn't responded to mine all day and all my calls have gone to voicemail. The last time I spoke to her was last night just before she went off to Clamities with Damien. She was so determined to drive over to Clearwater Marina despite my warnings. Which makes me think she knows that Katie is hidden on board The Phantasea. But her silence makes me fear for her safety too. The package handed over by a police officer to Christina at the Coco Shack may contain a little stash of candy dust that could be all that Damien needs to pay off his gambling debts. But at what cost? Who or what did she sacrifice in return? I've been tipped into this crazy universe where everything is so confusing and uncertain that I can't make up my mind who's the predator and who's the prey.

I'm sure of one thing. She's playing with fire.

The dining room's deserted by the time Costa drops me back at the hotel. I have to admit I enjoyed the dinner at Clamities, and all the more so because Costa stretched the meaning of 'strictly business' and treated me to a slap-up meal. We did get some useful information from our wine waiter who recalled that Damien and Christina had dinner there last night and left the restaurant at about ten-thirty in the evening. Before dinner Costa interviewed the harbour master who confirmed that The Phantasea had been docked in the harbour intermittently throughout June and left its moorings just before midnight last night. It was agreed that Costa would send one of his officers down tomorrow to view CCTV footage from three security cameras located along the quayside. No one we spoke to at Clearwater reported any sightings of Katie but if she had been taken onboard the yacht by Damien or Christina there was a chance that something would have been picked up on one of the cameras. The harbour master also promised to go back through the records of shipping movements logged by the marina since the beginning of June.

Now Costa's gone home to his wife and kids and I'm facing another miserable night alone in my hotel room. Despite my suspicions about Christina's role in all of this, I'm increasingly concerned for her welfare as I haven't had any contact from her for over twenty-four hours so I walk straight up to the front desk to ask whether there are any messages for me, and whether Miss Kenedey dined at the hotel this evening.

The receptionist looks at me in surprise.

'Mr and Mrs Kenedey checked out this morning,' she says. 'Mr Kenedey came to settle their bill first thing.'

So they can't have been onboard The Phantasea when it set sail just after midnight last night.

I don't even bother to correct her with the names.

'He said that Mrs Kenedey was finding it difficult to cope with the constant media attention and so they were going to transfer to a villa in the north of the island,' she continues.

Alarm bells start ringing in my head. Now that I've stopped fantasising about her being a predatory, drug-dealing, psycho-killer, I'm sure Christina would have told me if they were planning to leave.

'Did Miss Kenedey come down to say goodbye?' I say casually.

The receptionist tells me she only saw 'Mr Kenedey.'

'He ordered room service before their departure as the breakfast room was still closed. He said they wanted to leave early, before the press pack arrived.' She looks a little flustered. 'I respect her privacy. She must be very tired. She stayed up in her room. It was her husband who came down to make all the arrangements.'

'How about the porters?' I say. 'Didn't they go up to the room to bring down the luggage?' The receptionist goes into the office to ask.

'No, madam,' she says. 'The gentleman carried the cases himself. He said he didn't need any assistance.'

'How about last night? Did you speak to or see Christina late last night?'

She tells me she wasn't on late duty last night and goes back into the office to check with the other reception staff.

It seems that no-one has seen Christina since Damien took her out for dinner yesterday evening, *to Clamities, a secluded seafood restaurant, in a remote location, on the other side of the island…*

'Did they leave a forwarding address?'

Before she answers, I know what she's going to tell me. They left no forwarding address. 'They asked us to respect their privacy.' Her tone is frosty.

Well, that's great. Christina could at least have sent me a message to let me know. And who will be paying *my* bill?

'Mr Kenedey said you were going to stay on here at the hotel to act as a contact point for investigators and the media,' says the receptionist. Her patience is fraying as a queue of new arrivals forms at the desk. 'Miss Reyes. You have her phone number. I suggest you call her.'

I'm probably just being paranoid so I give up and go over to the bar to order a drink. But it's not like Christina to go off without telling me. She's so dependent – always has something or other she wants me to do for her. She's been unusually quiet.

Has Damien abducted her too?

I gulp down my diet Coke, shivering as the ice hits the back of my throat.

She could be in danger. He could have killed her already, dumped her body at sea. First Katie, then Christina.

I make my way slowly to my room, glancing over my shoulder as I walk down the corridor with that uncomfortable sensation of being watched. I feel so sad going back to an empty room alone. Katie should be tugging me by the hand, running in ahead of me to jump on the bed. It's so very quiet up here. All the guests are down below eating and drinking and taking part in the good-natured but naff entertainment laid on by the hotel.

I put on all the lights before stepping through the door.

Then I pull out my phone and text Costa.

Have you heard from Christina? She's gone.

21

Photograph Seven

21 September 2007: Rose Hill Private Hospital, Chelsea

You're the only person I've shown this photograph to, other than James, all those years ago. I printed this copy especially for your album. I want you to feel my pain. The original is in a mother-of-pearl frame, wrapped in dark blue velvet, locked in the drawer of my desk. The baby cradled in the image is so peaceful and content. Her eyes closed, lids fringed with downy lashes, rosebud lips almost smiling, and her miniature fingers resting softly on the cashmere shawl. It was taken in the delivery suite. In the background, you can see tubes and medical instruments and dials – the paraphernalia of birth and pain and death. She's perfect. We counted her fingers and her toes. She's mine. She belongs to me and James – our flesh and blood. If I hold my breath and sit absolutely still, I can feel her in my arms. Astonishingly pink, warm, fresh from my womb. My beautiful daughter. Juliet Rosalind. Born at sunrise on Friday 21 September 2007. Stillborn.

★

Gabrielle travelled to the hospital quite serenely in a black cab that morning. She'd even had time to put on her jewellery and a little light make-up to boost her confidence. Her consultant had told her to come in to the delivery suite as soon as she felt the first signs of labour. She had been monitored closely throughout the pregnancy and could not fault her care.

She called James from the taxi en route to the hospital and asked him to join her there. He came out of a meeting to take the call. He had recently been promoted to global research and product development director of the leading European international pharmaceutical company where he had worked for the last two years. It was flattering that the CEO, O'Sullivan, had entrusted him to clinch the deal, James told her. He would get away and join her at the first opportunity – he'd be at the hospital by lunchtime at the latest, he said.

Gabrielle's attempts to become a mother had been plagued with misfortune. They'd been trying for a baby for over four years and she had suffered from a series of miscarriages: early miscarriages, late miscarriages and mid-term miscarriages – she'd been through them all. In the face of these personal tragedies, it was a testament to her talent, energy and drive that she had achieved such renown and financial success in her career. She owned classy photography and film studios in London and New York that were fashionable with top models and the designer set (as well as providing her with a lucrative income from bondage and boudoir videos which she produced quietly on the side). She was also highly respected for the quality of her own distinctive black-and-white prints that she exhibited and sold on both sides of the Atlantic. She was successful in every aspect of her professional life. It was only in her attempt to become a mother that she had failed. But she'd been so strong and so brave! Everyone praised her for her resilience – everyone except for Lara.

Lara was brutal. She had told Gabrielle quite plainly that her difficulties were divine retribution: punishment for having forced and emotionally blackmailed Lara into having an abortion and lying about it to James all those years ago.

But this time finally things were going well. She had got past the critical dates and had felt as fit and energetic as could be expected throughout the pregnancy. For the last six weeks she had even begun to enjoy herself, redecorating the spare room and ordering baby clothes online. Though James preferred to wait, Gabrielle had insisted they should be told the sex of the baby, and they had chosen a name (or rather she had): Juliet Rosalind – named after Gabrielle's favourite Shakespearean heroines, the defiant, romantic and seductive young beauty in *Romeo and Juliet* and the feisty and enchanting mistress of disguise, Rosalind, in *As You Like It*.

She settled in to the private delivery suite on arrival and surrendered to the usual early labour hospital routines, the form-filling, the blood pressure checks, the pokings and the proddings. All seemed to be going to plan and she was coping well with the intermittent labour pains until the nurse asked her to lie down so she could listen to the baby's heartbeat.

Gabrielle lay back and looked up at the ceiling. It was white, clinical; a small black spider was crawling towards the light fitting. The cleaners must have missed its web. She closed her eyes trying to practise some of the mindfulness techniques she had been working on during her pregnancy.

The nurse smoothed cold gel over Gabrielle's swollen belly and began to roll the monitor over the taut skin. As Gabrielle tried to relax, she became aware that the woman (whose student ranking she had noticed on her badge with irritation earlier) seemed nervous, restless and fidgety. Her skirt rustled. She turned the monitor on and off, fiddled with the bank of switches, tutted to herself, and asked Gabrielle to shift her position on the bed.

Gabrielle's meditations were interrupted and she began to get impatient.

'Look, you're starting to get on my nerves,' she said. 'If you don't know how to work the equipment, you'd better go and get a qualified midwife to come and take over.'

Gabrielle glanced down from the ceiling to look at the nurse. There was an expression of barely contained panic on the woman's face.

'I'm just having a little trouble locating the heartbeat,' she said. 'I'm sure there's nothing wrong. I'm just going to call for Sister.' She half ran out of the room to the nurses' station while Gabrielle sat bolt upright, more angry than alarmed. The sister swept into the room within seconds and without so much as a word to Gabrielle, pushed her down onto the pillows, pulled up her gown and grabbed the monitoring equipment.

It would be nice to be treated like a human being once in a while, thought Gabrielle, as she lay there, feeling disembodied, listening to the nurses muttering to each other further down the bed.

'What's going on?' she shouted.

'We're trying to get a heartbeat,' said the sister. 'I'm going to call for help.'

She leaned across Gabrielle's face to press the red emergency button on the wall.

It was not until three in the afternoon that Gabrielle heard James' heavy footsteps in the corridor. A voice she didn't recognise was speaking as the door opened. The medical team must have changed shifts. 'She's resting,' said the nurse. 'We've given her strong sedatives to calm her down. They should also help to numb the pain.' The nurse stayed in the doorway. 'I'll give you some time,' she said, closing the door behind James.

Gabrielle was lying on the bed in the darkened room, facing away from the door curled up in the foetal position. She opened her eyes as he came into view carrying his briefcase in one hand and swinging a brand-new infant car seat in the other.

'Where the hell have you been?' said Gabrielle. She balled up the sheet in her fists as he burbled his excuses.

'I'm so sorry,' said James. 'O'Sullivan dropped me in it, pulled out of the lunch at the last minute and left me to entertain the clients. It's such an important pitch for us, the contract's worth millions. Our first breakthrough into the US market. I couldn't let him down.' He was slurring his words. He had left the table to call her, he said, but he couldn't find his phone. The damn thing must have dropped out in the taxi. He would have left immediately had he known the labour was really under way. 'I'm such a bloody idiot,' he concluded. 'Of all the days to lose my damn phone... must be the nerves!'

Gabrielle looked at him with contempt. Nobody had told him. The nurse coming on duty for the afternoon shift must have assumed he'd already heard the dreadful news from another member of staff. 'So why are you drunk?' she murmured. His words washed over her as he carried on digging himself a hole: the US clients had insisted on toasting the father-to-be with champagne over the starters, he said, but he could have done without the red wine (five bottles shared between six) and the two whiskies after the meal. Still, it was his last few hours of freedom before taking on his new responsibilities as a father. He should make the most of it, so the clients had said, as they kept refilling his glass. 'Anyway, I'm here now,' he assured her. 'I won't leave your side.'

'You're not going to be a father,' said Gabrielle. 'The baby's dead.' She watched his face break-up as her words hit like hammer blows. 'There was nothing they could do. Could have been dead more than twenty-four hours.'

James dropped the car seat on the floor and she watched him swaying over her bed as the colour drained from his face. When he bent down to place his fingers over her bulging stomach, she thrust his hand away, groaned and curled her knees up into a tighter ball. Her features were contorted.

'I've got to give birth to the baby. Go through with the labour. That's what they're telling me.' She spoke through gritted teeth. 'It's the safest way.'

She gasped, rigid again, as another contraction pulsed concentric waves of excruciating pain through her body. James fell back into the chair. He sat hunched over, his head in his hands. From the sedated depths of her own misery, she observed his distress as he grasped the full horror of the situation. His back shuddered. She knew he was desperate to comfort her but there was nothing he could say. He had dealt with many tragic cases when undergoing his medical training as a hospital intern but nothing could have prepared him for this soul destroying news.

'Pull yourself together, man,' she heard him mutter. 'Be strong for Gabrielle.' His mouth twisted and he knelt by Gabrielle's bed gripping on to her hand, struggling to compose himself as he groaned and sobbed into the sheets.

Neither spoke for several minutes until eventually he said,

'I'm sorry. I'm so sorry. That's all the words I have.' He stood up and walked over to the window and banged his forehead against the glass.

'I don't know what to do. I'm broken and I know my pain is nothing compared to yours...' He tailed off. She could imagine the words he left unsaid that were going through his doctor's brain. *My pain is nothing compared to the physical pain she's going to have to endure in the next few hours giving birth to our lifeless baby, and the emotional pain she's going to suffer for the rest of her life.*

He turned round. 'Shall I call your parents?' he said. 'I know you haven't spoken for a while but it may help to talk to your father. He of all people may be able to give you some comfort.'

She gave a rasping laugh. He should have known that this was a ridiculous suggestion. Gabrielle kept her parents out of their lives. This time she hadn't even told them she was pregnant.

'What about Lara? Should I call her? Do you want to speak to her?'

Gabrielle jerked her head. His words cut through the smog of her suffering. She couldn't believe what she was hearing.

'I didn't know you had her number,' she said.

Lara had changed all her contact details and cut off all communication with Gabrielle when she moved to her new place in New York.

'So, you've stayed in touch,' said Gabrielle with bitterness. 'Why does that not surprise me?' Gabrielle braced and screwed up her face as another contraction took hold. 'As you should know, Lara's the last person I want to speak to. I don't want to give her the satisfaction.'

As soon as the pain of the contraction began to ebb away, she ripped out the drips attached to her wrist, tore off her jade earrings, staggered to her feet and kicked away the car seat.

'Why the fuck did you have to bring that in?'

She picked it up and flung it as hard as she could at the window.

The safety glass shattered but did not fall, and the car seat bounced back onto the floor, where they watched it rocking until all was still.

22

Scarlett

I've had another fitful night. I couldn't get hold of Costa. His wife has probably got him under house arrest. And I couldn't get the idea out of my head that Damien might have driven Christina off to some remote location on the other side of the island and murdered her. I know it sounds crazy but ever since Katie disappeared anything seems possible.

Although it's still dark, I decide to go to the hotel gym for a morning workout before the heat gets up. I haven't had the heart to keep up with my usual exercise routines. The sadness and stress of losing Katie has sapped all my energy. But today I feel that a good pounding on the treadmill might help to calm my nerves.

By the time I'm finished, I'm dripping with sweat but feeling a lot more chilled. Now the sun's out and the birds are singing, my fears of last night seem absurd. Damien left a short message on the phone in my hotel room last night, effectively just telling me that he was taking good care of Christina and ordering me to hold the fort at the hotel and wait for further instructions. But I can't get hold of Christina. Still, there's no point imagining the worst. She's probably just ignoring my texts. Costa, on the other hand, finally replies to my text of last night – just a few brief words, but it's enough.

Relax. I've got the address of Christina's villa. I'll explain more later.

So, he's located them.

Perhaps my imagination has been running away with me. If it was Damien who took out The Phantasea the night before last it was probably only for a night cruise of boozing and gambling with his dodgy mates. Even so, I think it's weird that Christina hasn't called me. Have I done something to offend her? Other than losing her daughter, that is! But this is no time for black humour. I need to stay strong and one hundred percent focused on the search for Katie.

This morning I'm going to ask Marco in the hotel's marketing suite to print off five hundred A4 posters, with a blown-up image of Katie holding out the shells and the words STILL MISSING in large black letters at the top. I took the photograph just before I passed out under the parasol. It's the last photograph of Katie which Christina and I saw at the police station – but the police poster was too small and too limited in distribution. I'm going to make sure everyone round here gets to see it.

My plan is to walk into town and go to every shop and every market stall and every business, to ask them to put up the poster and call me if they have any information. I've put my number at the bottom.

There could be lots of reasons why people are scared to come forward. It's just possible that there's someone out there who knows something but doesn't want to have any contact with the police. They might be more willing to respond to this direct appeal from someone close to the family. What's more, with the exception of Brenda, I don't trust those lazy clerks in Costa's back office to deal with this. They wouldn't recognise a tip-off if it punched them in the face!

While I'm waiting for Marco to do my printing, I get a call from Costa.

'It's all in hand,' he says. Damien called him this morning with the address of the villa. It is part of his bail conditions that he has to provide his address at all times. 'I was able to speak to Christina,' Costa tells me. 'She is feeling unwell – emotionally and physically exhausted. She just wants us to respect her privacy and give her the chance to rest. They are going to lie low for a few days.'

I send a text to Christina.

I hope you manage to get some peace and quiet. You need to rest. Don't give up hope. We're hard at it here – we WILL find Katie – keep the faith. Any news, I'll let you know at once. Scarlett xx

Armed with my stack of posters, I walk up the dusty road into town. I don't have a driving licence or the money to hire a car otherwise I would drive out to the villa myself. There's no pavement so I'm walking in the road. A couple of motorists stop to offer me a lift but I'm not taking any chances. Others hoot as they speed by. I'm not sure if it's my skimpy shorts or they just want me to get off the road. One dodgy character brakes and leans out of the window as he drives past, making obscene hand gestures. It's scary enough for me but heart-breaking to think of Katie, God knows where, with people like him on the loose.

Once I've handed out all the posters around town, which takes me the best part of two hours as everyone wants to give me their opinion on the tragic situation, I decide to look in on Costa at the police station. I'm desperate for news of Katie. Also, I need to finish going through that file of witness statements and sightings sent in to the police.

The file is still open on his desk at the point I got to yesterday.

'Have you got the fingerprints from the sandals and the purse?' I ask him. Every procedure seems painfully slow on this island!

'They made a mistake with the transparencies,' he says. 'I've sent them back for review.'

'Well, you need to get them fast,' I say. 'Every minute counts. And you need to check the footage from the security cameras at the hotel. Unless it's a ghost, whoever came into my room can't be invisible.'

He gives me a frosty look.

'Don't tell me how to do my job, Scarlett. These things take time.'

'What about the CCTV at the harbour?' I ask.

'It's in hand,' says Costa and turns his back to me.

He's preoccupied this morning with another case involving extortion and corruption at the highest levels that's been entrusted to him by the Commissioner. He admitted last night that he's struggling to get to grips with the technicalities of the evidence, complex financial transactions involving international banks, a judge and a government minister. He told me he wants to do a good job because he's counting on a promotion at his next pay review in a few weeks' time. Besides, I know he's arrogant and conceited – he won't want to show his boss that he's out of his depth.

I can't believe he's wasting time on this new case when he should be channelling all his energy into finding Katie. 'The world keeps turning,' is his response.

'I might be able to speed things along,' I say impatiently, looking over his shoulder at the figures. 'I'm surprisingly good at maths.' He pushes me away and I go back to the file of evidence while he sits hunched at the desk, huffing and puffing over the compound financial calculations. The minutes pass. Every time I look up he's leaning back in the chair looking at me, his eyes half closed.

'For God's sake, please can you focus on the search for Katie! You've wasted enough time on that.'

'This won't do at all,' he murmurs to himself. 'She's one of my key witnesses.' He gathers up the banks' disclosure statements and locks them in the safe.

'I've got some business to attend to at the court house,' he says. 'I'll see you later.'

Not long after he goes, there's a loud rapping on the glass partition and I look up to see Brenda pressing a piece of paper to the pane and mouthing something at me, her eyes wide open. As I stand up, she leaps to her feet and runs round into the office. She slaps the sheet down on the table in front of me.

'You've got to read this. Just arrived in Costa's email. I printed it off for you.'

I've never seen Brenda move so fast.

The email is an electronic copy of a statement taken yesterday. I guess it must have been given in response to Costa's latest round of questioning and interviews – he was planning to contact all the hotel guests who've already left the island. I read through it three times with mounting excitement while Brenda sits watching me, drumming her long purple nails on the desk. If this doesn't validate my theory about Christina and Damien, I don't know what does. I can't wait for Costa to get back.

As soon as he walks through the door, I thrust the document into his hands.

Witness testimony of Stacey Jackson (the "Witness") dated 21 June 2015

The Witness states:

That she is a national of United States of America residing at Carrolton, Texas.

That she was on vacation to Grand Carmola in the British Leeward Isles between 8 and 16 June 2015 where she and her family were guests at The Palm Reef Beach Club (the 'Hotel').

That on 16 June 2015 she and her family spent the day within the grounds of the Hotel until their departure at 5.08 p.m. when they drove to Reef International Airport, Grand Carmola for their connecting flight to Dallas-Fort Worth airport which departed at 6.30 p.m.

Concerning the facts under investigation the Witness testifies as follows:

On 16 June 2015 the Witness was at the Hotel with her husband, Tom Jackson, and her daughters, Tayla, aged 7 and Sophie, aged 5. The family were at the Hotel pool from 10 a.m. until 12 p.m. where Tayla and Sophie, played with a girl, white, aged about four years, of slim build, height approximately 1.00 metres, with medium-length blonde wavy hair (the 'Child'). The Child's nanny introduced herself as 'Scarlett' and the Child as 'Katie.'

The Witness states that when she saw US media photographs and footage of missing person, 'Katie Kenedey' on her return to Texas she identified such images as being of the Child.

The Witness testifies that the girls played on the lilo with the Child's nanny. The Witness overheard the nanny explaining to her daughters that the Child didn't talk much because she found talking very difficult but that she would like to play with them. The Witness assumed that the Child had communication difficulties due to special needs and was pleased to see the three girls playing together so nicely.

At about 12 p.m. the family returned to their apartment for lunch on the terrace.

At about 2.30 p.m. the family arrived at the beach to relax for a couple of hours before their return flight to Dallas Fort Worth. At approximately 2.45 p.m. the Witness's husband, Tom, said it was too hot to sunbathe and told the Witness he was going for a walk along the beach to the lighthouse at Coral Bay. The Witness saw him exchange a few words with the nanny and wave to the Child who was playing near the water before he walked off in a westerly direction to the lighthouse.

The Witness read her book whilst her daughters played in the shade of their parasol. From time to time, they ran down to the water and the Witness observed them jumping in and out of the water with the Child. At approximately 3.30 p.m., the Witness and her daughters went to buy ice-creams which they ate on the beach.

At 4 p.m. the Witness and her daughters started packing up before heading to the hotel for showers. As the Witness was folding towels, she saw a woman she believed to be the Child's mother (the 'Woman') (she had overheard the nanny, Scarlett, referring to the Woman as 'Christina' and 'Mummy' that morning at the pool), walking past. The Woman looked preoccupied and did not acknowledge her greeting. Before resuming her packing up, the Witness saw the Woman approach the Child who was playing on the lilo in the shallow water.

A few minutes later, the Witness saw the Woman walking up the beach hand-in-hand with the Child. She was wearing blue-rimmed Tiffany sunglasses and had the Child's lilo under one arm and a camera round her neck. Tayla and Sophie asked to borrow the Witness's phone to take photos and ran up to the Child to say goodbye.

The girls took turns posing for photographs. The Witness also recalls the Woman taking one or more photographs with her camera. Then the Woman told the Child she would buy her an ice-cream and they walked up the beach towards the snack bar. That was the last sighting the Witness had of the Child and the Woman as she then left the beach with her two girls.

After the Witness and her daughters had showered in the Hotel gym her husband finally returned from the lighthouse at approximately 5 p.m. and changed from his trunks into a T- shirt and jeans. Then they loaded the suitcases into their hire car and set off at 5.08 p.m. The Witness recalls checking the precise time as she was worried they would miss their flight.

The Witness states that she did not notice anything unusual about the behaviour of the Woman or the Child, who did not seem to be distressed or coerced. Regarding the Woman, the Witness states that she was wearing a pale sundress and flat sandals. Her toenails were painted a bright coral red. The Witness describes her appearance as white, above average height, 168 to 175 cm, about 32 to 38 years old, slim build, mid-blonde shoulder-length hair swept back from her face, attractive features and a tanned complexion. The Witness also noted that she was wearing a large gold Michael Kors wristwatch and gold earrings with pale blue stones.

Regarding the Child, the Witness states further that the infant had 'bright blue eyes and an engaging smile'. She didn't speak and avoided eye contact with adults but was 'smiley and relaxed' with her daughters. She recalls that the Child was wearing a stripy pink one-piece swimsuit and pink jelly sandals.

The Witness states that she became aware of the victim's disappearance twenty-four hours after arriving home in Carrolton through the media campaign surrounding the Child's suspected abduction. She was later contacted via email by the BLI police force as part of their appeal for information from all guests at the Hotel.

This Witness Statement records the information the Witness gave to the police by telephone interview between 3 p.m. and 3.55 p.m. Eastern Time, 21 June 2015.

'Looks like I owe you an apology!' says Costa, when he finishes reading the statement. 'Your theory isn't so stupid after all.'

I look at him triumphantly.

'So you see my instincts were right! It's her. She's not a victim but a perpetrator – at the very least an accomplice.'

I remember that Texan woman and her little girls. And I vaguely remember her husband coming up to speak to me on the beach. It's all clouded by the effect of the drugs.

'I agree this doesn't look good for Christina,' he says, 'but we shouldn't jump to conclusions. After all, this is uncorroborated evidence. It could be a case of mistaken identity. Or the woman could have made it all up.'

That takes the wind out of my sails as I scan through the statement again.

'She does seem to have an unusually clear recollection of the details of Christina's appearance,' I point out. 'The *Michael Kors* watch – I know Christina wears one. And the earrings with pale blue stones. As you know, she has a pair of blue jade earrings that she wears all the time. Either this woman Samantha has a great eye for detail and great recall or she's trying to frame her.'

I turn the page to look down the Witness' personal details as recorded on the back of the Statement.

'Look here, *Employment Details* – she's a talent scout for Blitz, a Dallas-based modelling agency,' I say. 'That may explain her eye for designer labels and make-up.'

Modelling – that's a coincidence.

I keep that thought to myself.

'Perhaps her husband has something to hide?' I say. 'He seemed a bit weird, as far as I remember. His manner was very awkward.'

'I'll check him out, past convictions, sex offenders register, the usual checks,' says Costa, eyeing me coolly. 'Try and think back, what did he say to you on the beach?'

'Not much as far as I remember but he had no shame in looking me up and down.'

'Mrs Samantha Jackson could have made the whole thing up to distract police attention from Mr Jackson's unusual two-hours-and-fifteen-minutes' absence on the beach,' says Costa.

Stranger things have happened.

I flick through the rest of the file.

'Where are the photographs taken by the girls? They're not here. Get her to send them through, then at least we'll know whether the child was Katie.'

He walks out to the control room, and then returns.

There are no photographs, he tells me. So it could have been another little girl or it could have been another day. 'Don't jump to conclusions,' he says. 'She may be an unreliable witness.'

Apparently, the woman's phone was either lost or stolen while she and the girls were showering in the gym or on the way to the airport. She only discovered it was gone when they got to airport security and they didn't have time to do anything about it.

'Well, that's a bit odd in itself,' I say.

'We'll make enquiries at the hotel and at the airport,' says Costa, 'in case it has been found.'

One way or another this witness statement is the strongest proof yet that Christina was somehow involved in Katie's abduction. Suspicions spiral in my brain. Damien is controlling her, he forced her into this, Katie is the pawn in his ill-fated plan to get a shit-load of money to pay off his gambling debts whether through reward or ransom or insurance payout or some other shameful scheme in collaboration with a vicious drug-smuggling ring, in which one or more corrupt police officers are involved.

And it has all gone horribly wrong.

Which speculation all leads to a creeping new doubt, an uncomfortable thought. What is Kramer's role in all of this and why does Costa appear to be covering for him?

Can I trust Costa?

23

12 May 2009: The Neverland

Ah! The Neverland. How I loved that yacht. Dad let me choose the name, do you remember? Peter Pan was our favourite story that summer.

'So come with me where dreams are born and time is never planned.' He let me write that inscription inside the front cover of the Logbook when he took delivery of the new yacht and we lived by it all the summer long. We were mermaids, playing ball with bubbles in the rainbows, flirting with the boy who never grew up and torturing the dull, self-important Wendy.

This photograph brings back so many memories - smooth polished timber, the smell of salt and the sea, damp leather seats and the cool touch of brass fittings and blazing white painted metal. Father adored her – his one luxury – a throwback to the adventurous days of his youth when he and Grandpa took part in regattas together, sailing racing yachts in the Atlantic sea. They were proper sailors, not the sun-seeking, gin-slinging amateurs that we became.

Look, there in the distance, our rock, burning black and glorious in the setting sun. Marooners' Rock we called it in our games of make-believe. We spent hours combing our long golden tresses with imaginary shells, slapping our tails and diving into the water in search of Tinker Bell, and drowning men.

You're sitting at the polished table, next to James. The rock is behind you. There's a document in front of you and you have a pen in your right hand – you're looking down at the page, about to sign. James has his hand over the ring-less fingers of your left hand, and he's looking up at me, smiling, as I take the photograph. As the shutter closed, you succumbed, and signed your agreement to be our surrogate.

In the end, it was Gabrielle who made it happen. She was desperate to have a baby. She told Lara her marriage was cursed and only a baby could break the spell. She could be such a drama queen! Lara resisted. She knew Gabrielle had suffered from depression and post-partum psychosis but she didn't want to be dragged back into the toxic triangle, so she kept her distance and threw herself into life in New York.

If Gabrielle had had any kind of moral compass she would have laughed at the irony of the situation. Having forced Lara into having an abortion when she was pregnant with James' child, she was now in the humiliating position of having to beg and bully her into agreeing to act as a surrogate for herself and James. Lara was insultingly defiant, defending herself fiercely and refusing to cooperate. Gabrielle was infuriated by her moralistic interpretation of their childlessness. She called it 'divine retribution' for the supposed wrong that Gabrielle had done to her. Gabrielle was sick of her.

Indeed, Gabrielle was not the kind of person to indulge in feelings of guilt or self-doubt. She was acutely aware of wrongs done to her but sublimely oblivious to the distress she caused others. Since her marriage to James five years previously, she had experienced the devastating pain and anguish of multiple miscarriages, ending with the overwhelming heartache of Rose's tragic still birth. Further, she suspected with good reason that there had been more than one romantic dalliance between James and Lara during her disastrous pregnancies. All those business trips. Although she had no proof of it, she was convinced that he had combined business with pleasure on more than one occasion.

Lara owed her.

Gabrielle knew only too well that James was restless in their childless marriage. Fatherhood would 'anchor' him. After countless investigations and consultations, the medical experts had concluded that while she was not infertile, her womb was incapable of carrying a baby to term. Having exhausted all other medical procedures, the only remaining options were adoption or surrogacy. They both favoured surrogacy. The urge to pass on their genetic inheritance was compelling – a desire bordering on obsession in her case.

She had a plentiful supply of viable frozen eggs that she'd had the foresight to insist on preserving during the many IVF treatments she had endured, and the experts were confident that the couple were suitable candidates for a gestational surrogacy. James would have preferred a third-party arrangement but Gabrielle was not keen on the idea of entrusting the gestation of their baby to a stranger. Once the woman was impregnated, they would lose all control. If, on the other hand, Lara could be persuaded to act as their surrogate then Gabrielle knew she could retain command and control of the whole project: she could follow the implantation closely, be intimately involved all the way through, and make sure everything possible was being done to protect their baby. She had no qualms about using Lara in this way. The practical benefits of the proposed arrangement were all that mattered at the end of the day. It would be in the best interests of her baby. Lara's womb would be the perfect vessel for the gestation.

It had taken some serious bridge-building for Gabrielle to re-establish relations with Lara in New York. There had been more than three months of relentless transatlantic emotional blackmail before Lara had capitulated and agreed to a short 'reconciliation holiday' on the venerable old yacht *The Neverland* which now belonged to Gabrielle. Of course, Gabrielle had her own selfish agenda – the real reason was to get Lara to sign an agreement to act as surrogate mother for herself and James. According to her plan, it was to be a gestational surrogacy – using her previously frozen eggs, she and James would be the biological parents.

In preparation for the reunion, Gabrielle had instructed a lawyer in New York to deal with the necessary paperwork for the surrogacy. The lawyer had advised that paid or commercial surrogacy contracts were not legally enforceable in the state of New York but that he could draw up a memorandum of understanding formalising an altruistic surrogacy arrangement between the intended parents, Gabrielle and James, and their gestational surrogate, Lara. Once armed with this document, Gabrielle also investigated the procedural matters relating to the export of her frozen eggs to the United States. She contacted the medical facility in London where her eggs were stored and kicked off the formalities for their transfer to a fertility clinic in New York specialising in surrogacy where the fertilisation and embryo transfer procedures could take place. Gabrielle was determined not to leave anything to chance.

James was happy to go along with whatever the biology and Gabrielle required of him. It remained only for the couple to obtain Lara's agreement to the surrogacy. Gabrielle would then ensure that Lara made all the necessary arrangements for the embryo's transfer to be carried out successfully (with a prior visit by James to the fertility clinic to perform his part in the medical process, being factored into the plan). Initially Lara's response was to delete or ignore all communications. But Gabrielle was relentless, determined to get her own way come hell or high water. She bombarded Lara daily with messages in which she accused her of being selfish, cold, emotionally bankrupt. Finally, Lara responded to the barrage of emails and texts.

'I'll meet you in the BLI but I'm not making any promises.' She had a few days' holiday that she needed to take before her company's year-end, and she felt like a break in the sun. The trip would commit her to nothing. Anyway, she was longing to see James again.

So they had an alcohol-fuelled week together on the *The Neverland*, the three of them acting, as it happened, very much like over-excited teenagers living out a fantasy. It was the first time they had been together since that dreadful wedding day, almost exactly five years ago. Gabrielle was on her very best behaviour and James was at his most charming, romancing 'his girls' with the attentiveness and chivalry that came naturally to him. Although she loved his company, Lara couldn't stop herself analysing the situation and judging him.

He's not a stupid man, she thought. *But he has a rational and emotional blind spot where we're concerned. He doesn't see us as distinct individuals but rather as two interchangeable embodiments of the same person – he claims he loves us both and has even been 'in love' with us both, and yet he doesn't see anything wrong with that.* Lara had come to the conclusion that because he lacked the imagination to distinguish between them as individuals, he couldn't understand how his behaviour could be considered morally reprehensible or destructive. He was too lazy and lacking in self-discipline even to reflect upon it. It just came naturally to him, he followed his instincts, he couldn't help himself. For him, there was no boundary between friendship and infatuation.

And now they were making it easy for him, she realised. This 'reconciliation' would reignite the old flames. A surrogacy arrangement would forge an unbreakable bond between the three of them – a baby, the ultimate embodiment of the ties that bind – but would it be bonding or bondage? And who was the captor and who was the slave?

Someone's going to suffer, thought Lara. *But I won't let it be me.*

Would it be James? Was he a free agent or was he the one being ensnared into a trap, the sacrificial victim in this toxic triangle of love and hate?

During her first day on board The Neverland, Lara kept up her defences. But it was good to be together again with the two people in the world, who despite everything, she was closest to. She enjoyed the flirtatious attentions she received from James. She soaked up the solicitous care and calculated compliments from Gabrielle. What's more, they were easy in each other's company. They 'clicked' as a threesome. Even Gabrielle felt more contented and relaxed – the marriage was now complete. Where before there had been a gaping hole, which both she and James acknowledged as the longing for a child, for this brief happy spell it was, as the French say, a joyful *ménage à trois*. It was decadent and it was fun. They spent long days lazing out on deck, soaking up the sun. Even though in her late teens Lara had developed a phobia for being submerged in water (thanks to one of Gabrielle's more malicious pranks),

James strapped her into a life jacket and took her for thrilling rides on his jet-ski. Such was the confidence and trust he inspired in her, that there was nothing she enjoyed more than zooming across the bay with her arms clasped around his waist. She was exhilarated, more alive than she had felt in years. She didn't pause to wonder why. She and Gabrielle went shopping in the local markets and their dual beauty caused a stir among the locals. Lara enjoyed the wolf-whistles, and flashing smiles and turning heads. Her colleagues in New York were so dull in comparison.

On the fourth day, Gabrielle put James to work. He cooked a fabulous meal of exotic seafood and freshly caught fish, served with three different wines. They spent the evening reminiscing about the past and he kept the girls in fits of giggles with impersonations and stories about the eccentric private practice clients he had treated before his move from practising medicine to a sales management role in international pharma. Prompted by Gabrielle, he kept refilling Lara's glass. By the time Gabrielle brought out the dessert platter of fresh fruit and pastries and cream, Lara's head was spinning and she could scarcely stand. She lurched up from the table to get a glass of water and swayed her way over to the galley kitchen. Gabrielle nodded at James.

'It's time.'

James pushed the empty plates to one side and spread the document out on the table in front of Lara. He slid in beside her on the bench and handed her the pen.

'So there it is,' said Gabrielle. 'It's all very straightforward. I hired an attorney in New York.'

Lara slammed down her water glass, spilling water over the first page of the contract.

'So that's why you brought me here. You're giving me an ultimatum. And there was I, thinking that you just wanted us all to be friends again, to give me time to think about it and to make my own decision. I should have guessed your motives were entirely selfish!'

'Don't worry. It's really only the signature page that matters,' said Gabrielle, as she hurriedly soaked up the spillage with some paper towels. 'James and I have signed already. You need to sign here at the bottom of page three – that's all. Just below my signature… that's it, where James has got his finger. I'll fill out the rest for you. Don't worry about reading it now. It's getting late. You can read over the contract in the morning.'

Gabrielle handed Lara her pen.

Lara woke at midday with a searing headache and a bad feeling.

What have I done?

Out of habit and pity and love for James and too much red wine, she had capitulated and signed the agreement against her better judgment. The misgivings started immediately. What the hell had she let herself in for? How would a surrogate pregnancy impact on her social and working life in New York? She had a new circle of friends. She was in a 'thing' that was more than a 'thing,' with a guy she'd met a few weeks earlier at another hedge fund. She was getting on really well with her boss and angling for a promotion at work at her next annual review. Gabrielle's 'project' would mean taking time off work, losing the chance of promotion, wrecking her social life and probably sacrificing her 'more than a thing.' Save for the occasional 'throwback,' clandestine, business-trip close-encounter with James, this budding romance was the nearest she had come to a proper relationship in the past few years. The prospect of her surrogacy would strike it dead. She couldn't imagine a more effective passion-killer for a tentative boyfriend and potential lover.

Over breakfast, she said to Gabrielle,

'I've changed my mind, give me the document, I'm going to rip it up.'

'Too late,' said Gabrielle. 'You've signed it now. I've faxed it to my lawyer. You can't just pull out on a whim.'

'I don't even know what it says,' said Lara. 'You didn't give me a chance to read it. I was drunk last night. You forced me into it. You know that.'

'You can't do this,' said Gabrielle. 'We're counting on you now. James will never forgive you if you turn your back on us, and nor will I.'

She made Lara a cup of strong black coffee and banged it down on the table in front of her.

'Besides, it's all very fair and reasonable,' said Gabrielle. 'We'll compensate you for any loss of earnings due to time off work. We'll pay all your out-of-pocket expenses. And although it's not written in the agreement, I'll even pay you an extra twenty-five-thousand dollars to cover any inconvenience. It'll be our little secret. I'm being very generous.'

Gabrielle sat down at the table opposite Lara and eyed her like a cat watching its prey.

'Let's face it Lara, you're not going to get married. You're not the marrying type. This is your best chance of having a family. At the end of the day, we'll make you the godmother, you'll be known as the "auntie" and we'll give you the opportunity of seeing the child on a regular basis. If you don't do this for us, you're facing a sad and lonely old age.'

Don't do this, you bitch, thought Lara, although she didn't say it out loud, and fortunately just then James bounded up the steps from the cabin.

'Hey Lara, I'm riding the jet-ski over to the Mermaids' Lagoon. Want to come? The sea's like a mirror this morning.'

Lara tipped the coffee down the sink and followed James to the stern where she helped him lower the jet-ski onto the water. If nothing else, she was going to make the most of the remaining holiday. She wasn't going to allow Gabrielle's old bullying ways to spoil her fun.

The last two days on The Neverland were fraught with tension. Lara and Gabrielle barely spoke but James made valiant efforts to act as the go-between, smoothing things over and keeping everyone plied with drink. By the last evening, Lara had made up her mind.

'I'll do it, but on my own terms and in my own time – when it suits me,' she said over the last candlelit supper. She was determined not to miss out on holidays or lose her job or jeopardise her chances of furthering her career.

'I'm not giving up work and I'm staying in New York.' She glared at the couple. 'And I don't want any sentimental hand-holding ceremonies,' she said. 'I can do without you and James standing by the bedside looking all gooey-eyed while they do what they've got to do. I'll choose the clinic and I'll go to the clinic alone – you're not coming anywhere near it. I'm going to remain fully in control of anything that has to be done to my body. This time you're not going to interfere.'

'Whatever you want,' said Gabrielle. 'It's your call.'

'And you can keep that bloody camera away from me,' said Lara. 'I'm not about to become your next photographic exhibit.'

24

Scarlett

The villa is hidden away about five miles up a winding unmade road. If you are a little distracted and dulled by the heat, it's easy to miss. I catch sight of the broken sign for *Villa La Revanche* at the last minute and slam on the brakes.

The quad bike skids across the road with a sickening screech and I'm catapulted over the handlebars. I land with a heavy thump on to an overgrown bank of long grass and wild flowers. My helmet bangs against the turf. Maybe the quad bike wasn't such a great idea.

Having reached the conclusion I can't trust anyone, perhaps not even Costa, as I was leaving the police station, on a whim I decided to come and check things out at the villa for myself. Christina may have staged the abduction of her own daughter but for all we know she may be acting under duress. Her own life may be in peril.

On the way out of town, there's a scruffy little garage at the side of the road. I saw their sign:

QUAD BIKES FOR RENT
$25 AN HOUR

I was sure they wouldn't be too fussy about seeing a driving licence. I showed them my student card to prove I was over twenty-one and the fat old man in charge took me across to one of the rusty old bikes and told me to hop on. After a ten-minute tutorial in the saddle I was on my way, engine sputtering and roaring, speeding along gravelly roads winding up steep green hills, through unbelievably green and lush tracts of the Pine Mountain National Park, and across to the other side of the island, in search of the villa.

Sadly, the fat old man forgot to warn me to go easy on the brakes!

I stand up and take a few unsteady steps. My knees are bruised and bleeding, and my wrist is hurting but I'm more or less in one piece.

I look around nervously. Once again, I can't shake the uncanny feeling that someone's watching me. I spent most of the ride, checking over my shoulder every hundred metres or so, convinced I was being tailed. But I'm probably just imagining things. There's certainly not a soul in sight now. I can see why Damien chose this villa. It really is in the middle of nowhere.

I climb onto the quad bike and ride it gingerly in low gear back up to the turning for *La Revanche*. Strange name for a holiday home. If my schoolgirl French doesn't deceive me, I think it means the villa of 'revenge' or 'retribution.'

I steer the quad bike safely up the driveway that opens onto a sun-baked parking area. There's a rough stone wall running the length of the path leading to the ramshackle house. I park up next to it. A couple of lizards dash out as I follow the wall up towards the peeling front door. They're well camouflaged and I see only a flash of movement as they dart away into the gaps between the stones. This place is teeming with life but it's hidden away, furtive and secret. Even the reptiles are on the run. As I walk up the path, I pass a rickety wooden outbuilding and almost jump out of my skin as a dog just inside the rotting timbers starts up barking furiously and throws itself against the locked doors. I'm glad it's not on the loose. I can't see it behind the timbers but it sounds like the *Hound of the Baskervilles*.

Damien must have heard the engine and the rabid barking. He's waiting for me at the door. He's got a tumbler of whiskey in one hand. Not the first, judging by the way he sways over towards me. He kisses me on both cheeks and swings open the door with an extravagant gesture.

'Welcome to my humble abode.'

He doesn't look like a double murderer – more like a pathetic drunk this afternoon, with stubble on his cheeks and stains on his shirt.

Although the house itself is shabby and run down, its owners have begun to redevelop the property, starting with the pool area. The swimming pool is appealing, an infinity pool, set on a high point in the land overlooking the valley below. The pool is encircled by stone paving and a vast area of decking decorated with wood carvings, water features and hanging chairs. I can imagine the blurb in the brochure. *The perfect place to relax in complete isolation.*

Damien offers me a gin and tonic and asks if I would like to have a swim. It's too much to resist, so tempting after spending hours stuck in Costa's stuffy office.

'I need to clean myself up first,' I say, pointing to my scuffed knees. 'And I didn't bring my bikini. I can't go skinny dipping in broad daylight. Do you think Christina would lend me one?'

I want to go and talk to her as soon as possible so I'm looking for an excuse.

'Christina is resting,' he says. 'She went up about half an hour ago. Have a swim first. You can see her later. I think she left a bikini in the downstairs bathroom through there. Help yourself. I'm sure she won't mind.'

I go through to the bathroom and wash the blood off my knees. I look in the bathroom cabinet for some antiseptic to put on my wounds. Christina's medicine collection seems to have expanded since I last saw it. Alongside her usual brands of sleeping pills and sedatives, there are a couple of bottles with names I haven't seen before. I read the warning labels. I know enough from my aborted childcare studies to recognise that these are powerful anti-psychotic medications usually prescribed for schizophrenia. She must be in a bad way.

Her leopard-print bikini is hanging up to dry on the towel rail. Christina must have been for a swim. I thought she hated going in the water. It fits me pretty well though the cup size is a bit small. The odd thing is, I could have sworn she bought it from *Calvin Klein*, but the label on this is *Sauvage*. Anyway it looks great on me and I'm dying for a swim.

When I go back out to the pool, the grounds are deserted. Damien's left me a gin and tonic on a small table next to a sun lounger. Next to the glass there's a small silver bell – does he expect me to ring for service? It feels very *Great Gatsby*. There's also an open book on the table – *Hemingway's Death in the Afternoon*. Who reads a book about bullfighting in Spain when on holiday in the Caribbean? I'm sure it's not Christina's. Damien must have left it there on purpose. He's trying to impress (or intimidate) me.

I dive in the pool. The water's deliciously cool. I'm going to do forty lengths.

When I get out of the pool, there's still no one around so I settle myself down on the sunbed and reach for the gin and tonic. The ice has almost melted.

I'm about to take a sip when I notice something sparkling on the surface of the drink. I hold the glass up to the light. It's a silver jingle shell, gently curved and scintillating, floating on the top of my gin and tonic. It makes a tiny clinking sound as I swirl it round the rim. I stand up and call out to Damien but he's nowhere to be seen. The sound of my voice is enough to set off the hound in the outhouse. The alarming volley of barking and snarling sparks a recollection of the image in the police file of the dog photographed in front of The Phantasea. It occurs to me that someone is trying to communicate with me by leaving me a cryptic clue. Now I think maybe I get it – the floating jingle, the silver bell... Does that little floating shell on the surface of the water represent The Phantasea? Is the idea of the jingle and the silver bell intended to make me think of Katie's favourite fairy Tinker Bell in the story book of Peter Pan that I was reading to her the night before she disappeared?

Damien wouldn't have the imagination for this. If my instincts are right, it's Christina's work – Christina who bought the beautiful copy of Peter Pan that she found in the Book Cellar in New York for us to read to Katie on holiday. She told me it was her favourite children's' story when she was a little girl too. We were taking it in turns, reading Katie a chapter every evening at bedtime.

This message, that Christina's left for me right under Damien's nose, may help me to discover where Katie – our very own lost child – has been hidden. Could it be that this little shell is supposed to represent a boat floating in the sea, and could it be... that the lost girl...?

Yes, Katie's on the boat... The Phantasea must be where she's hidden.

Christina's the one who did this. I feel sure of it, just as she's the one who scrawled letters from Damien's name in lipstick on my mirror and took Katie's passport and her purse from my safe. God knows what her motives are but it's her. Perhaps she removed Katie's passport to stop Damien getting his hands on it. Maybe she's regretting having allowed Damien to force her into the dreadful conspiracy to stage Katie's disappearance. She wants this nightmare to be over as soon as possible and now that Damien's got her entrapped here at the villa, she's finding ways to communicate with me so that I can go and rescue Katie. Is this too far-fetched? Could this be true?

I can't face drinking the gin and tonic any more. It could be drugged or laced with poison if Damien got to it! So I decide to head up to the villa to get a towel and a glass of water. Damien must have gone up to join Christina. Looks like she was in a hurry to get undressed – her top, mini skirt, bra and briefs are abandoned on the floor. Christina's bathrobe is draped over the sofa. I wrap it round me. I've borrowed it before but there's something different about it today. It doesn't have that familiar Coco-Chanel-Christina-smell. She must have changed her perfume.

As I bend down automatically to pick up the scattered clothes (force of habit being a nanny), there's a loud thumping from upstairs. I go out into the hallway. More banging and screaming. God, he's attacking her. Maybe it was Damien who ripped off her clothes and dragged her up to the bedroom. I run up the stairs. There's a crash, something heavy falling to the floor, immediately followed by the sound of breaking glass. Then another scream. I grab the door handle and turn – it's locked. He's locked her in. I rap on the door.

'Open the door.'

Now, it's all gone quiet. I stand very still outside the door and listen. I can hear muffled talking, then panting and moans, and giggling. Unmistakably, it's the sounds of vigorous lovemaking ending with the high-pitched yelps of a woman, and a low groaning, 'God that was so good!' from Damien.

This isn't *Death in the Afternoon*. It's Sex in the Afternoon. Katie's disappearance clearly hasn't diminished Christina's sex drive – unless she's excellent at faking it! I stand out here on the landing for a few minutes, allowing a decent interval to pass then I rap on the door again. I'm determined to see Christina before leaving the villa.

'Piss off, Scarlett,' shouts Damien. 'We came here to get some privacy. Go away and leave us in peace.'

But I stand my ground. I'm not giving up that easily.

'I'm waiting here,' I say. 'I'm not moving until you unlock the door.'

'Fine, then enjoy the show.'

The banging and panting and moaning starts up again. They haven't any shame.

God, I've never heard anything like it. The three of us have shared an apartment for the last six months and I've never heard noises like that coming from their bedroom. It's carnage. He must have plied her with alcohol and legal highs (or more probably, illegal highs) – or it's that new anti-psychotic medication she's taking, driving her crazy, paradoxically!

When I can't take it any more, I go back downstairs into the garden. The noises off continue from the open window overlooking the swimming pool. I'm not leaving until I've spoken to Christina so I call her name and throw some pebbles up at the window where they splatter against the glass. Eventually Damien comes out onto the crumbling balcony wearing only a towel tied round his waist.

'You really are an insufferable pest, Scarlett. Just go away. And don't come back. You're supposed to be holding the fort at the hotel. If you keep coming over to spy on us, you're going to give away our hideout and lead the press pack over here. I'll have to ask Costa to keep you under control.'

'I'm not spying on you,' I shout up. 'I just want to make sure Christina's OK. I need to speak to her.'

'Well, as you've just heard, she's doing absolutely fine, much more positive about things. Now get lost'

'I'm not leaving until I've seen her,' I say.

'She's in the shower.'

When Christina eventually comes out onto the balcony about ten minutes later, she's wrapped only in a sheet, which reminds me that I'm still wearing her bathrobe.

'Hi Scarlett,' she says. 'How are things at the hotel? Are you still being hounded by the press?' She's swaying slightly and her words are slurred. 'Have you spoken to Costa today?' She's looking flushed from her shower and the sex.

I can't really tell her much about the investigation with Damien listening in the room so I just tell her everything is going fine and Costa's making good progress gathering witness reports and following up leads.

'I came here to make sure you're OK,' I say. 'I was worried about you because you didn't answer any of my texts.'

'I'm sorry' she says. 'I've lost my phone. Anyway I'm here. I'm OK. I'm coping.' With one hand she grips the balcony rail to keep herself upright, in the other she's holding a glass of red wine.

I fear she's talking and acting under duress, a victim of Damien's coercive control. I fear that Damien's putting her under pressure to say that she's fine but really, he's holding her hostage here, and subjecting her to psychological and sexual abuse. I'm also concerned she's off her head with a cocktail of medications, alcohol and drugs – that her judgment is impaired, that she's deluded.

I stand just below the balcony and say quietly, 'Are you sure? It seemed pretty wild in there. He's not forcing you, is he? Hurting you? It sounded like an orgy…'

That really provokes her. Suddenly she's on the attack.

'That's rich coming from you… flirtatious little tart… always flaunting your body in front of all the men. Damien told me you practically raped him in the Jeep… and why the hell are you wearing my bathrobe and my bikini?'

She's just clocked the fact I'm standing here in her gear. Abruptly, she switches to her most shrill, condescending tone – Christina does a good line in condescending.

'I don't think the star of that masterpiece of cinematic art *Made-in-Soho*, produced by Porn-R-Us, and ranked number 1 in the bisexual chart for short features on YouPorn is really in a position to lecture me about inappropriate behaviour in the bedroom.'

So perhaps she wasn't faking it!

She's floored me there.

She slings the wine glass down onto the stone terrace at my feet.

The white bathrobe and my legs are splattered and stained red with wine and blood and shards of glass.

Thank God she didn't sling it at my head.

I walk back into the house, rip off her bathrobe and bikini, drag on my own clothes, and run out the front door, down the driveway and past the raging guard dog.

As I swing the quad bike round and set off towards the road, there's a sudden crack and noise of creaking wood.

God, the evil hound must have broken down the rotting boards.

I turn and see a leaping mass of lolling tongue and flesh and dark gleaming fur and muscle. I crank up the gears and tear away in a cloud of dust and keep on going until all I can hear is the sound of frantic barking gradually merging with the puttering of the engine and then fading into the distance.

On the ride back to the hotel, I'm so angry and upset that I can scarcely control the bike. I take the bends too quickly and almost veer off the road as I swerve to avoid a pothole.

I pull over at a passing point to calm my nerves and gather my thoughts. The view from here is spectacular – verdant and tranquil, a vast canopy of green peaks, gradually falling away down to the sea.

How on earth does Christina know about my appearance on YouPorn? I thought I had managed to keep it absolutely secret. I can't imagine Christina is a user, but even if she had stumbled on the film or if Damien (who I have no doubt is a regular user) showed it to her, it doesn't feature my name and it certainly doesn't show my face – I made damn sure of that when I agreed to do it.

What's happened to Christina? Aside from the rampant sex which is completely out of character, I've never known her to be violent – apart from the day she lashed out at me on the beach but that was understandable. She must be off her head with the cocktail of alcohol and drugs she's taking. It's like she's had a personality change.

And what about the search for Katie? Has Christina lost her mind? What's she doing holed up here with Damien having sex in the afternoon, when she should be down at the police station, making a nuisance of herself and making sure the police are doing absolutely everything in their power to find her little girl?

Unless…Suddenly I remember Stacey Jackson's witness statement and Costa's warning about the notorious unreliability of witness evidence… Something's not quite right. For one thing, Christina doesn't take photographs. And she doesn't own a pair of Tiffany sunglasses. I'm quite sure of that. And come to think of it, last time I saw Christina, her toenails were painted purple, not coral red.

25

Scarlett

It's high noon by the time I get down to Coral Point, dump my quad bike in the scruffy car park of the Coco Shack and walk along the quayside to where the wooden motor boats are lined up for hire. Who should be there on the dockside but the hustler who made a play for me at the bar the other night! Looks like this is his day job – hiring out the boats. Does he use them on the night shift for smuggling dope? I wouldn't be surprised. I pretend not to recognise him.

'Hey, don't I know you?' He grins, flashing yellow teeth as I hand over a twenty-dollar bill. 'You're the chick who lost the kid, aren't you? We met at the Shack.'

'I need a boat for the day,' I say.

'Come on in,' he says. 'I can sort you out.' He stubs out his cigarette, and gives me a leery smile. 'It was a good haul last night.'

'Hey, don't get any ideas. The only thing I want from you is a boat to hire,' I want to make it absolutely clear I don't want him pushing anything else on me. 'And a map of the coastline if you've got one.'

'I don't sell maps,' he says. 'You're hiring a boat not a rental car. That's the ocean out there, not a frigging highway – just open your eyes.'

I take a deep breath.

'A tourist guide at the hotel told me about a place they call the Mermaids' Lagoon. Can you point me in the right direction.'

He laughs in my face. 'Wake up Wendy, I'm not Peter-fuckin'-Pan.'

God help me! I'm so sick of men... I wish someone would take me seriously!

I tried to get hold of Costa yesterday but his phone was going straight to voicemail all evening and when I dropped in at the police station this morning the duty officer smirked at me and told me that he'd be late in because Monday nights were his 'Singles Nights'.

'What does his wife have to say about that?'

'His wife don't say nothing 'cos his wife walked out on him last year – lives in San Juan with the kid.'

So he's been lying to me all this time! He's separated from his wife and child. And each time he told me he needed to get home to be with his family, it was just a fake excuse to cut short the working day. And to think I was beginning to put my trust in him! I don't know who to believe or what to believe about anyone or anything on this wretched island!

Brenda had a different story – but then maybe she's just covering for her boss? According to Brenda, Costa's in some high-level court hearing with the barristers and other big shots to do with the financial fraud case he's working on, and won't be free until five o'clock this afternoon. But this can't wait. Katie could be in immediate peril. If she's being held on the yacht her captors could sail out of local waters and over the horizon from one minute to the next.

Besides, why should Costa control everything? He's not my keeper. And I bet I'm still on his list of potential suspects. He didn't play it straight with me, so why should I wait for his approval? He lied to me about his family life. What else is he lying about?

So I make a snap decision. I'm going to have to make do with this joker with the crooked smile – even if he doesn't believe in mermaids! If he hires out boats, he must know something about navigating them. And if I've called it right that he moonlights on the nightshift then he should know every cove, and cave and hidden twist along the coast.

'Listen, I need your help.' I say. 'I've got to find a catamaran sailing yacht – a whopping great gin-palace called The Phantasea. Last seen moored at Clearwater Bay. It can't just have vanished into thin air. The police are supposed to be tracking it down but they don't seem to be making any progress. I think they're just stringing me along – not taking anything I tell them seriously. I believe the lost girl, Katie, may be on board. It's my hunch her abductors are hiding her on the boat.'

He's more interested now he sees there could be something in it for him.

SHE'S MINE

'And you may think I'm crazy but I believe the yacht is moored in a place called the Mermaids' Lagoon – at least that could be its nick name? Does it ring any bells?'

'You can ring my bell any time you like, sweetie,' he mutters. 'Come into my office and we'll look at the map.'

'Office' is a grand name for the pokey little shed I follow him into.

He flips the sign on the door to 'Closed' and shuts it behind me.

What have I let myself in for now?

Then he turns to me, his eyes glowering in the dim light. 'I hear there's a fifty-thousand-dollar reward on her head.' I nod.

'Yes, an anonymous donor – some billionaire in the financial services industry here – put up the reward in response to my online appeal.'

I feel very pleased with myself for getting that off the ground.

He puts his thumbs in his waistband and puffs out his chest.

'Well then, I'm your man,' he says. 'I'll help you find her.'

The entire back wall of the shed is covered by a yellowing map of the Leeward Isles roughly tacked up with drawing pins. As I peer at the map, reading out the names of beaches and towns, he runs his dirty forefinger along the outline of each of the islands. His stale breath is on the back of my neck and I suppress the urge to gag. After a couple of minutes his finger stops: Pelican Island – one of the smallest islands situated in the South East of the archipelago. He taps the map with his finger.

He grunts.

He goes over to a metal filing cabinet, yanks open the drawer and pulls out another dog-eared map that he spreads out on a small desk pushed against one side of the shed. It's a large-scale map of Pelican Island. He points to its southern shore.

'Here,' he says. Again, he runs his forefinger along the circular outline of the landmass in the south of the island, almost fully enclosing an expanse of inland sea. And now I can see what he's getting at. I can see it, the outline of a mermaid in the contours of the water – a dog leg, then a smooth bulge in the coastline resembling the head and long hair of a mermaid, falling into a curving inlet (the mermaid's sinuous body), which fans out at the innermost point into the symmetrical triangular shape of a mermaid's tail. For a man, who doesn't have a romantic sinew in his body, he's demonstrated commendable imagination.

'Yes, you're absolutely right,' I say. The lagoon resembles the shape of a mermaid. The way I used to draw them when I was a little kid. I turn and slap his palm.

'What's it called, that cove?' I ask

'Deadman's Cay.'

'Hmm... that sounds ominous. Well, maybe that's its real name...Can you take me there?'

He goes back to the filing cabinet, unlocks the bottom draw, and takes out a pistol and a fistful of bullets. He shoves the bullets in the front pocket of his jeans, and hooks the pistol into the back of his leather belt.

'Is that really necessary?' I say.

He grabs a faded denim jacket from the door and puts it on to hide the pistol.

'Let's go,' he says.

On the way out, he grabs a tourist leaflet from a tatty display.

Join us for a sunset cruise to the Mermaids' Lagoon.

'Here, have this.' He winks.

So his performance in front of the map was just that... a performance!

He turns and holds out his hand. 'By the way, it's Mitch.'

I remember that name...

'Mitch Stanley.'

'Scarlett Reyes,' I say. 'Thank you.'

The little blue-and-white motorboat is all too familiar as we strike out across the water towards Pelican Island. The distinctive smell of diesel and the feel of the splintering wooden bench against my skin brings back uncomfortable memories. But at least I've found a way of working with Costa that I can live with. I can't imagine ever reaching an accommodation with this rough diamond. Better the devil you know!

'So what makes you think the child may be hidden on a yacht at Deadman's Cay?' he asks, once the water flattens out, and we settle into the cruise.

'Well, it's complicated,' I say. 'For starters, Christina – that's Katie's mother – gave Katie a picture book of *Peter*

Pan to bring on holiday and I was reading the story to her the night before she disappeared. Christina told me she treasured the story as a little girl and now Katie loves it too.' My throat catches while I stumble on the present tense that I still need to believe in, as a memory of Katie dressed up as Tinker Bell and showing me how to 'fly' at the apartment in New York comes into my head.

I take out my phone. 'Christina sent me a message... She's always been a bit on the edge, and now with the shock, and the stress, and the sedatives she's doping herself up with...There's been radio silence from her for the past thirty-six hours, and suddenly this morning she sends me a quote from the storybook *Peter Pan*... wouldn't mean anything to you.'

He cuts the engine, sits down facing me and puts out the oars.

'Try me,' he says. 'All children, except one, grow up... that's me!'

I can't help laughing. 'More like one of the Lost Boys, I'd say.'

He starts pulling on the oars, taking long, strong strokes that propel the boat through the water. He tells me he wants to save on fuel as he forgot to load extra supplies but I think mainly he wants to show off his muscles.

'Don't judge a book by its cover,' he says in a tone of self–irony as he settles into the rhythm. 'Once upon a time I was a high school teacher. Got into a bit of trouble with one of the kids, so dropped out and washed up here. Believe me, I've got the soul of a poet.'

I've had my own 'bit of trouble' so I shouldn't jump to conclusions though it sounds as if his 'bit of trouble' involved inappropriate behaviour rather than illegal substances – or perhaps both?

'What happened?' I say.

'Usual story, got too close to one of the kids. Bright kid but failing at school. Cute-looking girl too. I wanted her to believe in herself, gave her extra tuition in the evenings.'

I bet he did!

'Turned out dad was beating her up. The girl was black and blue. I couldn't turn a blind eye so I reported him to the principal. The father accused me of abusing his daughter to hide the fact he was knocking her around. That's when the school closed ranks against me.'

He spits out the words.

'Didn't want a scandal. The mother was too scared of the bastard to speak up against him – she was his main target. The girl was getting caught in the crossfire. The charges against me didn't stick but the school kicked me out anyway.'

'That's tough,' I say. We've got something in common – we're both fall guys. If he's telling the truth that is. No smoke without fire. My gut reaction was to mistrust him when I first saw him at the Coco Shack – and they say you should trust your first instincts. And, oh God, then there's the sandals, Katie's sandals found stuffed in the bins of the Coco Shack the morning after I saw him there. The paranoia creeps up inside me.

Is it him? Has he got her? And if it's not him, how many other drop-outs and losers are there hanging out on this island? Any one of them could have taken Katie.

I look away from him and fix my eyes on one of the blades, cutting in and out of the water.

'Did you hear, the police have been making enquiries down at the Coco Shack?' I say. 'They're searching the premises today.'

'The police are always down at the Coco Shack,' says Mitch. 'The only thing they'll find down there is used needles.'

'They found her sandals,' I say. I might be making a very stupid mistake...

'Shit!' He pulls the oars in and rests them across his knees.

The boat bobs in the water and suddenly the land looks a very long way off but he doesn't seem to be faking his surprise.

'Have you come across DC Kramer?' I ask.

Mitch sniffs loudly. 'He's bad news – worst of a bad lot. Bent. Takes a cut on every drugs bust and does his own trafficking on the side at the Shack and plenty of other places. I've done some business with him myself in the past – but I don't trust him. Mind, he's not the only one,' he says pointedly.

I remember Costa's words: *It's only Mitch. I'll deal with him later.*

I must be looking anxious because as Mitch starts rowing again, he says, 'I would never lay a finger on a kid.'

I'm going to have to give him the benefit of the doubt as far as Katie is concerned. My 'first line of enquiry' as they say in detective stories, is still Damien – Damien with Christina as his accomplice (whether willing or coerced) caught up in some kind of gambling and drug smuggling ring involving extortion and blackmail.

'Look, I'll show you the text Christina sent me this morning – see what you think...'

I'm having to shout above the wind.

I clamber over to sit next to him on the bench and grab one of the oars in one hand, while holding out my phone in the other.

'She sent me this at 6 a.m. this morning.' I read it out to him.

'if you squeeze your eyes tighter, the pool begins to take shape, and the colours become so vivid that with another squeeze they must go on fire. But just before they go on fire you see the lagoon... just one heavenly moment; if there could be two moments you might see the surf and hear the mermaids singing...'

'That's a quote from the very chapter called "The Mermaids' Lagoon" that I was reading to Katie the night before she went missing.'

'If you want my opinion, the mother's off her head,' says Mitch.

'Well, she studied English Literature at university, so she's into that kind of thing. But I thought this might be her way of telling me that The Phantasea is moored at the Mermaids' Lagoon and that Katie is onboard and in danger. Her partner is controlling and abusive. I don't trust him. He's probably monitoring her texts – so that's why she's resorting to cryptic messages.'

'Have you replied?' says Mitch. 'Get some communication going.'

'I tried phoning her, no answer.'

'Well, keep trying.'

I punch out a couple of question marks and press Send.

A minute or two later, there's a ping on my phone.

I read the message out to Mitch.

'To die will be an awfully big adventure.'

'I told you she's nuts!'

Mitch pulls in the oars and starts up the engine again.

'We locals have our own legends for Deadman's Cay. There've been a number of fishermen drowned in shipwrecks on those rocks – they're treacherous.'

'Katie's father drowned, you know, in a dreadful car accident,' I say. 'That family seems plagued with misfortune.'

Mitch keeps his eyes ahead on the horizon as we navigate along the coast. 'Comes in threes, death...' he mutters darkly.

Eventually he pulls back the throttle and we glide between two rocky spurs into the mouth of the lagoon. We're not alone. Towards the far shore of the lagoon a large tourist boat is anchored and a crowd of booze cruisers are up on deck basking in the sun. The more adventurous are diving off the end of the boat and swimming out like a shoal of strange fish into the clear turquoise waters. The sound of brash American accents fills the air. The swimmers take their turn, hauling themselves up onto a large flat rock sticking up prominently out of the water, posing for photographs and diving sleekly back into the depths.

Mitch rows to a sheltered spot just off the beach and we anchor some distance from the cruise boat.

'There's the rock,' I shout.

While we wait in hope for the appearance of The Phantasea, he placidly sets up a fishing rod and I get out my phone and look up the tourist websites. Marooners' Rock – that's what they call it in the advertising blurbs I look up online. I was right – some of the sunset booze cruise websites say it's named after the rock in *Peter Pan* where the mermaids sit and comb their hair and dive in and out of the waves. It looks fun. It's a throwback to happier times watching the day-trippers. I wish I could be there with them sunbathing on the rock rather than being stuck here with my very own pirate looking for a lost girl – literally.

After the best part of an hour, the cruiser hoots its horn and the swimmers make their way back on deck. Music blares from its speakers now, shattering the peace. The cruiser drifts past our little boat. A group of Damien-lookalikes hang over the rails, beer bottles in hand. They wave and wolf-whistle as I raise my hand and smile.

'Hey gorgeous, come on board,' shouts Damien-lookalike-number-one. In my former life… But I turn away. Katie needs me now. I'm not giving up. This could be our last hope.

Now the lagoon is deserted. We listen to the thump of the music gradually receding across the waves. Mitch steers the boat into the shallow water behind an outcrop of rock.

'We'll slide the boat in here' he says. 'We can see the entrance to the lagoon from here and we're well hidden.

It's a waiting game now.

Time slows and I'm mesmerised by the changing sky as the sun goes down and the moon comes up. I didn't bring anything to eat or drink and it's getting cold and damp on the boat. The minutes drag by.

The lagoon is sinister. I imagine I can see the shapes of mermaids sitting on the rock and I remember the lines from Katie's storybook:

The most haunting time at which to see them is at the turn of the moon, when they utter strange wailing cries; but the lagoon is dangerous for mortals then...

I feel danger in the air now. Like a dog, I can almost smell it.

26

Scarlett

I'm woken by a shaft of sunlight striking my eyelids. I'm lying awkwardly on my side in the rowing boat, facing the rising sun. It must be well after dawn as the light is so intense. I'm aching all over. It's been a long night, with only a blanket for shelter and Mitch to keep me company. He's still sleeping, humped over and snoring at the other end of the rowing boat. Like a stray dog, sleeping rough doesn't seem to bother him.

After the anticipation of last night, I feel flat and despondent. We kept vigil until the early hours of the morning, exchanging stories and memories, watching and waiting and scanning the entrance to the lagoon for a yacht that never appeared. What a stupid, childish idea – chasing mermaids – when I should be at the police station helping Costa go through the files. We're still no closer to finding Katie and this quest for The Phantasea may well turn out to be no more than a fantasy and a fabulous waste of time. Why was I so sure I'd find The Phantasea at the Mermaids' Lagoon? I was foolish to embark on this escapade on the basis of a couple of cryptic clues given to me by a woman whose reason is clouded by tragedy and tranquillisers!

I'm feeling parched and sunburnt and just desperate to get back to the hotel for a cold drink and a hot shower and a few hours of decent sleep.

I stand up, lurch over to Mitch and shake his shoulder roughly.

'Wake up, Mitch, wake up, it's time to go. We're wasting our time here.'

I hadn't counted on Mitch being stubborn as a mule. He tells me that I've wasted enough of his time already, that he isn't a quitter and nor am I – we have to see it through. What's more he's just beginning to enjoy himself.

'Let's give it another day,' he says. 'Do you want to find Katie or don't you?'

I've had enough of taking orders from him, so I whip off the blanket and shout in his ear.

'For God's sake get up. I'm dying of heatstroke and thirst out here in the sun. We've got to get into the shade.'

Eventually Mitch sits up and pulls out a rucksack from under one of the seats. It's his secret stash of liquid – four litres of bottled water and a few beers. A pair of old-fashioned binoculars are at the bottom of the bag.

'Were you going to wait until I passed out before sharing?' I say, glugging down the best part of a litre of water. 'Glad to see you came prepared!' I add, nodding at the quaint binoculars – then it occurs to me that these are probably part of standard kit for his 'offshore business dealings'! Having slaked my thirst, I notice that I'm also starving. I haven't eaten anything since breakfast yesterday. Maybe he prides himself on being a self-styled Crocodile Dundee survival warrior, but I need regular sustenance.

'We can't survive on water and beer.' I say.

'No,' says Mitch, 'That's why I'm going to teach you how to fish.'

He pulls out a fishing rod and a tin of bait from under the seats, and good as his word, by lunchtime I've caught six sardines over the side of the boat and we're camped by the rocks grilling them over a makeshift barbecue using some driftwood I found when he sent me off beachcombing. It turns out Mitch is a pretty skilled fisherman and not a bad cook.

'Give me a week, and I could teach you how to survive a shipwreck,' he says.

We spend the afternoon stretched out on the sand in the shade of the rocks, sleeping off the beer and making up for the broken night. Mitch is supposed to be keeping a look out for the yacht but he keeps dozing off. Intermittently I scan the horizon but it's very quiet – only the occasional fishing boat passing out at sea. It must be a day off for the tourist cruisers.

It's only as the sun begins to lower in the sky and a cool breeze comes in from the sea that I start to get restless.

'I can't face another night in the rowing boat,' I say. 'If nothing happens by midnight, please take me back to the hotel.'

'They're most likely to sail here under cover of nightfall,' says Mitch. 'We're not giving up now.'

He packs our few belongings into the rucksack and we wade back out to the rowing boat. I row over to the rocks and steer the boat back to the rocky outcrop where we are hidden from view. We drop anchor. Mitch rummages around in the rucksack and retrieves a small bag of weed. He lights a spliff.

'This is a bit tame for you, isn't it?' I say. 'I thought you only dealt in the hard stuff?' He doesn't take the bait.

'Want one?' he says, as he sees me eyeing it longingly. 'Could be a long wait.'

I gave up smoking more than two years ago, but I need something to pass the time.

'OK, hand it over.'

I know it's risky. Drugs laws are strict in the BLI but who's going to see me here?

I don't know how long we sit there, but it's at least three joints later, and everything feels surreal when I become aware of vibrations in the air, then a rhythmic beat filling the horizon. I look out to sea and there it is, the shining silhouette of a catamaran yacht like a giant white swan, rounding the headland and entering the lagoon.

The reggae music gets closer and denser, waves of sound, rising and falling in the scarlet sunset above the lagoon. It's coming from the yacht. I lie down in the boat and shift my position for a better view. If I'm not mistaken, it's The Phantasea. I take a deep breath as the sleek lines of the catamaran come into focus. This is the moment I've been waiting for.

So we didn't miss the boat after all.

I'm terrified but excited.

Mitch must be reading my mind. '"To die will be a wonderful adventure!"' he says sardonically and punches the air.

I have to admit, I feel proud of myself. I'd love to see Costa's face when he gets to learn of this – he needs to know right now – but there's bad service here so I can't send him a message. I get out my mobile and snap away at the yacht coming towards us. Then I grab the binoculars and zoom in on the hull. Yes, sure enough it's The Phantasea. I take out a creased copy of the photograph of the mutt with-the-yacht that I've been carrying around with me since I found the original in the police file – it's a perfect match.

'That's it,' I say to Mitch triumphantly. 'We did it. That's the yacht we've been waiting for – luxury, best-in-class Ocean Lynx 560 catamaran sailing yacht – The Phantasea!' I've been doing my research.

As the yacht approaches, I lock on with the binoculars. Now my suspicions are confirmed. I always knew that gold-digger was in on this! Damien is on the sundeck, stretched out on a lounger in his coconut palm swimming trunks, cool as a cucumber. He's holding a glass of something in his right hand – probably a gin and tonic. I zoom in on his face. He stretches out his arm. Now I can see his lips moving – calling for a top up? The reggae is belting out of big black speakers positioned on each side of the sundeck.

In the outdoor lounge cockpit, standing up steering the boat, it's Christina. She's wearing white shorts and a billowing cotton shirt I haven't seen before. Her blonde hair is windswept and whips around her face when a gust catches it. I have to say she doesn't look as if she's in distress or acting under duress. When I zoom in on her features, she looks serene, happy even. What kind of mother embarks on a sunset booze cruise on a luxury catamaran when her child has been abducted? She's got to be mixed up in this somehow.

There's no sign of Katie. They must have hidden her away in one of the cabins. Perhaps she's already sleeping. It's past her bedtime. There's no time to lose. I think we're heading for a showdown. This feels like a trap, an ambush.

I take a few more pictures on my phone, zooming in on Christina and Damien.

I'm desperate to get aboard and see Katie, give her a huge hug and find out what the hell is going on. It's time to call a halt. I'm not taking the rap for their outrageous behaviour any longer. I scan the double hull of the catamaran with the binoculars, looking for any sign of Katie's presence.

Just then Christina switches the engine to neutral and drops the anchor. Damien calls out to her. She cuts the motor. Through the lens, I see her throw back her head, laughing. She sways over with a gin bottle and a glass tumbler to where he's lying spread-eagled on the deckchair, yanks off his trunks and slings them overboard. Then she kneels down between his legs like a prostitute.

'Oh my God!' I say to Mitch. 'I never knew it. That woman's sex mad.'

I put down the binoculars. Predictably enough, Mitch pounces on them.

'Ah, she's quite a dame.' He whistles softly. 'Sweet lord, I wish she'd deck me!'

'Don't get any bloody ideas,' I say. Even without the binoculars I can see more than I want to. Christina's getting up off the deck now, standing between his knees. She's pouring out the gin while Damien pulls down her shorts with his teeth. What a clown! It doesn't take her long to knock back the gin while Damien does his thing. Now she's straddling him.

'OK show's over,' I say, yanking the binoculars away from Mitch. 'We've got work to do. We're in luck, they shouldn't hear a thing, with that music raging up on deck.'

This is our best chance of getting on to the boat unseen, searching the cabins for Katie, and catching them off their guard – literally *in flagrante* if they keep at it for long enough.

As the red disc of the sun dips into the black line of sea at the horizon, Mitch pushes the rowing boat away from the rocks with the oar.

'Lie down,' he says, 'your top is catching the light.'

Slowly, he rows the boat in a wide arc behind The Phantasea and tucks into the shadows. Now Christina and Damien have rolled on to a canvas trampoline linking the two hulls of the catamaran at the front. The human circus is still in full swing, so this is my opportunity to climb the ladder at the stern and search inside.

I check my phone to see if Costa has responded.

Damn it, still no reply.

My phone is almost out of charge and I still can't get a signal

'Mitch, pass over your mobile, will you. I've got to get hold of Costa.'

'I don't own a mobile... tool of the devil.'

I can understand why. He doesn't want to be traceable 24/7. The only mobile device required to ply his trade is a pistol. But I don't want him coming on board gun-ho and trigger happy – that's just asking for trouble. He'll be more useful to me going back to alert the police.

'You're going to have to go back,' I say. 'As soon as you're on dry land, get to a phone and call 999 or just hotfoot it to the nearest police station. If I can get a signal, I'll keep trying to get hold of Costa until the battery dies.'

Somehow, we've got to raise the alarm. We need to get the police out here fast. Christina and Damien could sail off at any time and then we'll lose track of Katie again.

'Are you crazy?' he says. 'I can't leave you here on your own. It could be dangerous. If they've abducted the little girl, they could do anything.'

'Cool it, Mitch. I didn't know you cared.' I try to lighten the mood. 'Christina's not going to attack Katie – or me. She's Katie's mother, don't forget. It's not like this is stranger abduction. If Katie is there on board with them, she won't be in immediate danger. Christina loves Katie – she won't let Damien do her any harm. And Damien won't touch me when Christina's around.'

'I'm not taking any chances,' says Mitch, tying the rowing boat to the catamaran.

'Mitch, listen to me,' I say. 'He may be a coke head and a con artist, and she may be an alcoholic and a manic depressive – and a sex maniac, based on her recent performances! – but let's face it, they're not murderers, or predatory child abusers for that matter. At least, not Christina.'

Mitch takes out the pistol he's rolled up in a T-shirt stuffed in his bag and opens the cylinder.

'I need you to get the police – that's the best way you can help.'

He's not paying any attention.

'Get me five bullets,' he says. Enacting some kind of macho ritual, he sidesteps over to me and nods down towards his hip. I slip my fingers into the pocket of his jeans and pull out a handful of bullets. I count out five and he loads them into the chambers of the gun.

'They're off their heads on alcohol or drugs or something...' There's a hint of admiration in Mitch's voice. 'From what I saw going on up on the sun deck, they could do anything. She's on fire!'

Mitch is talking in a stage whisper. I see he's enjoying the drama of the situation and that fifty-thousand-dollar reward gives him a powerful incentive to play the part of superhero in the rescue. He hooks the loaded pistol into his belt.

'How would it look, if I left you here, all alone, to fend for yourself?' he says.

'Relax, Mitch, this isn't an Indiana Jones movie,' I say.

'I'll go onboard and search for the girl while you take the boat and go for help,' he says.

'Mitch – I know her. I lived with Christina for six months in New York, don't forget. I don't believe she could actually bring herself to hurt Katie, and I can look after myself. I'm not scared of her and I'm certainly not scared of Damien – I know now he's just a pathetic loser. I'm convinced this is some kind of botched plot all tied up with Damien's gambling debts and drugs deals. Look, you told me earlier, we're almost out of fuel and I'm not strong enough to row this bloody rowing boat back to shore.'

He pulls the pistol out of his belt and stretches out his hand to me.

'At least take the gun.'

I shrink away.

He gives me a stubborn look and slaps the gun and his hand into mine. His grip is as steely as the gun.

'Mitch, it's going to make things worse. You said it yourself, she's "on fire" – well, it's just going to inflame the situation if I go on board brandishing a pistol. I need to calm things down, read them the riot act and make them see sense. They're behaving like teenage delinquents. I'll tell them it's all over but it's not too late to give themselves up and avoid going to jail for a very long time. If they turn the boat, and sail back into port, it can be explained, a moment of madness, a huge mistake, the overwhelming pressure of Damien's compulsive gambling habit, mounting debts etcetera, etcetera…'

But Mitch is sticking to his guns – literally! 'Take the gun or I'm not going anywhere.'

I look down at Mitch's large tawny hand and my small white one, and the barrel of the pistol, poking out between them, gleaming in the setting rays of the sun.

'OK, you win. Let's do a swap – you take my mobile and the minute you get a signal, call the police. Make the

call as soon as you possibly can before the phone dies –
it's almost out of charge. As soon as you make the call,
come back. But if you can't get through or if the phone
conks out, you're just going to have to row all the way
back to dry land and then raise the alarm.'

I give my mobile to Mitch – it feels like handing over a
third limb – and close my fingers round the pistol.

'You're going to have to show me how to use it,' I say,
feeling the weight of the gun in the palm of my hand.

'Same here,' he says fingering my mobile. For the first
time, I see his real smile. And in fact, it quite suits him.

27

Scarlett

As Mitch turns the rowing boat and paddles silently away, I hoist myself up the ladder hanging off the platform in the stern of the boat and crawl onto one of the side decks, keeping low so that I'm hidden by the onboard dinghy chained up in the stern. Although I'm wearing only shorts and a cropped T-shirt, I feel weighted down by the responsibility of carrying a loaded pistol stuffed in the back pocket of my shorts where my mobile should be. The catamaran is rocking to the beat of the reggae. If the lovebirds are still working out on the trampoline, I should have a few minutes to search below deck for Katie before showing myself above deck and trying to make them come to their senses.

The entrance opens onto a spacious open plan saloon bathed in natural light – not unlike the lobby of a luxury boutique hotel with soft leather sofas and bar stools and shiny tables in shades of cream and beige. The whole pristine space is an echo chamber for the thumping beat of reggae and the slap of waves against the shell. But it doesn't look like a crime scene. It looks far too light and smooth and squeaky-clean for that.

There's a galley at the front end of the saloon, separating the open-air cockpit from the main lounge area. Down a short flight of wooden steps, there are two doors that I'm guessing must lead off to the cabins (en-suite, if I remember the sales blurb correctly!). In my previous life, I would have been thrilled to accompany them as Katie's nanny on a cruise... if only things hadn't turned out this way.

Swiftly, I make my way around the cabins. The first is clearly the master bedroom – it's circular in shape, a curved king-size bed filling almost all the space, loaded with silk cushions and quilts. The bed is unmade, the sheets tussled and twisted with vigorous love-making, I suspect. The concave walls are covered with large photographic prints – abstract patterns that look like collections of brightly coloured cells, photographed against a black background. Looking more closely, I can see that the collection of photographs circling the walls of the cabin represent a sequence of dividing cells – first two, then four, then eight. Of course. I see it now – I remember my GCSE biology – it's a human embryo, subdividing, in the first days of development. There's a signature scrawled at the bottom of each print: *Gabrielle Hamilton*, And then a branded logo: Embryonic Love. And below the signature and logo, a title on each print: Day One – Rose, Day Two –Rose, Day Three – Rose, and so on going round the room, ending with Day Five – Rose. The photographs are striking – I had no idea the beginnings of life could be so beautiful. Come to think of it, the translucent multi-coloured spheres look something like a blossoming rose. On the ceiling there's a big circular mirror – symbolic of an embryo too perhaps? If a little kinky, it's rather touching – a love nest celebration of fertility and passion.

I fling open all the cupboard doors. They're mostly empty, just a jumble of Christina and Damien's clothes heaped on the floor. They haven't bothered with hangers. Looks like they're planning a quick getaway, travelling light. On the top shelf, there's a camera and three passports belonging to Christina, Damien and Katie – so it *was* Christina who took Katie's passport out of my safe! My spirits soar... if Katie's passport is here, then she's alive and chances are she's hidden on board.

Shaking with excitement, I move on quickly to the next cabin door. It's locked. I cross to the second hull. There are two more doors. Both are unlocked and I fling them open one after the other. Checking each in turn, the cabins are smaller than the master, a pair of small functional doubles, with sleek furniture, built in cupboards and natural light from large portholes facing out to sea. The rooms look unoccupied, clinically clean and uncluttered. I'd happily have spent a few weeks living in one of these if things had been different! No one's hidden here. There's one more door, towards the rear of the vessel.

There's a sign on the door.

Dark Room - Keep Out

I try the handle.

If they're hiding her anywhere…

When my eyes adjust to the red lighting, I see that what was once a single cabin has been converted into a high-tech, state of the art dark room and digital processing lab. There's an array of sophisticated looking computers, printers and projectors on one wall of the cabin. The porthole is completely blacked out and below it there's a bench set up with an enlarger, three large trays and bottles of chemicals marked developer, stop bath and fixer. Above the shelf there's a drying rack on which several black-and-white prints have been pegged up to dry. I take a closer look and gasp in surprise. They're all images of Katie collecting shells in her red bucket, taken on the beach on the afternoon she disappeared. In one of the prints I can even see myself or at least my bottom half, stretched out on a towel under the parasol in my triangle bikini bottoms. I scan the remaining prints. My hands fly up to my mouth. It's a sequence of portraits of Katie that must have been taken after the abduction. She's alive… unsmiling and sad but alive… sitting on a sun lounger cuddling her blue bunny. The close-up angle has left no room for the background but there's timber decking all around the sun lounger. My guess is they must have been taken up on the deck of The Phantasea. My heart pounds with hope. So I was right, she must be hidden on board.

This cabin with the blacked out porthole would be a good hiding place. Although it seems empty, I check under the bench, behind storage containers and inside every cupboard, just to make sure. But there's no sign of Katie.

Defeated, I go back to the locked door in the first hull and try the handle again – there's no shifting it. Strange… there's no keyhole. Abruptly, the music stops. Any minute now, they might come down below deck. With no time to lose, I look round for something to break open the door. Chances are they'll hear me but I've got to find out if Katie's in there. I'm about to go back up to the galley to look for some kind of tool or kitchen implement that might work as a wrench, when I look up and notice the bolt that's been screwed on to the door right at the top edge. It's clearly a DIY job. Whoever fixed it has made a mess of the doorframe. But the fact it's a bolt and not a key, is significant: someone is being locked in, not locked out.

I reach up and pull back the bolt.

The room is in shadows as the porthole is screened with a makeshift blind. It takes a while for my eyes to adjust to the gloom. It's a small cabin, with a single bed along the starboard side. At one end, there's a mirror above a sink, an open door leading to a small toilet cubicle, and some wooden panels that look like built in full height cupboards. It appears empty and unoccupied. I step though the doorway to check under the bed and in the cupboards – just in case there's a big enough space to hide a small child. As I turn round to come out again a dark shape catches my eye, a hump of denser black low down behind the open door.

My God, is that Katie!

I press the light switch but nothing happens – maybe someone's removed the bulbs – so I rip open the blind that's been clumsily tacked to the wooden sill and the cabin floods with moonlight. The figure is not a young child but that of an adult, huddled on the floor.

It's not Katie...

She's sitting on the floor, hugging her knees, with her eyes closed and head back, resting against the wall. Her wrists are tied with cord. I sink down onto my knees in front of her.

It's Christina.

'Christina, what the hell is going on?' She opens her eyes.

'Oh, it's you,' she says wearily.

Her white shirt is torn and her lip is swollen and bleeding.

'Did that pig hit you?'

I put my arms around her gently. They must have come down while I was admiring the prints in the master cabin. Is it some kind of sado-masochistic sex thing they've got going on here?

'What's happening, Christina?'

He must have roughed her up on deck then shoved her in here and bolted the door.

'Did that bastard rape you?'

I touch her cheek gently.

'Oh my God, what has he done to you?'

Just as I'm helping her up onto the bed and leaning over to untie her wrists, I feel a presence darkening the doorway behind me like a spectral moonlight shadow. That prickling-flesh sensation, stock image of trashy ghost stories, spreads through me. I look back over my shoulder.

I double-take – literally. I'm seeing double – either that or the spliffs are kicking in and making me hallucinate.

It's Christina again, or her shadow, at least – same tall, lean figure, same bone structure, same profile, same long, wavy hair.

She's standing in my shadow, so I move to one side, to get a better view, still transfixed by what I see.

Now glowing in the moonlight, she too wears a white shirt, unbuttoned but not torn and her face is unblemished, perfect, a picture of happiness and health. The sex goddess of the sundeck smiles at me.

'Hello Scarlett. Welcome aboard The Phantasea. We've been expecting you. What took you so long?

What took you so long?

The words echo through my brain, as I stand there stunned, gaping.

I turn to Christina and see a pathetic, broken version of herself.

I'm shaking so much now that I can barely open my mouth to speak.

'What's happening? I don't understand. Who did this to you?' I look from Christina to her spectral twin. 'Was it her? Did she beat you up like this? Or was it that sadistic bastard up on deck?'

'Calm down, Scarlett. Don't be so melodramatic,' says the other woman. 'Just a few scratches… she'll live.'

She holds out her hand.

'By the way, it's Gabrielle, very pleased to meet you. I've heard so much about you.'

She smiles and those perfectly straight white teeth, the same as Christina's, glint in the moonlight.

I ignore her hand, shrink away from her and stand protectively in front of Christina, struck dumb with fear.

'I don't suppose she's told you much about me,' says Gabrielle, gesturing vaguely towards Christina. 'Lara likes to pretend I don't exist. She's written me out of her life story.'

Lara? Lara? What is this crazy woman talking about?

She's there in the doorway, an apparition, so charming and so civilised and so utterly terrifying.

Suddenly I find my voice.

'What have you done with her? Where's Katie? Where are you hiding her?' I'm screaming at her now. 'I know she's here somewhere.'

Gabrielle laughs haughtily.

'Calm down, you ridiculous, hysterical girl. I have absolutely no idea who you are talking about.'

And with that, she backs out of the room and bolts the door.

28

12 May 2010: The Bridge of Sighs, Venice

This faded black-and-white Polaroid makes me sick but the album wouldn't be complete without it.

Can you see the crease lines? It was folded into four, tucked away in James' wallet – that's where I found it, on that fatal day. You could say, this scrap of paper sealed his fate. You scrawled the date in pencil on the back – 12 May 2010 – so you were pregnant with my baby when this photograph was taken.

Look at you! Leaning back against his shoulder, rocking to his beating heart, rapt in easy ecstasy as you gaze at the intricate carvings above your heads.

You and James, together, rocking my baby in your belly, without me, in a gondola, in Venice. Treachery and fornication are imprinted on your up-turned faces, in the dancing shadows of the Bridge of Sighs.

*

Gabrielle drove James to Heathrow. He was going on a business trip to Milan for five days – at least that's what he'd told her. The pharmaceuticals conference was an important networking opportunity. He couldn't miss it, much as he hated to be leaving her alone again. It was unfortunate timing, just when she was feeling so stressed and anxious and the very morning after 'that day' which James so annoyingly insisted on referring to as 'Blast Off' – the date on which the blastocyst transfer of their genetic embryos into Lara's uterus (following the petri-dish fertilisation of Gabrielle's eggs) had been scheduled to take place in New York. The eggs, frozen through a procedure known as cryopreservation some years earlier, had previously been exported to the American fertility clinic chosen by Lara. Gabrielle had not been required to travel to New York at all. She would happily have made the journey but Lara had insisted that Gabrielle should have no contact with the clinic. Lara would take charge of everything and go through the medical procedures alone.

James, however, had been required to attend NYC Reproductive Medicine Associates in person some days earlier to perform his part in the surrogacy and being a practical man had combined this with a business trip to visit important medical associates in New York. He was empowered to deal with the medical and administrative formalities at the clinic on behalf of both genetic parents leaving his wife strangely excluded from this momentous event and more isolated than she had ever felt in her entire life. On his return, James found her in some distress. She had been waking up every day with nausea and a splitting headache – it was just like morning sickness in fact. She was suffering vicariously.

'You're bound to be feeling bad,' he said. 'We both want this so much and we've been through such tough times.'

But Gabrielle knew this was something more elemental than James could understand.

'You just don't get it,' she said. 'This is between her and me.' Although separated by thousands of miles and a vast ocean, Gabrielle felt as if the intense intimacy of the planned surrogacy, had unleashed some kind of telepathic response in her body and mind, something she hadn't experienced since they were little girls. Though so conflicted, they were so close, almost the same flesh and blood. She could imagine and visualise her twin's physical and emotional turmoil so vividly that it had become her own.

Gabrielle woke every night with excruciating lower back pain and stomach cramps. Then one night she woke screaming from a nightmare in which she herself, pregnant and in the throes of agony, gave birth to a horribly deformed creature. In the dream, James stood at her bedside, holding her hand, and laughing uncontrollably at the sight of the monster being pulled out from between her legs. And while he stood there laughing, she called out again and again, 'They've mixed up the eggs, it's not my baby... give me my baby.'

'This is getting out of control,' said James. 'I'm going to make an appointment for you to see your therapist. This surrogacy business is having a detrimental effect on your mental well-being. You need to increase your medication or get some extra mindfulness counselling or CBT or something…'

Gabrielle felt all the more bereft when James took off for Milan.

'I'll call you every day,' he promised. 'And I'll bring you back something special.'

'*Dolce et Gabbana* perfume please – The One,' called out Gabrielle, as she waved him off through security. 'I've almost run out.'

James kept his word, calling every evening to entertain her with amusing conference anecdotes. When he bounded out of the taxi on his return a week later and burst through the front door looking a million dollars in a new Italian leather jacket and tailored chinos, Gabrielle raced into his open arms, all the more welcoming as each hand was holding gift bags emblazoned with enticing Italian brand names.

'You're looking hot,' she said, taking in his suntanned face and sharp new jacket. 'So you found time for shopping, and it looks as if you've caught the sun. I hope you didn't enjoy yourself too much without me!'

She was delighted to discover that not only had he bought her a nice big bottle of her favourite fragrance but also a very stylish handbag in the best soft brown Florentine calfskin leather and a chic double-looping wide leather belt with a brass buckle.

'Love the bag,' said Gabrielle. 'It's exactly the style I would have chosen for myself.' It had a long leather shoulder strap so you could sling it casually across your body. It was both practical and the height of fashion. She was pleasantly surprised as James was not a handbag connoisseur! He laughed.

'I can't really take any credit for choosing it. Francesca picked it out for me.'

'And who is Francesca?' said Gabrielle, with a frosty smile.

'Ah! Francesca... she's the very pretty and sexy Italian shop assistant who took pity on this helpless Englishman.'

'Whatever... I love it,' said Gabrielle. She threw the handbag to one side and picked up the belt. 'Come here and stop teasing, or I'll strap you to the bed.' There was a hint of menace in her voice.

Playfully, she looped the belt around his waist and hers and pushed him roughly backwards onto the mattress, flipping onto his chest between his splayed legs.

'There, I've got you now,' she murmured, as she grabbed the buckle and tightened the belt until her hips were crushed against his loins.'

Later when Gabrielle began to suspect what had really happened in Italy, the smell of the perfume was enough to make her retch, and she couldn't stand the sight of the bag or the belt any longer, so she stuffed all three into the back of her wardrobe. Even though she couldn't prove it, she had a feeling in her gut that James was hiding something. He was such an incurable flirt. Was this Francesca really just a shop assistant? Or someone he had met at the conference and taken out on a date – or worse?

Of course, she was right – something had happened in Italy. However, Gabrielle's suspicions about Francesca were unfounded. There *was* no shop assistant called Francesca. It was Lara who had chosen the belt and handbag for Gabrielle – which was why they conformed so perfectly to her taste.

On the day in late April that James attended the clinic on Seventh Avenue, Lara had been surprised to hear from him. Gabrielle had stipulated in the surrogacy agreement that there should be no contact between James and Lara in New York. The protocol governing relations between the genetic father and the surrogate mother was designed to be as arms' length as possible. This suited Lara well. She was not in the mood for a sentimental reunion. She had spent the day shopping on Fifth Avenue, coming home somewhat perversely with an expensive designer bikini from *Calvin Klein*.

James apologised for telephoning but explained that the clinical procedure had been so cold and sterile that he couldn't help himself. He told her that as he had walked out of NYC Reproductive Medicine Associates on that beautiful spring morning, he had felt suddenly very lonely amongst the streaming crowd of commuters and had been compelled to call her.

'I know I'm not supposed to be contacting you but I think it's important to mark this day somehow. Let me take you out for dinner at least.'

'No, James,' she said firmly. 'That's not a good idea.'

'Oh come on. Don't be such a bore!' he said. 'It'll be miserable to be here on my last night in the Big Apple

dining alone! Just name the place – I'll take you wherever
you want to go, the most expensive, exclusive restaurant
in New York. Let's dine with the stars tonight. You deserve
to be spoilt. After all, you won't be wining and dining
once the pregnancy starts in a few days' time.'

Lara chose The View, New York's only revolving
restaurant, on the 48th floor of the Marriott Hotel, which
had spectacular views of the Empire State Building and
many other iconic buildings in the city. They met in the
lobby at eight o'clock. Lara chose an exotic salad with
vibrant colours and chiselled vegetable sculptures, while
James feasted on a twelve-ounce Texan char-grilled steak
and fries 'flown in this morning from the Lone-Star State.'

'I'm getting healthy for the pregnancy,' said Lara. 'Once
I've agreed to do something, I do it properly.'

Nevertheless, when James ordered the waiter to crack
open a bottle of champagne 'to toast the baby' she allowed
herself three glasses, and by the end of the meal she was
dizzy with drink, and laughter and the endlessly revolving
view.

'Weird to think that in a petri dish on Seventh Avenue
your baby has already been conceived,' she said.

James leant across and held her hand.

'Our baby,' he said.

Lara pulled her hand away.

'I've got some gifts for you,' he said, suddenly serious. 'I
know Gabrielle is going to pay you but I wanted to thank
you personally for your generosity in doing this for us.'

He placed a large brown envelope on the table then
reached into the pocket of his jacket and pulled out a

small turquoise box, marked with the Tiffany logo and tied with a white satin bow.

Lara opened it – a single solitaire diamond ring.

'What's this all about?' she said. Her eyes were fixed on the diamond, gleaming in the candlelight. 'Seriously?' She wasn't smiling any more.

'I bought it this evening – just as the shops were closing. It's the only way I could get a table,' said James with calculated flippancy. 'They told me you have to book six weeks in advance – but I begged them. I asked to speak to the manager and told him I was intending to propose to you over dinner. Look, they're over there, spying on us.'

He pointed at the waiters giving furtive looks in the direction of their table.

'Besides, it might come in useful,' he said. There may be times when you'd rather not be taken for a single mother once it becomes obvious that you're pregnant. Americans can be so reactionary in their views.'

Lara laughed bitterly.

'That's the most cynical and absurd "un-proposal" that I can possibly imagine. I feel like Alice at the Mad Hatter's "un-birthday" tea party!'

She tried on the ring. It fitted perfectly.

'How did you manage that, you clever man? Now let me guess, you checked the size of Gabrielle's engagement ring before you left for the airport.'

She twisted off the ring, placed it back in the box, and pushed the box back across the table.

'I'm not her clone, you know, James. We're not one and the same person. You're married to another woman.'

She got up and walked away from the table, ignoring the group of waiters standing expectantly at the side of the bar, ready to congratulate the happy pair.

James threw down a wodge of dollar bills and caught up with Lara at the lifts.

'OK, I'm sorry. I'm an idiot. But look, you forgot this. He handed over the brown envelope. I wanted to give you the ring first. But I think you'll be able to accept this – if you just let me explain.'

As they rode the elevator down the forty-eight floors, Lara ripped open the envelope. Inside was a small guidebook to Venice and a sheet of paper headed 'The Magic of Italy,' giving details of a reservation for a luxury twin bedroom at the Gritti Palace hotel – 'an opulent conversion of a fifteenth century palazzo in a spectacular setting overlooking the Grand Canal' – and a travel itinerary showing her return flight from New York to Venice airport with transfer by water taxi to the steps of the hotel.

'Don't get me wrong. See, I've booked you a twin room, to share with Gabrielle. But please don't tell her you'll be there. It's a surprise.'

'I haven't said I'm coming yet,' said Lara, glaring at him. 'I've done my homework. Transatlantic travel is not recommended in the early weeks of a gestational surrogacy. I'm sure you'll have the best interests of your baby at heart!'

But the 'yet' said it all. The allure of Venice and the Gritti Palace was working its magic.

'I've got a pharmaceuticals conference in Milan the week after next. This is my clever plan to bring you two girls together again. I know you've grown apart these past few years.'

Lara gave him a withering look.

'Listen, Gabrielle is in need of a holiday. I've persuaded her to come to Venice while I'm at the conference in Milan. I suggested she could have two or three days seeing the art exhibitions on her own and I would join her at the weekend when the conference finishes. And then, this afternoon, at the clinic, I thought of asking you. We'll keep it a secret from Gabrielle, so she'll be surprised to find you there. It will be perfect for the two of you to have some time together, alone, without me, before the baby is born.'

The lift reached the ground floor and the doors opened, just in time, as Lara began to feel a claustrophobic panic coming over her. She pushed past him and walked out briskly onto the street. He ran after her and continued, earnestly.

'You've seen so little of each other the past few years. And then I'm always there, and that causes tension for obvious reasons. She's feeling jealous and depressed. The idea of the surrogacy brings back so many painful memories of the miscarriages and our stillborn baby. She says she can't face seeing you, that just the thought of you being pregnant makes her hate you. It's understandable. But once you're together, I'm sure you'll work it out. You can make plans for the baby and Gabrielle can start to feel she's a part of it all. Besides, you deserve a holiday too. It's so good and unselfish of you to help us in this way. It's the very least that we can do. I'll come and join you both in Venice at the weekend and we can all have some fun.'

'I can make my own way home. Goodnight.' Lara was losing patience with him. 'I'll think about it and let you know.'

'Good luck,' said James, as they parted ways. 'I'll be thinking of you on Thursday.'

On the evening of 7 May 2010, Lara boarded the plane at JFK airport bound for Italy. Lara's new boyfriend was 'gutted' that she was going to Venice without him but since she had said she was going on holiday with her twin, he couldn't very well protest. He would have been still more dismayed had he known that the true reason she had bailed on their lunch date earlier that same day was not because she was behind with her packing (as she had told him) but in order to attend her follow-up appointment at NYC Reproductive Medicine Associates. She had been determined to keep the surrogacy secret from him for as long as possible. For now, more than ever, her life was a tangled web of secrets and lies.

In the event it was not until after her appointment at the clinic and with a heavy heart that Lara had finally made up her mind to go ahead with the Italian holiday. Her doctor had confirmed what she already knew from having carried out a home pregnancy test. Unfortunately, the implantation of Gabrielle and James's embryos had not been successful. She was not pregnant.

In view of the unique family circumstances of the planned surrogacy, Lara persuaded her doctor to allow her to be the one to communicate the sad news to the genetic parents that the embryo transfer had failed. Lara was not without empathy for her twin. She understood that Gabrielle would be bitterly disappointed, heartbroken even, and she resolved that it would be kinder to tell her in person, to discuss face-to-face the possibility of a second attempt and even to work towards a reconciliation by spending some time together in Venice before embarking on a second round of IVF.

Lara received VIP treatment when she checked in to the Gritti Palace on that sensational, sparkling morning in May. At reception Lara was greeted as 'Mrs Hamilton' and informed that her booking had been upgraded to the Hemingway Presidential Suite. She was not surprised to be mistaken for Gabrielle since this had happened on a regular basis throughout their childhood. She didn't bother to correct the lady who handed her the key – as she was sharing the suite with her twin, it was of no importance. Hardly auspicious, Lara mused to herself, reading the name in the plaque on the door. She knew that cursed with bad luck, Hemingway had almost died twice in two separate plane crashes in Africa and had ended his life with a botched, but nevertheless fatal suicide by shooting himself in the head. Nevertheless, the presidential suite sounded pretty classy.

Unlocking the door, she was delighted to find that the accommodation more than lived up to the description in the leaflet.

This sumptuous suite features five floor-to-ceiling
French doors that open onto a balcony affording
magical views of the Grand Canal

The views were indeed breath-taking. She threw down
her bag and looked out through the open French doors.

For once, the hyperbole was not an exaggeration. The
room was extravagant and ornate with Venetian Rococo
mouldings and Murano glass chandeliers. A collection
of works by Hemingway was lined up on mahogany
bookshelves. She ran her finger along the spines of the old-
fashioned volumes – pausing for a few seconds when she
reached the leather-bound edition of *For Whom The Bell
Tolls* – the feel of the dusty spine and the yellowing pages
making her nostalgic for her Oxford days, and those long
hours in musty libraries each week of term, pooled in the
glow of an old-fashioned lamp.

But the best thing was the view. The beauty of the scene
made her heart ache.

As she headed for the balcony, she almost tripped over
a suitcase and heard someone drawing back the curtains
in the adjoining bedroom. Gabrielle must already have
arrived.

She threw open the door, expecting to take her sister by
surprise, but stopped in her tracks.

'Oh... It's you!' she exclaimed. 'What are you doing
here?' Looking every bit like he'd just stepped out of a
Merchant Ivory film, in white cotton shirt and pressed
cream flannels, James was standing by the open window

watching the sunlight striking the silver dome of Santa Maria Della Salute. 'I might have guessed... of course, how stupid of me!' she said flatly.

He turned at the sound of her voice and drew her into his arms.

'Look, isn't this glorious.'.

'Where's Gabrielle?' said Lara. She pulled away. 'Don't tell me, she's gone shopping already.'

'She's not coming, is she?' said Lara, as they sat down to a candlelit supper at a table laid for three on the terrace of the hotel. 'You tricked me again. It was all lies.' James remained silent, watching the gondolas gliding past in the shadows. Just below the terrace, water lapped softly against the stone walls.

Angered by James' deception, Lara had deliberated all afternoon about whether and when to reveal that the embryo transfer had failed. She thought it only fair that Gabrielle should be the first to know.

'I'm sorry.' James had kept up the pretence all afternoon that Gabrielle had been delayed by work commitments and had made a last-minute change to her flight. 'I knew you'd never come unless I made up a story about Gabrielle coming too. She's at home. I thought of asking her but she's preoccupied with a new photography project. She's got an idea for a new exhibition at the gallery in Chelsea. Embryonic Love, I think it's going to be called – photographs and a film montage with music and coloured lights, gigantic prints of microscopic images she's managed to obtain from the New York clinic of the first few days' development of our pre-implantation embryo.'

'That woman is obsessed,' said Lara. She bit into a black olive. Despite her annoyance she felt sad for Gabrielle. 'What did you tell her?' She licked the oil off her fingertip.

'She thinks I'm at a conference in Milan – well that much is true. I did go to the conference. It isn't all lies.'

In such a beautiful place, Lara found it difficult to be mad at him for long. She didn't want to spoil the holiday for herself by telling James the truth. If she told him that the implantation procedure had failed, he would either cut short the holiday or spend it in a black mood. And she refused to feel guilty for her own part.

It wasn't her fault. Why should she beat herself up about it? They had forced her into this. So she said nothing. She'd tell them when she got back to New York. Then they'd just have to start all over again with a second attempt.

She was still planning to make a big sacrifice for Gabrielle – the most unselfish act she had ever contemplated in her life. She would be lending her body to her twin for a full nine months, putting herself through all sorts of physical and emotional traumas to give Gabrielle and James a child to complete their family. In return, it seemed only fair to 'borrow' her sister's husband for a few days. The planned surrogacy provided the perfect cover. Gabrielle need never know. James would certainly never tell her. He had engineered the whole situation. And now in full confidence that the gestational pregnancy was underway, he was treating her like his new bride – the precious bridal vessel for his longed-for unborn child.

'Come here,' said James. He tasted of olives and red wine. 'Like it or not, we're bound together forever now.'

'Are you kissing me or her?' said Lara. She understood that in his mind, she and Gabrielle were one and the same – merging in his imagination like concentric circles into a single identity with him at the epicentre, until he could make love to them both without any consciousness of committing an infidelity.

He didn't appear to be suffering any self-doubt or remorse. So why should she?

Carefree as young lovers, they spent the days basking in warm spring sunshine at over-priced cafes in the Piazza San Marco, gliding in gondolas though winding canals, wandering the maze of flower-fringed streets and bridges, shopping for perfume and leather goods and sinister carnival masks, sampling succulent Venetian cuisine, and making love in the opulence of their suite in the Gritti Palace hotel.

If Lara occasionally felt a frisson of guilt, like a cooling breeze in a shady canal, it simply added to the enticement of the romance. As she sat back on the balcony sipping prosecco and gazing over the panorama of palazzos, and bridges and boats, she fell easily into the role of the ill-fated romantic heroine of a late-nineteenth-century novel whose passions had been unleashed by the intense sunlight and brilliant colours, and overwhelming sensuality of the landscapes and the people encountered on her Grand Tour. She gave full reign to her literary imagination. It was delicious, so far from the frantic, yet mundane, reality of working life in the financial district of Manhattan.

Lara stopped James from taking any photographs – these days were for living, not recording, and it was too risky. She knew this passionate, technicolour sequence in their story could not make the final cut. So she was vigilant but, as it turned out, not vigilant enough. One moment of distraction, one pushy gondolier.

One image found its way into James' wallet, one unfocused photograph, beneath the Bridge of Sighs, folded and soon forgotten.

A couple of weeks after she returned to New York, Lara purchased a pregnancy test from her local drugstore. The next day she woke early, breakfasted and spent more than an hour putting on her make-up and adjusting her hair. She had to look just right to carry this off. From her apartment, she walked briskly across Central Park and on to Seventh Avenue for an unscheduled meeting at NYC Reproductive Medicine Associates. Now that she was pregnant, there was some unfinished business she needed to attend to, a settling of old scores that would give her peace of mind.

Some twenty minutes later, she walked out of the clinic with a new spring in her step. She made her way down to the subway, overtaking commuters as she ran down the steps, found a seat on the crowded train, rubbed off and reapplied her lipstick, and untied and brushed out her hair. That done, now she put on her headphones, closed her eyes, and filled her head with visions of Venice while she counted the five stops to her Wall Street destination.

Later that day she phoned James with the joyful news: 'Congratulations, we're pregnant.'

29

Scarlett

After Gabrielle locks us in, Christina collapses onto the bed, weak with emotion. I release her hands by biting through the cord binding her wrists, and swab her face improvising a cold compress with one of the towels hanging by the sink. I can scarcely trust myself to talk. Eventually I say, 'Why didn't you tell me you had a twin? Why didn't you tell the police? What have you dragged me into?'

She says nothing.

I search the room for something I can use to break down the door or smash open the porthole. There's nothing.

'How long have you been here?' I ask.

'I've lost track of time,' she says. 'I came onboard the night I had dinner with Damien at Clamities.

'I warned you that was a bad idea!' I mutter.

I hammer on the door with my fists and yell 'open the door' again and again, fighting a wave of panic as the claustrophobia of being trapped takes hold.

Get a grip, I tell myself.

I roll backwards on to the bed and try kicking the porthole with my feet. Not even a tremor. The safety glass is solid. It's not exactly a prison cell but we're well and truly her captives.

Surely it would only be a matter of time before Mitch told Costa. Costa will come and rescue us. I don't really believe it, but I've got to keep the panic down somehow.

As I roll off the bed, I feel something hard, digging into my back.

The gun.

I could kick myself. If I hadn't been so paralysed with shock at the sudden appearance of Christina's twin, I might have had the sense to make good use of the weapon. But it all happened so quickly.

Just then, there's a rumble above us, followed by a loud splash. I leap up and peer through the porthole. The water surrounding the yacht shimmers with light as its security lights come on. The dinghy comes into view. That's what made the splash – as they launched it into the water.

There are two people in the dinghy: that traitor Damien, now in jeans and a T-shirt, and Gabrielle – Gabrielle-not-Christina – wearing a thick sweater over her white shirt.

But there's no Katie. What have they done with her? Is she still alive?

I hammer on the porthole with the palms of my hands, and yell at the top of my voice.

'Stop, stop, let us out…'

I have no idea if they can hear me or not but Gabrielle turns briefly. I see her mouth move as she says something to Damien and they both laugh.

What a bitch!

My stomach starts to churn as the yacht rises and falls in the swell. They've anchored it here – with us imprisoned onboard. That woman abducted Katie. But if Katie's not hidden here, then she must be hidden somewhere else. Was this the plan all along? To lure Christina and I on to the boat leaving the coast clear for Gabrielle and Damien to collect Katie from wherever they've hidden her and make a quick getaway?

After the initial shock of seeing Christina's twin things are falling into place. Those things I've been grasping for like lost images from a dream, are now resurfacing in my head – the description of the woman in the witness statement, the vile parody of Christina I encountered at the villa, the images of 'Christina' that Costa identified on the CCTV footage carrying away Katie's birth certificate and other papers, the glimpses of someone in my room when Gabrielle defaced my mirror with lipstick, and even that morning at the apartment in New York where I caught Damien red-handed going through Christina's desk, rifling through her documents. Now it all makes sense. Gabrielle's been playing with us. It's all been part of a long-planned, elaborate charade to lure us onto the boat and make us her hostages while Katie is spirited away.

It's just after midnight but there's still no sign of Mitch or Costa.

'Come on boys, where the hell are you?'

How long does it take to send out a police patrol boat and a helicopter?

In this part of the world, it shouldn't be too difficult to find a way of getting Katie off the island. They'll simply disappear into some Latin American hellhole and wait for the trail to go cold.

With each passing second, I feel more despondent.

What if my phone ran out of charge? What if Mitch couldn't work out how to use it? What if the police don't launch a rescue operation until dawn or at all?

We lie side by side on the narrow bed, locked in the single cabin. I'm aching all over from my night under the stars in the rowing boat. Christina's battered and exhausted. She's mute, shivering and moaning. I stare at the ceiling wondering what to do next.

I pull the blanket up round her.

'Is your sister completely mad or just a very bad person?' I ask. 'If you want to find Katie and get out of this alive, you've got to talk – now.'

She covers her face with her hands.

'Come on, Christina. Tell me the truth. We've got to work out what the hell's going on, or she'll be gone, perhaps forever, you may never see her again.'

At last she sits up and leans against the glass porthole, looking out to sea.

'She's finally beaten me,' she says.

'I won't let you give up!' I scream at her. Then I take her hand and speak gently. 'You've known all along it was Gabrielle, haven't you? From the moment you heard Katie was missing, you knew that Gabrielle had taken her.'

She nods. 'Yes. I never really believed Katie had drowned. I know what she's capable of. She's my twin after all. That's why I've been trying to shake her off ever since Katie was born. She's a psychopath – it's as simple as that.'

Suddenly Christina leaps off the bed. 'There's got to be something we can use to break out of here,' she says, flinging open the cupboards and tugging uselessly at the pipes under the sink.

There's nothing.

'The only thing that might get us out of here is this gun,' I say. 'We could try and shoot the bolts off the door. But we've only got five bullets and I don't want to waste them.'

'Give me the gun!' she yells. 'I've got to get out. God only knows what's happening to Katie. I can't bear to think of it.'

She starts feeling her way manically round the walls of the cabin, beginning to pant and hyperventilate.

I grab her wrists and speak to her very firmly, as if to a child.

'Christina.' I make her look at me. 'I don't want to waste the bullets. We're safe for now. The police should be on their way. Costa won't abandon us here. Let's give them two more hours. If there's no sign of the police by 3 a.m., we'll blast our way out. Now, while we're waiting to be rescued, tell me everything you know. There might be something we've missed – some clue as to where Katie is hidden.'

Eventually she calms down and staring through the porthole into the blackness, the words come flooding out at last.

'It's not the only time Gabrielle's tried to kidnap Katie. The first time was when Katie was just five days old. There had been some complications at the birth so we had to stay in the hospital until I was fit enough to go home. I was taking a shower when Gabrielle came into my room. I had left the door to the shower room a few inches open. Katie was sleeping peacefully in the cot when Gabrielle walked in and just took her. The nurses on duty saw her going out of the room with Katie wrapped in the pink shawl and mistook her for me. As I was rinsing my hair I had a sudden surge of panic. Maybe it was that twin telepathy or I had felt her shadow passing behind me. Anyhow I leapt out of the shower and saw the empty cot. I ran out to the nurses' station screaming for my baby. Thank God, they radioed for security who stopped her just as she was heading for the exit. Brazen as ever, Gabrielle claimed she was taking the baby out for some fresh air while her sister took a shower. The hospital was happy to believe her despite my protests – she was family and she hadn't actually left the premises. It would have been difficult to prove intent to steal the baby, they told me. What's more, the breach of security on the maternity ward was embarrassing and the hospital preferred to hush it up. The attempted abduction wasn't even logged as a security incident. In fact, they made me feel like I was a hysterical new mother, overwrought with postnatal hormones and sleepless nights. The in-house psychologist came over to see me and every time I mentioned the word, 'abduction' she told me I was overreacting and suffering from post-partum anxiety that was 'distorting my view of reality'.'

Christina goes over to the sink and splashes water on her face. She looks at her reflection in the glass. 'She's my mirror-image.' She shudders. 'Identical but opposite. She's evil.' I guess she sees her twin looking back at her. She turns away.

'As you can imagine, I never felt safe after that,' continues Christina, matter of fact again. 'As soon as I got home, I changed the locks, my phone numbers and my email address. I deleted my Facebook account and anything that gave me an online identity. I ditched the name Lara and started using the name Christina. I changed the spelling of my surname. I didn't want to lose it altogether. I've always liked the name because of Jacqueline Kennedy – always admired her style. Anyway, I reverted to being a pre-digital individual – relying on paper and pen and exchanging emails and texts only when absolutely necessary. Within a few weeks, I had moved to a new apartment and handed in my notice at work. I tried to cut myself off from the family altogether, to break all contact with Gabrielle and to forge a new life under this new identity.'

She smiles ruefully.

'Being based in New York made it easier. But I had to be constantly vigilant especially as I knew that Gabrielle's design and marketing company had a photo studio in New York that she visited on a regular basis. There were two more scares when Katie was about eighteen months old. First, I found out that a woman pretending to be me had turned up to collect Katie at her day-care. Fortunately, Katie had been sick during the night and my nanny at the time had kept her home that day. Then a few months later the day-care manager called me at the office to give me a telling-off. Apparently, during an outing to Central Park I had been spotted standing behind a tree taking pictures with a long-lens camera "in contravention of nursery policy" which prohibited the taking of photographs of the children. Well, I was pleased to hear the day-care was so strict on security, but it gave me a scare all the same, and it made me look a fool.'

'Why on earth didn't you go to the police?' I say. 'These were serious incidents. The nursery could have backed you up.'

'I had my reasons. Let's just say I didn't want the police digging around in my private affairs or raking through my past. Anyway, I didn't think they'd take me seriously. Gabrielle's my twin and Katie's auntie after all.'

What is this dark secret in her past, I wonder. I'm tempted to ask but instead I say bitterly, 'Perhaps if you had gone to the police two years ago back in New York, I wouldn't be trapped with you right now in this God-damned floating prison.'

I sit up on the bed to look out of the porthole. A vast moon hangs above us glinting on the water and giving Christina a menacing look as shadows dapple through the cabin and across her face. This is beginning to resemble the set of a low-budget horror movie. I catch a glimpse of myself in the mirror. I look strangely sinister too.

Though it's the middle of the night the cabin is warm and stuffy. With the minibar stashed full of nothing but vodka, I thank God we've got the sink. It's probably not drinking water but at least we won't die of thirst. I put my mouth under the tap. The gushing water helps to clear my head and I'm struck by the thought that Christina must have known from day one that Damien was in on the abduction of Katie.

She doesn't attempt to deny it.

'When Damien didn't turn up at the play area I had a bad feeling – even before I knew that Katie was gone. But when I found out about his gambling debts at the Black Jack which seemed to give him an alibi, I knew he couldn't be acting alone. I decided not to let on that I suspected him. I thought if I could play my cards right there was a chance he would lead me to her. And I know Gabrielle will do anything to keep Katie away from me, so I didn't want the police blundering in. That's why I didn't hand over Damien's mobile. I wanted to find out whether he was acting for Gabrielle and I prayed that if he was I could intercept her texts and get to Katie first.'

Now I'm bubbling with self-righteous anger.

'You suspected Damien and yet you didn't tell me? I can't believe it! I put myself in danger with that brute and you didn't try to stop me. He practically raped me!'

'You can't blame me,' says Christina. 'I wasn't even awake when you went off that morning – you knocked me out with the sleeping pills remember!'

I can't argue with that, but I also can't let this go. Christina's silence and duplicity has hampered the investigation and all my efforts to find Katie.

'We've missed so many opportunities. I went to the villa. I thought he had kidnapped you. I had a whole conversation with Gabrielle thinking it was you. She slung a glass of red wine at my head.'

I'm so annoyed with her for not coming clean about her twin sister.

'It must have been her who put Katie's purse in your bag when you were at the spa. And it must have been her who came to your room and took away the documents when I was hiding in your bathroom pretending to be sick. And it must have been her who wrote on my mirror on the very first night. She's been haunting the hotel, caught on the CCTV images, mistaken for you, coming and going just as she pleases. She took Katie off the beach in plain daylight – it's all in that American woman's witness statement. I was sure you don't have a pair of Tiffany sunglasses! As your identical twin, it was so easy for her to take Katie away without anyone batting an eyelid. And now I understand why Katie went off with Gabrielle without staging a tantrum on the beach. In fact, Gabrielle wasn't a stranger to her at all. Gabrielle has been stalking her for years – and not only stalking her, but spending time with her, getting to know her, acting out the part of her mother. Poor Katie must have been so confused! No wonder Katie is always so anxious whenever you aren't around – always asking "Where's Mummy" again and again! All those long hours you spent working late at the office... there may have been many times Gabrielle went to the nursery without you finding out. Once Damien was your lover, there were more opportunities. You were so distracted. And then there were my days off when Damien offered to cover while you put in extra hours at work, and those Sunday afternoons when we went together to browse the second-hand bookshops in the Upper East Side, and that time you came to the Brooklyn Bowl hip hop festival. I bet Gabrielle was seeing Katie each time Damien was supposed to be babysitting!

My voice rises in anger and frustration.

'I just don't understand why you didn't tell me the truth until now?'

Christina takes a long drink from the cold tap, wipes her hand across her mouth and turns to face me.

'Because Scarlett, I couldn't trust anyone, not even you, especially not you. After Katie was taken, I feared you were in her pay too. If you must know, I thought you and Damien were acting together and working for Gabrielle. So when Costa interviewed me alone at the police station a few days after Katie's disappearance, I told him I thought your story about having been drugged was made-up. I believed you and Damien had been grooming Katie for months. And I believed that in accordance with Gabrielle's orders, you had staged the drowning scenario together while I was asleep in my room. Costa promised not to say anything to you about our conversations. Instead he decided to string you along and get you involved in the investigation, in the hope that you would give away some clue as to where Katie is hidden.'

Now I'm truly incensed. Here I am, a prisoner, literally risking life and limb for a woman who doesn't even trust me and has actually named me as a suspect!

So that explains why Costa felt justified in using his aggressive interrogation techniques on me and yet keeping me by his side, so close and confiding. He was trying to break me and keep an eye on me all at once.

'There's no point getting upset,' she says. 'Don't forget, you named *me* as a suspect. And I have no idea if Costa is playing it straight with me. For all I know, he's been stringing me along too. I don't trust the police. They've never helped me when I needed them in the past!'

30

Photograph Ten

20 August 2010: Lower Manhattan Maternity Hospital

Recognise this? Here she is! Rose – her image captured in the print of our last prenatal scan – named in loving memory of my first born, Juliet Rosalind Hamilton. I've seen so many. Little mermaids and mermen in their amniotic sacs.

'And not waving but drowning' – that's the way it always turned out in the end.

With a photographer's eye, I've learned to decipher them.

Now I'm skilled at detecting limbs and vital organs and the beating chambers of the heart.

Look carefully in amongst the shadows of the scan.

You'll find things that are hidden from those who don't know how to look.

Subtle shades of black-and-white and grey, reflecting variations in the density of substances through which the sound waves pass.

Solid tissues like bone appear white because the hard outer surface deflects the waves. Liquid-filled tissues like the uterus appear dark, a swirling sea absorbing waves of sound. Enhancement and attenuation, shadowing, contrast, clarity – the language of my trade – muted echoes of the structure of life itself.

Not the smallest detail escapes me. I seize on any imperfection with practised eyes – I've spent so many hours casting spells over submerged prints and negatives in a blacked-out cell, leaning over trays of pungent liquid, waiting for the alchemy to breathe life into the picture.

She is here, floating in the dark, inside your womb – 'and not drowning but waving' to transpose the verse.

She was your captive for a time...

But my creation... my Embryonic Love... and now at last she's free...

She's mine.

New York City was sweltering in the heat of summer. In Lara's opinion, it was not the greatest day for a pregnant woman to be walking the length of the Brooklyn Bridge like a tourist but Gabrielle had insisted. She and James had flown over for a short visit to see how Lara was getting on with the pregnancy and most importantly, to see images of their developing baby at the next prenatal scan. It was Gabrielle's third transatlantic trip since the start of the pregnancy – she was determined to keep a close eye on her surrogate for the sake of her baby.

Lara's appointment at the hospital was in the late afternoon which gave them time to walk to Brooklyn for lunch and then back for her four o'clock slot. Gabrielle had secured a photo assignment for a travel magazine featuring iconic walking tours in New York and needed to take photographs of the bridge, so it was a good way of combining business with pleasure.

'What's more, it's a healthy excursion for the surrogate-to-be,' she told Lara. 'You need to stay active.'

They set off from the Manhattan side of Brooklyn Bridge, joining the pedestrian walkway and making their way towards the Manhattan Tower. Lara was already flagging by the time they reached it.

'I was planning a pause here anyway,' said Gabrielle. She turned to James.

'It's a special day for us after all – seeing our baby together for the first time. I want to mark it.'

She opened her rucksack and pulled out a large stainless-steel padlock. Then she took James' hand and led him over to the bridge railings.

'Are you planning to lock me to the bridge?' said James 'Make me your prisoner!' he joked in mock submission.

'Hmm… tempting,' said Gabrielle. 'Look it's a tradition here.' She pointed at the collection of 'love-locks' hanging from the metalwork of the railings. 'Here, you do it,' she said, handing him the lock.

He took it from her, hooked it onto the metal wires, and clicked the lock shut. Then he held out the key to her in his open palm.

'I love you,' he said.

She took the key, kissed him softly on the lips, then kissed the key and flung it away as far as she could. It spun through the air, a glinting dart, before disappearing into the water below.

Lara watched with a pained look on her face.

'If you two have finished with your ridiculous pantomime, could we get going? I'm burning up.'

They walked on as far as the Brooklyn side of the bridge. Lara led the way while James and Gabrielle meandered hand-in-hand behind her, pausing at intervals for Gabrielle to take photographs.

Eventually they made it to the other side and wandered on to Grimaldi's where, to Lara's relief, they soon got a table.

'This is the best pizzeria in Brooklyn,' she said. 'You haven't lived till you've eaten pizza at Grimaldi's!'

Lara complained all the way back across the bridge. She was hot and bothered and bloated. Her back ached and her legs were heavy.

'I told you we should have taken a taxi to the hospital,' she said. 'This can't be good for your precious baby. You're going to give me a miscarriage at this rate.'

Gabrielle silenced her with a withering glare but when they reached the Manhattan end of the walkway, James hailed a yellow cab. Lara rode the few blocks to the hospital in a sullen, sweaty silence while James made occasional banal comments as they made slow progress along the fuming, gridlocked avenue. It was a relief to escape from the heat of the streets into the gleaming chill of the air-conditioned clinic. Soon, Lara was lying on a bed, her rounded stomach smothered with gel as a technician rolled a probe over her skin to reveal constantly shifting black-and-white ultrasound images on the monitor. Lara turned her face away from the screen but Gabrielle was transfixed. James just stood there grinning like a Cheshire cat and repeating, 'I've got a good feeling about this one,' until Lara told him to shut up.

'Don't you want to keep a copy?' said Gabrielle, as the technician handed over three copies of images from the scan at the end of the session.

'No, you keep them all,' said Lara

So Gabrielle kept them all, to tuck into her purse or stick up on her fridge, to show to any stranger who happened to sit next to her on the train or walk into her kitchen. But no, she would do none of those things. Her passion was too intense to share. She handed two of the copies to James for safekeeping and the third she tucked away inside the cup of her bra, next to the skin of her left breast. Her heart ached for that baby.

As they left the hospital, James held open the door for Lara. For a second their eyes locked and in that instant Lara knew that James had guessed the truth. The baby was hers – conceived in Venice, their love child. She – not Gabrielle – was the biological mother.

In the weeks following their Venetian 'honeymoon' Lara had found out that Venice (and the hormones she had been taking to improve the chances of a successful implantation for the surrogacy) had worked their charms and that she was pregnant through natural conception with James' baby. But she said nothing to him or Gabrielle.

She feared that Gabrielle would put pressure on her to abort the baby if she discovered the truth of the affair. Instead she resolved to make absolutely sure that there was no way that Gabrielle could force her to honour the memorandum of understanding she had signed up to for a gestational surrogacy. It didn't seem like such a great crime at the time – she was still planning to be her surrogate. She was still committed to give her the right to become the legal mother after the birth. This 'gift' of her baby would save their marriage.

She had said nothing to either Gabrielle or James about the failure of the embryo transfer procedure that she had undergone in New York. Let them remain in blissful ignorance. Let them believe they were both genetic parents of this longed-for child. If she could keep it a secret, no one need ever know. After all, she reasoned, as identical twins, she and Gabrielle shared almost identical DNA. It would be virtually impossible through genetic testing to prove which one of them was the biological mother. And although Lara considered herself morally (but as the birth mother, not legally) bound to hand over the baby at birth, by doing it her way, she would at least have the secret satisfaction of having 'made a baby' with James and passed on her genetic inheritance to the next generation.

However, this was also a time for righting past wrongs. The word 'revenge' was too crude but Lara believed in the adage 'vengeance is a dish best served cold.' She had made sure that even if Gabrielle were to find out what had happened in Venice there could be no chance of her forcing Lara into terminating this pregnancy and starting over with another surrogacy using Gabrielle's remaining eggs. Gabrielle was so consumed with the obsessive desire to conceive her own genetic offspring that there was no knowing how far she would go – and Lara was not taking any chances. It had been easy enough to sort things with the clinic by impersonating her twin, the way she had done on more than one occasion when they were little girls. It wasn't only Gabrielle who could pull that trick! True, she had had to perjure herself, forge a couple of signatures and attorneys' affidavits. In the stroke of a pen, her deceit had extinguished Gabrielle's last hope of becoming a biological mother. But at the end of the day, she had committed herself to an act of great altruism, and was intending to make the greatest sacrifice that could be asked of a mother – giving away her own baby.

Surely, a few venal sins along the way could be forgiven?

31

Scarlett

I whack my fists against the door until my fingers are numb with pain. I've got to get off this boat and back to England, out of Christina's life forever.

And yet? Could it be true that Gabrielle has been using me? Maybe I was indeed unwittingly duped by her, along with everyone else? I think back to my fight with Damien in the grounds of the hotel after he was released on bail. He seemed to know every detail concerning my past employment problems. After that confrontation, I suspected that Damien had had dealings with the New York modelling agency, just like me. I wondered if perhaps he had also been on their books as a model. But now I'm struck with another sneaking suspicion. Was Gabrielle the hidden face of e-Face? Was she, by chance, the extremely helpful woman I spoke to that time on the phone, who went out of her way to find me a placement as a nanny in New York, even though her main business was managing a modelling agency?

Exhausted, I sink to the floor with my back to the door and my head in my hands. Looking back over the last few months, the pieces start to fall into place. It seems that Gabrielle must have identified, groomed and recruited Damien before she identified and 'recruited' me. But why exactly did she select him? Gabrielle could have chosen any one of the models on her books, so how did she conclude that Damien was the perfect candidate to seduce Christina and do her dirty work? Was Damien a good choice because he was Christina's type? Being her twin, Gabrielle must have had a pretty good idea about Lara's taste in men! God knows, despite his flaws, he can be exceptionally charming and captivating when he wants to be. But Christina is so cultured and sophisticated, it seems counter-intuitive to assume she would fall for an arrogant hedonist like Damien (even if at the start she knew nothing of his gambling and drug taking habits).

I sit rocking gently, racking my brains to make sense of all this. Then suddenly I remember the faded photograph in Christina's old copy of Brideshead Revisited. It's obvious, of course. Gabrielle picked out Damien *precisely because* she was struck by his very strong physical likeness with Christina's first love. His image must have caught her attention for that very reason when she was scrolling through the models on her books looking for a suitable candidate. Gabrielle knew her twin would fall for him, no matter what his flaws. Now I can understand how Christina, who had closed herself off to the world in order to protect Katie, allowed her guard to fall and let this man into her life so easily.

Having selected her candidate, Gabrielle then needed to find a way to get him under her control so that she could coerce him into doing everything she wanted. Having witnessed her antics on the deck of The Phantasea, I can imagine that she first set out to seduce and entrap him with sex. Once they were in a relationship, she would have discovered his excessive drug and gambling habits and would then have found it easy to exploit these weaknesses in his character to corrupt and manipulate him into carrying out her orders. In addition, as he was trying to make a career for himself in modelling and film, she could trade favours with him by using her network to provide openings and introductions to influential people and interesting opportunities in the media world. Damien would be putty in her hands for such a master of manipulation as Gabrielle.

Once Damien had won over Christina's affections, Gabrielle would have looked for a suitable candidate among the many models registered on her e-Face database to install as a nanny in Christina's home. And that's where I came in. Gabrielle could have selected any number of girls on her modelling agency books to offer them an attractive position as a nanny. But I guess she chose me because she imagined that I was easily corruptible and vulnerable to manipulation given that I was virtually unemployable due to my previous drugs conviction. Seeing that my past employment history also included working as a waitress in a pole dancing club and a croupier in a casino, she would have assumed (not unreasonably) that my morals were none too strict. My damaged employment credentials must have caught her attention when I sent in my application.

'God, I think you could be right,' I say, recalling Christina's last words to me. 'I came to you through an agency. I was looking for modelling jobs and started out doing some boudoir photography but the woman at e-Face said she would be able to place me as a nanny with you. I remember at the time thinking it was a bit odd but I was just happy to be offered the position.' I spin round to face Christina. 'How much of a schemer is she? Is it beyond the realms of possibility that Gabrielle could have set up a fake nanny placement agency for the sole purpose of marketing her services to you and then picked me out as the ideal candidate to install as your nanny because of my damaged past?'

'Knowing the way her mind works, that's sounds exactly the kind of thing Gabrielle would do,' says Christina. 'There's nothing she enjoys more than scheming and manipulating people.' She sits biting her nails, then her eyes light up. 'Now I remember, it was Damien who told me about the nanny agency. He gave me a card with the name of the agency and the website –*Nanny Angels*, I think it was called. I looked up the website. The sales pitch sounded very professional – London-based nanny agency that places exceptional residential Nannies in New York and throughout the United States – something along those lines. He told me that his female "boss" used the agency for her own little girls and had passed him the details when he'd told her I'd had to fire my nanny. Damien's fictional boss even provided a fictional reference – faked by Gabrielle, I suppose! That man had turned my head. I was in such a spin that I was grateful for his help and didn't bother to check anything out.'

'Well, that figures,' I say. 'The modelling agency doesn't exist any more. There's no trace of it online. I tried to look it up a few days ago and there's nothing – e-Face has effaced itself. As for the nanny agency, I guess that never really existed except in Gabrielle's virtual reality universe.'

It looks like without me knowing it Gabrielle's been in the shadows pulling the strings for months leading up to this plan for the abduction of Katie. Now I understand why Christina always insisted on an absolute ban on posting photographs of Katie or anything about her on social media or anywhere online. And I understand why Christina told me she had sacked her former nanny, Hayley, when (thanks to Damien's ratting) she found out that the nanny had done just that, posting a photograph of 'Katie Kenedey' proudly holding up her Bright Star of the Week certificate Awarded by the Manhattan Bright Star Kindergarten.

We sit there, mulling over the last few months in New York. Christina tells me that she met Damien just a few weeks before I went to work for her. There had been a big row the first time Damien came to the apartment after Hayley accused him of trying to make a pass at her while Christina was in the shower.

'He was probably acting under Gabrielle's orders – to get her sacked,' I say.

Hayley's accusations (vigorously denied by Damien) didn't please Christina who was fiercely jealous. When

Damien showed Christina the photograph of Katie that Hayley had posted on her Facebook page, it gave Christina the perfect reason to get rid of her. Hayley left – under a cloud.

I also recall one of my outings to Central Park with Katie, when Damien insisted on tagging along and spent the afternoon flirting with me. I was taking photographs of Katie under the trees, some arty shots that I was planning to make into a traditional (strictly offline) collage for Christina's birthday. He was winding me up, horsing around and photo-bombing the shots. When I yelled at him, he started boasting that I should be paying him – that he'd worked as a male model and ladies' escort and I should be grateful to be getting his services for free. When I quizzed him about it – 'I thought you were a big-swinging-dick in the city'– he started back-pedalling madly and made out it was all a big joke. Now I think of it, he was probably telling the truth for once in his life.

'He took us all in. He's a class act,' says Christina bitterly.

'Did you ever meet any of Damien's work colleagues?' I ask Christina. Did you ever go to his office?'

'We always met in the downstairs lobby of "his bank." It was a big anonymous place, with hundreds of people streaming in and out. We sometimes went for a drink at a nearby bar, popular with the Wall Street crowd. He seemed to know them all, paying for drinks and exchanging banter with the best of them. But then, networking was always the skillset at which he excelled. People come and go in the financial world. Of course, now I know he succeeded in passing himself off as one of the crowd, even though he didn't work for that bank or for any of the banks. Why would anyone bother to check his credentials? Look at me! What a damned fool I've been! He was no more a Wall Street banker than you are!'

'He's such a con artist,' I say, 'Did you ever see *Catch Me if You Can*? He'd give DiCaprio a good run for his money!'

Christina manages a wry smile.

'You're right,' she says, 'Except that he's such a lousy poker player!'

As we talk through the night it becomes abundantly clear that Gabrielle's been planning this for months, if not years, like a poisonous spider spinning her web. She must have done her research meticulously. She discovered Christina's new identity, her new employer, the name of her little girl's day-care nursery and her new address – then it was simply a matter of installing her stooge (that was Damien) and her innocent operator (that was me) and watching and waiting until the opportunity arose to go in for the kill.

'If I've understood this, Christina,' I say 'It's not only Katie who is in grave danger but also you. Gabrielle's used Damien, and yes, she's even used me. Damien was vulnerable to blackmail because of his gambling debts and because he's obsessed with sex and has an ego the size of an elephant. And I was in desperate need of a job and struggling to get one because of my drugs conviction. She's played us all.

'She left all those clues that we thought were leading to Katie deliberately to entrap us. Like you, I was convinced Katie was hidden here on The Phantasea after I saw a photo of the catamaran on Costa's file.'

'She sent a photograph of the catamaran to me at the hotel too,' says Christina, 'in one of her trademark purple envelopes. It was delivered in person to my room by that loathsome hotel manager. I recognised the yacht, and I recognised the harbour. We used to dock at Clearwater Marina when we came on sailing holidays to the Caribbean as children. I knew it was a trick. I knew she was using Katie as bait and I was her prey. But I wanted to get onboard before the police – in case they botched the rescue and Gabrielle did something desperate. That's why I wouldn't listen when you warned me not to go to Clamities seafood restaurant with Damien. So of course, Damien drove me there for a candlelit dinner and at the end of the meal I suggested a walk to look at the yachts down in the marina. I made it so easy for him. But as we reached the bars, a guy called him over and started yelling about his winnings, something about a debt in a game of poker. Damien bluffed it, said the money was on its way but in the meantime he'd stand him a drink. I gave him the slip and walked on down to the waterfront. I found The Phantasea moored on the quayside. No one was around on deck but the deckhand on the adjoining yacht greeted me casually and wanted to chat. "What did you think of Clamities? I've heard the fried clams are to die for".'

'So I boarded the yacht – I knew I was walking into a trap but I had to find out if Katie was onboard.

'I searched everywhere. But she was nowhere to be seen. Of course, I waited. I waited and eventually Damien and Gabrielle came onboard together, drunk and in high spirits. Damien didn't even have the decency to look embarrassed. I started screaming and shouting at them, "Where's my baby? Where's my little girl?"

'I wanted to throttle Gabrielle.

'She just laughed, and said…

'"Have you checked under the beds?"

'That was her favourite gag when we shared a room as little girls – hiding under my bed and grabbing my ankle. So I got into the habit of always checking under the beds when I came into the room. Anyway, I raced back down to the cabins thinking that they'd done something dreadful to Katie. And while I was down here checking under the bed, Gabrielle followed me in and bolted the door. I've been trapped here ever since. So now she's got me. You could say I just gave myself up – my life for Katie's.'

'My God, the woman's completely mad,' I say.

'She's a psychopath,' says Christina simply. 'I mean that quite literally. When I was at university I was going out with a medical student, and sometimes when Gabrielle came to visit, we used to entertain ourselves doing those psychological diagnostic tests down at the pub after a few drinks – she always scored well into the psychopathic personality range, she took pride in it.' Christina turns towards me. 'She's been taking anti-psychotic medications for years.'

So that explains the shelf-full of bottles I saw in the bathroom cabinet at La Revanche!

'But why's she got it in for Katie?' I ask. 'That's just plain evil.'

'Because she believes Katie belongs to her,' says Christina, 'and the only way she can keep believing it and get everyone else to believe it is to kidnap her and get rid of me.'

Christina looks at me with something like compassion in her eyes.

'She wants Katie come hell or high water. I pray that she hasn't hurt her and is keeping her somewhere safe. I'm the one she wants to dispose of. But she won't let any person stand in her way.'

She takes my bruised hands gently in hers.

'You fell into her traps. You know too much. She won't let you go.'

She sits up and looks out at the looming dark mass of Marooner's Rock catching the moonlight.

'Once I was her hostage, she stole my phone and she sent you the lines from Peter Pan, knowing that you were smart enough to work out where The Phantasea was headed and to come in search of me and Katie. From Clearwater Marina we sailed all through the night and the next day to avoid a police boat that was patrolling the waters. I completely lost my bearings, as we went from one heading to another, round the islands, until we came here to the place the locals call the Mermaids' Lagoon. We moored here many times when we were kids on my father's yacht, The Neverland. The lagoon is so sheltered and secluded.' Christina points at the rock whose dark outline is just visible through the porthole. Her eyes go dreamy. 'Gabrielle almost drowned me there once in a game of make-believe where I was Wendy and she was Tinker Bell. That's why I never swim. I'm terrified of going under.' She gives a weary smile. 'If ever there was a psychotic fairy in children's literature, it's Tinker Bell!' Then she looks at me sadly. 'But, of course, Katie's not here. Gabrielle was too clever for that! She's arranged a hiding place for her somewhere else. When she's dealt with both of us, she can do what she likes with Katie. Finally, Katie will belong to her.'

'She must hate you so much to have behaved in this way,' I say.

'Oh yes, she hates me all right,' says Christina 'She thinks I stole her baby. And she wants me dead.'

32

15 December 2010: Pink Sands Bay

What a shame this is such a clichéd photograph! – me and James on a picture-postcard beach with palm trees and sand the colour of a Caribbean sunset, sipping a cocktail through straws from a shared coconut. We've positioned ourselves beautifully on a driftwood log so that the space between our bodies makes a sea-blue, heart shape in the background.

We could be honeymooners.

Even though the composition makes me cringe, I think perhaps we were truly happy that day, for the last time.

Gabrielle and James were spending Christmas in Stratford-Upon-Avon at the old family home. As the vicar in a local parish, it was the busiest time of year for Gabrielle's father, and impossible for him to get away. Lara had been persuaded to come over from New York to join them at the vicarage – a surprise visit. It was to be a family reunion, a time of good cheer and reconciliation. A time to break the joyful news to the parents - they were very soon to become grandparents.

Lara's pregnancy and the surrogacy arrangement had been kept a secret until now. Having deliberately cut herself off from family life and made her new life in New York, Lara had virtually no contact with her family back in England and had insisted that Gabrielle should say nothing until nearer the time of the birth. She didn't want them prying into her affairs. Gabrielle knew that her father would disapprove of the surrogacy on theological grounds and her mother (who seemed incapable of thinking for herself) would take the same line, so she had gone along with her sister's wishes. There was no point having them ranting on about it for the duration of the pregnancy. But they couldn't keep it a secret for much longer – the baby was due in six weeks' time.

So Lara was coming for Christmas (when, of course, her pregnancy would be impossible to conceal). The family would all be united in Stratford for the festivities. They would break the news of the surrogacy. And everyone would just have to get used to the idea that Gabrielle and James were having a baby.

Then on the morning of Christmas Eve, just after James had driven off to collect Lara from Heathrow airport, and as Gabrielle was in her mother's bedroom packing up Christmas presents to go under the tree, she received a text:

Nightmare scenario at work – project deadline 31 December – my boss being a dick as always – all leave cancelled. Sorry, I'm not going to make it.

Gabrielle stared at the text. She reread it three times in disbelief. It was two o'clock in the morning in New York – Lara was supposed to be on a plane touching down at Heathrow in less than an hour. But she must still be in her apartment on the other side of the Atlantic, awake, a monster in the night, unleashing her devastating blow. She punched out Lara's number. Three times it went to voicemail, then the fourth, the message came up *phone is disconnected, please try later.* The bitch had switched it off.

Gabrielle tossed the phone onto the bed and walked over to the dressing table. She looked in the mirror. Her twin stared back at her. She grabbed her mother's ivory hairbrush and hammered it into the mirror until Lara's face was fractured into a thousand pieces and her wild staring eyes shattered from the mahogany frame. Then she picked up the silver-framed rose garden wedding portrait (of herself, holding the dark red bridal bouquet, and Lara in her grey silk) from the bedside table, and hurled it at the wall. Splinters of glass flew in all directions to embed themselves in the carpet. A chunk of plaster was missing where the corner of the metal frame had hit the painted wall.

A few seconds later, she heard footsteps pounding up the stairs. The door was flung open and her mother stood there, wiping floury hands on her apron.

'What on earth is going on up here?'

'It's that bitch. That despicable, cold-hearted, scheming bitch. She's not coming.'

She bent down to pick up the long shards of glass, squeezing them into her palms until the blood began to drip down on to her mother's cream woollen shagpile.

A few hours later, a precarious calm had been restored and the family were sitting in the living room together. James had carefully tweezered out the glass from Gabrielle's flesh and bandaged up her palms with professional skill.

'Such a blessing having a medical expert in the family at a time like this,' said his mother-in-law gratefully.

'At least it will get you out of peeling the sprouts and all the usual Christmas chores,' said James ruefully to Gabrielle. 'Was this part of your cunning plan?'

Gabrielle was not amused. She was lying back on the sofa looking bored, sipping a glass of mulled wine and nibbling one of her mother's mince pies. James sat wedged in next to Mrs Kennedy, turning the pages of a photo book created by Gabrielle. It was an early Christmas present from Gabrielle to James containing photographs of their recent trip to the British Leeward Isles.

'Ah! What a lovely photo!' said Mrs Kennedy. 'You look like honeymooners. And what a beautiful beach.' She pointed. 'The sand is such an exquisite pink.'

'The photo rep at the hotel took that,' said Gabrielle absently. 'It cost us thirty dollars – a rip off.'

'Don't be so cynical,' said James. 'We had something to celebrate that evening.'

He turned to Mrs Kennedy.

'Did Christina tell you? We had a busy holiday. As well as taking delivery of The Phantasea, we put down a deposit on a villa. It's pretty run down. It's Gabrielle's new project – she's got all sorts of plans for the renovation.'

'How exciting!' said Mrs Kennedy, and she patted Gabrielle's knee. 'You must tell me all about it.'

Gabrielle banged her wine glass down on the sideboard.

'We've wasted enough time looking at those bloody holiday snaps. I'm going to watch a film. Hand me those DVDs could you please James?'

She had brought along a selection of classic black-and-white films to watch in place of the usual trashy Christmas TV that she despised.

'I'm going to expose you all to a bit of French culture,' she said. 'This is a good place to start. *Jules et Jim*.'

Obediently, her parents and James settled themselves on the faded sofas in the rectory sitting room to watch 'the most tragic and poetic love-triangle story ever made' (so said the blurb on the back of the DVD) by renowned French director Francois Truffaut, about the relationship between Catherine, seductive, charismatic, mentally unstable, and the two men who were captivated by the love of her.

'Do you see yourself as Catherine by any chance?' said James ironically, as he read the back of the DVD.

'Shush!' she said, impatiently. She was transfixed, listening intently to the French dialogue and reading the subtitles...

...It's a nightmare when night comes. I think of that child we can never have. I feel I'm being judged. I can't bear it any longer...

But we love each other Catherine, that's the only thing that matters...

There was a loud ping as a text message came in on James' mobile.

Jim was thinking of the children he could have had with Catherine... they made love once more not knowing why... perhaps to put an end to their passionate affair... it was like a funeral or as if they were already dead...

Another ping.

'For God's sake turn it off,' said Gabrielle, keeping her eyes fixed on the screen.

Jim received a letter from Jules.

'Your little baby is dead. Died in the first trimester of the pregnancy. She wants silence between you now.'

James got to his feet.

'Would you excuse me please. Something's come up at work. Could I use your office for a few minutes?'

I was scared she might try to kill herself. She had a gun...

Gabrielle's father nodded his agreement and James' left the room, just as his mobile pinged again.

Catherine believes at least one person must be faithful in a relationship – as for the other?

'Poor thing,' said Gabrielle's mother. 'You'd think they could leave him in peace on Christmas Eve.'

'Just shut up, Mother,' said Gabrielle. 'I'm trying to watch this.' Her eyes were glued to the black-and-white figures on the screen as the heroine, Catherine took out the gun and attempted to shoot her former lover, Jim

They would have been beautiful Jim! You're going to die! You disgust me! I'm going to kill you Jim! … Je vais te tuer!

Gabrielle sat up rigid as she listened to the deadpan voiceover.

Having asked her husband, Jules, to watch them closely – 'Jules, regarde-nous bien'– Catherine invites her former lover, Jim, to join her in the car, and drives the car off the end of a broken bridge, killing them both.

That phrase, 'Jules, regarde-nous bien!' echoed in Gabrielle's head. 'Jules, regarde-nous bien!'… and she sat entranced with tears running down her cheeks as the automobile sank into the river and the credits rolled.

★

Coming from behind the closed study door, Gabrielle could hear the muffled tones of James talking to his PA. It was so annoying. There seemed to be no escape from the demands of his work. Thanks to his bloody mobile phone, there was always someone else in the house.

He was shouting now. Even he was beginning to lose his cool. She heard the study door opening and he came in and sat down beside her.

'Problems at work?' said Gabrielle automatically – though she wasn't really interested in hearing about them.

The clanging of her parents' old-fashioned doorbell broke Gabrielle's reverie as she switched off the TV.

'Can you get that, James?' she said, giving him a prod with her elbow. 'Who the hell is it?' she muttered as he stood up. A few seconds later she got up and followed him into the hallway. He was at the front door, speaking to a deliveryman, who was carrying a large cardboard box and an oversized bouquet of red chrysanthemums.

Through the open doorway of the study, Gabrielle saw James's phone where he had left it on the desk. It was flashing on silent.

He walked down the hallway carrying the huge bouquet.

'They're from Lara,' he called out. 'For your mother.'

As he disappeared into the sitting room to hand over the bouquet, Gabrielle wandered over to the desk and saw the name, Francesca PA, displayed on the screen. That name set off bad vibes but she couldn't think why.

I've just about had enough of this, thought Gabrielle. She clicked the answer button and was on the point of giving Francesca a piece of her mind but before she could open her mouth, she heard the voice:

'Hello darling, I'm sorry. I lost my nerve. I know she's going to give you hell. I just can't face it, being in the spotlight in this condition, on top of all the usual stress and conflict of Christmas at home.'

It was Lara, unmistakably, Lara's voice. An echo of her own. The same texture and intonation but with the breath of an American accent. Devious bastard. But how cliched! He was so lacking in imagination even when he was cheating. She cut the phone, then scrolled back through the list of missed calls from 'Francesca PA' – eleven calls! The first at 3 a.m. then 6.30 a.m. – God, that was when he went down to get her a cup of tea just after they made love. A further three calls between 11 a.m. and noon when she went out shopping with her mother for some last-minute Christmas treats, and the remaining six just now while they were watching the film *Jules et Jim*.

Gabrielle slammed down the phone. Her ears were ringing with anger and she thought she would faint but she put on her habitual mask of indifference and when James returned saying, 'They're from Lara, for your mum. That was thoughtful of her.'

She replied nonchalantly, 'Symbol of death, what was she thinking of?' And then she flounced up the stairs.

James stood at the bottom of the stairs looking up at her with a pained expression on his face.

At the top, she turned and shouted, 'Does she think we're planning a bloody funeral?'

Then she went into the bedroom she had shared with Lara as a child and slammed the door.

33

Scarlett

It's three in the morning and still no sign of anyone coming to rescue us.

'We've waited long enough,' I say.

I take the gun from under the mattress.

'OK. This is the deal. Two shots at the door. That's all we can spare. That leaves us three bullets to defend ourselves if our escape plan fails and they come back.' Christina told me that she knows enough about yachting to work out how to skipper the catamaran. With a bit of luck and my help we should be able to navigate back to shore if only we can get out of this damn cabin!

I practise aiming at the top corner of the door, just the way Mitch told me to – *relax your shoulder, look down the barrel, hold your breath… and squeeze.*

I estimate that the bolts must be screwed in about two inches down on the outside of the door.

We twist the mattress on its side and crouch down behind it to protect ourselves as best we can. I take a shot. There's an almighty thud, as the bullet hits the door denting the wood, followed a split second later by the rip and scrunch of breaking glass as it ricochets off the door and flies into the mirror above the sink.

When all goes quiet, we throw ourselves against the door, and kick and pound. The bolts seem to loosen but it doesn't budge.

'I'll give it one more try,' I say.

This time I miss the door. The bullet hits the steel frame and shoots back in our direction.

Christina screams and clutches her right shoulder. Blood seeps through her fingers.

'Shit!' I drop the gun and support her in my arms. 'God, I'm sorry. I'm so, so sorry.'

She's gone ashen-white and looks as if she's about to pass out.

I should have trusted my instincts. I had a feeling taking the gun was a bad idea.

Dawn is breaking.

After spending the last two hours lying on the bed moaning and complaining of feeling sick and faint, Christina has revived sufficiently to roll herself into a sitting position and look out of the porthole. Fortunately, the wound in her shoulder seems to be only a flesh wound. With my basic first aid skills, learnt during my childcare studies, I've been able to stem the flow of blood by improvising a tourniquet with strips of cotton fabric torn from the sheet. But she needs to get to hospital fast.

Although I'm not a religious person, I gaze across the water and pray silently to the glowing disc of the sun, for Katie's safe return and for this nightmare to be over.

'That's the one thing we can be sure of in this uncertain world,' says Christina softly. 'Every day the sun will rise. Look. Isn't it beautiful? I read somewhere that there's always a sunrise and always a sunset and it's up to you to choose to be there for them.' She leans into the sun, throwing back her head so the warm rays coming through the porthole fall on her face. The numbing pain of her wound seems to have calmed her nerves. 'Put yourself in the way of beauty. That was the message.'

As if on cue, a dark shape comes into view at the entrance to the lagoon.

'Thank God! The police are on their way. Mitch must have raised the alarm.' I squeeze Christina's good hand until she pulls it away. 'I knew he wouldn't let me down.'

As the vessel approaches and comes into focus, euphoria turns to doubt, and then despair. 'It's the dinghy,' I say. 'They're back.' Why? It doesn't make any sense. With us trapped on board, this was the perfect opportunity for them to stage a getaway with Katie.

We see there's only one figure aboard – it's Gabrielle. No Damien. No Katie.

'Where's Katie now?' I say. 'She's not aboard The Phantasea so God knows who's looking after her?'

Christina's hands are shaking.

'Damien.' She almost chokes on the name. 'That bastard Damien is doing the babysitting.'

'What's she playing at?' I say. 'This is her chance, while you're out of the way, to pass herself off as Katie's mother and get her off the island.'

Christina's not even listening to me.

'She's coming back alone to take her revenge,' says Christina.

I don't know if it's Christina's use of the word 'revenge' or if the meditative beauty of the sunrise has worked its magic but a vision comes into my head. Katie's blue bunny lying on a sunbed – not a sunbed at the hotel but a bright green-and-yellow stripe cotton fabric – by the poolside at the Villa La Revanche.

I grip Christina's hand.

'Katie's at the villa. That's where they're hiding her. I saw the blue bunny left on a sunbed by the pool. At the time I thought you'd taken her soft toy because it made you feel closer to Katie. But, of course, it wasn't you at the villa, it was Gabrielle, and why would she have the blue bunny at the villa unless Katie was there too?' The more I think about it, the more sure I am. 'Katie must have been wailing for the bunny, you know how upset she gets when she loses it! Gabrielle must have come to fetch it from my room.'

So now it all makes sense – those photographs of Katie that I saw in the darkroom were taken at the villa.

'I'll bet my life on it, that's where they've hidden her. Your twin is so twisted, she's even signposted it with the name – the villa of revenge. For God's sake, what normal person, would give a holiday house a name like that? She wants her payback for what she sees as you stealing her baby. So she's kidnapped Katie and taken her back there.'

Damien must have returned to the villa to check up on Katie while Gabrielle deals with her twin. But far from babysitting, most likely Damien is busy plotting with Kramer or another of his dodgy drug-dealing associates, a way of smuggling Katie off the island.

The dinghy approaches.

Gabrielle steers the dinghy alongside the catamaran, and as she passes beneath our porthole, she looks up, smiles and gives a cheerful wave. Is she really hell bent on taking revenge on Christina? Maybe we're being absurd.

Looking down into the hull of the little boat I can see that she's brought provisions – but it's not our breakfast. I count more than twenty metal jerry cans of the kind used for carrying fuel. I can make out the words.

GASOLINE – HIGHLY FLAMMABLE

'She's refuelling,' I say. 'She must be planning to take us on a long journey with that quantity of fuel.'

I stand up and take hold of the gun.

'Christina, look at me. We're out of time. I'm going to shoot through the porthole'

She seems lost in a daydream watching the sunrise. Without taking her eyes away from the sky, she says quietly. 'Marine engines use diesel not gasoline.'

It takes me a second until the penny drops.

'Oh my God! Is your psychotic sister planning to torch the boat?' I put my hand to her cheek and turn her face towards me. 'Christina, for God's sake, listen to me – you can't just give in to her. I've got a new plan. Our lives may depend on it. More importantly, Katie's life may depend on it.' I talk slowly and clearly. 'As soon as she's out of sight, I shoot through the porthole. Then we climb out and swim round to the dinghy. After Gabrielle's unloaded the jerry cans, we grab the dinghy and sail back to shore.'

Christina's actually smiling when she finally turns to me and says,

'Oh Scarlett, you never give up, do you? Look at the state of me.' She points to her bandaged right shoulder. 'It's impossible. I can't move my arm. Anyway, I just told you. I'm terrified of swimming. I can't do it.'

Gently, I give her a hug. I know it's a desperate plan but I'm not giving up.

'Then I'll get the dinghy and come back for you. Just be ready to climb out of the porthole. You can manage that, can't you?'

As the dinghy disappears from view behind the catamaran, I carefully raise the gun using both hands and take two successive shots perfectly aimed at the fixings on the porthole.

'Bullseye!'

I toss the pistol down onto the bed.

'There's one bullet left. I'm off. If this doesn't work, you'll just have to use the gun to defend yourself.'

34

Scarlett

'You're going to have to be brave, and you might have to be brutal,' I say to Christina as I force open the broken porthole. 'If she comes down here, take control. Surprise her with the gun. Make her your hostage. Keep her here as long as you can. Better still, get out of the cabin and lock her in.' I try to sound more confident than I feel. Christina's not much of a fighter at the best of times. With only one good arm she'll be a pushover.

I crouch on the lower rim of the porthole and dive into the steely grey water. It's colder than I expected. The churning waves drag me back against the hull. Eventually I manage to kick myself away from the yacht and get into my stride for a long, hard swim round to the stern where the dinghy is tied up. Each stroke is painful as I fight against the current. It takes me so long battling the waves that when I get to the dinghy, spluttering and out of breath, I find Gabrielle has already unloaded all the gasoline cans, pulled it out of the water onto the trampoline and secured it to the yacht with a heavy-duty metal chain.

So that's that – there's no way I can release the dinghy. There's no escape.

I climb up until my head is just above the level of the deck and I can see into the saloon. Even out here with the sea breeze tangling my hair, the stink of gasoline reaches me. Gabrielle is strolling round the saloon, cigarette in one hand, and a jerry can in the other, pouring petrol out in a continuous stream over the wooden floorboards of the saloon. There's a heap of empty cans discarded in a corner on the deck. That woman really is nuts. If she drops her cigarette, the whole thing will go up like a flaming rocket.

She empties the last jerry can then casually kicks it out to the deck and heads down the steps to the cabins. This is my chance. Our only hope now is to get an SOS out to the coastguard. If the coastguard picks up our distress call, and alerts the police, there's a chance we'll be rescued. If not, we're done for. I just pray Christina can keep Gabrielle below deck long enough for me to send the message.

When Gabrielle is out of sight, I race to the control station and run my fingers over knobs and switches trying to figure out how to send out an SOS. As I do so, I hear raised voices coming from the cabin. At last I manage to activate the distress button. Thank God! Just then things start to kick off down below – screaming and shouting, the cabin door opening and slamming, followed by the clatter of footsteps on the stairs.

Gabrielle must have got hold of the gun… it's over!

I run for cover.

At the back of the saloon I find an empty store cupboard and squeeze inside.

I have no idea how long I've been crouching here in the dark – expecting to hear a gunshot ringing out any second. But it doesn't come. The Phantasea's been sailing under power for most of that time. I hear the rumble of the engine and the rush of water beneath me as the catamaran tacks upwind from one heading to another. I wonder where she's taking us? Is she heading for the open sea before setting fire to the boat?

I hear the grinding of the anchor being dropped and then the engine is switched off. Then all is still, save for the endless lapping of waves and the rise and fall of the catamaran in the swell – this combined with the intoxicating fug of petrol fumes, is truly nauseating.

My split-second decision to hide in the cupboard doesn't seem so smart now after someone – it must be Gabrielle – walked past the door that I'd left slightly ajar and kicked it closed. Now rather than a predator waiting for my moment to pounce, I'm a captive once again.

Fortunately, the door is slatted and made of plywood with a flimsy catch, so if I shove all my weight against it, I should be able to break it down. Trapped in the dark, I'm able to decipher two almost identical voices. There's Christina's, restrained, private school-educated tones, with the hint of a transatlantic accent over the top. And that must be Gabrielle, almost indistinguishable from Christina, but a touch more brittle and clipped – vintage

Made In Chelsea. Christina's gone silent now and Gabrielle is doing all the talking, speaking in a flat, relentless monotone as if she's reading from a text.

The cupboard's only just deep enough for me to sit down on the wooden floor with my knees bent up to my chin.

Relax. Breathe.

I've endured this claustrophobia once before in a performance of *The Tempest* when I was made to get inside a 'sea chest' while the whole cast leapt and vaulted over it as the ship went down in the storm.

Thump, thump, crash…Keep breathing, keep counting… When you get to one hundred it will all be over and you can push up the lid and leap out triumphantly onto the stage.

But that was playacting – this is for real. How did it come to this? Me, stuck here in a box, at the mercy of this psychotic woman?

I wriggle my toes as cramp sets in. Every muscle in my back and lower legs is killing me. Through the slats, I see two pairs of legs from mid-thigh downwards, slim, suntanned and shapely. Identical. The same firm line of muscle, the same curvature at the calf, the same structure of the knee. The sort of legs that belong to rich women. One pair of legs is sliding in and out of my field of vision, as Gabrielle (it must be her) moves round the cabin. The other pair of legs is bent at the knee – that must be Christina perched up on one of the leather bar stools – and bound at the ankle with several turns of thick rope. So now Gabrielle has tied her up. I see Christina's feet twisting round and round as she tries to loosen the rope.

The walking legs move into my field of vision. I hold my breath as a hand comes into view – it looks identical to Christina's hand but there's a wedding band and a large engagement ring on the fourth finger. The hand is clenching a knife, a short fisherman's knife, of a kind that might be used to gut a fish. It belongs to the walking legs.

Oh my God, she's going to stab her!

I kick my bent legs as hard as I can against the locked cupboard door. The wood splinters, the catch breaks and I tumble onto the floor. I leap to my feet and lunge towards Gabrielle, hoping that the shock of my sudden appearance will be enough to make her freeze. But instead of showing any sign of alarm, she turns to face me, the knife held in mid-air like the paintbrush of an artist interrupted in her work.

'I was wondering how long it would take for you to come out of your rat hole!'

She throws back her head and laughs while I stand there at a loss what to do next.

'I've been hearing you scratching away in there ever since we set sail.'

So, she knew I was there all the time. She's been playing cat-and-mouse with me again. It suited her to have me out of the way while she tied up Christina and set up her props. Instinctively, I sense that I have to confront this woman – any sign of weakness or vulnerability and she'll pounce.

'What the hell have you done with Katie?' I yell. 'Where is she?'

She feigns ignorance. 'You know exactly who I'm talking about.' I position myself between her and Christina. 'What have you done with her? The little girl you stole from the beach...'

Gabrielle steps right up to me, gesturing with the knife to emphasise her words. '*Rescued*. You insolent, irresponsible girl. I rescued her,' she says. 'Damien's taking good care of her. She's safe now, much safer than she ever was with you. It was on your watch that she almost drowned don't forget!'

Well, that hurt!

There's no point trying to have a sensible conversation with someone brandishing a knife. I turn my attention to Christina. She's leaning backwards with her eyes closed, rigid with pain. As well as having her feet bound, her arms are pinned behind the backrest of the bar stool, held fast by a thick belt strapped round her torso. Her shoulder must be killing her.

Gabrielle shoves me to one side and kicks her in the shins, hard.

'Wake up,' she orders. This is all your fault.' She punctuates her speech by hammering an empty vodka bottle down onto the table – bang, bang, bang – as she paces up and down the saloon. 'You destroyed my marriage... You broke my heart... You stole my husband... You stole my baby... I've taken back what was mine and now you're going to pay.'

Christina opens her eyes. 'You lying, vicious bitch,' she says.

It's astonishing. If it weren't for the knife and the belt and the rope, they could be mistaken for teenage sisters squabbling over a botched date after a boozy party.

'What's going on here?' I blurt out. 'Why have you tied her up?'

I dodge behind the barstool and struggle to undo the buckle of the belt.

'Don't you dare!' says Gabrielle. She speaks slowly, confident and in control. 'She chose that belt for me in Venice.' Her tone is hostile yet smooth. 'I always hated it. Finally I've found a good use for it.'

She smiles and drags over another bar stool.

'Do come and sit down,' she says, as if she's inviting me to join the Mad Hatter's Tea Party. 'In married life, three is company and two is none. Hey Lara – Oscar Wilde. You must remember that from your Oxford days. The same goes for us twins.' She pats Christina's knee. 'We always get along so much better when we're in a threesome, don't we Lara? We're not so good at being alone together.' She flicks the blade of the knife to direct me to the barstool next to Christina. 'Welcome to the Last Chance Saloon!' she says pointedly.

I'm scared she'll lose it if I challenge her, so I play along and sit down quietly.

A thick bundle of papers tied together with a black ribbon lies among the clutter of empty bottles on the bar in front of Christina.

IN THE CASE OF KENEDEY V HAMILTON

The heading reads. As Gabrielle pours herself a glass of vodka, I peer over to read the summary of proceedings at the top of the page. If I understand the legal jargon correctly, the documents relate to the legal battle over parental rights and custody of Katie in relation to the 'aborted' surrogacy.

So now I'm beginning to understand why Gabrielle lured Christina on to this yacht and is subjecting her to such intimidation and abuse. She's planning to keep her hostage, until she's broken her down and forced her to sign the legal papers giving herself adoption rights over Katie and the legal status as Katie's mother. She's taken the law into her own hands.

Ceremoniously, she frees one of Christina's arms from the belt and hands her a pen. She's not as crazy as she seems.

In one swift movement, Christina picks up the pen and hurls it as hard as she can across the saloon.

'You just made a big mistake, sister,' says Gabrielle without even turning to look at Christina. She hooks the knife inside her belt and pours me a shot.

I shake my head.

'Go on. Knock it back. Chill out.' she says. 'You look like a rabbit caught in the headlights. You're making me nervous.'

From the way Gabrielle's swaying around, I can tell she's had more than a few shots already even though she's speaking every word with absolute precision. The wild glint in her eyes also suggests she's been neglecting to take her medication!

She takes another cigarette from a packet of Lucky Strike open on the table and reaches for the matches. Her hands are shaking.

'Stop! Are you crazy?' I shout. The floor is drenched with petrol I remember with horror.

I make a grab for the matches but she gets there first.

'I always live dangerously.'

She strikes the match and the flame flickers before her eyes.

35

Newspaper Cutting

27 December 2010 The Stratford Herald

Have you seen this? It's the newspaper cutting from the Stratford Herald reporting the accident, with the headline, 'Christmas Day Tragedy at Clandon Bridge.' The local hack took a pretty good shot – interesting composition – angled down along the masonry arches of the bridge to the river below, and in the gloom of the pillars there's the plucky little red E-type Jag, almost fully submerged, only the boot visible above the swirling, murky water.

The print is grainy but you can just make out the personalised number plate,

'JAM1E' – so uncool but so James!

While I was locked away in the psychiatric hospital the year after the accident, I had time for introspection and remorse. Repent at leisure, they say. Well, I had time to relive every twist and turn in our drama.

It's very convenient to write my role as the 'wicked witch', or the 'bad fairy.' But this is no fairy tale, and you are no Snow White or Sleeping Beauty... no hapless damsel in distress. We are made of the same DNA.

At the time, I was so angry with you and with James that all I could think about was keeping out of jail. I was blind to the pity of it all.

We fought over him like a plaything. We tore him apart. Yes, Lara, you played your part. You must take your share of the blame.

You played your part in killing James as surely as if you had been the one to wrap the strap round his neck.

But he was also to blame. Loving us both. That was his vice. Two for the price of one. He thought he could get one of us for free – greedy, self-indulgent fool.

In the end, he paid the full price.

Now it's your turn.

After Gabrielle had had her fix of French cinema classics for the afternoon, the family sat down together for Mrs Kennedy's customary festive supper of poached salmon and cold salads followed by sherry trifle and Victoria sponge. Then Gabrielle and James set off to the village pub for their traditional Christmas Eve get together with old school friends of Gabrielle's. The plan was to spend the evening at the pub and then go onto the church in Stratford where Gabrielle's father was preaching at the Christmas midnight mass. James was driving the little red Jaguar, showing off as he tore round the bends on the country lanes.

'Slow down, you idiot,' said Gabrielle. 'You may have a death wish, but I don't want to die tonight.'

At the pub, they joined the group bunched around tables in the corner near the log fire. There was much kissing and banter and catching up on old times. Gabrielle's friends were also Lara's friends. To those who had stayed behind, they remained the beautiful, jet-setting, alpha-female Kennedy twins, who had escaped from a boring provincial setting to the glamour of Chelsea and New York. Gabrielle had kept up with a few of her Stratford friends but Lara had deliberately cut herself off – an attempt to break out of the toxic triangle in which she was trapped. The friends were curious. Where was Lara now? Did she have children? Was she married? What was she up to? Gabrielle answered curtly. The last person she wanted to talk about was her twin – the subject bored her to distraction.

Gabrielle offered to buy a round of drinks to get away from the inquisition.

'Give me your wallet,' she said to James. 'I haven't got any cash.'

He was deep in conversation with a man who had introduced himself as one of her former boyfriends. That wasn't the way she would have described him. They were discussing the merits of the latest edition of Jaguar sports car.

James dug into his jeans pocket for his wallet and handed it over without a pause in the conversation, without even giving her a glance.

'I'll take you out for a spin on Boxing Day,' he said to the man. 'It's a beautiful car.'

At the bar, Gabrielle opened the wallet and fingered awkwardly through the collection of random business cards and receipts with which it was stuffed until she found two crisp twenty pound notes. As she pulled them out, a couple of business cards fell out along with something else – a photograph, folded in four. Her bandaged fingers were making her clumsy. She opened it out.

A picture of her and James in Venice, just after they got engaged. Ah! That was such a wonderful trip. Rather sweet of James to keep that in his wallet after all these years. Perhaps she was being a bit hard on him. If only the bitch would stop harassing him the whole time, perhaps they could still work things out. Once the surrogacy was over and they were home with their new baby, they could make a fresh start.

The light was dim in the pub. She held the picture up to the wall light to take a closer look. Her face dropped. The photograph was of James and of the Bridge of Sighs in Venice, but she was not the woman leaning back against James in the gondola.

She had never worn French braids.

As she folded the photograph again, she noticed the date, written in pencil on the back.

12 May 2010.

The full horror of the affair dawned on her.

My God! She was carrying my baby. She was more than two weeks into the surrogacy.

She felt the urge to smash something, to grab the glasses and bottles resting on the bar and sling them to the floor. She wished Lara had never been born. *I should have wrapped the cord round her neck and strangled her in the womb. She's been the cause of all my misery since the very day we were born.*

She looked across to James, still boasting and bragging to his new best friend on the other side of the bar.

And as for him, I've always known he was a coward and a cheat but I never imagined that he could be such a moral degenerate. One of these days, I'm going to make him pay.

They drove in silence from the pub to the church for midnight mass. Gabrielle was driving – holding the steering wheel gingerly with her sore, bandaged hands.

'You could have laid off the drink for one night, in the circumstances,' she said crossly.

'What's wrong?' said James. 'I thought you'd be happy to have seen your friends.' He leaned his head back and slurred his words. 'We had a very nice evening with your friends; I was perfectly charming to them.'

Gabrielle wanted to scream. She had nothing to say to him. She was too enraged to argue. Lara's betrayal came as no surprise but she was incensed by James' stupidity. He didn't even have the mental agility to acknowledge his own infidelity.

She drove in silence, preoccupied with her murderous thoughts.

He couldn't even comprehend that they were two distinct individuals. In his eyes, they were just two identical incarnations of a woman he loved. She didn't exist as a separate person and if she didn't exist then he couldn't be unfaithful. What a jerk! She swung into the church car park and slammed on the brakes.

Well damn it, I'm going to show him that I exist. I'm going to make him appreciate me as a unique human being. He's got to learn. If I have to put a knife to his throat to make him understand that this flesh and blood and this beating heart belongs only to me, I'll do it. Whatever it takes.

During the service she regained her composure, smiled mechanically at members of the congregation who recognised her as the vicar's daughter, and murmured the words of the creed that she knew by rote. But her mind was elsewhere. She was incapable of joining in with the carols and while all round her sang enthusiastically she stood staring intently at the statue of the Madonna and Child to the right of the altar.

It was just after midnight as the congregation were singing 'For unto us a Child is born, Unto us a Son is given' that Gabrielle had her very own epiphany.

She felt as if she were sinking into a cool, dark river, the current swirling high above her head. It was refreshing, liberating, exhilarating. She didn't love James. She didn't need James any more.

She glanced across at him sitting a little further along the pew. He had grown scuffed, grey, soft round the edges. The lustre was gone. She was tired of him and it was time to get rid of him. The words: *Jim, je vais te tuer! Jules, regard-nous bien!* resonated in her head, like a mantra, drowning out the carol.

'He's served his purpose. I don't need him any more,' she said to herself.

'Mine' and 'More' – Gabrielle's mother had told her that until they were three years old, those were the only two 'intelligible' words she could make out in her little girls' babbling baby talk. They had invented their own private language and communicated in their own exclusive universe. But when it came to the adults, the only words they bothered with were 'mine' and 'more'. Gabrielle's mother feared they had learning difficulties and started consulting speech therapists and child psychologists. But then she came to realise, that in fact those two functional words were all they needed as toddlers to satisfy their needs and appeal to adults for assistance in regulating the endless power struggle that formed the basis of their relationship.

'You competed for everything, fought over everything,' said her mother. First the demands – more food, more attention, more love – and then the staking out of claims and the fight over the spoils: *it's mine, hands off, give it to me, it's mine*. It was the selfish gene – survival of the fittest, competing to the death with an identical copy of itself. 'I read something like that in those psychology books when expecting you girls,' she told Gabrielle.

Gabrielle's mindset had changed very little since those nursery battles over gifts and treats. The attachment she felt for all her prized possessions was bound up with the fact that they belonged to her and not to Lara – *mine, mine, mine*.

The satisfaction of owning any special thing was intimately connected with the pleasure of depriving Lara from the satisfaction of such ownership. It didn't matter whether 'the thing' was an object or a person. That's why, when Lara started going out with James, Gabrielle was determined to win him back – come hell or high water! And it followed that when Gabrielle tired of a toy, she never thought of giving it to her twin. The toy would be destroyed and thrown in the trash: denying her sister the pleasure gave her infinitely more happiness than owning the toy in the first place.

But James had violated this natural order of things. He thought he could have them both, thought he could make her share. What a reckless fool! And now she'd finally had enough of him. The romantic idealism of his younger days had ebbed away. He had grown too familiar and too worn. Threadbare – like her old teddy that she had ended up decapitating with her mother's needlework scissors and burning in the log fire.

She didn't love him. The love was gone. She was tired of his cheating and his lies. She didn't need this soft plaything any more. She wanted his baby, her baby. But now that the baby was on the way, he was of no further use to her. And she would make damn sure he didn't get the chance to share the baby with Lara. Come hell or high water, Lara was not to share in the joy of Gabrielle's baby. No way!

Gabrielle was driving the Jaguar. After three whiskies and five beers at the pub, followed by two glasses of mulled wine to accompany his mince pie after midnight mass, James was not only well over the limit but also well out of it, by the time they left the church hall.

'Happy Christmas. We'll see you back at the house,' called out Gabrielle as she steered James towards the car. Her father waved cheerily as he made his way back to the main building to thank the Dean and make sure all the candles had been extinguished and the doors locked.

James plonked himself down into the passenger seat and fumbled for the seatbelt.

'Here let me do it,' said Gabrielle. 'You're pathetic! Can't hold your drink. Worse than a teenage girl!'

The metal clasp of the seatbelt was bent from having been slammed in the car door but she managed to lean onto it and force it in to place. Then she threw her Florentine handbag into James' lap.

'Hold this'

He tried to kiss her cheek.

'Thanks for driving, darling. Happy Christmas.'

Gabrielle shoved him away.

'Your breath stinks,' she said.

She put the car into gear and released the handbrake, wincing as the pain shot through the lacerated palms of her hands.

James lay back against the seat and shut his eyes.

But if he thought she'd let him have a quiet snooze on the drive home, he could think again. As soon as she got onto the open road, Gabrielle started on him.

'I saw your messages. I answered her bloody phone call,' said Gabrielle. 'So there's no point trying to deny it.'

James kept his eyes closed. From the corner of her eye, she saw a muscle twitching near his jawline.

'I know you've been cheating with Lara.' The car veered across the road as she craned her neck to look at him.

He opened his eyes but they were dull with alcohol.

'You've got it all wrong...' began James.

'I found the photograph in your wallet,' said Gabrielle. 'So now I know why you were so keen on attending that conference in Milan.'

James turned away to look out of the window into the dark.

'I'm so done with you, James. You've grown tired... boring... shabby and unreliable. I don't need you any more. I don't want you any more.'

'Gabrielle, I can explain... I can't think now. Let's talk in the morning.'

His speech was stumbling and incoherent.

She didn't raise her voice but spoke with a steely calm.

'I've heard enough of your lies. I'm indifferent to you now. You've become a disposable item.'

She put her foot down on the accelerator until, even in his drunken stupor, James gripped on to the door handle fearing for his life. It was his turn to urge caution. Seventy miles per hour, on icy, winding country roads.

'Slow down, Gabrielle. It's too dangerous... shouldn't be driving with those bandages.'

'If you had a shred of self-control I wouldn't be driving,' she snapped back at him. Then she spoke through gritted teeth, in a hard tone, that he had never heard before. 'I want you out of my life, and out of Lara's life forever. If that whore thinks she's getting my leftovers, she can think again.'

Far ahead on the road, beyond the red mist inside her head, she could see red lights flashing. They were coming up to a level crossing. A train was approaching. On impulse, she decided to race it. The speedometer needle climbed to eighty, then ninety – the barriers were coming down.

'Fucking slow down, Gabrielle,' shouted James. 'Stop.'

'Too late.' said Gabrielle, and she pushed her foot right down to the floor.

The little sports car accelerated wildly and flew over the tracks just as the barriers closed over the boot, scraping the metalwork with a sickening screech as the car sped on and the train's whistle screamed down the track.

'Christ, Gabrielle, you're scaring the shit out of me.'

She eased off the accelerator and seemed to relax at the wheel.

'Well, that sobered you up,' she laughed, as he sat up straight and alert.

'There's something you need to know,' said James making an effort to speak slowly and clearly, enunciating every word painfully. 'It's not your baby.'

She made him say it again, just to make sure she'd heard him correctly. 'What did you say?'

'It's not your baby.' The words gushed out in a current of despair. 'The baby is hers. Hers and mine – a natural surrogacy. She's the biological mother. But she's going to give you the baby anyway. She's keeping her word. You've got the same DNA. It won't make any difference. She'll give us the baby... to save our marriage.'

Gabrielle didn't flinch. They drove in silence for a mile or so. Then she switched on the radio.

'You do talk a lot of tosh when you're drunk,' said Gabrielle. She glanced briefly at James who, having unburdened himself, had relapsed into an alcoholic daze. He was leaning back against the seat with his mouth hanging slightly open. 'You're disgusting,' she said.

The local radio station was playing the usual inane Christmas pop songs that were recycled every year.

'So here it is merry Christmas...everybody's having fun.' She sang along tunefully, as if she hadn't a care in the world. James stirred, reached out and squeezed her knee.

About a mile further on, she turned off the road into a layby. Now James was slumped in the seat, with his head thrown back, snoring. She cut the engine. She took her handbag off his lap and gently wrapped the long leather strap round his neck.

Then she pulled with all her strength.

'Because she's mine,' she said, very quietly.

She was driving carefully now along back roads taking the bends slowly and observing the speed limits as they came into the outskirts of the town.

A police car passed in the opposite direction.

'They're on the lookout for drunk drivers this evening,' she said out loud. 'Good thing I'm driving.'

James was slumped sideways in the seat, his head tilted forward, held up by the seatbelt.

As they approached Clandon Bridge, she slowed for the temporary lights.

'Road works. Must still be repairing the flood damage from last month.'

There were temporary barriers on one side of the bridge where the brick wall had been washed away by the force of the floodwaters and traffic was reduced to a single lane. The bridge was deserted. She stopped at the lights. The windows were misted up. She opened her window.

'That's better,' she said.

The lights changed to green. She moved away smoothly. 'Almost home,' she said quietly. She turned to James whose head was knocking against the window as they went over the ruts, 'Regarde moi, regarde moi,' she insisted.

As the car got to the middle of the bridge, she turned again and gave James her sweetest smile. Then she swung the wheel sharply onto full lock and rammed her foot down on the accelerator. The car lurched on a right angle. The temporary barriers crumpled on impact as the solid little Jaguar flew through the twisted metal and plunged gracefully into the inky water.

Gabrielle is a strong swimmer and she is sober. She braces as they fly through the air. When the car hits the water she is ready to unclip her seatbelt and wriggle out though the open window like a mermaid into the deep. Her head is throbbing where she hit the steering wheel. The river is at full flood and the current drags her away from the bridge further downstream towards the weir. Those many hours of training for her local club, competing with teenagers in other clubs, personal best pitched against personal best, every tenth of a second a matter of personal pride, survival of the fittest, and all the while, Lara standing on the sidelines clapping and cheering her on.

Now it pays off. Every tenth of a second counts for real this time, a matter of life and death. With every muscle and sinew, she fights the current. Stroke-by-stroke, she pulls back until she is able to haul herself up onto a concrete ledge at the base of a pillar beneath the bridge.

She doesn't know how long she lies there, coughing up river water, catching her breath, stunned, looking down at the boot of the Jaguar floating nose down in the water – it could be ten seconds, it could be ten minutes.

Eventually she hears a car pulling up on the bridge, a door slams, footsteps and voices, someone calling out. She comes to her senses. Now it's time for her best performance, her all-time personal best. She scrabbles around the base of the pillar for something hard or sharp. In amongst the debris she finds a broken brick. Then she stands up on the ledge and strips off her dress. She hears a man's voice shouting.

'Stop! Wait.'

She doesn't hesitate. She stretches up her arms, bends her knees and with broken brick in hand, dives gracefully into the water, down to the sunken car in a desperate underwater struggle to smash the window.

Battling the current, she hangs onto the door handle. His face is pressed against the glass. His eyes are open. His head is lolling from side-to-side in the water. She smashes the brick against the glass. She's good at this. The glass cracks, she strikes again and again, and pulls at the jagged edges, her flesh protected by the sodden bandages, until at last the opening is clear. She grabs the seatbelt, yanks at the broken catch. Good. It's well and truly jammed. He's trapped.

Clinging to the window opening, she pulls the seatbelt from his chest and lifts it over his arms and shoulders until it tightens and cuts into the flesh round his neck.

Feeling as if her lungs will burst, she comes up for air at the surface. Sirens fill the air, sirens and pulsing blue waves. She's flailing in the water. Someone flings a life buoy out from the bank. Just out of reach. Her head slides under, she gulps the rancid river water.

'Keep going. You can do it. You're almost there. Reach for it.'

That voice in her head. It's Lara, cheering her on, laughing, clapping, watching from the side of the pool...

A police officer grabs her arm and hauls her out of the water onto the bank. Another throws a metallic survival blanket round her shoulders and leads her away to the ambulance. She's exhausted and shaking. Her head bleeds from a gash above her eye. Blood streams down her forehead, into her eyelashes, clouding her vision with red. The bandages have come loose and her hands are raw.

As she collapses onto the couch in the ambulance, Lara's face floats above her. She's wearing a red silk evening gown – the very same one that Gabrielle borrowed that night she first met James.

'I asked for champagne. More champagne' says Gabrielle, as the apparition hands her a mug of tea. She toasts the lady in red.

'You'll be needing stitches, for that cut,' she hears her say.

A policeman stands to one side. He's saying something. 'You gave it your all. That was a splendid performance.'

'Thank you' says Gabrielle softly, as she sips her mug of tea. 'He had it coming.'

'What did she say?' says the policeman.

'Je vais te tuer Jim!' mutters Gabrielle manically. 'Je vais te tuer.'

'What's she on about?' says the policeman.

'I think it's French,' says the paramedic. 'She's in shock.'

Fortunately for Gabrielle, the policeman didn't speak French and he certainly wasn't a fan of French cinema.

It was on Christmas Day 2010 that Lara had finally made up her mind – when the rising sun hit the glass wall of her apartment in New York and she was woken by Mrs Kennedy's distraught phone call communicating the shattering news. Once she had eventually understood her mother's strangled message, not really understanding how it had happened, but only those dreadful words, 'James is dead, drowned…' that Lara made her repeat a hundred times – that was when she knew for sure. Struck with the immediate conviction that if she hadn't cancelled her trip, James would still be alive, Lara's world had changed. This baby stirring in her womb was her own flesh and blood. She could not give her away to Gabrielle.

'I'm keeping the baby.' said Lara.

'I don't understand. What on earth are you talking about?' she heard her mother say as she put down the phone.

I'm keeping the baby, because she's mine.

'I think she's in shock,' said Mrs Kennedy when she returned to the kitchen where her husband was busying himself making a cup of tea for the local police liaison officer who had come over to provide support. The Reverend Phil Kennedy looked up from the teapot that he was stirring mechanically, round and round.

'What dear?'

'I think she's in shock, or she was still half asleep. I must have woken her from a dream. I couldn't understand a word she was going on about, something about a baby.'

'Sit down and have a cup of tea,' said the Rev Kennedy. 'You look exhausted.' Mrs Kennedy, pulled up a chair, lent her elbows on the table and her head in her hands.

'She wouldn't listen to anything I said. I don't think she took it in – that James is dead. "She's mine" – that's all she kept saying, over and over again. "I'm keeping the baby, because she's mine."'

36

Scarlett

Even in danger and misery the pendulum swings.

Thank God, Gabrielle blows out the flame before tossing the match to the floor. Suddenly she is in a good mood and our situation feels slightly less desperate. She draws deeply on her cigarette and leans back in her chair.

'I've got a job for you,' she says, puffing into my face. I gag from the combination of petrol fumes and smoke. She pushes the legal papers to one side, reaches into a cupboard above her head and takes out a large, leather-bound photograph album, the sort that pretentious people like to display their artsy photographs in, using those fiddly little corners. It's embossed with the words THE ALBUM in large gold letters. It looks out of place lying there, along with the empty vodka bottle and the shot glasses. Then she turns to Christina. 'Do you remember that silly programme we used to watch when we were kids?' she says. '*This Is Your Life* – that's what it was called. They used to haul in old celebrities as they approached death, wheel in their long-lost friends – and enemies! – and present them with an album of photographs at the end of it. Well, this is for you– even though you're not old, and you're not a celebrity– at least not for the right reasons.' She pushes the album towards Christina and ends her little speech with a flourish. 'So, this is *our life*, and I hope you enjoy it!'

Our life – not your life or our lives but our life. That's how Gabrielle refers to the photo album. This is her testament of their shared existence, of their intertwined, singular identity. She's holding up a mirror to Christina's face and the truth is not pretty.

I glance across anxiously towards Christina.

Gabrielle leafs through the album, turning the thick ivory-coloured pages with care. She's laid it out artistically – a photograph on the right-hand side of each double page and on the left, a dense handwritten text in obsessively neat italic script, the letters beautifully formed in black ink. There they are, the ghosts from the past, the shadows of this drama – Gabrielle, Christina and the boy she was in love with – captured in their younger beauty, prisoners of the past.

'There's some unfinished business you can help with,' says Gabrielle, cutting short my reflections.

Catching sight of my grimy hands, she orders me to wash them at the galley sink. Absurdly, I feel ashamed of my chipped nail polish and dirty fingernails.

'Don't try any tricks,' she warns me, holding the fillet knife up to Christina's throat as I rinse my hands under the tap. Christina's eyes are wide open, shining with fear, like an animal caught in the headlights.

When I sit down again Gabrielle makes a theatrical sweep of the knife and tests the blade on her finger. For a second, I fear she's going to slash her sister's face but instead she runs the flat blade across her cheek like an old-fashioned barber.

Then she stands back to observe Christina's profile and says thoughtfully, 'No. I'm not finished with her yet. I don't want to spoil the photographs.'

With the knife now hitched in the belt of Gabrielle's jeans, I resolve to make a grab for the handle as she lights yet another cigarette. She's practically chain-smoking now, discarding the butts in a half-drunk cup of coffee, and adding to my sickening sense of impending disaster, in case she lets one drop to the petrol-drenched floor. As I kick back my chair, she thrusts the cigarette in front of my face.

'One false move, and this time The Phantasea goes up in flames.' My eyes are trained on the red ash which hangs perilously on the end of her cigarette. She turns back to Christina. 'Do you remember that show we did at school? *Sweeney Todd*,' she says. 'Of course, you got to play the beautiful, love-sick, Johanna.' Her tone is reflective, philosophical. 'And I got to play the mad, fire-obsessed, old hag, her mother.' She takes a deep drag on her cigarette. 'When I complained about the casting the teacher just banged on about family likeness.' She grabs a handful of Christina's hair. 'The murderous Mrs Lovatt would have suited me a lot better!' She laughs. 'I always was jealous of your long golden hair.' She holds the long strands up to the sunlight. 'Golden and scintillating. Mine always looked somehow mousy next to yours.' Suddenly, she sits forward, chattering manically. 'Remember that time when we were only three? I got hold of the kitchen scissors and started cutting off your golden locks while you were sleeping in the cot. Mother ran in screaming!'

'I don't remember,' says Christina, looking down at her bound hands. 'There were so many times…'

'Untie her,' I say. 'We need sit down together and talk this through calmly.'

'All in good time,' says Gabrielle. 'We've got work to do.' She jabs the cigarette at me. 'You're going to help me complete the album.' That sounds ominous! 'It will keep us entertained until your friends come to the rescue!' She must have heard me sending the SOS.

I glance across anxiously towards Christina. Her eyes are closed now. She seems to be almost fainting with the pain of the gunshot wound and the indignity of being tied up and humiliated.

'Open your eyes,' orders Gabrielle. 'We're not finished yet. Look, the last page is blank. Scarlett's going to read to you while I set up the cameras for the final photograph.' She flips back to the first page of the album and taps it with the blade of her knife. 'Now read,' she orders me. 'Then you'll understand.'

There's no getting out of this charade, so I start reading, deciphering with difficulty Gabrielle's intricate writing describing each of the photographs, speaking as slowly and clearly as I can, playing for time, praying my distress call got through to the coastguard, and was transmitted to the police and that Costa will get his act together fast before Gabrielle loses it completely and turns the knife on her twin.

As I turn the page, she casually aims a camera lens at me and clicks the shutter.

'There's no escape from our story. You're part of it now.'

Now Gabrielle's mood has turned as black as the weather. While I've been sitting here reading, the wind has changed. The air is electric and there are dark, menacing clouds on the horizon.

'There's a squall on the way,' I say. 'We need to get back to shore.' The waves are building steadily, making The Phantasea rise and fall like a seesaw. The sky lights up and the first crack of thunder explodes overhead. 'That sounds bad!'

Gabrielle swears and blasphemes like a squaddie as she struggles to set up a tripod at the back of the saloon. Meanwhile I seize on the chance to dash through the galley to the cockpit to see if I can work out how to start up the engines.

'Stop', screams Gabrielle. 'Get away from there.'

Gabrielle is not the sort of woman it's easy to say 'no' to – especially when she's got the blade of a fisherman's knife sticking out of her belt. But though I back off from the controls, I protest loudly,

'We're going to capsize. We need to find shelter fast. There's no time to lose.'

That really irks Gabrielle.

'I've been sailing these yachts since I was thirteen years old. I know what I'm doing,' she says. 'You've been a great help so far, Scarlett but you're really beginning to get on my nerves. Stop interfering. Get on with the reading or you can swim back to shore.'

So, while I continue to read from the album and Christina remains slumped, half fainting in her seat, Gabrielle saunters round the saloon, defying the thunder and lightning, setting up screens and lighting and making final adjustments to angles and profiles. She's in her element now, confident, in her professional comfort zone, mouthing the words I recite as she goes about setting up her photographic equipment. Walking past the galley, she tips the dregs of the vodka bottle into one of the shot glasses and tosses it back.

Once satisfied with her arrangements, Gabrielle decides to punish me for my aborted attempt at mutiny. She locks the doors and for good measure, holds the knife to my neck while she orders me to sit down and with one hand deftly binds my ankles to the legs of the stool.

'Any more false moves and she'll suffer for it,' says Gabrielle, flicking the knife towards Christina.

I'm feeling more and more seasick by the minute, desperate to get out on deck away from the reek of petrol.

'I need some fresh air,' I say. 'I'm going to be sick.'

'You're not going anywhere,' says Gabrielle. 'I haven't finished with you yet. You're part of our story now.'

This time, she makes it sound like a death sentence!

37

Photograph Twelve

14 February 2011: Maternity Ward,
New York City Hospital

*I found this photograph in the drawer of Mother's dressing
table when I went home last Christmas. It's of you,
propped up on the pillows of a hospital bed, dishevelled,
your hair damp with sweat and the sheets stained with
blood – the midwife can't have been too fastidious. I
suppose she must have taken the photograph for you.
It's time stamped 1.35 a.m. on 14 February 2011. I can't
imagine who else could have been there to hold your hand
at that ungodly hour of the night.*

*There you are, impersonating the blessed Virgin Mary
herself, a pastiche of maternal love. I've never seen you
looking so happy and serene. You're robed in hospital
blue, holding my newborn baby, swaddled in a white
sheet, her tiny face close to your breast.*

My darling Rose, born so poignantly on Valentine's Day, was already a prisoner in your arms.

With James dead and buried, who, other than me, could know the darkness that was in your thieving, cuckoo heart?

In the days following the drowning tragedy, Lara spent her time reminiscing about her past life in Oxford with James – heady days spent punting and pub crawling, drinking coffee in each other's rooms over shared essay crises, or getting drunk beneath the rose bushes in the Nuns' Garden on alcohol-drenched fruit picked from the bottom of a punch bowl. She smiled at the memory of those sweet debauched summer afternoons. The nuns would have blushed.

Ah! And then Venice – the agonising beauty of Venice. She could scarcely allow herself to dwell on memories of the reawakening of love she had shared with him there, winding along the sunny canals and under shady bridges. Reliving those images was like dipping her fingers into a black lagoon of grief – she dared not plunge beneath the shimmering surface for fear of being sucked under and drowned.

Unlike Gabrielle, all she had were her memories. There was no album to thumb, no images to peruse online. She had no interest in keeping pictures of the past. Life was for living in the moment. Lara's distrust for photography stemmed from her relationship as a twin. She had spent too much time when growing up confronted with a living image of herself. In her eyes, photography was just more unnecessary duplication.

In contrast, photography was Gabrielle's passion. From the age of six, she'd delighted in recording the minutiae of their lives. Lara saw this as part of her sister's obsessive need for control. Gabrielle wished to capture, process and document every aspect of their shared existence, to arrange it in the selection and order that she wanted – to own it. She was forever snapping away, first with her little instamatic, then with a sophisticated SLR camera that she had begged her parents to buy for her thirteenth birthday. A frequent target of Gabrielle's photo shooting projects, Lara felt no need to record their shared reality for herself. Now in the absence of photographs, and in fear of her memories, Lara focused on the new life that was growing inside her womb – experiencing every movement and sensation with renewed intensity.

As for Gabrielle, she found the inquest painful but she was excused from testifying on account of her precarious mental state. The coroner recorded a finding of accidental death by drowning. His report praised Gabrielle's bravery in having heroically risked her own life to attempt the rescue of James who had been trapped underwater in the car. The report noted that James's escape had been impeded by a faulty clasp on the passenger seatbelt. Bruising around the deceased's neck appeared to have been caused by the seatbelt becoming caught at the neckline either at the time of impact or in his struggle to escape from the car. The report also noted that high levels of alcohol found in the deceased's body may have contributed to his tragic death.

Gabrielle kept her emotions in check for the legal proceedings and the small private funeral but afterwards fell into a black depression. She took three months' leave of absence from work and moved back to the family home, spending hours each day locked in the bedroom that she used to share with Lara when they were girls.

She revived a few weeks later in time to plan a stylish memorial service for James to which more than two hundred of his friends and colleagues were invited. She insisted on taking control of everything, planning it meticulously like a VIP event organiser – she let her artistic instincts fly. It was to be an extravagant, vibrant, celebration of his life. Not some miserable, weak-tea-and-soggy-sandwiches affair. She would personally hand out glasses of James's vintage Claret to each of the guests as they stepped into the church. There was to be live music and dancing in the aisles.

She brought in professional photographic equipment from her studio in Chelsea and rigged up a vast projection screen behind the altar, so that life size black-and-white photographs and video sequences of herself and James, as the star-crossed lovers, could be projected up like an old-fashioned movie onto the back wall of the church. At the wake, they would drink buckets of champagne and eat smoked salmon and cupcakes.

'I'll make the cupcakes,' said Mrs Kennedy. 'I'd like to help.'

'I've got it covered,' said Gabrielle briskly. 'I've ordered them from our local patisserie on the King's Road – we go there for tea on Saturday afternoons.'

She planned her outfit meticulously – classic designer brands in retro-chic, complete with veiled hat, dark glasses, clutch bag and pearls like a 1950s star of the silver screen. She was going for the Grace Kelly look. No one was going to pity her. She was going to stun them all with her beauty and poise.

Her twin was not invited.

Back in New York, Lara remained absorbed in her own private mourning. After reading the report of the inquest that her mother sent to her, she reached her own conclusions. There were so many unanswered questions. She was appalled that the police had not launched a criminal investigation and thought cynically that the fact that Gabrielle was the daughter of a vicar had unjustly absolved her from suspicion. After the birth, she wrote to her mother, enclosing a photograph taken by the midwife of her baby daughter, Catherine Jamie. In her letter, she tried to explain why she was cutting herself off from the family but mostly she wrote to say goodbye:

She killed him, Mother. I'm sure of it. I knew as soon as I read the report of the inquest. She strangled him with the leather strap of a handbag I chose for her in Venice, and she drove the car off the bridge to hide her crime. If any of you ever try to track me down, I'm going straight to the police – I can prove it. She killed James to punish me. I know how her mind works. How could I give my baby girl to the woman who killed her father and my first love? We made her – James and I. She is unique, she is beautiful and she belongs to me. I can't blame

*Gabrielle for hating me, for wanting me dead too...
The power of maternal love – it's terrifying. Now I
understand why her desperation for that love, drove her
mad. I won't be coming back to England. I'm applying
for US citizenship and I'm staying here in New York.
Please don't try to contact me. I have a new identity. I'm
starting a new life to protect my baby. Though it breaks
my heart, I can never see you again.*

*Forget you ever had a daughter named Lara. She is
gone.*

38

Scarlett

Finally, she's ready.

'OK, let's go,' she says. 'Photograph Thirteen. This will be the last – a fitting ending to the album of our life.'

Without taking her eyes away from the viewfinder targeting Christina's face, she points to the Album and says,

'Scarlett, turn to the end.'

The last double page is blank. There's only a heading at the top on the right-hand side, written in black ink and underlined.

Photograph 13: Unlucky for Someone

Then below, the blank space, for a photograph.

'So, Scarlett,' says Gabrielle, with an ironic smile. 'What shall it be? You've done a little modelling yourself, haven't you? You should have some interesting ideas!'

Ouch!

Her swipe at my character confirms what I've known for some time – she was behind the YouPorn video and e-Face. She was the woman I corresponded with by email and spoke to on the phone.

Gabrielle swings the lens back round to Christina, and with professional ease, swiftly adjusts the exposure settings. She sings softly and I catch fragments of lyrics from one of last year's hits, 'You watching me…' She puts a hand under Christina's chin and tilts her head firmly towards the porthole to make the most of the remaining light. 'Hanging by a string this time…' Now Gabrielle is completely absorbed in composing the image. 'My smile's worth a hundred lies…' She adjusts the position of Christina's arms and Christina cries out in pain. 'Whatever happened to you?' says Gabrielle, noticing the blood-stained tourniquet underneath her shirt. She doesn't wait for the answer. She unbuckles the belt and loosens the rope around Christina's ankles. 'Stand up,' she says coldly, 'I want a full-length shot.'

As Christina struggles to her feet, she picks up the camera, spins the lens to focus and lock the settings, then clicks on the shutter button.

'Good girl, Lara, well done. That's beautiful. Really stunning.' The photographer's patter comes naturally to her.

'Now put your hands behind your head and lean away from the lens…'

I see Christina wince with pain as she moves into position but she knows better than to complain.

'One leg slightly forward, that's it… You're looking up dreamily at a stunning blue sky… Remember that day in the punt on the Cherwell? Willow branches arching overhead, sunlight on the water... passion shining in your eyes – or was it madness, like Ophelia?' She murmurs on tunelessly. 'Playing with desire... When it burns like fire.'

'If anyone's acting crazy round here, it's you,' I shout out from across the table. 'This madness has got to stop.'

Gabrielle turns to me with a smile worthy of Medusa. 'Nothing sweet about me,' she says.

Christina's face is a picture of misery as Gabrielle drags her wrists behind her head. Impatiently, Gabrielle slams the camera down on the table and her anger explodes,

'Come on Lara, I need you to try harder, we need some conviction here. You're a young woman in love. Not a bloody victim of gang rape.'

Christina shuts her eyes and rearranges her features. I see she's done this kind of thing for Gabrielle before. Swiftly, Gabrielle changes the lens on the camera and moves in for a close-up frame. 'Look at me Lara, open your eyes,' she says softly. 'I'm still waiting for that perfect shot. You always were my inspiration, my alter ego.'

As the yacht sways to one side, the knife slides across the floor of the saloon towards the side where I am tied up. I lunge down for it, but she pounces and grabs it first.

'Snap!' she yells in excitement as my hand thumps down a fraction of a second too late. Armed with the knife again a new idea seems to enter her head. Roughly she gathers up Christina's blonde hair in her right hand. 'You'll never get away from me, Lara.' For a second, I think she's rearranging Christina's hair for the next frame. 'Golden girl! You were always so proud of your golden curls, weren't you?' With a flick of her wrist, she twists Christina's hair into a ponytail and hacks it off with the knife.

'Stop!' I shout, desperately trying to kick my ankles free from the legs of the stool without tumbling onto the floor.

Gabrielle refocuses the viewfinder. 'That's so much better,' she says. 'We'll just have to make do with the gang-rape-victim-look, if we can't manage blissful-romantic today.'

I manage to free one leg. 'Are you mad?' I lurch towards Gabrielle, dragging the stool behind me. 'Give me the knife!' I succeed in grasping her right hand as she moves forward to pick it up. But I'm out of luck. Like a snake, Gabrielle whips around, seizes the knife in her left hand and slashes my outstretched forearm. Of course! She's left-handed being Christina's genetic mirror-image twin. I clutch my arm to staunch the blood streaming from the wound.

'Now look what you made me do!' she says. 'Be careful.' She nods towards Christina. 'It'll be her face next time.' She bends down and cuts through the rope still binding one of my ankles to the stool. 'Now for God's sake go to the sink and get a towel,' snaps Gabrielle. 'I don't want your blood dripping all over my floor.' The polished wooden floor is drenched in petrol so her concern about a few bloodstains strikes me as bizarre. As if reading my thoughts, she pats the packet of matches bulging in the pocket of her shorts. 'Don't do anything stupid. Any trouble from you, and we all go up in flames.'

Christina begins to shake and sob silently. Strands from her newly-styled bob stick to her cheeks. Gabrielle puts both hands up to her sister's neck and for one beat I fear she's going to strangle her. But then she grabs her shirt and rips it open, exposing her breasts. She stands back to look. The image pleases her.

'That's good,' she says, suddenly detached and professional again. 'Now, stretch your arms above your head, you're hanging from a tree... super... well done. Remember that day on the river in Oxford... Look up at the leaves, dappling against the sky... Hold it there ... Perfect... Now, look down... down into the black water swirling below. OK, at last we're getting somewhere.'

Christina sways from side to side as the catamaran is battered by the waves and what with Gabrielle vocalising her sadistic fantasy, I can't stop myself from imagining her swinging from a tree. Now I see what Gabrielle's playing at – trying to make me complicit, drawing me in to this 'toxic triangle' the way she's done with others before, making me feel tainted and dirty as a witness to this degrading spectacle of abuse.

At this moment, there's a sudden flash of lightning and a huge clap of thunder directly overhead. The power trips off, filling the saloon with shadows and gloom.

'The gods are smiling on us,' says Gabrielle. She changes the filter on the lens and switches the camera to video mode. 'We need some more action shots. I'm going to make the mood a little darker,' she says. 'Now, Lara, get on the floor. Hands and knees will do fine... Face the other way... Now look back at me... Just a few black-and-white stills and a video sequence then we're done.'

Gabrielle sits cross-legged on the floor, camera in hand, contented and relaxed.

'Ritual humiliation and sexual innuendo. We have to get some in somewhere,' she says, to no one in particular. 'Isn't that how every good story ends?' Then she turns to me with a smile. 'Hey Scarlett, this is your department, isn't it? Any suggestions? Any good creative twists?'

I'm lost for words, powerless to stop this madness. She's too far gone. All I can do is pray that the coastguard or the police will come to our rescue. Where the hell are they? They should have found us by now…

Gabrielle crouches forward to take some close-ups of her model, then slides the switch on the camera to video mode.

Christina is connecting with the lens now – she's on fire. Her eyes are hard as she says, 'This isn't one of your fantasy porn and bondage movies, Gabrielle. It's time to break out of your sick fictional universe and face the truth.'

'Keep your mouth shut,' says Gabrielle. 'It's the moving images I want to capture – not what you've got to say.'

Christina brings her face right up to the lens until her features blur in Gabrielle's viewfinder.

'No, you can't silence me any longer,' she says. 'You need to hear the truth from me, once and for all.'

Gabrielle is still filming – a video recording of Christina's confession, a strangely powerful voiceover montage. Even Gabrielle won't be able to deny the reality of that, I say to myself, when she plays it back in glorious technicolour.

Christina speaks very slowly and clearly to make sure she can be heard above the wind and the waves. 'Whatever happens to me,' she says, 'Katie will never be yours. I'm keeping her because she's mine. I'm her biological mother. She belongs to me.'

Gabrielle's face is as fixed and expressionless as a mask but there's a loud crack as she lets the camera drop to the floor.

Christina continues in a cold monotone. 'You found the photograph so you know it's true. James tricked me into going to Venice. He gave me the plane ticket. He told me you would be there and it would be a chance for us to bond before the baby was born.'

The camera slides across the petrol-soaked floorboards as the yacht tilts violently in the water but Gabrielle makes no attempt to retrieve it.

Christina continues with her 'confession'. 'I went ahead with the embryo implantation procedure as planned. Unfortunately for you it failed. I wasn't pregnant, the embryo had not survived, as I discovered on the day before my flight to Venice. I knew it would be a great disappointment so I decided that I would tell you both in person when I arrived in Venice, and in the meantime I booked in at the clinic to schedule an appointment for a second attempt at the implantation a few weeks after the trip.' Christina's eyes go all dreamy as she says, 'Thanks to James, it was not necessary. Two weeks after I got back from Venice, I discovered I was pregnant – but not as your surrogate. No, I was pregnant with my love child conceived with James in that enchanting Italian city of bridges and canals.' She observes the look of disgust and denial on Gabrielle's face. 'So I went to the clinic, impersonating you – you know we've played that game so many times, it comes to me quite naturally – to tell them the good news. My pregnancy was confirmed and the second embryo transfer procedure was cancelled. I informed the director of embryology that we would not be requiring the clinic's services any longer.' She looks out to sea. 'All my years of drama training saw me through that day. I gave my best-ever performance – worthy of an Oscar, so convincing, so authentic. They were completely taken in.'

At last, Christina pauses. Then she looks up into Gabrielle's eyes. 'I gave the clinic instructions to dispose of your remaining frozen eggs – all five held in storage were destroyed. It wasn't an appalling administrative error as you believed. The clinic was acting on my orders. I completed all the necessary formalities in your name.' She whispers sweetly, 'Blame it on Venice.'

There's a long silence. Gabrielle grabs the camera. The lens is cracked. She doesn't seem to care. 'Nice try!' she says, forcing her lips into a smile. 'I can see through your lies. I always could. Ever since you were in pigtails, you've been a nasty little liar.'

White-knuckled, Gabrielle's hands grip the camera. But her hands are shaking so much that she can't press the shutter.

'I'm so sick of you,' she says.

Their faces are within inches of each other now – confronting each other across an imaginary line, reflected and inverted in the black dilated pupils of each other's eyes. I'm struck by how interchangeable they remain despite Christina's shocking, convict-hair.

'That's the shot,' I say. 'Give me the camera. I'll take it for you. It's perfect. Photograph Thirteen. It's done.'

39

Scarlett

It seems ages since Gabrielle went down to the dark room to develop the pictures from the photoshoot. Before leaving the galley she tied us up again. I'm mortified at how impotent I have become to defend us from this madwoman but with her knife pointing at Christina's throat there was no room for heroics. This time Gabrielle's strapped us together back-to-back with the thick leather belt James bought for her in Venice, and our ankles bound to the legs of the bar stools.

The moment she left us on our own, I asked Christina the question that had been on my mind for hours: 'What did you do with the gun?' She sounded contrite. 'I couldn't use it. I'm sorry. But she doesn't know about it. I hid it in the cabin.' I lapsed into silence, exasperated by her faint-heartedness.

Ominous black storm clouds roll over the churning sea while gusts of wind whistle and howl across the decks. Christina slumps against my back, her body shuddering.

I decide the best thing is to keep talking, to keep her conscious and calm.

'Were you telling the truth?' I say, 'About the surrogacy… and the rest?'

'Yes,' she whispers. 'Do you hate me?'

'No,' I say. 'It's not my place to judge you. *The truth is rarely pure and never simple* – remember? You told me that.'

'Oscar Wilde,' says Christina in a toneless voice.

'It's clear Gabrielle thinks you're lying,' I say. 'She really believes Katie is her baby.'

'She's a fantasist as well as being a pathological liar,' says Christina.

She flinches in pain as she shifts her position on her chair.

'How is it?' I say. I can feel the exhaustion and strain in her voice.

'Bearable,' she says. 'In some ways it helps to have a focus for the pain, you know?'

I get it. She means the pain that's part of her very being now – since the day Katie disappeared.

'But surely Gabrielle must understand that taking Katie is child abduction, pure and simple?' I say.

'Gabrielle makes up her own reality,' says Christina. She believes what she wants to believe and rejects anything that doesn't fit in with her narrative. She thinks Katie is the surrogate baby that she planned to call Rose. She is convinced that she is the biological mother. The truth is too painful for her to contemplate so anything that contradicts her "truth" must be denied or destroyed. She'll be all the more determined now to take Katie away from me.'

I think of the collection of photographic prints lining the walls of the Master Cabin. Embryonic Love. Gabrielle wants to believe in her own version of the truth all right. It's an obsession.

God help us!

'One thing is for sure,' I say. 'As the birth mother, you've got the law on your side. Nobody can make you give her away – even if a DNA test can't be used to prove which of you is Katie's biological mother.'

I look down at the belt strapped around our torsos. Suddenly 'the truth' seems rather academic.

'You can't let her get away with this,' I say. 'You can't just let her keep on trying to bully and abuse you into submission.'

I nod towards the bundle of legal documents in the galley.

'She can't force you to sign some piece of paper making her the legal mother. If you sign under duress, it wouldn't stand up in a court of law.'

Christina gives a hollow laugh. 'I know that. But it's all part of her campaign of intimidation. Open your eyes and look around. I don't think Gabrielle concerns herself too much with legalities.'

For a moment, we are silent, listening to the gathering storm.

'I would fight back,' she says. 'I'm not scared of what she might do to me. But I'm scared of what she might do to Katie. That's why I've been hiding and running away from her since the day Katie was born. That's why I didn't want the police to get to her first. She's a sick woman. She's always been unstable, on anti-psychotics since she was a teenager. And now her sick obsession is not just about Katie, it's about me. She's been like this since we were little girls. She always thought I was the favoured twin – Daddy's golden girl, teacher's pet. She was insanely jealous of me. And she couldn't bear the thought of something or someone belonging to me and not her – that's why she smashed my dolls, that's why she stole my boyfriend, and that's why in the end she killed James.'

I look round the saloon, littered with debris, and empty jerry cans and vodka bottles, the luxurious décor wrecked and defaced with petrol and blood stains and smashed glass. I look down at us, hostages, tied to the chairs.

She's won.

'So, what will you do?' I ask Christina, shocked by this endless submission to her abusive twin. 'Sign the papers and let her have her way? Abandon Katie to this maniac?'

'I'll never sign the papers,' says Christina.

Gabrielle returns and slams the album down on the table in front of us.

'It's finished.' she says.

She pulls up a chair, lights a cigarette and pours herself another vodka from a new bottle.

'Haven't you had enough already?' I say, nodding towards the glass.

She yanks off the belt that binds us together, giving us the freedom to move our arms and torsos. She seems manically cheerful, which is no less frightening.

'I'm not an unreasonable woman. Would you like to join me girls? Let's all have a drink!'

She raises her glass in a toast.

'*To Our Life*,' she says, looking at Christina, and downs the vodka in one.

I twist round on my chair to face her. I've decided the last hope is to try to reason with her – to treat her as a rational human being.

'Gabrielle, it's over.' I say. 'We know you're hiding Katie. By now Damien will have been arrested and charged with her abduction. It's only a matter of time before the police find her. It's only a matter of time before the police catch up with you. This is your last chance. Give yourself up now before it's too late.'

I reprimand her in my best stern 'nanny voice' as if talking to a naughty child caught stealing sweets from the corner shop. 'Katie's not your little girl. She belongs to Christina.'

She looks at me as if I'm the one who's out of my mind.

'I know you're confused,' I say. 'If you give yourself up to the police, things won't be so bad. You can get psychiatrists' reports and evidence of mitigating circumstances – even what you've written in this album could be used in evidence to explain your disturbed state of mind and your desperate actions. You might escape a jail sentence on grounds of diminished responsibility. And you'll be able to get access to all the medical support you need.'

I almost feel sorry for Gabrielle now. She's clutching her stomach as if she's about to throw up.

'Traitor, liar.' She spits the words at me. 'The child's mine and I'm keeping her.'

She slips the loose prints into the album and stalks to the corner of the saloon where she flings open a cupboard door to reveal a safe. She inputs the code, slides in the album and slams the door.

'Fireproof,' she says. 'Just in case.'

She lights another cigarette and lets the flaring match drop to the floor before she grinds it under her heel not a microsecond too soon.

I'm not that easily intimidated so I carry on with my lecture.

'Even if Christina signed the adoption papers now, the court would never give you parental responsibility. Not after what's happened. You'll never be Katie's mother, never in a million years.'

Playing the drama queen to perfection, she sits down suddenly and holds her head in her hands. She starts murmuring to herself and I hear the words: 'One of us must die. That's the only way. One of us must die.'

Her head jerks up and she looks at me.

'You've read our life story. Now you can be the judge. Just like King Solomon in the bible story.'

'Have you been forgetting to take your medication?' I say. 'You've got to stop this ridiculous game now, Gabrielle, before it's too late. Give yourself up before something horrific happens.

'Don't they teach you anything in school these days?' she says. 'It's in the Old Testament. He called for his sword to cut the baby in two.' The look in her eyes sends a chill down my spine.

'That wasn't the way it ended,' I say hastily. 'The King understood that the baby's real mother was the woman who loved her baby so much that she chose to give her baby away rather than let it be harmed.'

'Well, I'm not that woman,' says Gabrielle, 'And nor is she.'

She smashes the vodka bottle on the surface of the bar and then turns to Christina, thrusting the broken glass at her chest.

'I would never harm my baby, you brainless idiot,' she spits out at me. 'King Solomon was a fool. It's not the baby who must die. It's one of the women. In our life, there's only space for one...'

Christina looks terrified. These are not empty threats – especially when Gabrielle's on her second bottle of vodka combined with God knows what cocktail of drugs.

'There's no point in harming Christina,' I cry, trying again to get through to her. 'It will only make things worse. You'll never have Katie now. The law's on Christina's side – she's the birth mother. The surrogacy agreement counts for nothing. She changed her mind about giving the baby away – there's nothing you can do.' Foolishly I add, 'Even if Christina were dead, you'd never be allowed to keep Katie after what you've done.'

Gabrielle slings the broken bottle across the lounge and spins the knife once more.

'You just don't get it, do you?' she says. 'Two's a crowd – that's my judgment.

The knife stops dead with the blade pointing at Christina.

Is this her variation on Russian roulette?

'Come on Scarlett! What's your verdict? We're running out of time. Who should it be? Her or me?'

She's smiling as she holds out the knife. The blade glints in sunlight from the setting sun breaking through the clouds

'I'm ready to die,' she says. 'To die will be a wonderful adventure!'

I sense a trap. Either that, or she's completely lost her mind. I take the knife and quick as a flash, I slash through the ropes at our ankles setting myself and Christina free.

'It has to be a fair contest,' I say.

Then I race out onto the deck and hurl the knife away as far as I can across the dark water.

Gabrielle follows me. To my surprise, she's laughing.

Her eyes are wild as she watches the knife spiralling in an arc through the air until the blade plunges into the water. I was expecting her to explode with anger but she turns to me quite cheerfully.

'I knew you would bottle it,' she shouts, above the noise of the wind and the waves. 'You kids are so soft these days.'

We stand side by side at the rail, facing out to sea, bracing against the wind that's whipping salt water into our eyes and tangling our hair. She seems exhilarated by the storm.

'It's OK, Scarlett. I've worked out the ending to our story now. And I won't be needing the knife.'

We're both gripping on to the balustrade as the catamaran lurches in the swell.

She reaches across and rests her hand on my wounded arm.

'Are you scared? Isn't it awesome? The power of the sea.'

A huge wave splashes up on to the deck. We're soaked.

She yells in my ear. 'Your friends are taking their time. Let's go back inside. I need your help to steer The Phantasea out of the eye of the storm.' At last she's coming to her senses. 'We don't want to capsize before they get here!'

40

Scarlett

Christina is nowhere to be seen when we step back into the saloon. She must have taken her opportunity to hide and I'm praying that she's had the sense to run below deck and grab the gun.

'Silly woman,' says Gabrielle. 'It's not as if she's got any hope of getting away.'

Gabrielle takes another cigarette. 'Go and get her will you,' she says, 'in case she does something stupid.' While she saunters over to the cockpit to raise the anchor and start the engines, I race down the stairs.

All the cabins are empty.

She must be hiding in the dark room.

I run to the dark room and slip through the door. Once the door closes behind me the room is pitch black.

'Christina,' I say softly. I can hear her breathing. 'It's Scarlett. Have you got the gun?'

'I can't,' she says. 'I can't do it. I left it in the cabin.'

I might have guessed Christina wouldn't have the guts to turn the tables on her twin. But I've made my decision to choose between the two of them, as Gabrielle pressed me to. I'm not about to let Christina die here like a rat in a hole.

'Don't be a bloody idiot!' I whisper. 'I'll be back,'

I start on a frantic search of the single cabin where Gabrielle held us captive.

'Christina must have hidden it somewhere in here,' I say to myself.

I rip back the bedding and search under the pillows, along the wall and under the mattress. I pull open every cupboard and drawer. I can't find the gun anywhere. Losing valuable time, I pull the panels off the shower and behind the sink. Still no luck! I'm worried about Christina, all this time defenceless and alone. Then I notice that the metal grille on the air-conditioning unit above the towel rail is very slightly out of place, just a millimetre or two ajar. I climb up onto the towel rail and pull the grille away from the wall, breaking my fingernails in the process. I grope round inside the unit. Sure enough – my fingertips brush against cold metal. The gun is there.

Seconds later I'm back in the dark room pushing open the blackout door, with the pistol concealed inside the waistband of my shorts. I peer into the gloom. Even though I know she's hiding there, when a hand reaches out to touch my arm, I can't stop myself from screaming and I fall back against the door.

'Hush Scarlett, it's OK. It's me, Christina.'

I hear a click and the safelight comes on. In the light of the lamp, I can make out Christina's silhouette through the shadows. I stifle a gasp. With her cropped hair and wild eyes and teeth glowing in the red beam she looks like a vision from a horror movie.

'You gave me a fright,' I whisper. There's something metal gleaming in her left hand. A large pair of scissors.

I hold out the gun. 'Here take this – you can't defend yourself from Gabrielle with a pair of scissors.' She lets the scissors drop to the floor and I thrust the gun into her empty palm. 'Don't be afraid to use it if you have to!' I say. 'After the shocking way she's treated you in the last twenty-four hours, you've got to learn how to stand up to her once and for all.'

'Don't worry,' she says softly, cocking the gun with surprising dexterity. 'I won't let her bully me again. I promise.'

There's a new conviction in her voice.

'Thank God, she seems to be calming down now,' I say. 'She's preparing to sail for shelter. She wants me to help crew the boat. Just keep out of her way down here. I'll go back up in case she changes her mind.'

When I open the door, I hear a crackling sound and the unmistakable acrid reek of burning paper. I run up the stairs and into a billowing cloud of smoke. There's no sign of Gabrielle but she can't be long gone. She's used the stack of legal papers as an ashtray and her latest cigarette is abandoned on the top, still burning its way through the heading:

IN THE CAS...KENEDEY V HAMIL...

As I run through the saloon to grab the fire extinguisher from the galley there's a sudden gust of wind and a plume of burning papers spirals into the air. To escape the burning cascade, I run on to the deck and become conscious of a wailing sound above the howl of the wind. The shrill noise becomes more insistent, closing in on The Phantasea like the Dementors in a *Harry Potter* movie.

For an instant, I think I'm going mad. Then a huge wave of relief floods over me – it's the sound I've been waiting for. Police sirens.

Now I hear new sounds from above – loud beating in the air, a throbbing engine approaching and receding and a shadow passing overhead.

I run onto the open bridge and look out to sea.

Thank God, though still some way off, three police boats are closing in on us from different angles, blue lights blazing, sirens screaming, and in the skies above, a helicopter circles the catamaran.

I start shouting into the wind as loud as I can and waving my arms frantically above my head.

'Help! Over here. Help!'

'Save your voice, lady! They'll never hear you.'

I recognise the loud hollering that comes from directly below where I'm standing waving my arms about on the deck.

'Relax, they've seen you. They're on their way.'

It's Mitch, riding the waves in a gleaming black speedboat that he's in the process of tethering to the catamaran.

'Where the hell did you steal that?'

'Mitch Stanley. At your service.' He touches his hand to his head in mock salute and gives his characteristic lopsided smirk. 'I borrowed it – called in a favour.'

'Get the hell up here fast,' I yell. 'I need your help. That madwoman's set fire to the boat. I've got to go back for Christina. She's down below deck.'

Just as I'm leaning out, throwing down a rope to Mitch so that he can pull himself up from the speed boat and on to the catamaran, a loud crack rings through the air.

'Shit – that sounded like a gunshot,' shouts Mitch.

'Fuck,' I say. 'She's done it.'

I'm in freeze-frame for a second before I turn to sprint inside.

'Stop!' shouts Mitch, as I drop the rope and he loses his grip on the deck and slithers down, landing on his back in the speedboat.

As I cross the deck, I hear a big splash above the sound of the fire and the sea.

What was that?

Inside the saloon flames dance across the petrol-drenched floor and a cloud of papers whirls in the wind.

Holding my T-shirt across my face, I take the stairs two-by-two then almost falling through the door into the dark room, I scream,

'Fire, fire, Christina, get out, the boat's on fire.'

Inside the smoked-filled darkroom, there's silence.

Thinking she might have passed out, I grope around on the floor until I'm almost overcome with smoke then drag myself back up the stairs on my hands and knees. Coming into the light, I look down at my palms. They are sticky with blood and cuttings of hair.

I reach the deck just in time. Only a few seconds later, while I'm still gasping for breath, there's a sickening, searing scrunch of ripping metal. I gape in horror as a black pall of smoke and flames erupts from the engine room, followed by an almighty bang. A fireball of debris and heat and pressure, a surge of shockwaves that rips through the catamaran, and flings me backwards off the deck into the sea.

Suddenly everything is in fast forward. Images and sensations flash before me and within me – first, the sudden, stomach-churning, fairground freefall from the deck, then the chilling descent into cold, bubbling-black brine, the stinging sensation of the waves engulfing me and my sea-weed hair floating up about my face. Then surfacing, gasping, coughing and choking on salt water, thrashing about in the surf, managing to get my equilibrium, coming up for air, floating on my back in the survival position. Slowly, the realisation that I'm still alive, looking up at the sky and the column of thick, pumping black smoke, rising from the engine room. Above The Phantasea, the air is alive with burning sheets of paper from Kenedey versus Hamilton, like giant fireflies swirling in the night sky. As I come to my senses, there's a grand finale, a monstrous explosion, spraying rockets and shells in the most spectacular, exquisite and deadly firework display I have ever seen.

I am struggling to keep afloat in the water, horrified, stunned and exhilarated – mesmerised by the firestorm overhead. But my strength is failing, waves break over my face and my head dips under the surface. My arms and legs flail, and the current sucks me down.

Just when I feel I'm losing my battle with the sea, I hear a shrill whistle, repeated several times and a brash voice calling to me on a loud hailer. Before I can turn, there's a flash of orange above my head and I hear the splash as something lands within a few feet of me in the water. Thank God – a lifebuoy! I summon all my strength and gradually, painfully, swim towards it – eventually I manage to grab it and position myself inside the ring. I feel the line go taut and hear, over the tannoy, another familiar voice.

'Hold on tight, we're bringing you in.'

I'm hauled in to the side of the police rescue boat.

I look up to see Costa staring down at me.

'Have you found Katie?' is the first thing I say to him.

He leans over, pulls me out of the water effortlessly and gathers me in. The Jackal is standing at the helm, the tannoy in his hand.

'She's not at the villa,' says Costa. 'My officers have been searching the premises since last night.'

It feels like he's just punched me in the chest...

He holds me very tightly, wrapped in the survival blanket while the Jackal steers away from The Phantasea. We turn to watch it going up in flames.

'What about Christina?' I shout. 'Turn around, go back.'

The tears stream down my cheeks. The Jackal pushes the throttle to full thrust.

'I'm sorry. There's nothing we can do,' says Costa rubbing my back while I struggle to break free. 'The helicopters are on their way with the water cannons.'

41

Scarlett

I'm at the police station most of the night being patched-up and checked over and interviewed and debriefed but as soon as the patrol car drops me back at the hotel, I hastily shower and change before ordering a taxi.

When the taxi drops me at the gate of Villa la Revanche just as dawn is breaking, all is quiet. There's no sign of Costa or the two police guards who are supposed to be here securing the site. I creep up the driveway, walking on the grass as I pass near the outhouse to avoid kicking the stones and waking the rabid Hound of the Baskervilles. Someone has done a poor DIY job of nailing back the timbers and between the gaps I can just make out the form of the dog curled up in the shadows in the far corner of the outhouse. When I get to the top of the driveway the peeling green shutters of the house are closed, so I can't see in to the property. But the front door is unlocked, so I let myself in.

The place looks as if it's been ransacked – cupboard drawers and doors ripped open and contents tipped unceremoniously on to the floor. Bookshelves empty and crooked stacks of books heaped round the sitting room. Pictures taken down and left leaning against the walls. Food from the fridge-freezer spills onto the worktop, left to defrost, drip onto the floor and rot in the heat. A trail of ants checks out the contents of the larder dumped in the overflowing bins. Every cushion on the leather sofa is slashed, handfuls of stuffing spewing out. It looks like wanton vandalism. I'm beginning to wonder if this is the aftermath of a burglary or a rave rather than the debris from the police investigation.

Whatever. It doesn't look as if the police officers have done a very professional job so I decide to look round the property myself. I don't care that this is a crime scene or that I'm leaving my fingerprints everywhere – this isn't the time to worry about legal protocol. We've got to find Katie fast – her life is in danger. If she's not hidden here, I may at least be able to find some clues as to where she's been taken.

When I go upstairs, I find the bedrooms are also in chaos: beds stripped and bedding left bundled in the corners, clothes dragged out of cupboards, and everything swept on to the floor. In short, whoever has been here, has made a shocking mess.

In among the jumble of clothes left at the foot of the bed in the single bedroom, I recognise some T-shirts and boxer shorts belonging to Damien and some of Christina's underwear and nightshirts. Incredibly, the police have also missed or discarded some of Katie's clothing down here on the floor. I work methodically through the pile and discover one of her nighties, a flowery T-shirt and a tiny pair of yellow shorts. I could cry! I lift Katie's clothes from the floor and hold them up to the light – looking for any mark or stain that could provide some clue to her whereabouts. Then I bury my face in the nightie – it still smells of Katie, her sweet just-out of-the-bath-and-dusted-with-talcum-powder smell. I fold up her clothes neatly and put them in my bag. Though appalled at the negligence of the police officers, perversely I'm filled with new energy and hope – if Katie's clothes are here, then at least there's a good chance that she was safe and well and here, not too long ago, and that she may not be too far away.

I hear creaking and a groan coming from the master bedroom. I push open the door. As I suspected, the police officers have made themselves at home. The two men are crashed out on the bed, using the house as an overnight squat. Surrounded by ravages of the previous day's search, they're fast asleep. This would never happen in England. Back home, I'm sure sleeping over at a forensic crime scene would be a sackable offence.

The older of the two, overweight, jowly and grey-skinned, is stretched out under the silk sheets, his boots, uniform and pistol, dumped on the chair next to the bed. He's snoring loudly – not a care in the world. The younger man rolls over to face the door. In a former life I could have appreciated this sleeping Adonis with his strong jaw, glorious suntan, kiss-me-now lips and morning-after stubble. He hasn't bothered to take off his uniform or his boots.

I walk out and make a point of slamming the door very loudly. A few seconds later the older officer runs out, a towel round his waist, pistol at the ready.

I step out from behind the door. It's almost farcical, as he jumps back, yells, cocks his gun and drops the towel.

'You left the back door open,' I say. 'So I let myself in. I'm meeting Detective Sergeant Costa here for breakfast.'

He's full of apologies as he covers his manhood, turns and flees back into the bedroom. I'd be laughing, if the situation weren't so tragic.

'I'll let him know you're here,' he says as he retreats behind the door. 'Help yourself to coffee. We've finished our investigations inside the house. There's only the forensic search of the grounds to be completed now, so you don't have to worry about disturbing the evidence.'

That's lucky, I think to myself, given the carnage you've left behind!

While I wait for Costa, I go outside to look round the pool and garden. There's yellow tickertape surrounding the swimming pool, the decking and the pool house. Keeping outside the tape I take care not to move anything or leave any fingerprints on the tables and sunbeds in case the police need to go back over the area. But I'm aching all over after the ordeals of yesterday and my blast-assisted backflip into the sea, so I give way to the temptation to lie down on one of the sunbeds and close my eyes. A great wave of exhaustion breaks over me – delayed trauma and sleep deprivation have caught up with me at last.

My recollection of what happened after Costa fished me out of the water is fragmented and confused but I can't get the searing images of the burning boat out of my head. Even now, lying here in the cool morning air on the sunbed, next to fragrant mimosa bushes, I can feel the heat of the flames and smell the acrid smoke in my nostrils. I recall a struggle with Costa on the police boat during which he restrained me while I screamed at him to turn back to rescue Christina and Gabrielle before the catamaran was consumed by fire. I don't know if it's because I'm in some kind of PTSD emotional shut down, but none of it seems real. I'm distanced from it – like I'm in a cinema watching the dramatic climax to an action thriller as I relive the memories of yesterday.

Abruptly, the peace is broken by the dog barking its head off down in the outhouse. A minute or two later, I sense a shadow looming over me and open my eyes to see Costa observing me from above.

'Hey Scarlett, how're you doing?' he says.

'Have you found Katie?' I say. He shakes his head. My heart sinks.

He's carrying a large brown paper bag.

'I bought you pastries for breakfast,' he says. 'From Betsy's, the best bakery in town.' His jollity is forced. He sits down on my sunbed and I shift to the side shielding my bandaged arm, which is still sore from the cut Gabrielle gave me with the knife.

'How's Christina?' I say.

He tells me he's just come from the hospital. 'She's doing OK,' he says. 'The doctor described her condition as stable. Apart from the gunshot wound, she got away remarkably lightly. Minor burns on her arms and legs. She had a lucky escape, jumping into the sea.' He hands me a pastry. 'But she looks a mess – I scarcely recognised her with her hair all cropped.'

'That was Gabrielle's doing,' I say.

'Why the hell didn't Christina tell me she had a twin sister?' says Costa.

Good question. 'More to the point, why the hell didn't she tell you her twin sister was a psycho?' I say.

Costa looks perplexed.

'Perhaps she thought she could deal with Gabrielle herself?' I say. 'Perhaps she thought it would endanger Katie even more if the police were involved. Perhaps even she didn't know what her identical twin was capable of?'

'She's got a lot of questions to answer when she's up to it,' says Costa.

The pastry sticks in my throat. I take a couple of bites and push it to one side.

'Was she able to talk?' I ask.

'She spoke a little, just a few words. She seems very confused. Not surprising with the head injuries and the gunshot wound and what she's been through. She was very distressed, asking for Katie every five minutes – "Give me my baby, she's stolen my baby" – like she was having a bad dream or hallucinating. The nurses said she was in and out of consciousness for most of last night. And of course, she's in a lot of pain with her shoulder. She's on sedatives and heavy-duty pain killers.'

'I feel so awful about that,' I say. 'It was my fault. I was trying to shoot the bolts off the door and she caught the ricochet. Is the wound infected?'

'They're going to operate later today, now that she's stable,' says Costa. It'll be a complex procedure but they've got some hotshot Miami-based surgeon seconded to our local hospital who'll be doing it. As you can imagine, coming from Miami he's got plenty of experience in dealing with gunshot wounds.'

'That sounds dreadful,' I say. 'I had no idea it was so bad. She was so very brave.'

Costa devours his pastry, scattering crumbs over my legs. 'The bullet's embedded in the shoulder joint. I've seen the X-ray.'

I thought it was only a flesh wound. Suddenly I feel sick.

'What about Gabrielle? Any news? Did your men find a body?' I ask.

Costa wanders over to the side of the pool. He looks down into the water.

'Nothing yet. Current status is missing, presumed dead. But we haven't given up.'

He tells me that they haven't found a body either in the water or on the burnt-out catamaran but it's early days. Forensics are still working their way through the yacht and they haven't got to the engine room and the darkroom as yet – that's where the fire was most intense due to the diesel tanks and the chemicals.

'So we have to prepare ourselves for the worst,' he says. It doesn't take much imagination to understand that he's preparing me for the possibility of a macabre discovery.

'The search and rescue helicopters are out this morning. Looking for anything on the surface. We've got divers in the water too. But the seas were rough last night – even if Christina's twin managed to escape the flames, chances are she drowned. We may never find a body.'

'She had it coming. She was completely off her head,' I say.

'There's evidence that fire accelerants were used in the saloon – irregular burn patterns and empty cans of gasoline,' continues Costa.

'I could have told you that. I saw her pouring out the gasoline myself.'

'That's hearsay. They want to prove it officially. They've taken away samples of the fire debris for chemical analysis,' says Costa. 'The recovery team are doing what they can to preserve the evidence. There's not much to go on since the fire was so fierce but they've found a fireproof safe which might contain some things of interest.'

He comes back to the sunbed and pulls me up.

'Your hands are so cold,' he says. 'You must be in shock. You really should get yourself checked out properly. Come on, let's go and make some coffee. You look in need of it.'

While he brews the coffee, he tells me his plan for the day. The focus of the investigation is to keep searching for Katie. It's small comfort that I'm now off his official list of suspects. His main task this morning is to interview Damien in the hope he'll finally crack and reveal where she's hidden. Damien's been rearrested and held in custody on charges of suspected abduction and perverting the course of justice.

'After breakfast, I'm going straight back to the police station to question him again – and this time I'm going to make the bastard squeal. He knows where she is. I'm convinced of it,' he says. 'He led me on a wild goose chase yesterday, pretending to cooperate. I believed he was on the point of making a confession and might be leading me to where Katie was hidden, or in the worst-case scenario to the scene of the ultimate crime. But the bastard was faking it. We lost valuable time while I drove him to spots round the island – supposedly retracing their movements. It was a false trail, of course – each time we drew blanks. He'll pay for it today. I'm going to nail him.'

I'm only half listening to him. I've got my hands in my lap and my eyes fixed on the unusual ribbed pattern scoured into the wooden decking at my feet. I remember that pattern, and it's not from my previous visit. I recognise it from the prints of Katie I saw in the darkroom. I thought the pictures had been taken on the deck of The Phantasea. But now I'm sure the pictures must have been taken here.

'Katie was here,' I say, jumping up to check the viewpoint and scrutinise the fabric of the sunbeds.

'There were prints in the dark room of her sitting right here by the swimming pool in broad daylight on this very sunbed. How could you all be so incompetent as to let her slip away? We've all failed her.'

'It's not over yet,' says Costa. 'Those "good-for-nothing" officers you scared the wits out of this morning, made an important discovery yesterday. They found plane tickets hidden in a Cheerios packet in the larder – for tomorrow, three tickets for a flight from San Juan airport in Puerto Rico to Panama City. My hunch is that Gabrielle and Damien's original plan was to sail to Puerto Rico today with Katie before catching the flight to Panama posing as holidaymakers, and to lie low there for a few months in Central America until the scent went cold.'

'Surely they didn't think they could get away with it?' I say. 'What about border controls?'

'They're not too hot on border controls in Puerto Rico or Panama,' says Costa with a scowl. He sits back in the chair and wipes a few crumbs off his chin. 'What I don't understand is why the sister took off in the boat without taking Katie with her?'

'Her sadistic instincts got the better of her,' I say. 'In the end, the thing that mattered most to her was to punish Christina. She was a psychopath.'

'Well, I agree with you. It certainly looks like the poor woman was mad! Died in the flames of her own conflagration. As for Varcoe, he's just scum. Her creature – and a pathetic gambling addict – would do anything to get money to pay off his debts. In my line of work, I've come across a few men like him before. Anyway, he's facing years in prison and he deserves it.'

Costa's looking pleased with himself now. This is a bit premature, I feel.

'Before you start congratulating yourself too much, we need to find Katie,' I say. 'She's not on a boat heading to Puerto Rico – the original escape plan has literally gone up in flames.'

'We can't be sure of that,' says Costa. 'There are plenty of boats all round these shores and plenty of people willing to earn a quick buck without asking any questions. She could be anywhere by now if she was handed over to a third party.'

'I still believe it's more likely Katie's hidden somewhere close by – maybe in the surrounding woods,' I say. Costa told me he's had roadblocks on all the roads leading from the villa so it's unlikely she could have been driven away. 'Look, I found some of her clothes on the floor in the bedroom.' I hand the clothes to him. 'Your crack team of investigators missed them!' Costa can't hide his embarrassment. 'Katie must have been here not so long ago.' I reflect that Costa arrested Damien here at the villa yesterday morning, so if the bastard had locked her away somewhere, that means she's been alone for over twenty-four hours. 'She's going to suffocate or die of dehydration. It's a race against time.'

'You're right' says Costa. He jumps to his feet. 'I'm off to get the truth out of Damien. He's in for a good kicking. I'm going to make him talk, if it kills me – or him, if that's what it takes.' He takes out his radio. 'In the meantime, I'll order the team to start searching the woods.'

He squeezes my hand.

'You'll be the first to know.'

As he strides away, he turns.

'By the way, your pal Mitch Hunter did well yesterday. He was the one who pulled Christina out of the sea. Found her flailing around in the water surrounded by burning debris. She practically drowned. Fair play to him – he saved her life.'

So I was right to give Mitch the benefit of the doubt.

'So will he get a share of the fifty thousand reward?' I ask Costa.

He smiles sardonically.

'Don't be so cynical. The reward is for finding Katie, not saving her mother,' he says. 'But… yes… I'll make sure he gets something – that's how things work round here.'

There's a burst of barking from the outhouse as Costa marches off down the driveway. He reaches the gate, then I watch him turn and walk back again, provoking another outburst from the hound.

'You need to have a rest today, stay here away from the press, there's a gang of them hanging out at the gate. Have a shower, relax by the pool…' He gives me a wink. 'The boys'll look after you.'

As he leaves, the dog barks again.

'That bloody dog is driving me nuts,' I say to myself.

There's something about the insistent, frantic barking that's nagging at me, hammering into my brain, but I can't quite grasp it. That dog just won't leave me in peace. I wander down the lane, to take a closer look at it, to check if it is indeed the dog in the photograph in Costa's file that helped us to identify The Phantasea.

When I approach the outhouse, the great slavering hound goes completely mental and flings itself against the stable door. The door creaks. Any minute now the botched repair is going to give way. Sure enough when the dog lunges again there's a sickening crack as the rotting wood splinters into two and it forces its way through the gap. It pelts towards me and I turn to run but I'm not quick enough. The dog bounds up, striking me at shoulder height and throws me backwards so that I'm sprawled on my back, with my face and neck exposed, about to get mauled. I shut my eyes in horror and suddenly it's all over me, licking my face, tail wagging, jumping about in excitement. I can't help laughing as I push its muzzle away from my face and roll over, sprawling in the dust.

As I open my eyes and scramble to get up, something catches my eye – a tiny blue plastic slipper, so tiny that I can hold it between my finger and thumb. It's a Barbie doll's shoe – dropped just at the entrance to the outhouse. And I've seen it before. It's part of an outfit worn by Katie's *Sleeping Beauty* Barbie doll that Christina bought for her last Christmas. I remember, on more than one occasion, scrabbling round on the floor in Katie's bedroom looking for a lost Barbie shoe while she sat crying her eyes out on the bed.

Now if you are looking for a place to hide a little girl, what better place than behind a door, guarded by a slavering hound, whose vicious bark suggests it'll eat anything that comes close, but who is really just a stupid old mutt who wants to jump all over you and lick your face?! More Nana than *Hound of the Baskervilles*.

Costa told me his men had searched the buildings – but I know that macho type. I bet they're scared of dogs and didn't venture in here!

I go in. The place stinks – the dog obviously hasn't been let out for a while. The outhouse is an L-shaped, mouldering concrete structure, the long part of the L about the size of a single garage. There are no windows or openings in the walls other than the now-broken wooden door at the front, and so I can see as soon as I round the corner that no one is hidden inside. In the smaller section of the L-shaped building, the dirt-encrusted concrete floor is covered with straw and old newspapers, stained with wet patches and dog excrement. I hold my breath and drag the papers to one side with my foot. Concealed beneath, there's a metal trap door cut into the concrete. It's bolted. I draw the bolt and hinge the trap door open to reveal a narrow metal spiral staircase leading down into the dark.

It's got to be…

It's very dark and I almost trip as I go down the staircase. At the bottom I reach for the walls to feel my way round the room. My hand fumbles over a light switch and now the room is flooded with light – I'm blinded by it. When my eyes adapt, I find myself in a bright, clean underground space that from the hundreds of empty racks, looks as if it has been used as a wine cellar in the past. The room has been transformed into a bedsit, decorated for a child with a series of *Peter Pan* murals depicting scenes of islands and seas and the underwater world in the background, and Wendy and Tinker Bell and Tiger Lily and the wicked mermaids in the foreground. Although the theme is *Peter Pan*, there's not a lost boy in sight. The walls feature only female characters. This is indeed, a fitting underground prison cell for a lost girl!

In one corner of the room there's a bunk bed. The top bunk is neatly made up with a pink duvet. The bottom bunk is filled with a mountain of soft toys. And Katie's picture book copy of *Peter Pan* is lying on the floor. Now I'm sure! This is where they've been hiding Katie. In another corner of the room is a child-sized table, strewn with an assortment of paper and pens. I walk over to it. The floor is peppered with pen caps (now that looks familiar!), and to one side there's a big untidy stack of drawings, simple outlines of crude human figures and mermaids and fishes and shells. I recognise Katie's hand immediately – it's her way of processing her thoughts, visualising her day dreams and experiences, by spending hours absorbed in making pictures of her day. This is her work.

Round the corner, there's a door leading to a small shower room with a barred opening right at the top providing ventilation. There's also a kitchenette with a fridge stuffed with bottled water and children's yogurts and bread, half-eaten packets of sliced cheese and ham, apples and grapes. Three or four used spoons have been dropped in the sink. The door to the fridge is ajar, and discarded on the floor are empty yogurt pots, plastic water bottles and half-chewed apple cores.

If I'm not mistaken, Katie's been left here to fend for herself. I'm relieved and horrified to discover the place of her captivity. What kind of warped obsession could have led to this? What kind of sick imagination could spend so much time on creating a picture-book fantasy as a prison for a little girl? How long has this been planned?

And she's not here. So where is she now?

I run over to the bunk bed – it's the only place I haven't searched properly. First I lie down on the floor and look underneath it, then I lean in between the bunks and delve into the mound of soft toys on the lower mattress.

Yes...

Could it be...?

I can scarcely breathe.

I can scarcely believe it.

My hand touches soft warm flesh burrowed in among the toys, rising and falling beneath my palm. I scatter the toys to one side.

It's Katie and she's alive. Thank God.

I'm not a regular church-goer, and I'm not a great Christian, but if there's a God then He'll know I'm thanking him with all my heart right now.

'Katie, Katie. Are you OK?' I call out, bundling her still sleeping into my arms and lifting her out of the bunk, settling her round my hips and holding her tighter than I've ever held her before.

'I'm sorry, I'm so sorry...'

She stirs, opens her bright blue eyes, and looks up at me.

She is so fragile and so pale.

'I've got you. You're safe now. I'll never let you go.'

Then she reaches up to stoke her little fingers though my hair.

'Scarlett,' she says.

It's the first time I've ever heard her say my name.

42

Scarlett

We've come full circle.

Back here on the beach it all seems unreal. We're in exactly the same spot where I fell asleep on the sand when Katie vanished. I'm kneeling right next to her – within touching distance, not taking any chances. Last night she slept in my bed at the hotel and I held her in my arms all night long.

She's got the red bucket and once again we're sifting through the sand for shells, naming them, counting them, adding to her collection. I could almost imagine the events of the last two weeks were all nothing but wild hallucinations – a bad trip caused by sunstroke and a spiked cocktail.

Today, there's a cool breeze, my wits are razor-sharp and there's no chance I'm going crash out again on the sand.

I went to visit Christina in hospital first thing this morning. She's out of intensive care now and recovering well from her injuries, though she still looks rough. The burns on her arms and legs are healing up well and the medics are hopeful that she may escape permanent scarring. Fortunately, the operation on her shoulder was a great success. The surgeon managed to extract the bullet. She should regain full movement of the joint.

The nurses tell me she hasn't stop smiling since Costa told her the wonderful news about Katie. We didn't talk much, she just thanked me, and cried, and asked me if I could do one more thing for her – take Katie home to New York. She's going to have to spend a few more days in hospital and she wants to know Katie's safely back home, back to her kindergarten routine and normality. She thinks this will help her to get over the trauma of what she's been through.

I think she's right.

In the last twenty-four hours since we rescued Katie from her Disney-princess prison, she's hardly spoken, save for two incessant refrains: 'Where's Mummy?' and 'Go home!' She knows what she wants. She spent much of yesterday with a child psychologist and a female police officer, being 'debriefed,' or 'counselled' as they preferred to call it. But I don't think it will have helped her much – she's not the most communicative of little girls at the best of times. She needs to get back to her own familiar space. The psych accompanied Katie on a short visit to see Christina but apparently the poor little thing was so overwhelmed and distressed by the hospital environment and the sight of her injured and disfigured mother that she spent most of the time curled up on the chair with her head in her arms.

Before saying goodbye to Christina at the hospital, I summoned up the courage to ask her what had happened in the dark room and how she had managed to escape. Understandably she found it difficult to talk about but she told me there'd been a struggle with the gun when Gabrielle had tried to grab it off her.

'I was weak and in so much pain but I clung on,' said Christina. 'Gabrielle was frantic, screaming hysterically that one of us had to die and challenging me to shoot her or shoot myself. The room was filling with smoke and we were both coughing and choking. I knew we had to get out so I let go of the gun and fled. I yelled at her to follow me up the stairs but she had completely lost her head. I shouldn't have left her, I know, but it was survival instinct, I suppose.'

'There's no need to feel guilty,' I said. 'It was all her fault. She was trying to kill you.' She went on to tell me how she had summoned the courage to throw herself into the sea despite her phobia of water. 'I should have been terrified of jumping into the sea,' Christina said, 'But I didn't have time to think about it. And just before I jumped into the water to save myself from the fire, I heard a shot. My sad crazy twin must have turned the gun on herself.'

Oh God! What a thought.

I tip out a perfect sandcastle.

I have a nagging pain deep in my gut. After all, I was the one who provided her with the weapon. And I knew there was a bullet left in the gun. One shot to kill herself. I hope that doesn't put me in breach of some crime. It seems I may have unwittingly assisted a suicide!

I follow Katie down to the water's edge and take her hand. I can't wait to get on that plane and out of here.

After visiting Christina in hospital, I spent the rest of the morning being interviewed by Costa's deputy and a family liaison officer. An 'interrogation' would be the more accurate way of describing it. With the possible exception of Costa, I don't think the police have any belief in my innocence. Anyway, with all this interviewing and debriefing and counselling, I could see it taking a good few days before we were free to leave the island, but Costa has cut through the red tape and given me permission to take Katie home today. His one condition is that I agree to travel back to the island for more interviews 'if deemed necessary to further the ongoing investigation.' The investigation is, of course, 'ongoing', as there is still a missing person search underway for Gabrielle.

Before we checked out of the hotel, we had another visitor. Mitch called in to say goodbye. He insisted on seeing Katie.

'I've bought you something very special,' he said to Katie. 'A pair of Angel Wings for a very special kid.' He unwrapped the delicate white shells that he had folded carefully in newspaper. 'They'll bring you luck. Look, they're still joined in the middle – that's very rare.'

Even though she didn't have a clue what he was on about, Katie was thrilled with the gift. I knew perfectly well that those beautiful shells shouldn't be removed from the beach (and that Mitch couldn't care less about ecological trivia like that!) but I was touched all the same. It was kind of him.

Mitch stayed for a coffee and was keen to fill me in on what had happened after he left me on the yacht to go back and alert the police.

'I rowed back towards the harbour and as soon as I managed to get a signal on that God-damned phone of yours I put a call through to Costa to raise the alarm, then I put in a call to one of my "business partners". Let's just say we've done a few deals together and he owes me. He met me at the harbour and lent me his speedboat.'

'How did you find us?' I asked.

'I had a pretty good idea where you'd be headed,' said Mitch. 'Round the bay to Puerto Rico. I figured if Christina's sister was trying to get away with the girl, she'd be making for Puerto Rican territorial waters – police and surveillance are much slacker over there.' He should know – must be one of his bootlegging patches. 'It wasn't that hard to find you – that speedboat had some pretty sophisticated satellite tracking equipment on board!'

'Well, I can't thank you enough for coming back for us,' I said. 'And for rescuing Christina from the sea. You're a hero.'

He looked pleased with himself. 'I couldn't miss out on the chance of a share in that fifty-thousand-dollars reward, now could I?'

After Mitch had said his goodbyes, I brought Katie down to the beach for one last time before we leave. Katie and I are catching a flight to New York this evening, so (with the blessing of the psych) we have just a couple more hours to erase the bad memories of this place and to replace them with some good memories of the sun, sea and sand. I glance up from the shells we're collecting to decorate Katie's sandcastle and catch sight of Costa, backlit by the sun, strolling over towards us, holding a clear plastic bag. I've become quite close to him in a weird kind of way. He's in uniform, looking very handsome but more officious than usual. He's promised to escort us to the airport. He squats down next to us, and I see the bag contains the album. Suddenly, I shiver in the breeze.

'We managed to salvage this photo album from The Phantasea,' he says. It was in a fireproof safe in the galley. Christina's asked me to give it to you for safekeeping.'

I can't bear the sight of it. 'You should have thrown it into the ashes to burn.'

He stands up and looks out to sea. 'Maybe all this madness could have been prevented if I'd known Christina was a twin.'

'It sounds like you've got things all wrapped up now,' I say. 'Well done.'

'I have to admit I was baffled by the fingerprints that we were getting all through our investigations,' he says. 'At first I assumed they were Christina's prints but then I realised that most of them were mirror-images of hers. I kept referring back to forensics thinking that the images had been mistakenly inverted. But, of course, it makes sense. The fingerprints belong to Gabrielle – Christina's and Gabrielle's DNA is very nearly identical but as they were mirror-image twins the prints are identical but opposite.'

Costa gives me a hug and this time I don't object. 'Gabrielle was a very clever woman. She may have been a psychopath but she always stayed one step ahead of us,' he says. That's the most perceptive thing I've heard him say.

Costa picks up Katie and swings her round while I start to pack up our beach bag.

'So, it turns out Gabrielle fooled us both. You were wrong about Christina and I was wrong about you. But we were both right about Varcoe. That loser will get what he deserves. I'll make sure of that. He's facing a long jail term.'

Katie squeals in delight as Costa lifts her up in the air.

'Oh, and you were right not to trust DC Kramer,' he says. 'He's crooked as you suspected – but it wasn't Christina he met at the Coco Shack, it was Gabrielle. She was buying crack cocaine off him. Her drug addiction must have contributed to her loss of sanity. Anyway, Kramer's been busted and the Commissioner's taken his badge away. He's on bail awaiting trial for dealing in drugs'

He looks at me with uncharacteristic humility.

'I'm sorry. I owe you an apology – for doubting you and for allowing you to put yourself in danger. I was so desperate to get a conviction in this case. I broke all the rules.'

I stand up and take Katie from him into my arms.

'Well, in the beginning you behaved like a jerk, but in the end, you saved my life.'

I kiss him chastely on the cheek.

'Are you sure of me now?'

He backs away, laughing.

'Hey, I'm on duty, people will talk.'

Never stopped him before, funny that!

I sit back down on the sand with Katie. 'Five more minutes. It's almost time for us to go.'

I take the album from the bag and turn to the blank page headed Photograph Thirteen.

'She never did fill in the blank,' I say.

'Well,' he says, taking out his phone. 'This is the perfect shot to end it with – happy ending.'

He snaps a picture of Katie and me playing with shells in the sand.

'Stop,' I yell at him. 'No more photographs – that album is poisonous. It should never be completed and I certainly don't want to feature in it.'

'The photo's for me then, something to remember you by.' He holds out the screen for me to see, and there we are, with the red bucket full of shells in the foreground, and the turquoise Caribbean Sea behind.

There we are, me, with auburn hair, glowing in the sun, athletic and tanned, looking pretty dammed hot (if I say so myself!), and Katie, the sea breeze playing with her wispy blonde curls, pale from her captivity, delicate and so extraordinarily beautiful with that faraway look in her dreamy blue eyes.

This chapter of my life is over.

'Give it to me,' I say.

He hands me the phone and I press delete.

After

Scarlett

It's almost four o'clock in the afternoon when I ring the doorbell of No 17 Larch Avenue, Greenhaven-in-Rye. The brass nameplate is inscribed with the words *Chelsea Mews Cottage* in large italic lettering but the house is nothing like a cottage. It's a grand and imposing pile, approached by a sweeping gravel driveway, built in colonial style of red brick with white pillars on either side of the wide, raised porch and decorative blue shutters. It's typical of the neighbourhood, which is – according to my taxi driver – one of the most exclusive districts of Westchester County along the Long Island sound.

I hear the bells echoing within but no one comes to the door. Perhaps Christina is still at work but I had hoped Katie would be home from school by now. Of course, I should have called before jumping in a taxi on impulse at JFK airport and taking a ride out here. But I wanted it to be a surprise visit.

I should at least have rung the doorbell before paying off the taxi and sending it away.

After the trials and tribulations of last summer, I was desperate to take a break and have a fresh start. So I took a gap year and I've been spending the last few months working on ecological projects in Belize and Costa Rica. I'm homeward bound now, heading back to England, planning to spend this coming summer working in a bar in London before taking up my place to study Criminology at Nottingham University – it's my second attempt at getting a university degree and nothing's going to stop me now. I'm done with childcare.

There were problems with my flights back home to London resulting in me being re-routed via New York with four hours to kill at JKF airport. It seemed like fate. I couldn't pass by this chance opportunity to drop in on Christina and Katie for a flying visit to see how they're doing.

I've had very little contact with Christina since I left – just a few emails. She's given up her job in the city and found a new job working in a local art gallery on Long Island where they now live. She wants to spend as much time as she can at home with Katie.

A couple of weeks after I accompanied Katie back home to the apartment in Manhattan, Costa sent me an email attaching the official report he had received from his forensics investigators. This was in breach of protocol, of course, but Costa was never one for playing by the rules. The report documented that the badly disfigured remains of a female body had been recovered beneath a workbench on the floor of the boat's darkroom. Due to the condition of the human remains it was not possible to establish the cause of death with any certainty. A gun and a pair of scissors of the type used for cutting photographic prints had been found on the floor close to the body. It was not possible to obtain fingerprints from either the gun or the scissors as these were charred by the fire. Investigators had, however, found traces of blood and human hair outside the door of the darkroom and on the stairs, in addition to traces of darkroom chemicals.

The blood I could understand – but the hair?

Inevitably, a DNA test of the particles of blood and hair had produced a nonsensical result – a 99.9 per cent match for both Gabrielle and Christina!

Taking account of witness statements provided by both me and Christina in the immediate aftermath, the forensic report concluded that the probable cause of death was asphyxiation due to smoke inhalation from the fire. The report also noted that in light of Christina's testimony about the precarious mental state of Gabrielle at the time of the incident, the finding of the gun was indicative of suicide as a possible cause of death, although a bullet had not been identified in the bodily remains.

Costa had added a personal message at the bottom to say that he hoped that life was treating me well and that as for him, he was looking forward to his wife and daughter returning to the island and moving back into the family home. He wrote that the kidnapping of Katie had taught him the importance of valuing human relationships and he was now determined to put his little girl at the centre of his life. For once, I believed he was being sincere.

Well, that email left me distraught and tortured with anxiety for reasons I could not fully process or verbalise to myself. It seemed the report raised as many questions as it answered and I was left with the feeling that the authorities wanted to hush up the whole affair to avoid any negative publicity that would tarnish the image of the BLI as an island paradise.

However, given that I was the person who had supplied the gun, I was thankful that Costa had not ordered a full autopsy. Suicide was not the only possible explanation for the dead body. I had no wish to discuss what had happened in that dark room with Christina. I had no wish to be extradited back to the BLI on suspicion of having acted as an accessory to murder.

Anyway, the resurgence of those traumatic memories strengthened my resolve to go travelling and to put it all behind me.

But it's impossible to escape the past absolutely.

So now here I am at last – ringing the doorbell – with a sinking feeling that no one is home.

I ring for the third time and peer through the letterbox. A figure moves into my line of vision padding down the stairs and I hear a foreign voice I don't recognise.

'Is that someone at the door, Katie? Why didn't you come and get me, sweetie?'

I step back, and a young woman who's probably from the Philippines and I guess must be Katie's new nanny, opens the door.

'Miss Kenedey is still at work,' says the woman, who seems gentle and nice. 'She won't be home until five.'

'I've come to see Katie,' I say. 'I'm Scarlett – Scarlett Reyes. I used to be her nanny last year. Could I see her for a few minutes, please? I've got a present for her.'

The woman wavers – not wanting to be rude by refusing the request, but nervous of letting me in. Any minute now she's going to close the door in my face.

I look past her through the open doorway leading from the hallway to another room where I can see Katie sitting by the window in front of a large whiteboard easel, drawing pictures with a black marker pen. I'm so excited I can hardly restrain myself from rushing in, but I keep talking to try and win the woman's confidence.

'I can see she still loves drawing,' I say. 'When I was her nanny, I taught her how to draw mermaids. She used to spend hours drawing them.'

The woman relaxes and smiles though she's not about to invite me in. But just then Katie turns away from the board and glances towards the front door. She throws down her pen and kicks back her chair.

'Scarlett, Scarlett!' she calls out, as she runs into my arms.

Katie tugs me by the hand out into the garden to the sandpit that's been installed for her under the trees next to the swimming pool. It's been transformed into a blanket-sized beach, decorated with her collection of Caribbean shells, complete with sunbeds and parasols made of fuse wire and fabric samples, and miniature rowing boats made of lacquered lollipop sticks. I'm pleased to see that Mitch's Angel Wings have pride of place in the display. This must be Christina's handiwork. Hidden talents – I never knew she was so creative.

There are three Barbie dolls lying down on a stripy facecloth that's doubling as a beach towel on the sand. Katie picks up the Barbie doll with the long blonde hair.

'Here's Mummy,' she says.

'I've got something to show you,' I say, rummaging through my daypack as we sit together on the grass.

'It's a special shell called a conch. I found it on a golden sandy beach in a country called Belize where I've been travelling. Here you are. I wrapped it in my T-shirt so it wouldn't get broken.'

Katie unrolls the T-shirt to reveal the conch shell, bigger than my fist, brilliant white on the outside and the palest of pinks on the inside.

'It's for you,' I say, 'to add to your collection.'

I hold the shell up to Katie's ear.

'Listen. You can hear the sea.'

Back in the living room, while the new nanny makes tea, I sit alongside Katie as she draws on the whiteboard, intensely absorbed in her work, a series of drawings showing three figures – female (I can tell from the long hair!) – holding hands: a child in the middle, and a taller figure on either side.

'Who's that?' I ask, pointing to each figure in turn.

'Mummy, Katie and Scarlett,' says Katie, before rubbing out the picture and starting all over again.

'Is it the beach?' I ask, pointing to the wavy line representing the sea.

Katie smiles.

'It's a hot, sunny day,' I say, pointing to the circle surrounded by lines representing the sun in the sky.

While Katie draws, and rubs out and draws again, I look around the grand living room. My eyes are attracted to a large gilt-framed mirror on the wall above an antique, lacquered sideboard. I wander over and look at myself in the glass. Out in the Costa Rican jungle where I've spent much of the last few weeks, there aren't many mirrors, and I'm quite happy with what I see – my features chiselled by exercise and outdoor pursuits and the diet of tropical fruits, copper highlights in my hair, eyes shining and teeth sparkling white, all set off by a golden tan. I am literally glowing with health.

I glance down, and then I see it. The album. I'm surprised Christina would want to have it out on display. She's set it up almost like a shrine – the album in the middle, surrounded by little bowls of rose petals and a candle burning on either side.

I leaf through the pages – despite the rose petals, there's a faint smell of smoke still clinging to the paper. I get to Photograph Thirteen – the blank page. Gabrielle never did get to choose the last image. But the page isn't blank any more. Christina must have decided to complete the album her way.

She's amended Gabrielle's heading for Photograph Thirteen so that it now reads, *Lucky, lucky me!*

Instead of one photograph, she's stuck in a sequence of three – pictures of Katie's birthday party, a couple of months ago.

The first is a portrait of Katie dressed in a pretty, pale-blue silk party dress, looking on in wonder, in front of a large pink birthday cake lit with five candles, decorated with mermaids, and ringed with rosebuds and shells. The second picture shows Katie blowing out the candles with a handful of little girls on either side, clapping and laughing. The third is another close-up shot, this time of Christina herself, sporting a short, stylish Lady Diana haircut. She must have overcome her long-standing aversion to being photographed. She looks well. Her smile is confident and flirtatious, as if she's sharing a joke with one of the dads, her right hand resting on Katie's shoulder and her left hand (beautifully manicured and adorned with a large diamond solitaire), slicing into the soft pink icing with the long silver blade of a cake knife.

She never told me she was getting engaged!

I can't think why, but as I return to Katie's side, the words of Lennie, the casino manager, pop into my head.

I never forget hands.

An image of a hand, sporting a sparkling platinum engagement ring, bearing an uncanny resemblance to the one in the photograph, a hand holding a different blade, flashes into my consciousness but I delete it instantly. I can't allow myself to dwell on that.

James bought two pairs of jade earrings, so why not two engagement rings? Or perhaps in that final confrontation Christina simply took back what she believed was rightfully hers?

We drink tea, and Katie shows me her bedroom – all pretty pink rosebuds and pastel paints – and she places the conch shell beside her pillow so she can listen to the sea before she goes to sleep, and I read her a story, and I draw her a mermaid... and then I look at my watch and it's time to go.

I'm sorry to miss Christina but maybe it's no bad thing that she's been delayed at work. Some things are best left uncertain and unsaid.

'I have to go to the airport now, Katie,' I say. 'I'm catching a plane back to my home in England.'

As we cross the landing, I pause outside Christina's room and look around, imagining her new life here. I go into the room. Katie waits outside on the landing, looking the other way.

In contrast to the living rooms downstairs, Christina's bedroom is decorated in a modern and minimalist style – no books or paintings on the walls, just cool linen curtains and grey silk sheets on the enormous bed and a large frameless mirror above a desk that is clear of clutter, save for one photograph of Katie as a tiny newborn baby set in a mother-of-pearl frame.

It feels a little lonely and oppressive in here. The window is open. The curtain smells faintly of cigarettes.

It's time to go. I don't want to miss my plane.

My taxi is parked at the end of the drive. Katie follows me down the stairs to the front door. She's still holding the Barbie with the long blonde hair that she calls 'Mummy'.

She tugs on my hand.

'I want to go home.'

She says the words slowly and clearly and it occurs to me that this is the first time ever that I've heard her speak a proper sentence.

I crouch down beside her.

'This is your home now.'

'Where's Mummy?' she says. She fixes me with those searching blue eyes I remember so well – as clear and as deep as the Caribbean Sea.

I could drown in those eyes. So I look up to the dark outline of the nanny waiting in the shadows, anxious to close the door.

'Mummy's at work. She'll be here very soon.'

I throw my arms round Katie and kiss her goodbye.

'Give Mummy a hug for me.'

I stand up. I don't want her to see me cry.

'Mummy's gone,' says Katie softly as I turn and walk away.

Acknowledgements

So many people have helped in the writing of this book and I am endlessly grateful to you all. My heartfelt thanks goes out...

To the team at Aria and in particular, my brilliant editor Hannah Smith who called me out of the blue last summer with the news that she would like to publish this story. Ever since that surreal phone conversation (partly drowned out so fittingly by the sound of breaking waves on a sun-scorched beach), she's been fabulous to work with and I am so very thankful for her boundless enthusiasm and expertise, as well as her inspired editorial notes! Huge thanks also to Vicky Joss and the marketing and production gurus at Aria who created such an eye-catching cover for *She's Mine* and are always on hand to help with all-things social media.

To the hardworking professionals behind the scenes – Aria copyeditors and proof-reader extraordinaire Sue Lamprell who transformed the text from a manuscript into a real book!

To my wonderful agent Hayley Steed for responding so positively to my first submission and for giving me a second chance when I returned with a complete manuscript two years later, having made the rookie mistake first time round of sending in the first three chapters when they were all I had written! I am incredibly lucky to be represented by the Madeleine Milburn agency.

To Jamilah and Barbara for their early faith in this book. I'll always be grateful for their patience, guidance and professional help on the first stage of its journey to publication. Also, to Mike for editing the original text.

To my 'Faber Grad' and 'Faberite' friends for constructive feedback and great company both in class and beyond and especially to Karen, Elizabeth and Sam who read and commented on the novel at different stages of its development. You are all such brilliantly talented writers and perceptive critics – looking forward to a succession of book launches over the coming months and years!

To Faber tutor Shelley Weiner who taught us the fundamentals of creative writing and started us on this journey, and to Helen Francis and Sam Copeland who gave us many fascinating insights into the world of publishing. The courses were massively motivating and so much fun! Also, to the lovely people at the Blue Pencil Agency who run such great retreats!

To other 'literary' friends who so kindly and generously gave up their time to read, critique and comment on my drafts, including 'Queenswomen' Sara, Rose, Sarah and Janet for whom the backstory may have rung some bells, and 'RGS mums' Carol, Allison, Denise, Helena and Karen.

Most especially, to Sara who read and reviewed the book not once but twice! What a star! Also, to author Kerry Fisher, my 'grown-up' writing friend who is a fabulous mentor. And to Ilinka for being keen enough to read the story with a dictionary as English is not her first language!

To new friends - some of whom I have met in person including authors of Aria/Head of Zeus and Madeleine Milburn, and others in the Twittersphere (special shout out to Barbara Bos of Women Writers) – what a lovely friendly community of writers, book bloggers, reviewers and readers!

To my father Graham, a rock of encouragement and support in so many ways for me and all the family, and to my parents-in-law Sylvia and Peter for their enthusiastic interest in my work.

To my sister Christine who was my very first reader and revealed impeccable editorial skills in correcting my grammar mistakes and plot inconsistencies in the early drafts! – I loved our transatlantic phone calls in the middle of the night. Your endorsement gave me the first hope I might be on to something!

To my husband Nigel for embracing (and bank-rolling!) my dream of becoming a writer and putting up with all my shortcomings on the domestic front with great fortitude and good humour! I couldn't have done it without you...

To my girls, Clara and Louisa for reviewing my manuscript and liking it (that meant so much to me!) and for being the best sounding-boards imaginable for story lines, possible endings, plot twists and character traits. Needless to say, all my best ideas were stolen from you!

To my son, Jack, who inspired certain scenes in this book and kept me company in the writing of it as I tapped away to the soundtrack of his David Attenborough wildlife DVDs.

To all of you. In unique and varied ways, each of you has spurred me on to write this book.

THANK YOU! THANK YOU! THANK YOU!

And finally:

To new readers of *She's Mine* – if you're reading this, you made it to the end!

Thank you so much for that and I hope you enjoyed it!

Hello from Aria

We hope you enjoyed this book! Let us know, we'd love to hear from you.

We are Aria, a dynamic digital-first fiction imprint from award-winning independent publishers Head of Zeus. At heart, we're avid readers committed to publishing exactly the kind of books we love to read — from romance and sagas to crime, thrillers and historical adventures. Visit us online and discover a community of like-minded fiction fans!

We're also on the look out for tomorrow's superstar authors. So, if you're a budding writer looking for a publisher, we'd love to hear from you. You can submit your book online at ariafiction.com/we-want-read-your-book

You can find us at:
Email: aria@headofzeus.com
Website: www.ariafiction.com
Submissions: www.ariafiction.com/
we-want-read-your-book
Facebook: @ariafiction
Twitter: @Aria_Fiction
Instagram: @ariafiction

37972089R00271

Printed in Poland
by Amazon Fulfillment
Poland Sp. z o.o., Wrocław